The COURTSHIP
of
PRINCESS LEIA

Dave Wolverton

BANTAM BOOKS
NEW YORK • TORONTO • LONDON • SYDNEY • AUCKLAND

STAR WARS: THE COURTSHIP OF PRINCESS LEIA

A Bantam Spectra Book / May 1994

Library of Congress Cataloging-in-Publication Data

Wolverton, Dave.
   The courtship of Princess Leia / by Dave Wolverton.
     p.   cm. — (Star wars)
   ISBN 0-553-08928-5
   1. Leia, Princess (Fictitious character)—Fiction.   I. Title.
  II. Series: Star wars (Bantam Books (Firm) : Unnumbered)
PS3573.0572C68   1994
813'.54—dc20   93-20977
                                       CIP

Published simultaneously in the United States and Canada

PRINTED IN THE UNITED STATES OF AMERICA

BVG   0 9 8 7 6 5 4 3 2 1

Chapter

1

Genernal Han Solo stood at the command console viewport of the Mon Calamari Star Cruiser *Mon Remonda*. Warning sounds tinkled like wind chimes as the ship prepared to drop out of hyperspace at the New Republic's capital on Coruscant. It had been so long since Han had last seen Leia: five months, five months hunting the warlord Zsinj's Super Star Destroyer, *Iron Fist*. Five months ago, the New Republic had seemed so secure, so in control. Maybe now, with the *Iron Fist* gone, warlord Zsinj would be crippled and things would go smoother. Han longed to get off the humid Calamarian ship, longed even more for the taste of Leia's kisses, the caress of her hand on his brow. He'd seen too much darkness lately.

The white starfield on the screen resolved as the hyperdrive engines cut, and Chewbacca roared in alarm: across the blue velvet of space where the city night lights of Coruscant blazed from a dark world were dozens of enormous, saucershaped starships that Han recognized immediately as Hapan Battle Dragons. Among them were dozens of slate gray Imperial Star Destroyers.

"Get us out of here!" Han shouted. He'd seen a Hapan

Battle Dragon only once before, but it had been enough. "Full shields! Evasive action!"

He watched the three dorsal ion guns of the nearest Dragon, expecting them to knock him from the sky. The blaster turrets on the saucer's rim all swiveled toward him.

The *Mon Remonda* twisted and dove planetward, toward the lights of Coruscant. Han's stomach wrenched. His Mon Calamari pilot was well schooled, and knowing that they could not run before setting a new course, he surged into the thick of the Hapan warships so that they could not fire without the risk of hitting one another.

Like all the technology on the Mon Calamari ship, the viewport was exceptional, a work of art, so that as they hurtled past the command port of a Hapan Battle Dragon, Han could make out the startled faces of three Hapan officers, the silver name tags sewn into their collars. Han had never seen a Hapan. Their star sector was renowned for its wealth, and the Hapans guarded their borders jealously. He'd known that they were human—for humans had scattered like weeds across the galaxy —but he was surprised to discover that without exception, all three of the female officers were astonishingly beautiful—like fragile, living ornaments.

"Cease evasive action!" shouted Captain Onoma, a salmon-colored Calamarian officer who sat at a control console, monitoring sensors.

"What?" Han shouted, surprised that the lower-ranked Calamarian would reverse his orders.

"The Hapans are not firing, and they are broadcasting as friendlies," Onoma answered, swiveling a large golden eye at Han. The Calamarian cruiser ceased its crazy headlong dive and slowed.

"Friendlies?" Han asked. "They're Hapans! Hapans are never friendly!"

"Nevertheless, they've apparently come to negotiate a treaty of some sort with the New Republic. The accompanying Star Destroyers are theirs, captured from the Imperials. As you can see, our planetary defense forces are still intact." Captain Onoma nodded up toward a Star Destroyer in another quadrant, and Han recognized its markings. Leia's flagship, the *Rebel Dream*. It had seemed so huge, so vast when they'd captured it from the Imperials, but here beside this Hapan fleet, it looked small, insignificant. Huddled around the *Rebel Dream*, he saw a dozen smaller Republic Dreadnaughts, their hulls still painted with the markings of the old Rebel Alliance.

The first time Han had seen a Hapan warship, he had been smuggling guns with a small convoy fleet under the command of Captain Rula. Since the Hapans hadn't yet fallen to the Empire, the smugglers had been using an outpost in neutral territory near the borders of the Hapan star cluster, hoping that their proximity to the Hapans would keep the Empire off their back. But one day they came out of hyperspace and found a Hapan Battle Dragon hovering in their path. Even though they were in neutral territory, even though they made no aggressive moves, only three of the twenty smuggler ships managed to survive the Hapan attack.

A communications officer said, "General Solo, we're receiving a call from Ambassador Leia Organa."

"I'll go to my quarters and pick it up there," Han said, and he hurried to punch up the call. Leia's image appeared on the small screen.

Leia was smiling, euphoric, and her dark eyes had a dreamy look to them. "Oh, Han," she said in a breath, her voice mellifluous. "I'm so glad you're here." She wore the pure white uniform of an Alderaanian ambassador, and her hair was down. In the past months it had grown longer than Han had ever seen it. In her hair she wore the combs he had given her, made from silver and opal mined on Alderaan before Grand Moff Tarkin blasted the planet to cinders with the first Death Star.

"I missed you, too," Han said huskily.

"Come down to Coruscant, to the Grand Reception Hall," Leia said. "The Hapan ambassadors are about to arrive."

"What do they want?"

"It's not what they want, it's what they're offering. I went to Hapes and spoke with the queen mother three months ago," Leia said. "I asked her for aid in our fight against Warlord Zsinj. She seemed very distant, noncommittal, but promised to think about it. I can only guess they've come to give that aid."

Lately, Han had begun to realize that the war against the remnants of the Empire might take years, even decades to win.

Zsinj and some lesser warlords were firmly entrenched in over a third of the galaxy, but the warlords now seemed to be on the move—pillaging entire star systems as they swept toward the free worlds. The New Republic could not patrol such a vast front. Just as the old Empire had struggled to repel the Rebel Alliance, the New Republic battled the might of the warlords and their vast fleets. Han didn't want Leia to get her hopes raised for a Hapan alliance. He said, "Don't expect too much from the Hapans. I've never heard of them giving anyone anything—except a hard time."

"You don't even know them. Just come to the Grand Reception Hall," Leia said, suddenly all business. "Oh, and welcome back." She turned away. The transmission ended.

"Yeah," Han whispered. "I missed you, too."

Han and Chewbacca hurried through the streets toward the Grand Reception Hall on Coruscant. They were in an ancient part of Coruscant where the planetwide city had not built over the top of ruins, so that all around them plasteel buildings rose up like the walls of a canyon. The shadows thrown by the steep buildings were so deep that overhead the shuttles streaming through the spaces between buildings were forced to keep their running lights on even in the daytime, creating a massive tapestry of light. By the time Han and Chewie reached the Grand Reception Hall, the processional band was already playing an oddly mincing marching song, using janglers and deep woot horns.

The Grand Reception Hall was an enormous building, more than a thousand meters long, with fourteen levels for seating, but as Han neared the entrance, he found that all of the portals were jammed with curious onlookers, eager to see the Hapans. Han ran past the first five entrances, then suddenly saw a golden protocol droid nervously trying to jump or stand on tiptoe to see over the crowd. Many people claimed that all droids of a certain model looked alike, but Han recognized See-Threepio instantly—no other protocol unit ever managed to look quite as nervous or excited.

"Threepio, you hunk of tin!" Han shouted to be heard over the crowd. Chewbacca roared in greeting.

"General Solo!" Threepio responded, a note of relief in his voice. "Princess Leia asked that I find you and escort you to the Alderaanian ambassador's balcony. I was afraid I'd missed you in the crowd! You're fortunate that I had the foresight to wait for you here. This way, sir, this way!" Threepio led them back across a broad street and up a side ramp, past several guards.

As they climbed a long winding corridor, passing door after door, Chewbacca sniffed the air and growled. They rounded the corner and Threepio halted by a balcony entrance. Within, only a few people stood looking through the glass onto the procession below. Han recognized some of them: Carlist Rieekan, the Alderaanian general who had commanded Hoth base; Threkin Horm, president of the powerful Alderaanian Council, an immensely fat man who rested in a repulsor chair rather than try to carry his own weight. And Mon Mothma, commander of the New Republic, stood next to a bearded gray Gotal, who gazed dispassionately toward the main floor, head tilted, aiming his sensor horns in Leia's direction.

The diplomats were all speaking softly, listening to comlinks and watching Leia, who sat on a dais, regally gazing on a Hapan diplomatic shuttle that had landed on a pad built within the great open-air hall. Perhaps five hundred thousand beings had gathered on the main floors, eager to catch a glimpse of the Hapans. Tens of thousands of security guards had cleared the gold carpet between the shuttle and Leia, and Han looked up to the balconies. Nearly every star system in the old Empire had had its own balcony here, and beside each balcony was the nation's standard. Over six hundred thousand of those standards hung now on the ancient marble walls, showing the membership of the New Republic. Down on the floor, silence fell as the shuttle dropped its loading ramps.

Han went to Mon Mothma. "What's going on?" he asked. "Why aren't you down on the dais with Leia?"

"I was not invited to meet the Hapan ambassadors," Mon Mothma replied. "They asked only to see Leia. Since even the Old Republic had very limited contact with Hapan's monarchs over the past three thousand years, I felt it best to remain aloof until invited."

"That's very considerate," Han said, "but you are the elected leader of the New Republic—"

"And Queen Mother Ta'a Chume feels threatened by our democratic ways. No, I think it best that Ta'a Chume's ambassadors speak through Leia, if she makes them feel more comfortable. Have you counted the number of Battle Dragons in the Hapan fleet? There are sixty-three—one for each inhabited planet in the Hapes cluster. Never have the Hapans initiated contact with us on such a grand scale. I suspect that this is to be the most important contact our peoples have made in the past three millennia."

Han would not say it, but he felt slighted at not being seated by Leia's side. The fact that Mon Mothma had been similarly treated added to the offense. They waited only a moment before the Hapans began to disembark.

First from the shuttle came a woman with long dark hair and onyx eyes that glittered in the lights. She wore a light dress of peach-colored shimmering material that left her long legs exposed. Microphones on the floor fed into the balcony, and Han could hear a sigh pass through the crowd as the beautiful woman made her way up the promenade.

She approached Leia and dropped gracefully to one knee, keeping her eyes on Leia. In a strong voice she spoke in Hapan, *"Ellene sellibeth e Ta'a Chume. 'Shakal Leia, ereneseth a'apelle seranel Hapes. Rennithelle saroon.' "* She turned and clapped her hands six times, and dozens of women in shimmering gold dresses began descending from the shuttle, running quickly and playing silver flutes or drums while others sang over and over in clear high voices, "Hapes, Hapes, Hapes."

Mon Mothma listened intently to her comlink as a translator broadcast the words in Basic, but Han couldn't hear the translator.

"Do you speak this stuff?" Han asked Threepio.

"I am fluent in over six million forms of communication, sir," Threepio said regretfully, "but I think I must be experiencing a malfunction. The Hapan ambassador cannot have said what I heard." He turned and started to walk off. "Darn these rusty logic circuits! Excuse me while I report for repairs."

"Wait!" Han said. "Forget about the repairs. What did she say?"

"Sir, I think I must have misunderstood," Threepio said.

"Tell me!" Han added more forcefully and Chewbacca growled a warning.

"Well, if you're going to be that way about it!" Threepio affected a hurt tone. "If my sensors monitored her correctly, the delegate reported the words of the great queen mother: 'Worthy Leia, I offer gifts from the sixty-three worlds of Hapes. Take joy in them.' "

"Gifts?" Han said. "That sounds pretty straightforward to me."

"Indeed it is. The Hapans never ask a favor without offering a gift of equal value first," Threepio said condescendingly. "No, what troubles me is the use of the word *shakal*, 'worthy.' The queen mother would never apply that word to Leia, for the Hapans use it only when speaking to equals."

"Well," Han hazarded a guess, "they are both royalty."

"True," Threepio said, "but the Hapans practically worship their queen mother. Indeed, one of their names for her is *Ereneda*, 'she who has *no* equal.' So you see, it would not be logical for the queen mother to refer to Leia as her equal."

Han looked back down to the unloading ramp and shivered as a sense of foreboding washed through him. The sounds of drums thundered. Three women in bright, almost garish silks rushed from the shuttle bearing a large container the color of mother-of-pearl. Threepio still spoke to himself, shaking his head and saying "I really must have these logic circuits repaired," as the three women spilled the contents onto the floor. The whole crowd gasped. "Rainbow gems from Gallinore!"

The gems glittered with their own fire in dozens of shades from brilliant cardinal to blazing emerald. Indeed, the invaluable gems were not gems at all, but a silicon-based life form that glowed with its own brilliant inner light. The creatures, often worn on medallions, matured only after thousands of years. One gem could buy a Calamarian cruiser, yet the Hapans had thrown hundreds of mated pairs to the floor. Leia showed no surprise.

A second trio of women, far taller than the others, descended from the diplomatic shuttle wearing leathers in colors of tawny ocher and cinnamon. They danced lightly to the sounds of the flutes and drums, and between them floated a platform that bore a small, gnarled tree with ruddy brown fruits. Twin lights floated above it, beaming steadily like the suns of some desert world. The crowd murmured quietly until the ambassador explained, *"Selabah, terrefel n lasarla."* ("From Selab, a tree of wisdom, bearing fruits.") The crowd suddenly shouted and cheered in delight, and Han stood dumbfounded. He had thought the wisdom trees of Selab to be only a legend. It was said that the fruit of the wisdom trees could greatly boost the intelligence of those who had passed into old age.

Han's blood pounded in his veins, and he felt lightheaded. A man came forward to the sound of the music, a cyborg warrior dressed in full Hapan body armor, black with silver trim. He stood nearly as tall as Chewbacca, and strode purposely, pulled some sort of mechanical device from his arm, and laid it on the ground before Leia. *"Charubah endara, mella n sesseltar."* ("From the high-tech world Charubah, we offer a Gun of Command.")

Han leaned against the glass for support. The Gun of Command had made the Hapan troops nearly irresistible in small-arms combat, for it released an electromagnetic wave field that virtually neutralized an enemy's voluntary thought processes. Those shot with the Gun of Command stood helpless as invalids, unaware of their surroundings, and tended to follow any orders given them, for they could not distinguish the command of an enemy from their own voluntary thoughts. Han began sweating. *Their every world, each planet in the Hapes system, is offering its greatest treasures,* Han realized. *What could they hope to gain? What could they want in return?*

He watched over the next hour. The music of the drums and flutes and the high, clear calls of the women singing "Hapes, Hapes, Hapes," over and over again seemed to pound through his veins, through his temples. Twelve of the poorer worlds each gave Leia Star Destroyers captured from the Empire, while others brought things that held more esoteric value. From Arabanth came an old woman who spoke only a few words on the importance of embracing life while accepting death, offering a "thought puzzle" that her people held to be of great value. Ut sent a woman who sang a song so beautiful that the sound seemed to carry Han away to her world on a warm breeze.

At one point, Han heard Mon Mothma whisper, "I knew Leia had asked for money to help fight the warlords, but I never imagined . . ."

And finally, the singers stopped singing and the drums stopped beating and a portion of the wealth of the hidden worlds of Hapes lay scattered on the floor of the Grand Reception Hall. Han found that his breathing came ragged from his lungs, for he kept unconsciously holding his breath as the gifts were offered.

The silence on the floor of the hall seemed heavy, ominous. More than two hundred ambassadors from the worlds of Hapes stood on the promenade, and Han marveled at them, for once again he was impressed by their grace, by their beauty, by their strength. Until today, he had never seen a Hapan. Now he would never forget them.

No one spoke as the Hapans held their silence. Han waited to hear what they would ask in return. His blood thrilled, for he realized they could only want one thing: a pact with the Republic. The Hapans would ask the Republic to join an all-out war against the combined might of warlords who served as the last remnants of the Empire.

Leia leaned forward from her throne, looked over the gifts approvingly. "You said that you had gifts from all sixty-three of your worlds," Leia told the ambassador, "but I see here gifts from only sixty-two. You have offered me nothing from Hapes itself."

Han was shocked by the remark. He had lost count of the gifts long ago, stunned by the wealth the Hapans offered, and now Leia's comments seemed churlish, greedy. He expected the Hapans to scoff at her bad manners, take everything, and leave.

Instead, the Hapan ambassador smiled warmly, as if pleased that Leia had noticed, and looked up and held Leia's eyes. She spoke, and Threepio translated, "That is because we have saved our greatest gift for last."

She motioned with her hand, and all the Hapan ambassadors stepped aside, clearing the aisle. Without fanfare, without the music of horns, only in silence did they bring their last gift.

Two women, modestly dressed in black with silver ringlets in their dark hair, came from the ship. A man walked between them. He wore a silver circlet that held a black veil in front of his face, and his long, blond hair fell down around his shoulders. The man was bare-chested except for a small silk half-cloak fastened with silver clasps, and in his muscular arms he carried a large, ornate box of ebony inlaid with silver.

He brought the box and set it on the floor. He sat on his haunches, hands resting lightly on his knees, and the women pulled back his black veil. Beneath it was the most incredibly handsome man that Han had ever seen. His deep-set eyes were a dark blue-gray, like the color of the sea on the horizon, and promised wit, humor, wisdom; his powerful shoulders and firm jawline were strong. Han realized that this must be some high dignitary from the royal house of Hapes itself. The ambassador spoke, *"Hapesah, rurahsen Ta'a Chume, elesa Isolder Chume'da."* ("From Hapes, the queen mother offers her greatest treasure, her son Isolder, the Chume'da, whose wife shall reign as queen.")

Chewbacca growled and in the crowd below everyone seemed to talk at once, an uproar that swelled in Han's ears like the sound of a storm.

Mon Mothma pulled off her headset and gazed at Leia thoughtfully, one of the generals in the room swore and grinned, and Han stepped away from the window. "What?" Han asked. "What does that mean?"

"Ta'a Chume wants Leia to marry her son," Mon Mothma answered softly.

"But, she won't do it, will she?" Han said, and then his certainty faltered. Sixty-three of the wealthiest planets in the galaxy. To rule as matriarch over billions of people, with that man beside her. . . .

Mon Mothma looked up into Han's eyes, as if gauging him. "With the wealth of Hapes to help fund the war, Leia could overthrow the last remnants of the Empire quickly, saving billions of lives in the process. I know how you have felt about her in the past, General Solo. Still, I think I speak for everyone in the New Republic when I say that, for all our sakes, I hope she accepts the offer."

Chapter

2

L uke could sense the ruins of the ancient Jedi Master's
home before his Whiphid guide brought him to the place.
Like the landscape of Toola itself—a barren plain where
the short purple lichens thrust up from patches of thin winter ice
—the ruins felt clean and refreshing, yet empty, almost as if they
had never been visited by humans. The clean feeling assured
Luke that the ruins had once been inhabited by a good Jedi.

The huge Whiphid, its ivory fur ruffling under the spring
winds, trudged over the purple moss, a vibro-ax fitted in its
paw. It stopped and raised its long snout in the air so that its
massive tusks pointed up at a distant purple sun, then gave a
trumpeting whistle, glaring ahead with small black eyes.

Luke pulled back the hood of his snowsuit and glimpsed
the danger on the horizon. A flock of snow demons was dropping from the shelter of storm clouds, hairy wings flashing gray
in the slanting sunlight. The Whiphid whistled a battle cry,
afraid they would attack, but Luke reached out with his mind
and felt the snow demons' hunger. They were hunting a herd of
shaggy motmots that moved like icy hills on the horizon, seeking a calf small enough to slaughter.

"Peace," Luke said, reaching up to touch the Whiphid's elbow. "Show me the ruins." Luke tried to use the Force to calm the warrior. But the Whiphid quivered, clenching its vibro-ax, eager for battle.

The Whiphid whistled a long reply, pointing north, and Luke translated by power of the Force: "Search the Jedi's tomb if you must, little one, but I go to hunt. Having sighted an enemy, honor demands that I attack. My clan will feast on a snow demon tonight." The Whiphid wore a weapon belt as its only article of clothing, and from the array hanging there, it pulled free a blackened iron morning star. With a weapon in each huge fist, it charged over the tundra faster than Luke would have believed possible.

Luke shook his head, pitying the snow demons. Artoo whistled from behind, asking Luke to slow his pace as the little droid negotiated a treacherous patch of ice. Together, Luke and Artoo traveled north until they reached three huge flat rocks that rose from the ground to form the roof and sides of a tunnel. The tunnel smelled dry, and Luke pulled a minilantern from his utility belt and made his way down. A short distance from the surface, the tunnel had been caved in. A huge boulder blocked the path. Black soot on the boulder showed where a thermal detonator had blown the stone free in ages past, closing off whatever lay beyond.

Luke closed his eyes and reached out with his mind until the Force channeled through him. He shifted the rock, lifted it free, and held it. "Go ahead, Artoo," Luke whispered, and the droid rolled forward, whistling in dismay as it passed beneath the floating rock. Luke ducked under the hovering boulder, then let it settle behind him.

On the dirt floor immediately behind the rock, Luke found the boot prints of Imperial stormtroopers, still preserved after all these years. Luke studied the prints, wondering if any would have belonged to his father. Darth Vader probably would have had to come. Only he could have killed the Jedi Master who had lived in these caverns. But the footprints told him nothing.

The tunnels wound down through storage rooms carved deep beneath the ground. The air carried the stale scent of rodent dung and fur. A small, square power droid lay dead in one hallway, long since drained of energy. A thermal heater filled another room, its power cables chewed away by small animals. Luke followed the tunnels toward the clean feeling of the Jedi, and finally found the dead Master's room. The body was gone, dissipated as Yoda's and Ben's had, but Luke could feel the residue of the Master's force, and he discovered a snowsuit, slashed and burned, with a lightsaber nearby. Luke picked up the lightsaber, flipped it on. A stream of opalescent energy shot out as the lightsaber hummed to life.

Luke wondered momentarily about the man who had owned the lightsaber, then flipped it off. He knew little except that the Jedi Master had served the Old Republic in its final hours. For months now, Luke had followed the man's trail. As curator of records for the Jedi at Coruscant, the man had seemed only a minor functionary, hardly worthy of notice by the invading Imperials. Yet he had fled Coruscant with the records of a thousand generations of Jedi.

Such records, Luke hoped, would be more than a mere catalog of the Jedis' deeds. Instead, they might contain the wisdom of the ancient masters, their thoughts, their aspirations. As a young Jedi who had not been thoroughly educated in the ways of the Force, Luke hoped to learn the deeper mysteries of how the Jedi had trained their warriors, their healers, their seers.

Luke cast about the room, looking in the feeble light of his minilantern for anything that might provide a clue. Artoo had gone down a side passage, guiding himself through the dark using his headlamps. From the passage Luke heard a mournful whistle and followed.

It was a hallway that led to blackened rooms carved in the stone where cell after cell of holographic video recordings had been stored. But the recordings were blasted and burned to cinders. Computer cylinders lay in piles of molten slag, their memory cores fried. Thermal detonators had melted the things, but Luke also found chunks from EMP grenades. Whoever had destroyed the holo vids had done his or her best to erase them first.

Luke paced the tunnel, passing dozens upon dozens of cells, gazing into each cell in turn, and his heart went from him. Nothing was left. All of it gone. The knowledge and deeds of a thousand generations of Jedi.

"It's no use, Artoo," Luke said, and his words seemed to be swallowed by the darkness, the silence of the empty tunnels. Artoo whistled sadly, rolled on down the corridor, lifting up on his wheels to peek over the lip of each cell.

Gone. All of it gone, Luke realized. The Emperor had not been content to hunt down and murder the Jedi. He had felt the need, in his bid to gain absolute control of the galaxy, not only to extinguish their fire from the universe but to crush their embers, scatter their ashes, so that the Jedi would never rise again. So that after months of searching, Luke found only ashes.

Luke sat on the floor, put a hand over his eyes, wondering what his next move should be. Certainly there had been other records, other copies. He would need to go back to Coruscant and begin the search there.

From down the hall, near the end of the tunnel, Artoo began to whistle excitedly. "Found something?" Luke asked, and he got up, dusted cinders from his clothing, forced himself to walk slowly. Artoo had found a cell where the records were not melted. A thermal detonator still lay atop them, an obvious dud. The EMP grenade had fragmented, but Luke wondered how effective it had been. He took a computer cylinder from the top, plugged it into Artoo. The droid whistled and bent forward, preparing to display the hologram, but after a moment ejected the cube with a grinding wheeze.

"Come on," Luke whispered hopefully. Reaching near the bottom of the pile, Luke freed a second cylinder, popped it into the droid, and Artoo flashed the image of a man dressed in flowing, pale green robes. Yet static so interfered that the holo image soon broke up. Artoo spat out the cylinder, and light from his headlamp shone once again into the cell, urging Luke to try again.

"Okay," Luke sighed, and he searched for a cylinder farthest from the EMP grenade. He dug through the pile, found one in a far corner on the floor, and was about to pull it free when he felt the Force tug him in another direction. He fumbled among the cylinders, until his fingers brushed one. Very distinctly, he felt a sense of peace. *This one, this one,* a voice seemed to whisper. *This is what you seek.*

Luke grasped it, pulled it free, and stepped away. Somehow, he knew that to search the caverns further would be useless. If any answers were to be found here, they were in his hand.

He popped the cylinder into Artoo, and almost immediately Artoo caught a signal. Images flashed in the air before the droid: an ancient throne room where, one by one, Jedi came before their high master to give reports. Yet the holo was fragmented, so thoroughly erased that Luke got only bits and pieces —a blue-skinned man describing details of a grueling space battle against pirateers; a yellow-eyed Twi'lek with lashing headtails who told of discovering a plot to kill an ambassador. A date and time flashed on the holo vid before each report. The report was nearly four hundred standard years old.

Then Yoda appeared on the video, gazing up at the throne. His color was more vibrantly green than Luke remembered, and he did not use his walking stick. At middle age, Yoda had looked almost perky, carefree—not the bent, troubled old Jedi Luke had known. Most of the audio was erased, but through the background hiss Yoda clearly said, "We tried to free the Chu'unthor from Dathomir, but were repulsed by the witches . . . skirmish, with Masters Gra'aton and Vulatan. . . . Fourteen acolytes killed . . . go back to retrieve . . ." The audio hissed away, and soon the holo image dissolved to blue static with popping lights.

Other people gave reports, but none of their words seemed to offer hope. Again and again, Luke reflected on the words *Chu'unthor from Dathomir.* Was the Chu'unthor a single person, perhaps a political leader, or could it have been a whole race of beings? And Dathomir—where was it?

"Artoo," Luke said. "Run through your astrogation files and tell me if you find any reference to a place named Dathomir. It could be a star system, a single planet . . ." *Maybe even a person,* he thought with dismay.

Artoo took a moment, then whistled a negative. "I thought not," Luke said. "I've never heard of it, either." During the Clone Wars, so many planets had been destroyed, made uninhabitable. Perhaps Dathomir was one of those, a world so ravaged that it had been forgotten. Or perhaps it was a small place, a moon on some planet on the Outer Rim, so far from civilization that it had merely been lost from the records. Maybe even less than a moon—a continent, an island, a city? Whatever the

case, Luke felt certain that he would find it, sometime, somewhere.

They went up topside, found that night had fallen while
they worked underground. Their Whiphid guide soon returned,
dragging the body of a gutted snow demon. The demon's white
talons curled in the air, and its long purple tongue snaked out
from between its massive fangs. Luke was amazed that the
Whiphid could haul such a monster, yet the Whiphid held the
demon's long hairy tail in one hand and managed to pull it
back to camp.

There, Luke stayed the night with the Whiphids in a huge
shelter made from the rib cage of a motmot, covered over with
hides to keep out the wind. The Whiphids built a bonfire and
roasted the snow demon, and the young danced while the el-
ders played their claw harps. As Luke sat, watching the writh-
ing flames and listening to the twang of harps, he meditated.
"The future you will see, and the past. Old friends long forgotten . . ." Those were the words Yoda had said long ago while
training Luke to peer beyond the mists of time.

Luke looked up at the rib bones of the motmot. The
Whiphids had carved stick letters into the bone, ten and twelve
meters in the air, giving the lineage of their ancestors. Luke
could not read the letters, but they seemed to dance in the firelight, as if they were sticks and stones falling from the sky. The
rib bones curved toward him, and Luke followed the curve of
bones with his eyes. The tumbling sticks and boulders seemed
to gyrate, all of them falling toward him as if they would crush
him. He could see boulders hurtling through the air, too,
smashing toward him. Luke's nostrils flared, and even Toola's
chill could not keep a thin film of perspiration from dotting his
forehead. A vision came to Luke then.

Luke stood in a mountain fortress of stone, looking over a
plain with a sea of dark forested hills beyond, and a storm rose
—a magnificent wind that brought with it towering walls of
black clouds and dust, trees hurtling toward him and twisting
through the sky. The clouds thundered overhead, filled with
purple flames, obliterating all sunlight, and Luke could feel a
malevolence hidden in those clouds and knew that they had
been raised through the power of the dark side of the Force.

Dust and stones whistled through the air like autumn

leaves. Luke tried to hold on to the stone parapet overlooking the plain to keep from being swept from the fortress walls. Winds pounded in his ears like the roar of an ocean, howling.

It was as if a storm of pure dark Force raged over the countryside, and suddenly, amid the towering clouds of darkness that thundered toward him, Luke could hear laughing, the sweet sound of women laughing. He looked above into the dark clouds, and saw the women borne through the air along with the rocks and debris, like motes of dust, laughing. A voice seemed to whisper, "the witches of Dathomir."

Chapter

3

L eia unplugged the comlink from her ear and gazed at the
Hapan ambassador in shock. Hapans were hard to deal
with—so culturally distant, easily offended. The roar of
the hundreds of thousands in the crowd began to swell, and
Leia looked up to the windows of the Alderaanian balcony,
wondering what to answer. Han had turned away and was
speaking excitedly to Mon Mothma.

Above the uproar, Leia said to the ambassador, "Tell Ta'a
Chume that her gifts are exquisite, her generosity unbounded.
Still, I need time to consider the offer." She paused, wondering
how long she could legitimately take. The Hapans were a deci-
sive people. Ta'a Chume had a reputation for making decisions
of monumental importance in the space of hours. Could Leia
take a day? She felt dizzy, almost giddy.

"Please, may I speak?" Prince Isolder asked in accented
Basic, and Leia halted, surprised that Isolder could speak her
language at all. She looked into his gray eyes, remembering the
warm thunderheads over the tropical mountains of Hapes.

Isolder smiled apologetically. There was a certain strength
to his face, a ranginess. "I know your customs differ from ours.

Among the ancients, this is how we arranged our royal marriages. But I want you to feel comfortable with any decision. Please, take time to get to know Hapes, our worlds, our customs—take time to know me."

Something in the way he spoke made Leia realize that this was an unusual offer. "Thirty days?" she asked. "I would take less time, but I must leave for the Roche system in a couple of days. A diplomatic mission."

Prince Isolder lowered his eyes in acceptance. "Of course. A queen must forever be at the call of her people." Then he added apologetically, "If you are leaving on a diplomatic mission, will I have time to meet with you previous to it, under less formal circumstances?"

Leia considered furiously. She had a great deal of studying to do before she left—trade agreements, registered complaints, studies in exobiology. The Verpines, an insect race, had apparently broken dozens of contracts to build warships for the carnivorous Barabels, and it was very unhealthy to break a contract with a Barabel. Meanwhile, the Verpines claimed the ships had been taken by one of their mad hive mothers and felt no obligation to force the hive mother to return the merchandise. The whole affair was complicated by substantiated rumors that the Barabels had begun negotiating to sell Verpine body parts to chefs among the insect-loving Kubazis. Leia simply felt that she had no business letting her personal life interfere with her work, at least not now.

Leia glanced up at the observation deck. Han had left with Chewbacca, and now Mon Mothma stood, holding the comlink to her ear. Mon Mothma did not move, but beside her sat Threkin Horm, president of the Alderaanian Council. Threkin nodded the affirmative, urging Leia on.

"Yes, of course," Leia said. "If you are free to join me before the mission."

"My days and nights are yours," the prince said, smiling gently.

"Then please," Leia asked, "join me for dinner tonight, in my stateroom aboard the *Rebel Dream*?"

Isolder lowered his eyes again, used the thumbs and index fingers of both hands to pull the black veil over his face. Leia had marveled at the beauty of the Hapans during her visit, but now felt a twinge of regret that Isolder hid his face, felt guilty for wanting to gaze at him longer.

Leia left the Grand Reception Hall, thousands watching her departure. Leia felt anxious, and only wanted to find Han. She went to her quarters at the embassy, hoping Han would be there, but the apartments were empty. Perplexed, she used her comlink on the military frequency, found he had left Coruscant on his way to the *Rebel Dream*. That was a bad sign. The *Millennium Falcon* had been docked aboard the *Rebel Dream*, awaiting Han's return. When Han felt worried or frustrated, he liked to work on the *Falcon*. Working with his hands, solving familiar problems, seemed to ease his mind. So he had run to his ship, to work. This proposal must have disturbed him deeply, probably more deeply than even Han knew. Leia was bone weary, but she could see why Han would be in a bad mood. She summoned her personal shuttle.

She found the *Falcon* at docking bay ninety. Han and Chewie were in the main cabin at the control panels, worrying over the tangled mass of wires that connected to various projectile and energy shields. Chewie looked up and roared in greeting, but Han sat holding a plasma torch, facing away. He switched off the torch, but did not shift in the captain's chair to look at her.

"Hi," Leia said softly. "I was hoping to find you back in my room on Coruscant."

"Yeah, well, there were some things I needed to check into," Han said. Leia didn't answer for a long moment. Chewbacca got up and hugged Leia, pressing the fur of his tawny belly into her face, then went down below, leaving them alone. Han turned to face her. His forehead was sweaty, though she knew he couldn't have been working long enough to perspire. "So, uh, how did it go down there? What did you tell the Hapans?"

"I asked them to give me a few days to think," Leia answered. She didn't feel ready to tell him that Isolder would be visiting aboard the *Rebel Dream* that night.

"Hmmm. . . ." Han nodded.

Leia took his grimy hands in hers. She said softly, "I couldn't just send them away—it would be rude. Even if I don't want to marry their prince, I can't destroy our chance to build a relationship with them. The Hapans are very powerful. The whole reason I went to Hapes was to see if they would aid in our fight against the warlords."

"I know," Han sighed. "You would do just about anything to win against them."

"Now what is that supposed to mean?"

"You hated the Empire, but now Zsinj and the warlords are all that is left of it. You've risked your life fighting them a dozen times. You would give your life for the New Republic in a moment, wouldn't you—without thinking, without regrets?"

"Of course," Leia answered. "But—"

"Then I suspect you'll give your life now," Han said, "give it to the Hapans. But instead of dying for them, you'll live for them."

"I, I couldn't do that," Leia assured him.

Han stared at her, breathing hard, and all the pain and accusation went out of his voice. "Of course not," Han sighed, setting the torch down on the floorboard. "I don't know what I was thinking. I just . . ."

Leia stroked his forehead. After five months away from him, she felt a little clumsy. Normally, she imagined, he would take something like the Hapan proposal as a joke, but he was quiet. Something more was going on. Something was hurting him very deeply. "What's wrong? You aren't acting like yourself."

"I don't know," Han whispered. "It's just—this last mission. Coming back to this. I'm so tired. You saw what the *Iron Fist* did on Selaggis. It turned the whole colony into rubble. I kept following it for months, and everywhere we went it was the same: star stations obliterated, shipyards ruined. Just one Super Star Destroyer with a murderer at the helm.

"Back when the Emperor died, I thought we'd won. But I keep finding that we're fighting something so huge, so monstrous. Every time we blink, another Grand Moff announces another lofty unification scheme, or some ragtag sector general rears his or her ugly head. I have dreams at night that I'm fighting this beast in the fog, this huge beast that's roaring and devouring. I can't see its body, but its head comes out of the mist, eyes flaming, and I battle it with an ax, and I finally strike off the head. Then within moments I hear roaring in the fog as the beast grows a new head. I can't see where it's coming from, I can't see the body. I know it's out there, but it's all invisible. We've lost so much, and we're still losing."

"The war?" Leia said. "It must feel that way, out on the front lines," she soothed him. "The warlords, like the Empire they served, thrive on fear and greed. But as a diplomat, almost all I see are victories. Every day another world joins the New Republic. Every day we make some small inroads. We may be losing some battles, but we're winning the war."

"What if the Empire were perfecting the cloaking devices for their Star Destroyers?" Han asked. "We keep hearing rumors. Or what if Zsinj or some other Grand Moff just builds another ship like the *Iron Fist*, or a fleet of them?"

Leia swallowed. "Then we'd keep fighting. It takes so much energy to run a Super Star Destroyer of that size, Zsinj could not afford to run more than one or two at a time. The expenses are too high. Eventually, we would wear him down."

"This war isn't over," Han said. "It might not end during our lifetimes."

She had never seen Han like this, looking so drained. "If we can't win peace for ourselves, then we'll fight for our children," Leia answered. Han leaned back, rested his head against Leia's breast, and she knew what he was thinking. She had said *our children*. Han would be thinking about the Hapans.

"I have to admit," Han said, "the Hapans sure made a tempting offer today. You hear rumors about the riches of the 'hidden worlds,' but wow! Did you get to see much of Hapes when you were there?"

"Yes," Leia answered firmly. "You should see what the queen mothers have built over the centuries: Their cities are beautiful, stately, serene. But it's not just the homes or factories, it's their people, their ideals. It feels like . . . peace."

Han looked up into her dreamy eyes. "You're in love."

"No, I'm not," Leia said.

But Han twisted around, grabbed her shoulders. "Yes, you are." He looked into her eyes. "Listen, sweetheart, you may not be in love with Isolder, but you're in love with his world! When the Emperor destroyed Alderaan, he destroyed everything you loved, everything you were fighting for. You can't put that behind you. You're homesick!"

Leia caught her breath, realizing it was true. She had never quit grieving for Alderaan, for friends lost. And there was a certain similarity between the two worlds in the simplicity and grace of the architecture. The people of Alderaan had had such a respect for life that they refused to build their cities in the plains where the inhabitants would trample the grasses. Instead, their majestic cities rose from the tops of sandstone bluffs among the rolling fields or were wedged into crevices under polar ice or stood on gigantic stilts in Alderaan's shallow seas.

Leia put her hand over her eyes. The tears started to well up. Those had been simpler times.

"Here, here," Han whispered, and he pulled down her hand and kissed it. "There's no need to cry."

"Everything is such a mess—" Leia said, "this mission to the Verpines, the battles with the warlords. I've been working so hard, taking on one mission after another. And through it all I keep hoping we'll find a home world, but nothing seems to work."

"What about New Alderaan? Support Services found you a nice place."

"And five months ago some of Zsinj's agents discovered it. We had to evacuate, at least temporarily."

"I'm sure something else will turn up."

"Maybe, but even if we find something, it won't be like home," Leia said. "We've been holding meetings with the Alderaanian Council every month. We've discussed terraforming one of the worlds from our own system, starting a space station, or buying another world, but most of the refugees from Alderaan are poor traders or diplomats who were offplanet when the Empire attacked. We don't have the kind of money it takes to buy or terraform. It would impoverish us for generations. Meanwhile the scouts are looking for some unmapped world on the fringe of the galaxy, but our traders rightfully don't want any part of that. They've already established trade routes on other worlds, and we can't ask them to isolate themselves from their sources of income. We're reaching an impasse, and some of the council members are just giving up."

"What about the gifts the Hapans gave you today? They would go a long way toward making a big down payment on a planet."

"You don't know the Hapans. Their customs are very strict. If I accept their gifts, it's an all-or-nothing deal. Unless I marry Isolder, I have to give it all back."

"Then give it back," Han said. "I don't think you want to get involved with the Hapans. They're a bad lot."

"You don't even know them," Leia answered, astonished that he would speak that way about an entire culture that spanned dozens of star systems.

"And I suppose you do?" Han countered. "Does a week getting brainwashed by their propaganda chiefs on Hapes make you an expert on their civilization?"

"You're talking about an entire cluster here," Leia said, "billions of people. You've never seen a Hapan before today. How could you talk about them that way?"

"The Hapans have kept closed borders for over three thousand years," Han said. "I've seen firsthand what happens when you get too close to them. Believe me, they're hiding something."

"Hiding something? They've got nothing to hide. All they have is a peaceful way of life that they feel is threatened by outside influences."

"If this queen mother is so fantastic, why would she feel threatened by us?" Han asked. "Nah, Princess—she's hiding something. She's scared."

"I can't believe this," Leia said. "How could you even think that? If things were so terrible in the Hapes cluster, don't you think we'd see defectors, refugees? Nobody ever leaves."

"Maybe it's because they can't get out," Han said. "Maybe those Hapan patrols don't just keep out the troublemakers."

"That's absurd," Leia said. "You're paranoid."

"Paranoid, huh? What about you, Princess? Have a few baubles and trinkets so blinded you that you can't see straight?"

"Oh, you sound so sure of yourself. Do you really feel so threatened by Isolder?"

"Threatened? By that big lout? Me?" Han pointed at himself. "Of course not!"

She knew he was lying. "Then you won't mind that I'm having a private dinner with him tonight?"

"Dinner?" Han asked. "Why should I mind that he's dining with the woman I love, the woman who claims to be in love with me?"

"You're so cute," Leia said sarcastically. "I came here to invite you to dinner, too, but now I think that maybe, just maybe, I should just let you sit up here and gnaw on your own petty jealous fantasies."

Leia stormed from the control room of the *Millennium Falcon*, and Han shouted at her back, "Well, fine—I'll see you at dinner!" He banged a wall with his fist.

After Leia left, Han threw his heart into working on the *Falcon* so that his mind numbed and the sweat poured from his face. He used a few tricks he'd learned to boost the rear energy deflector shields 14 percent over their peak efficiency rating, then went under the ship to work on the swivel guns while Chewie stayed inside, pulling out the main focusing lenses for the ventral blasters. Two hours of hard work later, an entourage entered the docking bay with fat old Threkin Horm in the lead. The president of the Alderaanian Council floated in his repulsor chair as he led Prince Isolder, the prince's bodyguards, and half a dozen curious minor officials around the hangar bay.

"This, as you can see, is one of our repair docks," Threkin Horm said in his nasal voice, planting a thumb firmly between his third and fourth chins. "And this is our esteemed General Han Solo, a hero of the New Republic, working on his private— er, uh—ship, the *Millennium Falcon*."

Prince Isolder scrutinized the *Falcon*, gazing at the rusting metal exterior, the odd panoply of components. Somehow, in all his years running the *Falcon*, Han had never felt quite so embarrassed by the thing. It truly did look like a hunk of junk, sitting there on the gleaming black floors of a Star Destroyer. Isolder stood taller than Han, and his thick chest and arms seemed somehow intimidating, but not as intimidating as his regal manners or the calm strength of his face, the sea-gray eyes, the straight nose, and the thick hair hanging around his shoulders. He wore a different outfit now, another silk half-cape, over a white top that did not conceal the sculpted muscles of his belly or the prince's dark tan. Isolder looked like some barbaric god come to life.

"Han here is an old friend to Her Highness Princess Leia Organa," Threkin Horm added. "He has, in fact, saved her life a number of times, if I am not mistaken."

Isolder shifted his attention to Han and smiled warmly. "So, you are not only Leia's friend but her savior?" Isolder asked, and in his eyes Han thought he saw true gratitude. "Our people owe you a great debt." Isolder's strong, soft voice had an odd accent. The long vowels were deeply inflected, as if the prince were afraid he would cut them short.

"Oh, I guess you could say I'm more than her savior," Han answered. "We're lovers, to be precise."

"General Solo!" Threkin sputtered, but Prince Isolder raised a hand.

"That is all right," Isolder said. "She is a lovely woman. I can understand why you would be attracted to her. I hope my appearance here hasn't been too . . . unsettling."

"*Annoying* is the word," Han answered. "I mean, it's not as if I wished you were dead or anything. Neutered perhaps—not dead."

"I apologize, Prince Isolder!" Threkin stuttered, then shot a venomous glance at Han. "I rather expected more civility from a general in the New Republic. I thought he would at least know how to behave himself." Threkin's frown suggested that Han was seriously in jeopardy of losing his rank, if Threkin had any control over it.

Isolder studied Han a moment, then bowed slightly so that his long, sandy blond locks danced around his shoulders. He smiled at Han, "Believe me, no offense is taken. General Solo is a warrior, and he wishes to do battle for the woman he loves. That is the warrior's way.

"General Solo, would you kindly show me the inside of your ship?"

"Gladly, Your Highness," Han answered, and he led Isolder up the gangplank. Threkin Horm sputtered and tried to follow, but two of Isolder's female bodyguards stepped in Horm's path. One beautiful redhead casually dropped her hand to her blaster, and a silent alarm sounded in Han's head. He'd seen people like her before, people who were confident, people so familiar with their weapons that the blaster seemed almost an extension of their bodies. This woman was dangerous.

Threkin Horm must have realized this, too, for he stopped in his tracks.

As Han climbed up into the ship, he kept waiting for Isolder to slug him from behind. Instead, the prince simply followed, listened attentively as Han showed off his hyperdrive unit, the sublight engines, and the weaponry and defenses that he'd slowly built up through accretion over the years.

When Han had finished, Isolder leaned toward him and asked, seeming bewildered, "Do you mean to say that it actually flies?"

"Oh yes," Han said, wondering if the prince was truly astonished or if he were merely impudent. "And she's fast."

"The fact that you can keep this ship together at all speaks very highly of your skills. This is a smuggler's ship, no? Fast speeds, secret compartments, hidden weaponry?"

Han shrugged.

"I'm familiar with smugglers. I left home when I was young and worked for a few seasons as a profiteer," Isolder said. "Have you seen one of our Hapes Nova-class battle cruisers?"

"No," Han answered, looking at Isolder, feeling curiosity and a sudden sense of respect for the prince.

The prince clasped his hands behind his back, said thoughtfully, "They are over four hundred meters long, go without refueling for over a year, are very fast, and could blow this ship out of the sky before you had time to cry out."

"Are you threatening me?" Han asked.

"No," Isolder said, then whispered conspiratorially, "I will give one to you, if you promise to use it to fly far, far away from here."

Han leaned forward, whispered back in the same tone, "No deal."

Isolder grinned, admiration shining from his eyes. "Good, you are a man of principles. Then let me appeal to those principles. General Solo, what can you really offer Leia?"

Han faltered a moment, unprepared to answer. "She loves me and I love her. That's enough."

"If you love her, then leave her to me," Isolder said. "She wants the security that Hapes offers her people. But loving you would only cramp her, give her a smaller life than she de-

serves." He began to leave, edging past Han in the small hallway, but Han grabbed the prince by the shoulder and spun him
around.

"Wait a minute!" Han said. "What's going on here? Let's
put all our weapons on the table."

"What do you mean?" Isolder asked.

"I mean there are a lot of princesses in the universe, and I
want to know why you're here. Why did your mother choose
Leia? She has no wealth, nothing to offer Hapes. If you want a
treaty with the New Republic, there are easier ways to get it."

Isolder looked down into Han's eyes, and smiled, "I understand that Leia has invited you to dine with us this evening. I
think, perhaps, both of you should hear what I have to say."

Chapter

4

W hen Han arrived at Leia's stateroom for dinner, dressed in his finest military blues with all the appropriate bangles, the party was already into its second course. It was obvious that Leia had not expected him. Prince Isolder sat to Leia's left, dressed in a conservative dinner jacket, with his amazon guards at his back. Han couldn't help staring at the women for a moment—both of them were dressed in seductive outfits of fiery red silk, with silver-plated blasters sheathed on one hip and intricately decorated vibro-swords on the other. Threkin Horm sat to Leia's right in his repulsor chair, acting as a dinner escort. As the servers hurriedly set a place for Han, Leia introduced him to Isolder.

Threkin Horm blurted rather icily, "They've already met."

Leia looked at Threkin, whose face was reddening in anger, and Han said, "Yeah, the prince stopped by for a chat while I was working on the *Millennium Falcon*. We, uh, found that we have some things in common."

Han turned away rather quickly as he took his seat, hoping that Leia wouldn't see his embarrassment.

"Oh, really, I'd like to hear all about it." Leia's tone hinted at reprisal.

"Yes, General Solo, why don't you tell her *all* about it," Threkin growled.

There was an uncomfortable silence, and Prince Isolder cut in, "Well, for one thing, I was fascinated to learn that both General Solo and I had once worked as privateers. It really is a small universe."

"As privateers?" Threkin asked suspiciously. Han released a breath in relief.

"Yes," Isolder said. "When I was a boy, still in my teens, privateers attacked the royal flagship and murdered my older brother. That is when I became the Chume'da, the heir. I was young, idealistic, so I secretly left home, assumed a new identity. For two years I plied the trade lines as a privateer, working on ship after ship, hunting for the pirate who killed my brother."

"What an intriguing story," Leia said. "Did you ever find him?"

"Yes," Isolder said. "I did. His name was Harravan. I arrested him, and we held him in a prison on Hapes."

"Working with pirates must have been very dangerous," Threkin interjected. "Why, if they had ever discovered your identity . . ."

"The pirates were not so dangerous as one might think," Isolder said. "The greatest threat came from my mother's naval forces. We had frequent . . . encounters."

"You mean your own mother didn't know where you were?" Leia asked.

"No. The media believed I was hiding in fear, and since my own mother did not know where I had gone, she downplayed my disappearance, hoping I would resurface."

"And the pirate that you captured, Harravan, what became of him?" Han asked.

"He was murdered in prison while awaiting trial," Isolder said heavily, "before he could ever name his accomplices."

There was an uncomfortable silence for a moment, and Leia looked at Han. She obviously recognized that Isolder had changed the topic to protect him from her anger. Han cleared his throat. "Do you have a lot of problems with privateers in the Hapes cluster?"

"Not really," Isolder said. "The interior of the cluster is remarkably secure, but we consistently have problems on the rim, no matter how well we patrol. Our encounters on the rim are frequent, and frequently bloody."

"I survived one of those encounters as a privateer," Han said. "After what we went through, I'm amazed that pirates would work your cluster." Han wondered at Isolder. He had worked as a privateer, risking his life against the might of his mother's own navy, risking that the pirates he worked with might discover his identity. Isolder was handsome and rich, and those traits in themselves made him a threat, but Han began to realize that this foreign prince must have a great deal of grit hidden beneath his smooth exterior. He wasn't the kind of man who needed to hide behind amazon bodyguards.

Isolder shrugged. "The Hapes cluster is very rich, and that always attracts interest from outsiders. But I'm sure you know our history. Certain young men tend to glorify the old lifestyle."

"Your history?" Han asked.

Leia smiled. "Didn't you learn anything at the academy?"

"I learned how to pilot a fighter ship," Han said. "As for politics, I leave that to the diplomats."

Leia said, "The Hapes cluster was originally settled by pirates, a group called the Lorell Raiders. For hundreds of years they stalked the trade routes of the Old Republic, seizing ships, stealing cargo. And when they found a beautiful woman, some raider would take her as a prize to the hidden worlds of Hapes. In short, Han, the raiders were your kind of people." Han began to protest, but Leia smiled warmly, teasing him.

Threkin Horm said in his high voice, "So the women of Hapes raised their children as best they could. The pirates would steal the boys, making them pirates in turn. They would leave for months at a time, then come back to rest." Han looked up. Threkin Horm was studying Isolder's bodyguards with as much interest as he usually showed food, and Han suddenly understood why so many of the Hapans were beautiful—they had been bred for it over generations.

Prince Isolder said, "When the Jedi finally wiped out the Lorell Raiders, the pirate fleets never returned. The worlds of Hapes were forgotten for a time, and the women of Hapes took control of their own destiny and vowed that no man would ever rule them again. For thousands of years now, the queen mothers have kept that vow."

"And they've done a fine job for their worlds," Leia said.

"Still, sadly, a few of our young men feel powerless in our society," Isolder added. "And so they glorify the old ways. When they rebel, often they become pirates. Thus we have a perennial problem."

Han ate a few bites of dinner, some type of meat that tasted spicy and amphibious, and he realized he had no idea what he was eating.

"But we are off the subject," Threkin Horm said. "I believe Leia asked only a few minutes ago what you two talked about today." He glared at Han.

"Ah, yes," Prince Isolder said. "Han asked a question that I believe deserves an answer. He wondered, with all the other princesses in the galaxy, including many that are far more wealthy than Leia, why my mother would choose her.

"The truth is, the queen mother did not choose Leia," Isolder said calmly, gazing at Han. "*I* chose her." Threkin Horm must have inhaled some food, for he began coughing into his napkin. Isolder turned to Leia. "When Leia's shuttle landed on Hapes, she met my mother for a soiree in the gardens. They were so surrounded by dignitaries from the worlds of Hapes that Leia did not speak to me, perhaps never even saw me. I do not think she even knew I was alive. But I became enamored of her. I have never done anything like this. I've never been so impulsive. No other woman has captivated me this way. It was not my mother's idea to arrange a marriage with Leia. She only consented to my request." Isolder took Leia's hand and kissed it. Leia blushed, simply staring at Prince Isolder.

Han looked at Isolder's gray eyes, at the golden hair cascading down his shoulders and the strong, handsome face, and he could not see how Leia could resist such a man.

Then Han's mind went blank, and the next thing he knew, he was rising from the table, stumbling out of his chair. All eyes turned to him, and he felt clumsy, stupid, like a little boy. His tongue felt thick in his mouth, and he sat down. His mind was in such a turmoil that he said nothing, practically heard nothing through the rest of the dinner.

As they prepared to leave an hour later, Han kissed Leia good night, swiftly, and wondered afterward how it had felt to Leia, as if kissing were some athletic event she would judge. Threkin Horm shook Leia's hand warmly and left first, while Prince Isolder stood and talked quietly with Leia for a moment, thanking her for the dinner, thanking her for the time she had spent with him. He made some small joke, and Leia laughed quietly. Just as Han realized that Isolder was hesitant to leave Leia, the prince kissed her good night, holding her close. It started as a friendly kiss, the kind that dignitaries often exchange, but he lingered a second, and then for a second more. He stepped away, and Leia gazed into his eyes.

Isolder thanked her again for a wonderful night, glanced at Han, and a moment later Han and Isolder were outside her door, Isolder walking off with his bodyguards at his back.

"I'm going to fight you for her," Han said to the prince's back. It was an oafish thing to say, but Han's head was spinning, and he could think of nothing else.

The prince stiffened, turned. "I know," he said. "But I promise you, General Solo, I intend to win her. Much is at stake here, more than you know."

Long after dinner with Prince Isolder, Leia lay in bed luxuriating. She nearly fell asleep once, but the whining of the ship's engines as technicians tested the hyperdrive awakened her. On her dresser the rainbow gems of Gallinore smoldered in their dull lights, and in a corner, the Selab tree gave off an exotic, nutty scent that suffused the room. Threkin had insisted on storing the treasures in Leia's room, but Leia tried not to dwell on the riches. Instead, Isolder filled her thoughts—his courtesy to Han during dinner, his attentiveness, his small jokes and easy laughter. And finally, his profession of love.

In the middle of her normal sleep cycle Leia rose from bed. In an attempt to get her mind off Isolder, she sat down at a computer console and studied the Verpines. The large insects had long been a spacefaring race and had colonized the Roche asteroid belts before the Old Republic was born. They had developed an odd form of government. Because they communicated via radio waves using a strange organ in their chests, a single Verpine could talk with the entire race within seconds, allowing the Verpines to develop something of a communal mind. Yet each Verpine considered itself completely aloof from the group, not controlled by the hive. A Verpine who made a decision that might be considered "wrong" by the group was never punished, never condemned. The acts of the "mad" hive mother who had sabotaged the Barabel contracts weren't seen as a crime to be rectified but only as a sickness to be pitied.

Leia looked through the files and found ample evidence of Verpine criminals in the history books—murderers, thieves. And she discovered something very interesting. Nearly all of them had one thing in common: a set of damaged antennae. This fact made Leia wonder if the Verpines hadn't developed more of a communal mind than they realized. A Verpine without antennae was forever alone, unreachable.

Whatever the reason for the Verpines' behavior, the Barabels were mad enough to slaughter the whole species and chop them into hors d'oeuvres. Leia knew she wouldn't find an answer until she reached the Roche system and met the Verpines. She probably wouldn't understand the whole truth even if she met the mad hive queen herself.

Leia rubbed her weary eyes, but was too wound up to sleep. Instead, she walked the long corridors to the holo vid room and said to the operator, "I would like to arrange a broadcast to Luke Skywalker. You should be able to reach him at the New Republic embassy on Toola."

The operator nodded, made the connection, and spoke with an operator there. "Skywalker is in the wilderness. We can have him at the holo vid screen within an hour, if it is an emergency."

"Please do," Leia said. "I'll wait for him here. I can't sleep anyway." She took a seat nearby, then waited for Luke. When he appeared, he stood in a tall building wearing a dark wool greatcoat. Behind him was a huge window of cut glass. A pale red sun shone coldly through the glass, scattering light all around him in a fiery halo.

"What's the emergency?" Luke asked, breathless.

Leia suddenly felt embarrassed, shy. She told him about Isolder, about the treasures piled in her room and the Hapan's proposal. Luke remained calm, studied her face a moment.

"Isolder frightens you? I can feel your fright."

"Yes," Leia said.

"And you feel tenderness for him, something that might even turn into love. But you don't want to hurt either Han or the prince?"

"Yes," Leia said. "Oh, I'm almost sorry I called you with something so trivial."

"No, this isn't trivial," Luke said, and suddenly his pale blue eyes seemed to look beyond her, focusing on something in the distance. "Have you ever heard of a planet called Dathomir?"

"No," Leia answered. "Why?"

"I don't know," Luke said, "just a feeling. I'm coming to you. I sense an urgency. I should reach Coruscant in four days."

"I'll be to the Roche system in three."

"I'll meet you there, then."

"Good," Leia said. "I'd like you nearby."

"In the meantime," Luke offered, "take things slowly. Find out how you feel. You don't have to decide between the two in a day. Forget about Isolder's wealth. You wouldn't be marrying his planets, you would be marrying him. Just give him the same consideration you would give to any other man, okay?"

Leia nodded, suddenly became conscious of how much this call would cost. "Thank you," she said. "I'll see you soon."

"I love you," Luke said, and he faded.

Leia went back to her room, lay in bed for a long time before she fell asleep.

She was wakened in the early morning by door chimes. She found Han at the door, holding a starburst plant.

"I came to apologize for yesterday," Han said, offering the plant. The brilliant yellow flowers on their dark stalks seemed to twinkle as they opened and closed. Leia took it, smiled warmly, and Han kissed her.

"How do you think dinner went?" he asked.

"Fine," Leia said. "Isolder was a perfect gentleman."

"Not too perfect, I hope," Han said. Leia didn't laugh at his joke, and he hurried to add, "After dinner last night, I went to my room and gnawed on my own petty jealous fantasies for a while.''

"How did they taste?'' Leia asked.

"Oh, you know. I ended up going to one of the ship's galleys in the middle of the night, looking for something tastier to eat.'' Leia laughed, and Han stroked her cheek. "There's that smile. I love you, you know.''

"I know.''

"Good,'' Han said, taking a deep breath. "So how do you think the dinner went?''

"You aren't going to give up, are you?'' Leia asked.

Han shrugged.

"Well, he seemed nice enough,'' Leia answered. "I guess. I plan to invite him to stay here on the ship while we go to the Roche system.''

"You what?''

"I'm going to invite him to stay here on the ship.''

"Why?''

"Because he's only going to be here for a few weeks, then he'll leave and I'll never see him again. That's why.''

Han began shaking his head. "I hope you didn't fall for that line about how he fell in love with you from a distance,'' he said a little loudly, "and how he begged his mother for the chance to marry you.''

"Does that bother you?''

"Of course it bothers me!'' Han shouted. "Why shouldn't it bother me?'' His gaze turned inward, and he clenched his fist. "I'll tell you, as soon as I saw that guy, I knew he was trouble. There's something seriously wrong with him''—he glanced up, as if suddenly remembering that Leia was in the room—"Your Majesty. That guy is, uh—I don't know—slime.''

"*Slime?*'' Leia exclaimed. "You're calling the prince of Hapes slime? Come off it, Han, you're just jealous!''

"You're right! Maybe I am jealous!'' Han admitted. "But that doesn't change my feelings. Something is wrong here. I can't shake this feeling that something's wrong.'' Again he took on that same inward look. "Believe me, Your Highness. I've lived in the gutter most of my life. I'm slime. Most of my friends are slime. And when you've been among slime as long as I have, you learn to spot it at a distance!''

Leia didn't understand how Han could say such things. First to insult her by saying that he found it suspicious that another man might find her attractive, then to call the man a slime—all of it ran against her most deeply ingrained beliefs about how people should act toward one another.

"I think," Leia said, shaking with anger, "that maybe you ought to take your *stupid* plant and give it to the prince with your apologies! You know, someday your slow wit and quick tongue are really going to get you in trouble!"

"Ah, you've been listening to Threkin Horm too much! It's obvious he's trying to get you two cozy. Did you know that your precious prince offered to give me a new battle cruiser if I promised to fly away and leave you two alone? I tell you, the guy is slime!"

Leia glared at Han, stuck a finger in his face. "Maybe—just maybe—you should accept his offer while you can still get something out of this deal!"

Han stepped back a pace, wrinkled brow showing his frustration at the way the conversation was going. "Hey, look, Leia," Han apologized. "I . . . I don't know what's going on here. I'm not trying to be difficult. I know Isolder seems like a nice guy, but . . . last night in the galley I listened to people talk. Everyone is talking. As far as they're concerned, they've got you two married already. And I'm here trying to hold on to you, and the harder I hold, the more you slip through my fingers."

Leia considered what to say. Han was trying to apologize, but he didn't seem to realize that at this moment, she found his whole manner offensive. "Look, I don't know why people would even begin to think that I'd marry the prince. I certainly haven't given anyone that impression. So don't listen to them. Listen to me. I love you for what you are—remember? A rebel, a scoundrel, a braggart. That won't ever change. But I think I need some time to myself for a few days. All right?"

In the silence that followed, communicator tones sounded. Leia went to the little holo unit in the corner, flipped the switch. "Yes?"

A small image of Threkin Horm expanded in the air in front of her. The old ambassador was resting his enormous weight on a daybed. Folds of fat nearly concealed his pale blue eyes. "Princess," Threkin said jovially, "we are convening a special session of the Alderaanian Council tomorrow. I've already taken the liberty of calling the usual celebrities."

"A special session of the council?" Leia asked. "But why? What's wrong?"

"Nothing's wrong!" Threkin said. "Everyone has heard the good news of the Hapan's proposal. Since the marriage of Alderaan's princess into one of the wealthiest families in the galaxy will affect all of us refugees, we thought it best to convene the council so that we could discuss the details of your impending marriage."

"Thank you," Leia said angrily, "I'll be sure to attend." She punched the off button with disdain. Han gave her a knowing look, turned, and stormed from the room.

In the sterile white corridors of the *Rebel Dream*, Han leaned against a wall and considered his options. His attempt at an apology had failed miserably, and Leia was probably right about Isolder. He seemed like a nice enough guy, and Han's concerns were probably bred out of jealousy.

Yet Han had seen the yearning in Leia's eyes as she spoke of the peaceful worlds of Hapes. And Isolder was right. Even if Han won Leia's hand, what could he really give her? Certainly not the kind of wealth the Hapans offered. If Han convinced Leia to marry him, Alderaan's refugees would only lose in the end, and Threkin Horm stood at Leia's shoulder, reminding her of that fact every step of the way. Leia was endlessly loyal to her people.

Han chuckled to himself. *I think I just need some time to myself for a few days,* Leia had said. He'd heard that line before. It's the one that is always followed a few days later by, "Have a nice life."

Han could see only one way to match Isolder's wealth. Yet his heart hammered and his mouth went dry at the thought. He pulled a handheld communicator from his belt and thumbed a number, contacting an old acquaintance. The image of a huge, rubbery brown Hutt appeared on screen, looking out at Han with dark, drugged eyes.

"Dalla, you old thief," Han said with false enthusiasm. "I

need your help. I'd like to take out a loan on the *Millennium Falcon,* and I want you to get me into a card game tonight. A big one."

Captain Astarta, the prince's personal guard, woke Isolder in his room. She was a woman of rare beauty, with long, dark red hair and eyes as dark blue as the skies of her planet Terephon. *"Flarett a rellaren?"* ("Was dinner spiced well?") she asked almost casually. As Isolder lay in bed, he watched her eyes scan the room more thoroughly than normal, her scrutiny moving from dresser to bed to closets. Her movements were fluid, catlike.

"Dinner was spiced well," Isolder answered. "I found the princess to be charming, good company. What is wrong?"

"We picked up a coded message just an hour ago. It was beamed to all the ships in our fleet. We suspect it was an assassination order."

"The signal came from Hapes?"

"No. It was beamed up to our fleet from Coruscant."

"Who was to be assassinated?"

"The order did not name the target, or the time or place," Captain Astarta answered. "The complete message reads, 'The temptress seems too interested. Take action.' I know it's cryptic, but to me at least the meaning is clear."

"Did you notify New Republic Security that Leia is in jeopardy?"

Astarta hesitated. "I'm not convinced that Princess Leia is the target."

Isolder did not say anything. If he died, the royal line would fall to his aunt Secciah's daughter. Someone had also killed Isolder's betrothed once before, Lady Elliar. They had found her drowned in a reflecting pool. Isolder could not prove his beliefs, but he was sure that his aunt Secciah was behind the killing, just as he was sure that his aunt had hired the pirates who had assassinated his older brother after sacking the royal flagship. The pirates would have known that the Chume'da was worth a great deal to his mother, yet they had killed the boy without seeking a ransom. Isolder asked, "So you think I am to be the target this time?"

"I think so, my lord," Astarta answered. "Your aunt could blame it on the outsiders—on factions within the New Republic, on some warlord who feared the marriage union, even on General Solo."

Isolder sat up in bed, closed his eyes, thinking. His aunts and his mother—all were vicious women, cunning and deceitful. He had hoped that by marrying outside the Hapes royal line he would find someone like Leia, someone untainted by the avarice that plagued the women of his family. It hurt him to think that someone had managed to plant assassins in his own fleet.

"You will notify New Republic Security of the threat. If my aunt has managed to plant an assassin on this ship, perhaps they can help uncover her identity. Beyond that, you will assign half of my personal guard to protect Leia."

"And who will protect you?" Astarta asked. Isolder could see the sense of betrayal in her eyes. She loved him, could not neglect him. He had always known that. It was what made her so good at her job. Perhaps Astarta even hoped a little that Leia would die. Yet Isolder knew that Captain Astarta would follow his orders. Above all, Astarta was an excellent soldier.

He pulled a blaster from under the covers of his bed, saw the flicker of surprise in Astarta's eyes at having missed the presence of a gun pointed at her chest. "As always," Isolder said, "I will watch my own back."

Chapter

5

That evening Han found himself in a seamy dive in Coruscant's underworld—a casino that literally had not seen sunlight in more than ninety thousand years because layer upon layer of buildings and streets had been constructed over it, until the casino became wedged like a fossil in its layer of sediment. The moist air down here smelled of decay, yet for many races in the galaxy, those bred for life beneath ground, the underworld provided a habitat that they could thrive in. Deep within the gloomy shadows of the casino, Han could make out many pairs of large eyes, furtively watching.

Han had asked to get into a high-stakes card game and had worked his way up through three lesser games, but he had never been prepared for anything like this. To his left sat a Columi counselor in an antigrav harness, with a head so large that the blue, throbbing, wormlike veins around his cerebrum were far longer than his scrawny, useless legs. The Columi's vast intellect had made him one of the most feared gambling opponents in the galaxy. Across from Han sat Omogg, a Drackmarian warlord known for her incredible wealth. Her pale blue scales were polished to a high gloss, and green clouds of methane inside her helmet hid her vicious teeth and snout. To his left sat the ambassador from Gotal that Han had seen the day before, a gray-skinned, gray-bearded creature who played with his eyes closed, relying on the two huge sensory horns atop his head to probe the other players' emotions, hoping to read their minds.

Han had never played sabacc among such company. In fact, Han had not played sabacc in years, and now sweat poured down his body, moistening his uniform. They played a variation on the game that hailed back millennia, a variation called Force sabacc. In normal sabacc, a randomizer built into the table periodically altered the values of cards, giving the game an intensity and excitement that had kept it alive for generations. But under the rules of Force sabacc, no randomizer was used. Instead, the randomness of the game was provided by the other players. After drawing the first card for a hand, each player had to call out if his or her hand would be light or dark. The player who played the strongest light or dark hand would win, but only if the combined strength of his or her chosen side won. For example, if Han chose to play a dark hand while all others played light, he would surely lose. Han stared at his cards, mixed cards—the two of sabers, the Evil One, and the Idiot. Altogether, a weak hand in the dark suit, and he didn't think it would be good enough. Han had won the last several pots by playing cards from the light arcana. Perhaps it was just superstition, but he felt that it wasn't a good time to be switching to the dark suit. Still, Han could only take the cards he had been dealt.

"I will call your bet," the Gotal whispered to Han, not opening his red-rimmed eyes, "and I'll raise you forty million credits."

Behind Han, Chewbacca whined, and Threepio bent close and whispered in Han's ear, "May I remind you, sir, that the odds are sixty-five thousand five hundred and thirty-six to one against anyone winning eight hands in a row?"

He didn't have to say it aloud, but Han finished for him: *And they are significantly less when the hand looks like this.* "I'll call," Han said, pushing forward the deed to the mineral rights of a dead star system whose name only the Columi could pronounce. "And I'll raise you eighty million." He pushed over a stock chip that held a large percentage interest in the spice mines of Kessel. Han's nervousness must have overwhelmed the Gotal, for the ambassador suddenly shielded his left sensory horn with his hand.

The others saw how the Gotal registered Han's sheer desperation and eagerly called the bet. "Would anyone like to call the game now?" Han asked. He hoped they would wait until another round had been dealt.

"I'll call the game," the Gotal said. Each player laid his cards on the table. The Gotal was playing a dark suit, but for the moment his was weaker than Han's. The two others were playing light suits and could potentially beat Han. They waited for the dealer droid, which was bolted to the ceiling above the table, to give each of them a last card.

Overhead, gears squeaked as the arms of the ancient dealer rotated to place one in front of the Columi. The Columi touched it. The heat from his body activated the microcircuits in the card so that it displayed its picture and Han's heart nearly stopped: The commander of coins, the commander of flasks, and the queen of air and darkness. At twenty-two points it was nearly an unbeatable hand. Han only hoped that the combined strength of the dark hands might outweigh it.

The dealer dealt the final card to the Drackmarian. A picture of a Jedi Knight blossomed under her touch—Moderation, upside down. The fact that Moderation had been dealt upside down reversed the Drackmarian's light hand, twisted it so that power was added to the dark hands of Han and the Gotal. Han's heart leaped. This could turn it, this could turn the whole game. But under the rules, the Drackmarian could choose to discard one card. She pushed the upside-down Moderation card away, keeping her light hand at only sixteen points.

The mechanical arms shifted over to the Gotal, dropping a seven of staves onto his deck. It was a minor card, but it served to strengthen the dark hand. The Gotal held the queen of air and darkness, Balance, and Demise. He came in at negative nineteen points. Han felt a surge of elation, realizing that the dark hands would probably win. The Gotal must have sensed Han's elation and mistaken it to mean that Han believed he personally had won. The Gotal looked at Han's winnings jealously, then discarded his seven of staves. Since his dark hand now totaled below negative twenty-three points, the hand was declared a bust, meaning that the dark arcana would automatically lose—unless Han could hit a natural twenty-three, either positive or negative.

Han studied his cards again. The Idiot was worth nothing, the two of sabers was worth two points, while the Evil One was worth negative fifteen. Han's best chance to win would be an idiot's array—he could keep his Idiot card, plus the two of sabers, plus a three of any suit—thus making a literal twenty-three. He figured the odds of getting a three were pretty bad—about one in fifteen, but it was the only shot in town.

The mechanical hands rotated over Han, squeaking suddenly loud. The metal hands pulled out the top card from the deck, set it on the table, and Han reached out hesitantly, touched it. The second Endurance card blossomed under his fingers. Negative eight points. Han looked at his cards in disbelief, discarded the two. At negative twenty-three, he had a natural sabacc.

"You've won!" Threepio shouted, and the Gotal ambassador collapsed and began making small barking noises that Han guessed could only be sobs. The Columi regarded Han coldly from enormous black eyes.

"Congratulations, General Solo," the Columi said in a clipped tone. "I regret that this game has become too expensive for my tastes." The engines on his antigrav unit fired, and he began to maneuver carefully from the room, taking care that his enlarged brain did not collide with any of the furnishings.

The Gotal ambassador pushed himself from the table, lunged away into the shadows of the underworld.

"You arrre verrry rrrich, hhooooman," the Drackmarian warlord hissed through the speakers of her helmet. She set two gigantic paws on the table, scraping her talons over the ancient black metal. "Toooo rrrich. Youuuu mmmay nottt mmake ittt outtt of the underrrworld alllive."

"I'll take my chances," Han said, slapping his hand against the blaster holstered at his side and gazing into the warlord's helmet. He could make out dark eyes, gleaming like wet stones through the green clouds of gas. Han pulled all of the credit chips, stock certificates, and deeds into a single enormous pile.

Over eight hundred million credits. More credits than he had ever dreamed of owning. Yet still not enough.

The Drackmarian reached across the table, and her claws dug into his wrist. "Sssstop," she hissed. "Annnotherrr hh-hannnd."

Han considered, trying to appear calm. His mouth and tongue felt dry, but rather than lick his lips, he downed a mug of Corellian spiced ale. "Double or nothing?" he asked.

The Drackmarian nodded, and the methane tubes leading to her helmet jiggled. Among the opponents that Han had been playing, she alone might possess what he wanted. A world. With so much money on the table, Omogg could offer nothing less than a habitable world.

Omogg whispered to a security droid in the shadows at her back, and the droid swiveled guns toward Han, then popped open a vault in its belly. The Drackmarian pulled out a holo cube. "Thisss hasss been in fammmily forrr mmmany generrrationsss," the Drackmarian said. "It issss worth two poinnnt four billion creditsss. I will ssssell you onnne-third interesssst in it nnnow. If you winnn the next gammme, you will ownnnn the plannnnet. If I winnnn, I will ownnn both the plannnnet annnd the creditsss." She clawed a button on the cube, and the image of a planet appeared in the air. Class M, nitrogen and oxygen atmosphere. Three continents in a vast ocean. The holo began rotating through a series of shots of two-legged herd beasts squatting to graze on a wide purple plain, a bluish sun setting over a tropical jungle, a flight of dazzling birds sweeping over the ocean like colored glass spilling across a blue tile floor. Perfect.

Han began sweating again. "What's it called?"

"Daaathommmirrrrrr," the Drackmarian breathed.

"Dathomir?" Han repeated, mesmerized. Chewbacca growled in warning, placed a restraining claw on Han's arm, begging him to be cautious.

Threepio leaned close and his prissy vocalizers cut through the clouds of smoke. "May I remind you, sir, that the odds are one hundred thirty-one thousand and seventy-two to one against you taking nine hands in a row?"

.   .   .

When Leia answered her door chimes at the Alderaanian consulate, she found Han there, bathed in sweat, his hair a mess, his clothes looking baggy. He reeked of smoke and he smiled at her enormously, his bloodshot eyes gleaming with joy. He had a small box in his hand, wrapped in gold-colored foil.

"Look, Han, if you've come back to apologize, I forgive you, but I really don't have time for this now. I'm supposed to meet Prince Isolder in a few minutes and some Barabel spy wants to talk to me—"

"Open it," Han said, shoving the box into her hand. "Open it."

"What is it?" Leia asked. She suddenly realized that the box wasn't just wrapped in gold-colored foil, it was wrapped in gold.

"It's yours," Han said.

Leia untied the strings, pulled the foil open. It was a registry chip, one of the old kind with a holo cube built in. She thumbed the switch, watched the planet materialize in the air before her, a scene from space showing the planet: Thin pink clouds shone at the edge of the terminus, dividing night from day, and generous storm clouds swirled out from the ocean. In the background, four small moons hovered. She studied the continents, green with life, vast purple savannahs, exquisitely small ice caps at the poles. "Oh, Han," she said, her breath coming ragged with excitement. Her whole face seemed to be lit up, glowing. "What is its name?"

"Dathomir."

"Dathomir?" She frowned in concentration. "I've heard of it . . . somewhere. Where is it located?" She suddenly turned all business.

"In the Drackmar system. I won it from warlord Omogg."

She looked at the holo, watched it sequence into its first picture: giant green herd beasts, possibly reptilian, grazing on a blue plain. "This can't be in the Drackmar system," Leia said with certainty. "It's only got one sun."

She went to her console, locked into Coruscant's computer network, asking for the coordinates to Dathomir. It must have taken the huge computer banks some time to locate the files, for they waited nearly a minute before coordinates came up on screen. Leia looked into Han's face, saw his manic joy turn into a frown. "But, but that can't be!" Han said. "That's in the Quelii sector—warlord Zsinj's territory!"

Leia smiled regretfully, rubbed Han's hair as if he were a kid. "Oh, you sweet, shaggy nerf-herder. I knew it was too good to be true. Still, it was kind of you to offer. You know, you really are so kind to me!" She gave him a quick peck on the cheek.

He stepped back in shock. "The . . . the Quelii sector?"

"Go on home and get some sleep," Leia said, as if distracted. "You won't do yourself any good thinking about it. This ought to teach you *never* to play cards with a Drackmarian." She escorted him out the door of the Alderaanian consulate, and Han stood for a moment, rubbing his eyes, trying to keep awake and think at the same time. He looked up at the towering buildings above him, and the sunlight was thin, as if he were locked deep under a jungle canopy.

He had imagined that Leia would love her new world, had imagined how she would collapse in his arms with joy. He'd planned to wait till that moment, then ask her to marry him. Yet now all he had won was a worthless piece of real estate, and Leia had tousled his hair as if he were a kid brother. *I probably look pretty stupid right now,* Han thought. *Stupid and grungy.* He jingled the money in his pocket, enough credit chips so he could get the *Falcon* out of hock. Fortunately, Chewbacca had had the foresight to pull that much out of the pot. Nearly two billion credits won and lost. Han was feeling too old to cry—almost. He stumbled back through the gray streets of Coruscant to a small apartment that he kept onplanet, just hoping for some sleep.

"You really shouldn't go to this meeting," Isolder said. "I don't like the idea of you traveling alone in the underworld."

Leia smiled tolerantly at the prince. He was, after all, interested only in protecting her, but after tripping over his bodyguards for the past two days, she was beginning to wonder if he weren't overly protective. "I'll be all right," she said. "I've handled his kind before."

"If his information is so important," Isolder said, "then

why hasn't he given it to you already? Why insist on this meeting?"

"He's a Barabel. You know how paranoid predators get when they're convinced someone is hunting them. Besides, if he really does have information about attack dates and battle plans, I'll need that information before we go to the Roche system. The Verpines have got to be warned."

Isolder studied her with his clear, profound gaze. He wore a yellow half cape, an enormous golden belt, and wide golden bracelets that accented the bronze color of his skin. He stepped forward, rested his hands lightly on her shoulders, and Leia's skin tingled at the contact. "If you insist on going into the underworld, then I am coming with you." Leia started to object, but he touched his finger to his lips. "Please, allow me this. I suspect you are right. I suspect that nothing will happen, but I could not live with myself if anything should happen to you."

Leia studied his eyes, wanted to object, but there *had* been threats against her life. Isolder hinted that factions on Hapes would object to the union, and already she had heard reports through the New Republic spy networks that warlords on the far side of the galaxy were making efforts to sabotage the union. They didn't want the Hapan fleets adding their ships to the New Republic. Leia was already getting a taste of what it would be like to be the queen mother, wielding her might.

"All right, you can accompany me," Leia said, and she admired Isolder for having the courtesy to *ask* to accompany her. Han would have demanded it. She wondered if Isolder's good manners were a natural part of his personality or if they had become ingrained simply because he was reared in a matriarchal society where women were shown greater respect. Whatever the case, she found it charming.

He took Leia's arm, and they strolled out to the curb, flanked by Isolder's amazon bodyguards, to wait under the marble porte cochere for Leia's hover car. Old Threkin Horm came humming up the street in his repulsor chair. The broad streets here were fairly empty at this time in the morning, a couple of Ishi Tibs strolling, an old droid painting the lampposts. Threkin greeted them casually, as if he just happened to be passing by, but he did not volunteer to leave. Instead, he thumbed the switch that stopped his chair and just sat, waiting for the hover car. "I hear that it's such a nice day up top," Threkin said, nodding toward the towering buildings above them, hover cars moving through slants of sunlight, "that I'm almost tempted to go sunbathing. Almost."

Isolder tenderly gripped Leia's arm, and Leia suddenly wished that Threkin would just get lost. She looked up at Isolder, and he smiled down as if sharing her thought.

"Ah, here's your car now!" Threkin said. A black hover car plowed down the street, slowed, swerved in close. The tinted glass in the passenger's window shattered as someone shoved a blaster barrel through.

"Down!" one of Isolder's bodyguards shouted, and the woman leaped in front of Leia as the first volley of red bolts cut through the air. One of the bolts caught the woman in the chest, lifted her and threw her back. Gouts of blood glittered in the air, and Leia smelled the familiar stench of ozone and charred flesh.

Threkin Horm cried out and hit a button on his repulsor chair—he went hurtling south as fast as if he were in a land speeder, shouting at the top of his lungs.

Isolder pushed Leia back behind one of the broad pillars of the porte cochere and was a blur of motion as he whipped off his belt. Part of it—a small gold shield—he held in his left hand, and from somewhere he drew a small blaster. Leia heard a humming noise and a second volley issued from the car--but the red flaming bolts hit the air in front of them, exploded harmlessly.

A thin, blue, circular haze shimmered before Isolder, white at the edges, like a ring around a moon on a cold night. *Personal shielding,* she realized. Leia was suddenly conscious that the remaining amazon bodyguard was behind her, taking momentary advantage of the shielding to shout into a hand-held comlink for a backup.

A burst of blaster fire whizzed past Leia's head, hitting the marble above them, and Leia turned. The droid that had been painting on the corner fired a blaster at them.

"Astarta! Get the droid!" Isolder shouted. The prince's shield couldn't cover them in the crossfire, and they couldn't count on the marble pillars for much protection. Leia lunged for the dead amazon's blaster, fired off two quick rounds, enough so that the droid hid behind his lamppost. It was only then that

Leia registered the oddly erect main body, the bullet-shaped head and long legs. An Eliminator assassin droid, model 434. Astarta joined her in opening fire on it.

The hover car stopped, and two men leaped out, firing. Leia knew that Isolder's personal shield couldn't hold for more than a couple more seconds. Personal shielding tended to provide minimal protection, because you couldn't get a power source strong enough to deflect enemy fire and still last for more than a moment. The second danger came from the shield itself—the energy shield got so hot that the wielders risked frying themselves if they accidentally touched it. Isolder held the shield before him, lunged at his attackers.

Two more bolts whizzed past his head, and Astarta fired. Leia looked just in time to see the amazon's single bolt hit the assassin droid at midtorso. Metal bits flew into the air, followed by a massive explosion as the droid's power plant exploded.

The prince swung his shield as a weapon, and its energy field knocked his attackers backward. Blue sparks erupted in the air as it made contact. One man cried out and dropped his blaster, holding his burned face. Isolder raised the shield over his head, spun it and tossed it at the last attacker. The shielding caught the assassin in the chest, sliced through him like a lightsaber, and then Isolder stood alone with his blaster, aiming it at the remaining assassin, who was screaming in agony, clutching his face. He once had been a handsome man, Leia thought. Too handsome. A Hapan.

"Who hired you?" Isolder demanded.

The assassin screamed out, *"Llarel! Remarme!"*

"Teba illarven?" Isolder asked in Hapan.

"At! Remarme!" the assassin begged.

Isolder kept the gun leveled at the assassin a second longer, and the man shouted again. A piece of burned flesh tore away from his face. The man leaped into the gutter for his gun, and Isolder hesitated. The assassin fumbled for the gun, pointed it at his own face, and pulled the trigger.

Leia turned away. Suddenly Isolder's bodyguard was pulling at Leia's arm, yelling, "Inside, get inside!" and Isolder grabbed Leia, took her back into the house. There was an alcove by the door where guests could hang their coats, and Isolder pulled Leia toward the alcove, then stood protecting her, breathing hard and looking out into the hallway. The body-guard, Astarta, had bolted the door. As on most of the consul-ates, Leia's door was made of ancient blastplate and could withstand even a sustained assault. The bodyguard was yelling into her communicator again. Leia couldn't understand Hapan, but the guard was making a lot of noise.

"Who sent them?" Leia asked.

"He wouldn't say," Isolder answered briefly. "He only begged me to kill him."

Outside, through the walls, Leia could hear New Republic forces shouting as they sought to secure the area.

Isolder stood panting, listening intently, probably trying to eavesdrop on both his bodyguard and the police outside, make sure it was safe. He held Leia lightly, protectively, and her heart hammered. She pushed at him gently, and said, "Thank you for saving me."

Prince Isolder focused on the sounds around him so strongly that at first he seemed not to notice that she was push-ing him away. Then he looked down into her eyes. He lifted her chin and kissed her forcefully, passionately, and stepped in closer so that the entire length of him pressed against her.

Leia's mind seemed to go white, and her whole body felt electric. Her jaw was trembling, but she kissed him long and slowly, the seconds ticking away far slower than the pounding in her chest. With each second she could think of only one thing, *I'm betraying Han. I don't want to hurt Han.* But then Isolder whispered into her ear, demanding. "Come away with me to Hapes! Come see the worlds you will rule!"

Leia found herself crying, had never really imagined that she would let something like this happen. But at that moment, whatever attachment she had ever felt for Han suddenly seemed to become as insubstantial as fog, as a gentle white mist, and Isolder was the sun, burning it all away. With tears running down her cheeks she tangled her arms around Isolder and promised, "I'll come with you!"

Chapter

6

I don't know why I asked you here," Han said to Threepio, waving his hand in an expansive gesture. They sat in a booth in a cantina on Coruscant. It was a tame place by any standards—clear air, couples dancing slowly to the sound of Ludurian nose flutes.

Chewbacca looked up from his drink with weary eyes and growled. Chewie knew Han was lying. He knew exactly why Han asked Threepio there.

Threepio glanced at both of them, and his logic drive told him to probe further. "Is there anything I can help you with, sir?"

"Well, see . . . you've been closer to Leia over the last couple of days than I have," Han said, hunching his shoulders. "She hasn't exactly been happy with me . . . and she's spending all of her time with that prince, and after what happened to them this morning, they are so tightly surrounded by bodyguards that you can hardly get a glimpse of them. And now Leia left me a holo message to say she might be going to Hapes."

Threepio studied the words for 3.12 seconds, searching

through layer after layer of innuendo and unspoken meanings. "I see!" he said. "You two are having diplomatic problems!" Although Threepio was a translator with some of the finest programming in the galaxy, his human friends seldom called on his talents when dealing with their own complex emotional entanglements. Threepio perceived immediately that Han was placing an inordinate amount of trust in his abilities. This would be a rare opportunity to prove himself. "You've certainly come to the right droid! How may I help you?"

"I don't know . . ." Han said. "You see them together a lot. I was just wondering, you know, how things are going. Are they really getting that close?"

Threepio immediately accessed all visual records where he'd seen Leia and Isolder together over the last couple of days: dinners three nights in a row, council meetings where the two of them discussed potential difficulties in negotiating a settlement between the Verpines and the Barabels, just walking, dancing at a party for a minor dignitary. "Well, sir, during their first day together, Prince Isolder kept an average distance of point five six two decimeters between himself and Leia," See-Threepio said, "but that space is closing rapidly. I would say that the two of them are becoming very close indeed."

"How close?" Han asked.

"Over the past eight standard hours, the two have been touching nearly eighty-six percent of the time." Threepio's infrared optical sensors picked up a slight brightening as blood rushed to Han's face. He quickly apologized, "I'm sorry if this news disturbs you."

Han downed a mug of Corellian rum. Since it was his second in the past few minutes, Threepio quickly calculated Han's body mass and the alcohol content of the rum and decided that Han was more than mildly inebriated. Yet the primary manifestation of the intoxication seemed to be only a slight slowing of his speech.

Han placed a hand on Threepio's metal arm. "You're a good droid, Threepio. You're a good droid. There's not many droids I like as much as I like you. I don't know, what would you do if some droid prince was trying to muscle in on the woman you loved?"

Threepio's sensors picked up heavy emanations of alcohol from Han's breath, and he leaned away to avoid any corrosion to his processors.

"The first thing I would do," Threepio proffered, "would be to gauge the opposition and see what I have to give that the opposing party does not. Any good counselor droid could tell you that."

"Uh-huh," Han said. "So, what do I have to offer Leia that Isolder doesn't?"

"Well, let's see . . ." Threepio said. "Isolder is extremely wealthy, generous, well-mannered, and—at least by human standards—attractive. So, now all that we need to do is see what you have to offer that he doesn't have." Threepio searched his files for several moments, overheating his memory drives.

"Oh dear!" he whined at last. "I see your problem! Well, there's always emotional attachment, I suppose. I'm certain that Leia won't forget about you just because a better man has come along!"

"I love her," Han said emphatically. "I love her more than I love my own life, more than breath. When she touches me I feel like . . . I don't know how to say it."

"Have you told her?" Threepio asked.

"Like I say," Han sighed, "I just don't know how to say it. You're a counselor droid." He poured another rum, just stared at it. "Do you know how to say it? Do you know any songs or poems?"

"Indeed! I carry masterpieces from over five million cultures in my memory banks. Here is one of my favorites, from the Tchuukthai:

"Shah rupah shantenar
shan erah pathar
thulath entarpa

Uta, emarrah spar tane
arratha urr thur shaparrah
Uta, Uta, sahvarahhhh
harahh sahvarauul e thutha
res tarra hah durrrr—"

Han listened to the gentle music of the words, the soft curling snarls, the muted thunder. "That sounds pretty good," Han admitted. "What does it mean?"

See-Threepio translated it as closely as possible.

> *"When lightning rushes over the evening plains,*
> *I return to my cold den*
> *with a thula rat in my jaws.*
>
> *Then, I smell your sweet spoor*
> *smeared on the bones by the cave's maw.*
> *Then, then my head fins begin to tremble*
> *And my tail sways majestically as my mating howl*
> *begins to fill the hollow of the night—"*

Han stopped him with a wave of the hand. "All right, all right, I get the picture."

"There's much, much more," Threepio assured him. "It really is a beautiful epic, all five hundred thousand lines of it!"

"Yeah, yeah, thanks," Han said, sounding as disheartened as ever. He sat, listening to a foursome who had just sat down at another table, and Threepio realized that over the past minute, Han had been focusing on them. Threepio downloaded his auditory tracks and played back the conversation of those at the other table to find out what so intrigued Han.

FIRST WOMAN: "Oh, look, there's General Solo!"

SECOND WOMAN: "Gee, he looks pretty bad. Look at those bags under his eyes."

FIRST MAN: "Kind of scruffy looking, if you ask me."

SECOND WOMAN: "It makes you wonder what Leia ever saw in him, anyway."

FIRST WOMAN: "Now that prince from Hapes, he is *so* gorgeous! Down on Coruscant, street merchants are selling posters of him!"

SECOND MAN: "Yeah, I bought one for my sister."

FIRST MAN: "As for me, I'd take one of his bodyguards any day."

FIRST WOMAN: "With a body like his, I'd *kill* to be his guard."

SECOND WOMAN: "Well, you can guard that body all you

want—I'd rather be his masseuse. Can you imagine kneading that hot flesh all day long?"

Han said angrily, "Look, Threepio, why don't you keep an eye on Leia. If she asks about me, tell her I miss her. All right?"

Threepio stored the request. "As you wish, sir," he said, rising to leave the bar.

Chewbacca growled a good-bye to the spy. Threepio made his way out into the streets, wandered down chasms toward one of Coruscant's central computers that had a reputation as something of a gossip. Such a computer would gladly tell a droid secrets that it would never reveal to a biological life form. So Han needed a diplomatic counselor. This would be a wonderful opportunity for See-Threepio to prove himself! A wonderful opportunity!

Threkin Horm looked his best—dressed in a long, dark green waistcoat and white pants, his thinning hair meticulously curled so that ringlets danced around his ears. Leia noticed that he didn't look as fat as usual when he stood under his own power, and he was standing now at the podium. "As you all know, I have called this session of the Alderaanian Council so that we can discuss preparations for Princess Leia's marriage to Prince Isolder, the Chume'da of Hapes."

The crowd erupted into vigorous applause. The plush council room with its curtained walls and plum-colored chairs could hold nearly two thousand people, yet only a hundred members of the council were present. The rest of the seating was occupied by curious onlookers, while the back of the hall was a gleaming forest of metallic media droids. Leia sat in her seat on the front row, only a couple of meters from where Threkin stood on the podium. Han sat in a back row, dressed casually in a white shirt and vest, looking very much the way he had when they'd first met, years ago. Chewbacca sat beside him.

Leia had intended to discuss her plans here bluntly but hadn't been prepared for so much media attention. In the past day she suddenly found her entire life in the spotlight—the attempted assassination of the morning before had been covertly filmed from eight different angles and was playing on all the stations. New Republic Intelligence officers had swept the embassy for bugs this morning and found microphones with open channels to fifteen networks. It seemed that the only thing the public liked better than a royal marriage was a royal assassination, and the media hounds were lapping this up. Leia's only consolation was that if another assassin struck, he or she would have to shoot through the camera operators to get her.

Ah well, best to get this over with. "Threkin, members of the council," Leia said, standing. "I would like to thank you all for coming here, but don't you think this is a bit premature? I agree that this seems like a marvelous offer, but I haven't consented to marry Prince Isolder yet." She sat down again.

"Oh, Leia," Threkin said with a condescending smile. "Often in the past your clear head and cautiousness have served you well, but in this particular case . . . ?" He shrugged. "I've seen how you two look at each other, and you have agreed to a six-month excursion with Isolder, touring the worlds of Hapes. I think it's a grand idea! It will give you and Isolder a little time to grow closer while the royal house of Hapes gets an opportunity to see how well that pretty little head of yours wears a crown!" The crowd tittered with nervous laughter at the jest. "Let's put it before the council." Threkin waved at the seated assemblage. "Don't you all think that Leia and Isolder make a beautiful couple?"

Most of the professional politicians remained somewhat somber, but many of the traders snickered while members of the media and audience cheered and clapped. This didn't look at all to Leia like a normal council meeting, this looked like a carnival.

"You can't plan my wedding without me!" Leia interrupted, rising from her seat, astonished at Threkin's audacity. "Isolder understands, as I'm sure that you must, that we aren't engaged—either formally or informally. I'm going to Hapes simply to . . . ."

And she realized the truth. Isolder was taking her to Hapes so that the planetary dignitaries she might someday rule could study her, measure her for the crown. And she was going so that she could have time to get closer to Isolder. It was just as Threkin said. No matter how she might try to deny it, everyone else in the galaxy could see what was happening. She glanced over at Han. He looked miserable. She sat down, tried not to blush, intensely conscious that this encounter was already being carried live over dozens of news nets. She knew she should argue against Threkin, if only to save face, but right now she just couldn't think. For the first time in her life, Leia was at a loss for words.

"Indeed, indeed we can't plan your wedding without you," Threkin assured her from the podium. "We wouldn't think of it. We are only making plans *in the eventuality* that you marry Isolder—"

"Councilman Horm?" See-Threepio's voice cut through the council room. Leia turned, saw the golden droid standing on tiptoe and waving from the back of the room excitedly. "Oh, Councilman Horm, may I address the council?"

"What?" Horm asked in disdain. "Let a droid address the council?"

Leia smiled inwardly. The droid rights lobbyists would have a field day with that comment. It might well be the first nail in the coffin for Horm's political career. Leia stood quickly. "He may only be a counselor droid, but I think we should let him speak!"

There was grumbled assent from the general assembly, along with deafening cheers from the forest of media droids in the back.

"I, I, I see nothing wrong with that!" Horm sputtered, waving his arms. "I yield the podium to, to, to—that droid!"

The media droids cheered and Threepio walked up to the podium, scanning the crowd on his left and right as he did so. Leia had never seen a droid take such initiative. She wondered what he wanted. Threepio reached the podium and turned to address the crowd.

"Well," he said, "I would like to propose that the council *should* begin planning Leia's wedding—to General Han Solo!"

"What!" shouted Horm. "Why, why this is preposterous! General Solo isn't even royalty! He's just, he's just . . ." Horm must have realized that he had better not say anything libelous, but he shrugged in disgust. All through the crowd, a wave of grumbling began, and Leia wondered if she hadn't misjudged in letting poor Threepio address the council.

"I beg to differ!" Threepio answered. "I have been communicating with various computers through Coruscant's network all morning, and I've discovered some startling facts that all of you seem to have overlooked—possibly because General Solo has labored intensely to hide them: although the Corellians became a republic nearly three centuries ago, by birthright Han Solo is the king of Corellia!"

The room erupted in a dull roar and media droids began hitting Han Solo with spotlights. Threkin Horm's nasal voice sliced through the chatter with, "What? What? What?" Leia turned and looked to the back of the room in shock. The back seats of the auditorium were raised in tiers, and she could see Han plainly, blushing, trying to scrunch down into his seat. From the look on his face, she could tell that Han was indeed trying to hide something. And Leia knew that Threepio's programming as a counselor droid made him incapable of lying. Han put his hand up over his eyes and looked down at the floor. *In all these years, why didn't he ever tell me?* Leia wondered.

Aboard the Bith counselor ship *Thpfftht,* Luke watched the holo vid with interest, surprised that even on a backwater world like Toola the doings of Leia and Isolder—and now Han —could be of enough interest to warrant the enormous expense it cost to send the news clips through hyperspace. Well, Leia *was* living every woman's fantasy—attracting the interest of an incredibly rich and handsome prince. And the intrigue of the assassination attempt had escalated the worth of the story so that now Luke could watch his sister live, nearly three hundred light-years distant.

The Bith ship was scheduled to jump into hyperdrive within a few moments, and Luke studied the video with interest. The holo vid cameras were focused on Han now, and Solo sat scrunched in his chair, hand over his face. Even Chewbacca, sitting next to Han, opened his eyes wide in surprise, a throaty roar of astonishment escaping from between his canines.

Luke smiled inwardly. *Of course,* he thought, *Han is a king. I should have recognized it before. But why did he hide it?* In spite of his smile, Luke felt troubled. He could feel something odd, something distant and dark stirring. Too many in the galaxy would resist Leia's union to Isolder. He could feel the force of their malevolent intent, and Luke silently willed the Bith technicians to hurry and finish their equipment tests before making the jump to hyperdrive. Luke wouldn't reach the Roche system any too soon.

"Indeed," Threepio went on. "Han is the royal heir! Birth records indicate that Han's paternal ancestry goes back to Berethron e Solo, who introduced democracy in the Corellian empire. You can easily track the birthright for the next six generations, to Korol Solo, but records from Korol's period were destroyed in the Clone Wars and the lineage became lost.

"But Korol Solo married and fathered his first son on Duro nearly sixty years ago, and because of the wars and turmoil, that son never returned home. His name was Dalla Solo, but he changed his name to Dalla Suul to hide his identity during the Clone Wars. His firstborn son was Jonash Suul, and the first son of Jonash Suul was named Han Suul—who changed his name back to Han Solo. Obviously, Han knew of his royal lineage, but for reasons that are quite beyond me, he's also tampered with records back on Corellia in an effort to hide that lineage!"

There was an audible gasp from the crowd, and Threkin Horm shouted for order. Han got up slowly and walked out of the auditorium as the roar in the background diminished. Leia half-stood, watching Han leave, and the crowd quieted enough for Threkin to cry out, "But wasn't Dalla Suul also known as Dalla the Black? The famous murderer?"

"Well, yes, I suppose," Threepio admitted, "though the history texts describe him more accurately as a kidnapper and a pirate."

"And, well," Threkin said, "well, what kind of lineage is that? I mean—Dalla Suul was one of the most notorious kingpins in organized crime! You can't expect respectable people to give any credence to Han's claims of royal lineage."

"Well, I am just an ignorant droid and confess that I don't really understand how the actions of one's ancestors enhance or detract from one's respectability," Threepio apologized to Threkin Horm. "Such concepts are beyond the ability of a model AA-One Verbobrain to process. But since Dalla Suul's illegitimate daughter was your mother, I expect that you are infinitely more familiar with the logic of the arguments than I am.''

Threkin Horm's face paled, and he stood shaking.

The holo vid clip ended, and a droid announcer began commenting on it. Luke flipped off the holo and sat back in a thick chair, folded his hands on his lap. In only a couple of generations, Han's line had diminished from kingship to underworld kingpin. No wonder Han had hidden his lineage, had turned his back on the Alderaanian Council and stormed away before his secret was revealed. Poor Han.

Chapter

7

That afternoon, Leia and Isolder strolled through a secluded forest in the botanical gardens of Coruscant, a garden where plants from hundreds of thousands of New
Republic worlds flourished. Leia was showing Isolder the oro
woods of Alderaan—forests where the graceful, clean-limbed
trees climbed hundreds of feet into the air, but every inch of the
trees' bark was covered with iridescent lichen colonies that
glimmered in colors of cinnabar, violet, and canary—like the
effluent of rainbows. White cairoka birds fluttered from limb to
limb, while tiny brilliant red deer with golden stripes fed
among foliage on the ground. On Alderaan the oro woods had
occupied only a dozen small islands, and Leia had only traveled
there once as a child. Still, seeing that even a piece of her home
world still thrived lightened her heart.

Isolder walked hand in hand with her. He said, "I called
my mother on holo vid. She was pleased that you planned to
come visit. She's bringing her own personal vehicle to carry you
back to Hapes."

"Vehicle?" Leia wondered aloud at his choice of words.
"You mean she's bringing her own personal ship?"

"In this case," Isolder said, "I think the word *vehicle* is more appropriate. It's thousands of years old and rather eccentric in design. Still, you will like it." The woods were quiet. Isolder's bodyguards had spread out among the trees, except for the woman Astarta, who walked at their backs.

Leia smiled, stopped to smell a violet, trumpet-shaped flower. The flower had been uncommon on the plains of her home world, a pungent-smelling weed. "This is an arallute," Leia said. "Folktales said that if a new bride found one growing in her yard, it was a sign that she would soon have a child. Of course, the bride's mother and sisters always made it a point to plant an arallute in the newlyweds' lawn after the wedding, and of course they had to do it at night. It was considered bad luck to get caught." Isolder smiled, fingered the flower. "When it dries," Leia said, "the petals fold in and the seeds get trapped in the dry flower. Mothers then give the dry flowers to their babies to use as rattles."

"How charming," Isolder said, and he sighed. "It's sad to know that it's all gone, all destroyed. Except for what's here on Coruscant."

"When our refugees find a new home," Leia said, "we plan to take some of these specimens with us, establish another garden on a new world."

Comlink tones sounded, and Leia flipped her comlink on reluctantly. "Leia, Threkin Horm here. I have great news! The New Republic has canceled your mission to the Roche system!"

"What?" Leia asked, stunned. She had never been pulled from an assignment. "How did this happen?"

"It seems that relations between the Verpines and the Barabels are disintegrating at a faster rate than we anticipated," Threkin answered. "So Mon Mothma has escalated the level of intervention in hopes that we can avert a war. General Han Solo will be assigned to lead a fleet of Star Destroyers to the Roche system to protect the Verpines until the crisis is resolved. Meanwhile, Mon Mothma personally will be handling this crisis with a team of her most trusted counselors."

"What crisis?" Leia asked.

"Customs agents boarded a Barabel cargo ship outside the Roche system this morning and found the thing we all feared."

Leia's stomach turned at the thought of lockers filled with

Verpine body parts, hard frozen in the depths of space. In spite of her attempts to overcome such prejudices, the more Leia dealt with species of carnivorous reptiles, the more she anticipated such atrocities. Still, she told herself, you couldn't judge an entire species by the actions of a few. "What of Mon Mothma? Won't she need my help?"

"She and I both feel that there are . . . better ways for you to serve the New Republic," Threkin said. "Mon Mothma has temporarily relieved you from duty for the next eight standard months. I trust your time will be well spent." The undertone to his voice clearly indicated what he desired, but he said it outright. "You may leave for Hapes at your earliest convenience."

Threkin's image flicked off the communicator, and Isolder squeezed Leia's hand. Leia considered momentarily, and knew she could not argue against Horm—the Verpines really would be better off with a New Republic fleet at their side, and Leia had felt overwhelmed by the assignment all along. As a diplomatic counselor, she had great skills, but the Barabels were never impressed by stirring speeches or elaborate arguments. The Barabels, who had evolved as communal predators dominated by a pack leader, would respect Mon Mothma for handling the affair. The simple fact that the "pack leader" for the entire New Republic had jumped into the fray would disorient the Barabels, force them to regroup and rethink the situation.

In fact, now that Leia looked at it, she realized that Mon Mothma didn't need her at all. Leia had been so curious, trying to understand why a Verpine hive mother would be allowed to go feral, that she had been planning to attack the problem from the wrong angle. She should have been looking at the Barabels all along.

Perhaps the only thing that didn't make a great deal of sense would be to send a New Republic fleet to the Roche system. The Verpines could protect their hives. With their ability to communicate via radio waves, the fact that their colonies were built in an asteroid belt that was nonnavigable (at least by human pilots), and their swarming attack style in high-speed B-wing bombers, the Verpines would make a formidable foe.

Isolder stepped in closer. "Why are you frowning, little one?"

"Just wondering about something."

"No, you are worrying," Isolder said. "Don't you think Mon Mothma has things in control?"

"Too much control," Leia said, and she looked up into the stormy seas of his gray eyes.

"You aren't ready to leave yet, are you?" Isolder asked. Leia started to speak, but Isolder added, "No, no, that is all right. Leaving all of this behind," he gestured to the oro woods around him, "will be a big step for you. It will feel as if you are leaving it for good—and perhaps, if you so choose, you will indeed be leaving these worlds, this life, behind."

He held her hands, and Leia smiled wistfully. Isolder said, "Take a few days. Spend some time with your friends. Say your good-byes if you feel that you must. I understand. And if it makes you feel any better, then just repeat what you said to the Alderaanian Council: You are coming to Hapes for a visit, nothing more. There are no strings attached, no obligations."

His words slid over her like a wave of warm water, buoying her spirits. "Oh, Isolder, thank you for understanding." She leaned into his chest, and Isolder put his arms around her. For a moment, Leia was tempted to add, "I love you," but knew it was too soon to speak those words, knew it was too much of a commitment.

Isolder whispered softly into her ear, "I love you."

Han Solo sat at the console of the *Millennium Falcon*, running dodge maneuvers through an orbital junkyard of space debris off Coruscant's smallest moon. Doing computer checks of all flight systems on his ship was one thing—but Han had long ago decided that only a live test was sufficient.

Flying through a junkyard was much like negotiating through an asteroid field, except that the junk here tended to be all heavy metal, unlike those nice, soft carbonaceous asteroids. Threading his way through the debris somehow seemed to ease Han, tranquilize him. He dipped under the slowly tumbling busted stabilizer wing of a TIE fighter and then came up to the skeletal hull of an old Victory Star Destroyer, long since gutted for salvage.

Just what I want, he thought. There were some systems aboard the *Falcon* that just couldn't be tested in friendly space, and where Han was headed, he didn't expect to meet any friendlies. He slowed to match the Star Destroyer's velocity, nosed into the main exhaust nacelle up to where its turbodrive generator had once been housed, then carefully set the *Millennium Falcon* down.

Han flipped on his modified Imperial IFF Transponder, switched it to option fourteen. As his ship's radio signals bounced against the metal shielding of the fission chamber, Han's proximity indicators screamed in warning of approaching enemy Incom Y4 passenger ships in every direction, their blue-gray metallic images flickering on the head-up holo display. Han had salvaged the transponder code from a military transport ship attached to warlord Zsinj's marines. The transport ship had been carrying a twelve-member team from Zsinj's Raptors—a special forces organization supposedly devoted to surveying planetary defense systems, then infiltrating said planets and demolishing their defenses. But the Raptors were developing a nasty reputation as the strong arm of Zsinj's secret police. Ultimately, on many thousand worlds, the Raptors ruled.

Secure in the knowledge that his new transponder signal would identify him as one of Zsinj's ships, Han flipped on his jammers—and so much static and radio traffic came over his sensors that the ghost ships blanked out on his head-up display. Han smiled inwardly. Both the new transponder and the high-powered jammers were working fine. He'd need them in unfriendly space.

Now that he'd tested his hardware, Han fired his sublight engines and carefully lifted the *Falcon* out of the rusting innards of the old destroyer. As he maneuvered through the orbiting junkyard, the call he'd been waiting for came on audio.

Leia said, "General Solo, I hear that you'll be taking a fleet to the Roche system tonight."

"Yeah, that's what they tell me," Han said.

"I'll be sorry to see you go. I was hoping we could get together for a few hours before you leave."

A fleet? She thought he was leading a fleet? One Star Destroyer could hardly be called a fleet. Han knew who was behind the orders, who had stabbed him in the back. Threkin Horm. Han had underestimated the fat man, and now they planned to ship him off, far, far away, so that Leia would forget about him. "Yes," Han said. "That would be nice. I'm kind of busy right now, trying to get a grip on a few things. I can't come down planetside. Maybe I could meet you at fifteen hundred hours at your place? Aboard the *Rebel Dream*? We could maybe talk a little, go out for a drink."

"That sounds good. I'll see you then." Leia signed off.

Han glanced at the timepiece on his console. Chewbacca and Threepio were supposed to meet him on the *Millennium Falcon* at seventeen hundred hours. Time was running out.

When Han came to Leia's door, he had a tired smile on his face. He gave Leia a quick hug, then entered the hallway to her quarters, glancing around nervously. She stepped back to look at him. His hair was mussed, eyes fatigued. He didn't look happy at all.

"Can I get you a drink or something?" Leia asked.

Han shook his head. "Uh, no." He didn't say anything else, just stood, looking at the walls and glancing into the living quarters. In Leia's bedroom, the dull lights shone from the gems of Gallinore on her dresser. The twin suns above the Selab tree had gone dark, as if they were on a night cycle.

"You aren't happy about your transfer to the Roche system, are you?" Leia asked.

"Well, uh, to tell the truth, I'm not going," Han admitted.

"Not going?" Leia asked.

"I resigned my commission."

"When did this happen?" Leia asked.

Han shrugged. "Five minutes ago." He walked into her bedroom, stood staring down at the bed, glanced at the gems on her dresser, the piles of treasure from Hapes. Part of Leia was still surprised to have it here. If she'd had any sense, she told herself, she would have had it locked up.

"Well, where will you go?" Leia demanded. "What will you do?"

"I'm going to Dathomir," Han said, and Leia stood with her mouth open a moment.

"You can't go there," she said. "That's in Zsinj's territory. It's too dangerous."

"Before I resigned, I ordered the *Indomitable* to run a strike-and-fade against some of Zsinj's outposts on the edge of New Republic space. Zsinj will be forced to fortify those outposts, drawing any ships away from Dathomir, and I should be able to just slip between the cracks. He won't even know that I'm there."

"*That*," Leia said loudly, "is an abuse of authority!"

Han turned his interest from the gems, looked up at her and grinned. "I know." Leia didn't say anything else. When he got in one of these headstrong moods, she knew she couldn't talk any sense into him. He shrugged again. "No one will get hurt. I ordered them to attack only with long-range drones. Our soldiers will be okay. You know, I think I must have been looking at that holo of the planet too long. I dreamed about it last night: running on the beach, the wind in my face, water slapping against my ankles. It was all so sweet. So when I got my orders today, I just decided. I'm going."

"What will you do there?"

"If I like it, maybe I'll just stay. It's been a long time since I've felt sand beneath my feet. Too long."

"You're burned out," Leia said. "Don't resign your commission. I'll pull some strings, get you reassigned. You can have a few weeks off . . ."

Han had been looking at the floor, but now he turned his attention to her, studied her face. "We're both tired," he said. "We're both burned out. Why don't you come with me, run away?"

"I can't do that," Leia said.

"That's what you're planning to do with Isolder. Run away. Why can't you give me equal time? Chewie and Threepio are going to meet me at the *Falcon* in an hour. You could come with us. Who knows, maybe you'd fall in love with Dathomir. Maybe you would fall back in love with me."

He sounded so pitiable. Leia felt guilty for the past few days, for ignoring him, deserting him. She remembered how she'd felt the day that Vader had encased Han in carbonite, shipping him back to Jabba the Hutt, the joy they had shared when the Emperor was vanquished. She'd loved him then. *But that was a long time ago,* she told herself. "Look, Han, I'll always be fond of you," Leia found herself saying. "I know it's hard."

"But have a nice life?" Han asked.

Leia found herself shaking. Han strolled over to her dresser, and Leia saw that he was looking at the polished black metal of the Gun of Command. "Does this really work?" he asked. He started to reach for it, and Leia realized what he planned, shouted, "Don't touch that!"

Han snatched the gun and spun, faster than she would have believed possible. He stood pointing it at her. "Come with me to Dathomir!"

"You can't do this!" Leia pleaded, raising a hand as if it could ward off the blast.

"I thought you loved rogues," Han said. A spray of blue sparks erupted from the gun, bringing forgetfulness and the night.

"Are you sure that General Solo kidnapped the princess?" the queen mother asked. Even though his mother's image was only carried on holo vid, Prince Isolder dared not look up at her veiled face.

"Yes, Ta'a Chume," he answered. "A news network planted a fly eye in the hallway leading to her quarters, and it filmed Leia leaving her quarters with the general. She walked like one who is dreaming, and Solo was armed with the Gun of Command."

"So, what steps will you take to recover the princess?" Isolder could feel the weight of the Ta'a Chume's stare. The queen mother was testing him. On Hapes, the women in authority often spoke deprecatingly of the "ineptitude of men," their seeming inability to ever do anything right.

"The New Republic has already assembled a thousand of their best detectives to track down Han Solo. Astarta has secured hourly progress reports, and we have put out calls for bounty hunters."

The Ta'a Chume spoke softly, menacingly. "Look into my eyes."

Isolder gazed up at her, tried to relax. His mother wore a circlet of gold, and a thin yellow veil obscured her features. The lights around her lit the gold so that she seemed almost to gen-

erate an aura of power. Isolder focused beyond the veil, at her
dark eyes boring into him.

"This General Solo is a desperate man," she said. "I know
what you are thinking. You want to rescue Princess Leia from
his clutches yourself. But you must remember your duty to
your people: You are the Chume'da. Your wife and daughters
must someday reign. If you place yourself in jeopardy, you will
be betraying the hopes and dreams of your people. You must let
our assassins handle General Solo. Promise me!"

Isolder stared hard into his mother's face, tried to hide his
intent, but it was no use. She knew him too well. She knew
everyone too well. "I *will* hunt down General Solo," Isolder
said. "And I *will* bring home my bride."

Isolder waited for his mother to explode, waited for the hot
wrath in her voice to pour over him like magma. He could feel
it in the silence that followed, but the Ta'a Chume was not the
kind of woman to show her anger. She said calmly, almost with
a sigh, "You disobey me lightly, but no matter what you think,
your tendency toward selfless heroics is no virtue. I would cure
you of it if I could." She did not speak for a moment, and
Isolder waited for her to pronounce his punishment. "I suppose
you are too much like your father. General Solo will probably
seek refuge with one of the warlords, someone who might hope
to withstand the might of the New Republic. I will gather my
assassins and bring a fleet to Coruscant immediately. It goes
without saying that if I find Solo before you do, I will kill him."

Isolder let his gaze drop to the floor. Isolder had wildly
hoped that now that Leia had been abducted, his mother would
forgo this trip, stay away. But it made sense: Solo had kidnapped her successor. Honor demanded that she take all steps
to recover the princess. "I know you are displeased. Yet when I
was a child you often said, 'Hapes can only be as strong as
those who lead her.' I often reflect on your words, and I've
taken them to heart." He ended the communication, sat back
and considered. Isolder almost pitied Han. General Solo could
not possibly guess the kind of resources his mother would bring
to bear on him.

.   .   .

Corporal Reezen had somehow managed to work in the military for seven years in relative obscurity, never attracting the praise or attention he felt to be his due. All too often, that is how it went in military intelligence. You scraped and slaved for years to break a big case, hoping that some useful information might cross your way.

That is why he planned to send this report to warlord Zsinj directly, for his eyes only, signing his name to the documents so that none of his superiors could take credit. It was only fair. Corporal Reezen was the only person to notice it—three strike-and-fades over a period of nine days, maneuvers designed to draw off Zsinj's fleet. Obviously the New Republic was planning some sort of an attack, hoping to open enough of a hole to send a fleet through. And it had to be a fleet—something more important than a mere spy ship—for anyone to have spent so much money ensuring that the ships got through the corridor safely.

Reezen could feel it in his bones—something big was coming. So he had calculated the vectors, gauging possible military targets, had narrowed his list to six, ranking them by possibility. So much territory to cover, and so much uncertainty. Reezen pondered the possible targets one last time, and looked beyond the obvious possibilities. There, far off on his charts, was Dathomir, and Reezen studied the planet, felt an odd tingling in his bones.

Dathomir was already well protected, so far within Zsinj's territory that the New Republic could not possibly know of the warlord's operations there. The shipyards? Could the New Republic be planning to attack the shipyards? No, that didn't feel right. They wanted something on the planet. Such a rugged, dangerous place. There were a number of prisoners on the planet that the New Republic might want—if the New Republic even knew of the penal colony—but no one would be stupid enough to try to land there. Reezen had met the natives, and the very notion of landing on Dathomir sent a chill creeping down his spine. Still, the planet seemed to beckon to Reezen. *Here, here. They are coming here!*

Once, when Reezen was in his early teens, he'd watched a military parade on Coruscant with his father, and during the parade Darth Vader, Dark Lord of the Sith, had stalked by—

nearly. Instead, Lord Vader had halted the parade, stopped to look at Reezen, pat him on the head. Reezen remembered how his frightened image had been reflected in the Dark Lord's helmet, remembered the cold terror as that armored hand patted his head, but Vader had only said softly, "As you serve the Empire, trust your sensitivity," and then he moved on.

Hesitantly, Reezen suggested reinforcements for Dathomir despite his belief that the New Republic would not attack, then keyed in the sequence on his computer terminal that would send the encrypted warning to Zsinj.

The warlord was a thorough man. Zsinj would take care of it.

Chapter

8

L eia awoke to darkness. She had been lying still for a long time, staring up into blackness, unmoving. She had been concentrating on being still, concentrating so hard that her head ached and her muscles cramped. Han's last words had been "Lie still and be quiet," and with all her might she had struggled to comply.

With the sudden realization of that betrayal, she screamed, "Han!" and tried to sit up. Her head hit something hard, and she had to lie back down. She felt a grate beneath her and the familiar, subdued rumble of the *Millennium Falcon*'s hyperdrive engines. It had been five years since she'd last hidden in the *Falcon*'s smuggling compartment, and it still smelled the same.

Han Solo, I'm going to kill you, she thought. *No, on second thought, you'll be lucky if you only die.* She felt in the dark around her for the latch, found it, tried to pull it back. It wouldn't open. She fingered it, found that it was broken. She rolled over, found something small and metal, banged it against the roof.

"Han Solo, you let me out of here this minute!" she shouted, felt the thing in her hand vibrate and emit a hissing noise. Leia held it to her ear. *Oh great! An air exchanger! At least he didn't want me to suffocate.* She shook it, listened to the rattling of the air exchanger's busted innards. "All right, Solo. You let me out of here! This is no way to treat a princess!" She banged on the ceiling of the compartment, kept banging, but got no response.

As the air got warmer, Leia began to wonder if Han could even hear her. Was background noise drowning out her calls? She lay next to the Quadex power core, the main power source for the ship, and every few moments the piping above her head would hiss as coolant surged toward the core. The compartments weren't large, but they circled a third of the interior of the ship—from the entry ramp, over to the cockpit corridor, and around to the passenger bunkbeds. Leia closed her eyes and considered. Han and Chewie normally bunked over by the technical station in the lounge. There was a wall separating her from the technical station, but Han should have heard her pounding if he were there. He might, however, still be in the cockpit, a good seven or eight meters away. If they were in the cockpit, and the bulkhead door was closed, there would be no way for Han or Chewie to hear her calls.

And now her air was running out. Leia picked up the busted air exchanger, banged against the ceiling harder and harder, but resisted the impulse to yell for fear that her oxygen would run out all the faster. After only a few minutes, her arms burned with fatigue, and Leia stopped to rest. She felt like crying. Han knew she didn't trust this faulty metallic mélange gleaned from forgotten junkyards and cut-rate dealers. Sure, the *Falcon* was fast and well armed, but it was also always falling apart. Han had three droid brains running all his jury-rigged, modified systems, and Leia felt sure that all his technical problems couldn't come by mere accident. Han said that the brains bickered, but those droid brains had to be sabotaging each other's systems. Someday, one of them would do something really bad, and the whole ship would blow. It was just a matter of time. She banged on the ceiling again.

The hatch above her opened a crack. Chewbacca growled.

"What do you mean the sound couldn't be coming from here?" Threepio said, his voice muffled by the hatch. "I'm sure I heard something banging right under here. Why you don't scrap this old bucket of space debris is far beyond me!"

The hatch flipped open, and Chewie and Threepio peered in. Chewie's eyes widened in surprise, and Threepio lurched back. Chewie howled, and Threepio said, "Princess Leia Organa, why are you hiding in there?"

"I've come to kill Han," Leia said, "and this is the only way I could sneak aboard the ship. What do you think I'm doing in here, you turbopowered dummy, Han kidnapped me!"

"Oh dear!" Threepio muttered, and he and Chewie looked at each other, then hurried to help her from the hold.

Leia got up, feeling a bit dizzy, and Chewbacca looked off toward the cockpit. His eyes were hard, and the fur on the back of his neck had raised. He growled menacingly, and for one moment Leia thought that surely Chewie would rip off Han's arms in typical Wookiee fashion. Chewie stalked toward the cockpit, and Leia ran after him, saying, "Wait, wait . . ."

Han was sitting in the captain's chair, his fingers flying over the instrument panels. The wash of stars in the viewscreens was a brilliant white—signifying that they were hurtling through hyperspace at the *Falcon*'s top speed of point six above lightspeed. Chewie growled, and Han didn't turn to face them.

"So, did you figure out what that banging noise was?" Han asked.

"You bet he did!" Leia said.

At her back Threepio shouted, "I suggest you return the princess immediately, before we all wind up in the brig!"

Han turned calmly, swiveling in his chair, and put his hands behind his head. "I'm afraid we can't return just yet. We're locked on course for Dathomir, and the helm won't respond to any other orders."

Chewbacca rushed forward to the copilot's seat, hit a sequence of keys, growled questioningly at Leia. Threepio translated, "Chewbacca wants to know if you would like him to beat Han for you."

Leia looked at the Wookiee, knew how much that question must have cost him. Chewbacca owed a life debt to Han, and was bound by his code of honor to protect Solo. But perhaps, under the extreme circumstances, the Wookiee felt Han needed a little correction.

Han raised a hand in warning. "You can beat me if you want, Chewie, and I doubt I could stop you. But before you knock me senseless, I want you to think about something: it takes two people to bring this ship out of hyperdrive, and you can't do it without me."

Chewie looked at Leia and shrugged.

"You think you're so smart," Leia said. "You think you have all the answers. Chewie, keep him in here. He brought a Hapan Gun of Command aboard, and I'm going to shoot him with it."

Han pulled a gun from his holster, and Leia realized it wasn't his normal blaster. It was the Hapan gun—but Han had broken off the circuitry on the barrel. "I'm sorry, Princess, I think it's busted."

He let it drop to the floor.

"All right, what is it you want from me?" Leia asked, feeling somewhat defeated.

"Seven days," Han said. "I want you to spend seven days with me on Dathomir. I'm not even asking for equal time with Isolder, just a mere seven days. After that—I'll take you straight back to Coruscant."

Leia folded her arms and tapped her foot nervously, looked at the floor, made herself stop tapping, then looked up at Han. "What's the point?"

"The point is, Princess, that five months ago you told me you loved me, and it wasn't the first time. You used to love me. You believed it, and you made me believe it. I thought our love was something special, something I would gladly die for, and I'm not going to let you throw away *our* future just because some other prince comes along!"

Other prince, he'd said. Leia tapped her foot, had to consciously will herself to stop. "Then you admit it? You are the king of Corellia?"

"I never said that."

Leia looked away at Threepio, glared back at Han. "What if I don't love you anymore? What if I really have changed my mind?"

"The news nets are already reporting that I've abducted you," Han said. "They began broadcasting the story just before we bugged out. If you don't love me, then I'll bring you back in seven days, and I'll serve my time in prison. But if you do love me," Han paused, "then I want you to kiss Isolder good-bye and marry me." He jerked his thumb, pointing at his chest.

Leia found her head shaking in frustration. "You've got a lot of nerve."

Han stared into her eyes. "I've got nothing to lose."

He really was putting everything on the line, as he had done for her time and time again. A few years ago she had thought he was dashing and bold, perhaps a bit reckless. Now that she thought about it, he had only seemed reckless because he so often risked his life for her. Han would almost throw it away at her whim. What she had once deemed an almost inhuman courage was really a sign of his unflagging devotion. And Leia found her heart pounding in fear at the thought that someone could love her *that* much.

"All right," Leia swallowed. "You have a deal—"

"Princess Leia!" Threepio said in consternation.

Leia added, "—but I hope you like prison food."

As soon as the Bith ship dropped out of hyperspace near the maelstrom of rubble that circled the Roche system, Luke knew there was trouble. He couldn't *feel* Leia anywhere nearby. He went to his room, called the New Republic's ambassador to the Verpines over subspace radio, and got the old man out of bed.

"What's so important?" the ambassador snapped.

"What has happened to Princess Leia Organa?" Luke asked. "I was supposed to meet her here."

The ambassador frowned. "She got kidnapped a couple of days ago, by General Solo. I watch the holo vids when I can, but I'm a busy man! I don't have much time for such nonsense. You could always call Coruscant, if it's that important to you."

Luke frowned. His status as a war hero didn't give him enough pull to make hyperspace calls on holo vid. Besides, a call wouldn't get him any closer to Leia. He needed to go back to Coruscant, start from there. "Do you have any ideas where I might find Han and Leia?"

The ambassador yawned, scratched his bald head. "Who do you think I am, the chief of espionage? Nobody knows where they are. Eyewitnesses claim to have sighted Solo on at least a hundred worlds. Invariably it turns out to be only a rumor, or some lookalike gets nabbed. I'm sorry, son, I can't be any help." The ambassador flipped off the communicator, and Luke sat, puzzled. He seldom received such rude treatment from anyone, much less dignitaries. He guessed that the operator hadn't told the ambassador who was calling.

Luke closed his eyes, stretched with his senses. Sometimes, in his sleep he would dream about Leia. Usually, if she was within the same star system, Luke could feel her presence. She was nowhere nearby. He decided to get his fighter out of storage and head for Coruscant.

Han was working in the galley aboard the *Falcon*, trying to put together his fourth candlelight dinner in as many days. The smell of spiced aric tongue wafted up, and Han was busy spooning some pudding into cora shells when the pudding bowl tipped over and dropped on the floor, spattering the walls and Han's pant leg. Chewbacca had been standing at the viewport, and the Wookiee turned and laughed.

"Go ahead," Han said. "Laugh it up, fur brain. But let me tell you something: by the end of this trip, Leia is going to realize she loves me. In case you haven't noticed, it's only been four days, and she's already warming up to me nicely."

Chewbacca growled disparagingly.

"You're right," Han said with a tone of dejection, "Hoth will warm up before she will. And I suppose mating rituals are much simpler where you come from. When you love a woman, you probably just bite her on the neck and drag her to your tree. But we handle things differently where I come from. We make our women nice dinners, we compliment them, treat them like ladies."

Chewie laughed derisively.

"So we shoot them and drag them into our spaceships," Han admitted. "All right, so maybe I'm not *that* much more civilized than you, but I'm trying. I'm really trying."

"Han, oh Han," Leia called from the lounge. "By any chance, do you have that first course ready? I am getting so hungry, and you know how irritable I get when I'm hungry."

"Coming, Princess," Han called sweetly as he opened the oven. He tried to pull out the pan of spiced aric tongue with the bottom of his apron, burned his fingers. He yelped and stuck his hot fingers in his mouth, got a hot pad and dumped the tongue on a plate. Somehow, the tongue looked bluer than it should, and he wasn't sure if he had overcooked it, if the tongue was just bad, or if maybe he'd put in too much ju powder.

"Are you about done in there?" Leia called.

"Coming!" Han shouted, and he brought the tongue to her. He'd set a nice red tablecloth over the hologram board, and the candelabra was all aglow. Leia looked spectacular in a dazzling white dress jumpsuit and pearls, the flames dancing in her dark eyes. He set the plate down, and said, "Dinner is served."

Leia looked at him questioningly, raising an eyebrow.

"What?" Han said. "What is it this time?"

"Aren't you going to slice it for me?" she asked. Han looked at the vibro-blade on the table. He'd seen Leia hack her way through a jungle with a dull machete. He'd seen her slice ropes off her hands with a piece of broken glass. He'd even seen her dispatch some kind of swamp monster with a pointed stick that wasn't anywhere near as sharp as that vibro-blade. "Of course I'll slice it for you," Han said. "It would be my pleasure."

He took the blade, began slicing the tongue into portions. When he was halfway done he decided he'd better check his progress. "Are these slices all right for you? Would you like them thicker, thinner, sliced lengthwise instead of sideways?"

"The portions look fine," Leia said, and Han finished slicing the tongue, sat down to the table and picked up a napkin.

Leia cleared her throat, looked up at him.

"What now, my pet?" Han asked.

"Are you going to sit at this table with your dirty apron on?" Leia asked. "I mean, that is a little disgusting."

Han remembered a moment when they had shared stale rations in a battlefield on Mindar, dead stormtroopers all around. "You're right," Han said. "I'll take it off." He got up, removed the apron, took it and hung it on a peg in the galley. He came back and sat down. Leia cleared her throat.

"What now?" Han asked.

"You forgot the wine," Leia said, looking at her glass. Han glanced at her plate, noticed that she'd already begun eating without him.

"Would you prefer white, red, green, or purple?"

"Red," Leia answered.

"Dry or wet?"

"Dry!"

"Temperature?"

"Thirty-nine degrees."

"You aren't going to let me eat with you again tonight, are you?"

"No," Leia said firmly.

"I don't get it," Han said. "It's been four days now, and outside of ordering me around, you haven't said one word to me. I know you are mad at me. You've got a right to be. Maybe I've ruined it for you, and you're never going to be able to like me. Or maybe you're getting so used to having servants around, that you just want to turn me into your slave. But I would hope, if nothing else comes out of this, that at the very least you would still like me as a friend."

"Maybe you're asking too much of me," Leia said.

"I'm asking too much of you?" Han said. "I'm the one who has been cooking and cleaning and taking care of your clothes and making your bed and flying this ship. Just tell me this. Just answer me this, and answer honestly: isn't there anything you like about me anymore? Isn't there just one thing? Something? Anything?"

Leia didn't answer.

"Maybe I should just turn the ship around," Han said.

"Maybe you should," Leia agreed.

"But I don't get it," Han said. "You agreed to come on this trip," he shrugged, "albeit under duress, I'll grant you that. But you're madder than you should be. If you want to take it out on me, then go ahead. I'm right here. Han Solo, in the flesh." He leaned his face forward. "Go ahead, slap me. Or kiss me. Or talk to me."

"You're right," Leia said. "You don't get it."

"Get what?" Han said. "Get what? Give me a clue!"

"All right!" Leia said. "I'll spell it out for you: you, Han

Solo the man, I can forgive. But when you brought me on this ship, you betrayed the New Republic that we serve. You're not just Han Solo the man anymore. You were Han Solo the hero of the Rebel Alliance, Han Solo the General of the New Republic. And that Han Solo I can't forgive, I refuse to forgive. Sometimes what you represent is so important that you can't let your standards down. You become respected as an icon, as much for *what* you are as who you are."

"That's not my fault," Han said. "I refuse to be bound by anyone's preconceived images of me."

"Fine," Leia said. "Maybe you don't think the universe should work that way. Maybe you want to be free to run off to be a pirate again or play around like a little boy, but that's not how the universe works! You're going to have to face up to that."

"Fine," Han said throwing his napkin on the table, "so I'll face up to it. After dinner. You tell me what you want me to do, how you want me to act. I'll change—forever. I promise. Okay?"

Leia stared up at him, and something in her features softened. "Okay."

Four days later the *Millennium Falcon* dropped out of hyperspace above Dathomir and the proximity indicators screamed in warning. Leia came running, leaned over Han's pilot seat to look out: Star Destroyers littered the sky while shuttles and barges plodded up from a small red moon in a solid line toward a huge mass of metal piping and struts—ten kilometers of gleaming scaffolding that floated in space at an L5 point. It looked like some giant insect, but docked around it were thousands of craft—one Super Star Destroyer, dozens of old Victory-class models and escort frigates, thousands of box-like barges. For one moment, Han stared at them in awe and then breathed angrily, "Trespassers!"

Leia drew a deep breath. "Well, Han, you've certainly struck the jackpot this time. Why, this planet must have more enemy fighters than a Hutt has ticks."

Han glanced over at Chewie. The Wookiee was trying to

pull up the nav charts for the Ottega star system. On the head-up holo display, two red fighters began vectoring up from a Star Destroyer. "Can the sarcasm, Princess, and get yourself up to the gun well, we've got company."

Han nodded out the viewscreen to the TIE interceptors screaming toward them. Leia knew enough not to ask if Han could outrun them. He couldn't. "Seriously, Leia, you better get up there," Han said. "Once they get close enough to see that we're not an Incom Y-four, they won't wait to shoot." Leia ran up the corridor to the stairwell.

Over the *Falcon*'s radio, a controller began querying, "Incom Y-four Raptor, please identify yourself and your destination. Incom Raptor, please identify."

"Captain Brovar," Han answered, "carrying an inspection team for the planetary defense systems?" Han wiped the sweat from his forehead. This was the part he always hated, waiting to see if they'd swallow his story.

After a delay of four seconds, Han knew the flight controller was querying his supervisor. Always a bad sign. "Uh," the controller said after a moment, "this planet doesn't have a defense system."

Chewbacca glared at Han, and Han keyed the mike. "I know. We're here to inspect the sites to *install* the planetary defense system." The controller remained quiet too long, so Han added lamely, "We have an extra one, or parts of an extra one. I mean, you've got to store these defense systems somewhere, right?"

"Incom Y-four Raptor," a gravelly voice called over the same frequency. "Do you have some kind of *strange* modifications to your ship?"

The interceptors were coming into visual range and Han couldn't rely on stealth anymore. He reached up to switch on the signal jammers, and Chewie winced. "It's all right," Han promised. "We won't fry our own circuitry this time. I tested it before we left."

Han flipped the switch and prayed. Chewbacca roared in fright and Han glanced over—the nav computer had gone down. As Han watched, the run lights for the hyperdrive motivator died, along with the rear targeting computer. Han realized belatedly that he hadn't tested the jammers *with* the nav computer working. They wouldn't be jumping to hyperspace anytime soon.

Chewie growled in terror, and Han dipped toward the glittering shipyard, diving toward a Kuat escort Frigate. All that metal would have to play hell with the sensors, and even though the TIE interceptors were technically faster and more maneuverable than the *Falcon*, Han would match his flying skills against these academy jocks any day.

Bolts of blue blaster fire ripped across the *Falcon*'s prow, bounced off the hull, and Leia shouted over her radio, "They're in range!" Threepio stood behind the pilot's seat watching the blaster fire, shouting, "Oooh, aah!" and ducking with every near miss.

Han heard the welcome *blam, blam, blam* of the quad cannons as Leia returned fire. The *Falcon* screamed toward the scaffolding and the Frigate beyond. Huge beams of plasteel flashed past, and Han flipped the *Falcon* sideways to slip through the scaffolding. Han locked his forward targeting computer onto the Frigate's primary sensor array. Without active shielding on, the huge Frigate was just another hunk of space debris, and Han's first blast enveloped the sensor array in blue lightning. He fired his proton torpedoes in rapid succession, and they flashed in a brilliant ball that would have fried Han's eyes if he hadn't looked away.

Among the brightening mushroom clouds, Han reversed thrusters, fired two concussion missiles into the thin stem of the Frigate, the walkways that joined the Frigate's monstrous engines with its forward arsenal. As the slowing *Falcon* dove for the breach in the Frigate's hull, chunks of shrapnel burst against the forward concussion shielding.

Chewie roared and shielded his face with his hands. The *Falcon* slammed into the yawning hold of the Frigate, and warning sirens screamed. The control panels darkened as the concussion shielding overloaded, brightened again as it died. Smoke was rising from Chewie's panel, and he growled.

"Shhh . . ." Han hissed, putting his hand over Chewie's mouth. Both of the TIE interceptors screamed into the Frigate and exploded. The corridor that the *Falcon* had crashed into filled with light and fire.

That's the problem with those transparisteel windows on the TIE fighters, Han thought. *The worthless things darken when they detect a blast, and then you can't see anything for the next two seconds.* He'd counted on it.

Han flipped off his radio jamming, began shutting down the *Falcon.* Leia came running down the corridor. "What in the hell do you think you're doing? You almost got us killed!"

"Listen!" Han said, raising a hand for quiet. Between the concussion of the torpedoes and the fighters, and a few well-placed ion blasts, the Frigate's orbit was already destabilizing. The ship was peeling away from the docks as Dathomir's gravity well sucked it down.

"Oh, great!" Leia said. "I'm supposed to be happy that we're going to crash into the planet instead of blow up in space?"

"No," Han said. "Our concussion shielding should have kept us from damaging the *Falcon* too badly, and now that our sensor jamming is off, Chewie should be able to get the nav computer back on line. Meanwhile, Zsinj's navy thinks we all crashed, and as the Frigate drops toward the planet, we'll quietly move out of their interception range for ten minutes or so—plenty of time for us to plot a course. Then we just casually ease our way out of here and head for home. Trust me, I've done this before!"

Han took a deep breath and prayed. "Go ahead, Chewie, turn the nav computer back on. Show her."

Chewie growled, shot Han a nasty look and flipped the switch. The monitor stayed dim. Chewie frantically began testing other switches. The hyperdrive motivator stayed off, as did the rear deflector shields. Threepio had been watching behind the pilot's seat and he began gesticulating wildly but refrained from speaking. When he saw that the motivators wouldn't go on, he shouted, "We're doomed!"

Han jumped out of his seat. "It's okay, it's okay, nobody panic. We just have a little fried circuitry here. I'll fix it." He shoved his way past Threepio and ran down the corridor to the engineering station and pulled off a face plate to get to the motivator circuitry. The nav computer he could sort of live without—for ten minutes. Just make a quick jump to get out of the solar system, then take a few days to try to fix it nice and leisurely in the cold of space. But the motivators, he needed those now.

He pulled off his vest, wrapped it around his fist, jerked back the face plate. Fire erupted from the charred slag in the circuit box, and Leia appeared behind him with a fire extinguisher. She began spraying the circuitry and Han stepped back, saw that it was useless.

"It's okay, it's okay," he muttered and ran back to the cockpit, fired all his circuits and let the diagnostics computer begin a readout. The forward sensor arrays had been smashed during the crash. "That's okay, I don't need sensors as long as I can see where I'm going," he groaned.

Concussion shielding gone. Top radio dishes clipped off. Most of the rest of it looked pretty good. As long as the diagnostics were correct, they could fly out of here—as long as they could break free of the wreck and no one shot at them and no one caught them and they didn't try to make it offplanet.

Han's head began to whirl, and he realized that the Frigate must be spinning as it sank toward Dathomir. "Hang on, folks, it's going to be a rough ride down!" he muttered. He glanced back at Leia, saw that she wasn't mad, wasn't berating him. Instead, her pale face was set in fear, and her eyes seemed dilated. The hair on her scalp had raised. Han had never seen her so scared.

"What? What?" he asked, glancing frantically at the diagnostics display.

"I feel something down there," Leia said, "on the planet. Something . . ."

"What?" Han asked.

Leia closed her eyes. She didn't have Luke's sensitivity yet. But Han knew she had the potential. "I see . . . drops of blood on a white tablecloth. No—more like sunspots, black against the brilliance. Only the black spots are filthier than that—loathsome . . ." Leia frowned in concentration, inhaled, sucking deep breaths, her lower lip trembling.

Leia's eyes blinked open, and her face was pale again, stark with terror. "Oh, Han, we can't go down there!"

Chapter

9

At Han's apartment on Coruscant, Luke felt the walls. It was an odd apartment, one without decorations, without warmth, the kind of place that a person sometimes *inhabits* but does not *live* in. The building had been ransacked. Han's military uniforms lay scattered on the floor with a ripped mattress, torn pillows. The floors were littered. Dozens of people had already searched the place, but not the way Luke planned to search it.

Luke touched the pillow, closed his eyes. He could feel Han's desperation on the pillow, and something older and odd —a trace of manic glee, of hope.

Luke stood. Such strong emotions carry a unique scent, and he ran his fingers along the wall, tasting it, followed the scent down Coruscant's long avenues. Sometimes the scent would elude him at a corner, and Luke would stop for a moment, concentrating.

After hours of following the taste of that manic hope, he found himself in the upper layers of the underworld, in an ancient gambling hall. He stood, looking at a sabacc table where a trio of rodents played while a mechanical dealer dropped cards into their hands.

He went to the manager, a batlike Ri'dar who watched over his domain with half-open eyes while gripping an overhead cable with his toes. Luke asked, "Do your dealer droids keep a visual record of games, to make sure there is no cheating?"

"Why?" the Ri'dar asked. "I run an honessst placcce. Are you trying to imply that my dealersss cheat?"

Luke was tempted to roll his eyes at the Ri'dar. Their paranoia was a species trait and could lead to problems if Luke didn't placate the creature quickly. "Of course not," Luke said, "the thought never crossed my mind. But I have reason to believe that a friend was here recently, and that he played cards at the corner table. If the films are available, I'd like to see the video. I could pay you."

The Ri'dar's dark eyes flashed, and he looked around furtively. He reached up with one winged hand, grasped the cable, and dropped to the floor. "Thisss way."

Luke followed him to a back room, and the Ri'dar glanced at him suspiciously. "Money firssst."

Luke handed him a credit chip worth a hundred. The Ri'dar shoved the chip into some hidden pocket in its vest, showed Luke how to scan through the video display unit that could not have been less than a hundred years old. It was rusting and crusted with dirt, but the rewind on it went incredibly fast. Luke hit pay dirt within moments, stopped the video, and watched Han win his planet. There was no sound to the video, only the holograph of the planet on the table, gleaming. So that was the source of his joy.

"Who is the Drackmarian here?" Luke asked.

The Ri'dar looked at the Drackmarian, his eyes flickering furtively between the image and Luke. "Hard to sssay. They all look alike to me."

Luke pulled out another credit chip.

"Yesss, I remember now," the Ri'dar said. "Warlord Omogg."

Luke knew the name. "Of course. Only she would lose a planet in a card game. Where can I find her?"

"Gambling," the Ri'dar said. "When she isss not here, she playsss elsssewhere. Drackmarianss do not sssleep."

Luke got the names of Omogg's haunts, closed his eyes and let his forefinger drift down the list. It stopped at the third name on the list—a nearby place down four more levels in the underworld.

He drew his robes tight around him, felt the lightsaber hanging at his side. Something in the air warned him to keep it handy, so he unclipped it, put it in a pocket.

The trip down took only a few minutes, but it seemed as if he'd entered a different world. The air down lower was stale, the lights dimmer than above. Hundreds of levels down, there were places in the underworld where even the bravest humans wouldn't venture. Already living down here were aliens from races that Luke had never seen—a large turquoise, bioluminescent amphibian walked by, flapping on webbed feet, eating some type of fungus in its broad mouth. Something huge, with tentacles, slithered over the wet stones. Luke didn't know if it was sentient or some form of vermin. Luke found the place he was searching for by a dim light over its door: "The Stowaway."

He walked in, squinted into the gloom. The only light in the place came from the headlamps of a cleaning droid and from bioluminescent amphibians like the one Luke had seen outside. Down here, the creatures did not use artificial lights.

And in the depths of the shadows, Luke heard choking sobs that could only have been death cries.

Luke whipped out his lightsaber, and its brilliant blue glow cut through the shadows. Dozens of aliens screamed and covered their eyes in pain, and many shouted in dismay as they leaped for the door. A dozen rat people scurried deeper into the shadows to watch the fray with glittering eyes.

At the far back of the gambling room, at a table, three humans stood over the Drackmarian. Two of them held her with her back pinned to the table, while the third worked desperately to pull off her helmet, open her to the oxygen atmosphere that would surely poison her. The Drackmarian fought them, digging into their arms with her talons till she drew blood, kicking at them with clawed feet, batting at them with her tail.

Two other humans were already on the floor, but the Drack-marian was near the end of her struggle. The men had her pinned now. All three of the men wore infrared goggles, a sign that they were not accustomed to life here in the underworld.

"Let her go," Luke ordered them.

"You stay out of this," one of the men said in Basic, using an odd accent Luke had never heard. "This one has informa-tion."

Luke stepped forward, and the inquisitor who had been ripping off Omogg's helmet pulled up a gun, fired at him. Blue sparks shot from the gun and enveloped Luke, and for a por-tion of a second Luke's mind went blank—it felt almost as if his head were immersed in freezing ice water. He blinked and let the Force flow through him. The three men had turned back to their task, apparently satisfied that the confrontation was over.

"Let her go," Luke repeated, louder.

The inquisitor glanced up at Luke in surprise, pulled the gun again. Luke waved, used the Force to rip the weapon from his hand.

"Get out of here, all three of you—" Luke warned.

The men stopped, stepped back from the Drackmarian. She lay gasping on the table, fighting the effects of the oxygen that leaked past her helmet seal. One man said, "This *creature* has information that could lead us to a woman who has been kid-napped. We will get that information."

"This *woman* is a citizen of the New Republic," Luke said, "and if you do not take your hands off her, I will take your hands off you." Luke swung the lightsaber threateningly.

The men looked nervously at each other, backed away. One pulled up a communicator, began speaking into it quickly in a foreign language, obviously calling for reinforcements. The rat people in the corner scurried away, unwilling to brave the situation any longer, and the room seemed strangely quiet, with only the dull hum of food processors in the background.

Within ten seconds, a female voice spoke behind Luke. "What is going on here?"

All three of Omogg's attackers folded their arms, bowed their heads. "O Queen Mother, we found the Drackmarian war-lord as you requested, but she has been loath to answer us. We could get no information from her." Luke turned to look at their leader. She was a tall woman with a gold circlet and a golden veil to hide her face. Every inch of her spoke of regality and wealth. She wore a long flowing dress that could not disguise her shapely figure. Behind her were at least a dozen armed guards, blasters at the ready.

"You tortured her, a foreign dignitary?" the queen mother asked, eyes flashing behind her veil. Luke could feel her wrath, but he wasn't sure if she was truly angry at her men, or angry that they had failed.

"Yes," one of the men muttered. "We thought it best."

The queen mother grunted in disgust. "Get out, all three of you. Place yourselves under arrest." For a moment Luke wondered if this were all an act, and he further tested the Force of the newcomer. She was not surprised or appalled by her men's actions, but that told him little. Leaders tend to become jaded, hardened.

"I owe you a debt of gratitude for stepping in here," she told Luke. She gestured, and two of her guards hurried to the fallen Drackmarian, made sure her gas mask fit snugly over her snout. Omogg was still gasping but seemed to be coming around. She moved her arms, and her tail twitched feebly. The guards lifted her to a sitting position, adjusted the valves on her backpack, increasing the amount of methane she received. She inhaled deeply.

"I'm terribly sorry," the queen mother said to the Drackmarian. "I'm Ta'a Chume, of Hapes, and I asked my men to find you, but I did not order them to question you like this. They are already under arrest. Name whatever punishment you think just."

"Mmmake themmm breathe mmmethanne," Omogg hissed.

The queen mother bowed her head slightly in sign of acceptance. "It will be done." She paused a moment. "You already know why I have come. I need to know where Han Solo is. It is said that you are organizing your own private party to follow him. I will pay whatever price you ask, within reason. Do you know where he is?"

Omogg studied Ta'a Chume for a moment. The Drackmarians were noted for their generosity, but they were an independent people and could not be coerced. They had been fearless opponents of the Empire and could only loosely be considered allied to the New Republic. They resisted coercion to the death. Omogg glanced at Luke. "Isss thisss what you wannnt, too?"

"Yes," Luke answered.

The Drackmarian studied Luke a moment. "You have saved mmmy lllife, Jedi. Yourrr rrreputationnn prrrecedes you. Nnnammme yourrr rrrewarrrd."

The Drackmarian hesitated, and Luke understood. She would tell him where Han had gone, but she did not want to speak in the presence of Ta'a Chume. Yet Luke could feel something from the queen mother. Confidence? If Omogg truly had planned to send a party after Han—and the New Republic was offering enough of a bounty to make that reasonable—then Ta'a Chume had probably already done her homework. She knew which ship Omogg would take, perhaps had even questioned crew members and bugged the ship so that they could follow it.

"As my reward, I ask that you leave General Solo to me, and that you not reveal the name of the planet to anyone, but that you look into my eyes and think of the name."

Omogg glanced up, and the dark orbs of her eyes shone from behind the wisps of green methane in her helmet. Luke let the Force connect him to her, and distinctly heard the name of the planet in his mind. *Dathomir.*

The name struck Luke, and for a second he recalled the holo of Yoda in a younger shade of green saying, *We tried to free the Chu'unthor from Dathomir . . .*

"What do you know of the place?" Luke asked.

Omogg said. "Forrr a mmmethannne breatherrr, it hass little valllue . . ."

"Thank you, Omogg," Luke said. "The Drackmarian reputation for graciousness is well deserved. Do you need a doctor? Anything?"

Omogg waved Luke's thanks away, began coughing again.

Ta'a Chume studied Luke openly as if Luke were some slave she might buy in a market, and finally he felt her nervousness. She wanted something from him. "Thank you for coming when you did," she said. "I suppose you are a bounty hunter of some type, looking for a reward?"

"No," Luke said defensively. "You might say I'm a friend to Leia—and Han."

The queen mother nodded, seemed loath to leave him. "Our fleet will leave tonight"—she glanced at the room, empty of all but her guards, Luke, and Omogg—"for Dathomir." She must have seen Luke's startlement when she spoke the name, for her voice took on a note of confidence. "Omogg made the mistake of running a course check on her nav computer. Once we learned that she planned to make the trip, we had no trouble finding where she might go. Yet I see no reason that Han would choose to go to such a world."

"Perhaps it holds . . . sentimental value," Luke said.

"Of course," Ta'a Chume agreed. "A probable choice for a crazed lover who has just kidnapped a mate. So you agree that it is worth checking out?"

"I'm not sure," Luke said.

"I'll check it out," Ta'a Chume said thoughtfully. "I have not seen a Jedi since I was a small child. Even then, the one that I met was an old man, balding. Nothing like you—but interesting. I would like you to join me on my ship for an hour or two, for dinner. You will come tonight."

Her tone did not invite refusal, though Luke sensed that it would be permissible to decline her offer. But something else struck him—the casualness with which this woman served out life or death, the way she accepted the execution of her own men. This woman was dangerous, and Luke wanted to probe her mind further.

"I would be . . . honored to join you," Luke said.

Chapter

10

As the *Millennium Falcon* plunged toward Dathomir, Chewbacca roared in fear and clung to his chair. The spinning of the ship nauseated Leia, but the Wookiee, having been raised in the trees, perhaps felt more distress from the free fall.

"It's getting hot in here," Leia said, stating the obvious. They had hit the atmosphere, and without much in the way of atmospheric shielding the big Frigate would burn. "Han, I don't know how I let you talk me into this! I don't care if you do go to prison, get me home, right now!"

Han leaned forward over his control panel. "Sorry about this, Princess, but it looks to me like Dathomir is going to be your new home—at least until I can get this thing fixed." Han pressed a button, turned on the *Falcon*'s acceleration compensator, and the sense of falling abruptly stopped. He began pushing more buttons, pulling levers. The engines roared to life, and Han said, "Let's get out of here."

The *Falcon* lifted and made loud crunching sounds as something metal scraped the roof. Han began backing out of the wrecked Frigate to the accompaniment of screaming metal.

"Nothing to worry about," he said. "It's just our antenna getting pulled off." He muttered under his breath. "We have to pull out slowly, stay near the Frigate so they can't pick up our exhaust trail. I figure that when the Frigate hits, the heat from the explosion will hide us pretty well for a moment. Still, we'll have to land nearby."

The *Falcon* eased free of the wreck, and Leia saw that they were still several thousand kilometers above ground. The *Falcon* tumbled as it dropped, and for a moment they would see the stars and moons that looked very distant now, then they'd glimpse the planet.

It was night down there. *At least we're falling toward land rather than water,* Leia thought. They were over what looked like a temperate zone, a huge area of rolling hills and mountains on the edge of a dune sea. It didn't look hospitable, but it might be livable. The mountains were dark with trees. Leia had flown over hundreds of planets, and ones like this always gave her the creeps. It was so dark down there, so lonely looking, without the cheerful lights of cities.

The recognition of how desolate this place was sent a chill through her. "Han, stabilize us before we get any lower," Leia said, "and get a readout from the sensors. Look for any sign of life."

Han flipped some buttons. "We don't *have* any sensors."

"We've got to have sensors!" Leia shouted. "Where are you going to get the parts to fix this thing?"

"Over there!" Threepio shouted. "I see a city over there!"

"Where?" Leia asked, following the vector of Threepio's pointing finger. There was something on the horizon, a slight glowing, maybe a hundred and fifty kilometers off.

"Take us that direction!" Leia shouted.

"I can't just fly in there!" Han said. "We've got to land within half a kilometer of the crash site, or else the infrared scanners on those Star Destroyers will pick us up."

"Then take us half a kilometer in that direction," Leia shouted.

Han grumbled something under his breath about bossy princesses. The ground rushed toward them, and in only seconds they were falling between the peaks of incredibly tall mountains. The night sky was clear, and by the ample light of the moons Leia could make out forests of high, twisted trees.

They were almost at ground level when Han pulled them out of the dive. The sky filled with brilliant white light as the Frigate crashed, and the *Falcon* whisked over the treetops for a portion of a second, skimmed over a mountain lake and dipped in under the forest canopy. They skidded through some thick underbrush, came to a jarring halt. A fireball rose behind them, shooting its light across the lake.

Han looked up through the viewscreen at the tall trees. "Well, this is the place." He shut down the *Falcon*.

"Oh, Han," Leia said. "Even if we can get parts to fix the *Falcon*, you've seen all that fried circuitry. How are we going to carry it back here?"

"That's what droids and Wookiees are for," Han said.

Chewbacca grumbled, shot Han a feral look.

"I quite agree," Threepio told Chewbacca. "No one would blame a Wookiee for eating a lazy pilot."

"Do you think we made it?" Leia asked. "Are you sure they didn't pick us up on their scanners?"

"I'm not sure of anything," Han said. "But if Zsinj's men follow Imperial procedure, they'll come down here to check out that slag heap of a Frigate as soon as it cools. At the very least we'll need to get out and cover our skid marks, hide the *Falcon*."

"Pardon me, sir," Threepio interjected, "but might I point out that Zsinj's men *aren't* Imperials, at least not in the strictest sense, not since the Empire has been overthrown."

"Yeah," Han grimaced, without stating the obvious fact that most of Zsinj's men had been trained by the Empire, "but look at it this way: what space jockey could possibly pass up the chance to come down and look at a really neat wreck? Believe me, we've got plenty of company coming, and unless you want to throw a picnic for them, we'd better get to work."

The four of them went down into the hold and got out the camouflage nets. The nets worked in two stages: A baffle net of thin metallic mesh went over the *Falcon* to hide its electronics from detection by sensors, and then a second camouflage net went over that to hide the ship from visual inspection.

Then they stepped outside. The air here was warmer than Leia had expected, the stars fiercely bright. The night felt liquid, as if it could melt the knots in the corded muscles of her back and neck. The woods were quiet. They could hear the fire from the wreck burning on the other side of the ridge, but there were no bird calls, no strangled cries of hunted animals. The smell of leaf mold and live sap came rich to her nostrils. All in all, Dathomir did not seem like a bad place.

The four quickly threw down the mesh, then took out the camouflage net. It was a thirty-five-meter-long piece of photo-sensitive netting attached to an activating strip. They pulled off the activating strip, then placed the netting over the leafy soil for a minute so that it would take a picture of the ground. Then they flipped the netting right-side up and covered the *Falcon*. Generally, the chameleonlike quality of the netting would hide the ship from even the closest fly over. There were even cases where searchers had climbed over ships set in shallow depressions, never realizing that they were standing on top of their target.

When they finished, they raked leaves over the skid marks in the brush, cut out a few of the badly mangled bushes and hid them. By dawn Leia felt weary, stood in the brush by the small lake, looking up at the fiery stars. Steam rose from the lake, a small fog threading its way up through the woods, and a light wind began to rattle the tree leaves up on the hilltops.

She was tired, and Han came up behind her, kneaded her back.

"So, how do you like my planet so far?" Han asked.

"I think . . . I like it better than I like you," Leia said playfully.

"Then you must love it an awful lot," Han whispered in her ear.

"That's not what I meant," Leia said, pulling away. "I'm not sure whether to be furious with you for bringing me here in the first place, or if I should thank you for getting us down alive."

"So you're confused. I seem to affect a lot of women that way," Han said.

"Did you really use that tactic once before?" Leia asked,

"—of crashing into a larger ship and letting the wreck drop you into a blockaded planet?"

"Well," Han admitted, "it didn't quite work as good back then as it did this time."

"You call *this* good?"

"It's better than the alternative." Han nodded up at the sky. "We'd better get under cover. They're coming."

Leia looked up. Four stars seemed to be falling in unison out on the horizon. They twisted in the sky and vectored toward them. The little group hid in the *Falcon* for the rest of the following day, unable to see how large the search party was, whether a band of stormtroopers might be surrounding the *Falcon* as the fugitives fed on cold rations. Han kept the automatic blaster cannon lowered, just in case. Dozens of times during the early morning they heard fighters flying over, skimming the treetops. And at mid-morning, a steady barrage of missiles dropped for an hour, decimating the downed Frigate. The *Falcon* rocked from the explosions, and the whole group sat there stunned, amazed that Zsinj's men would go to so much trouble to demolish a wrecked ship, wondering if some of the missiles might eventually be dropped on them.

Once the bombardment stopped, the ship became quiet. But after half an hour, another group of fighters circled. Threepio ventured, "They're searching for us!"

Han sat, staring up at the ceiling, listening for the return of the fighters. Some of those craft had sensors that could hear a whisper at a thousand yards. Leia closed her eyes, straining her senses. She could no longer feel the presence of the dark beings she had felt earlier, could feel nothing at all, and she wondered if it had been a hallucination.

Early in the afternoon the fighters apparently gave up the hunt, and Leia wondered at that. If Zsinj's men believed they had made it to the planet, surely they wouldn't give up so easily. Certainly they would never have given up if they'd known that a New Republic general and an ambassador were aboard the ship. So obviously they didn't know the *Falcon* had landed safely and they didn't know who its passengers had been. But then a more troubling thought occurred to her: perhaps Zsinj's men weren't hunting because they didn't believe the group could survive on this wild planet. There had to be some reason that a planet this beneficent wasn't more settled.

As the sun began to set, Han got up and stretched, put on a flak jacket and helmet, got out a blaster rifle. "I'm going to go on out and have a look around, make sure that Zsinj's men have left."

Leia, Threepio, and Chewie waited in the ship. Chewbacca began to get nervous after half an hour. The Wookiee whined plaintively.

Threepio said, "Chewbacca suggests that we go look for Han."

"Wait," Leia said. "A big Wookiee and a golden droid are too easily spotted. *I'll* go look for him."

She pulled on some combat fatigues, threw on a flak jacket and helmet, then went outside, blaster turned to full power. She set off down a trail toward the lake, watching for stormtroopers. At the very least, she expected some kind of patrol on speeder bikes. But she found Han only a hundred meters from the ship, standing by the muddy bank of the lake, watching the sun set in a wash of vibrant reds and yellows with muted purples.

He picked up a rock, tossed it out over the lake and watched it skip five times. Some creature called in the distance, making a whooping sound. It was all very restful.

"What are you doing out there in the open?" Leia asked, mad as hell at finding him in such reverie.

"Oh, just looking around." He glanced down at the mud puddle by his feet, kicked over another flat stone.

"Get back here under cover!"

Han put his hands in his pockets and simply watched the sunset. "Well, I guess this is the end of our first day on Dathomir," he said. "It's been kind of uneventful. Do you love me yet? Are you ready to marry me?"

"Oh, please, get off it, Han! And get back here under cover!"

"It's all right," Han said. "I have reason to believe that Zsinj's troops have left already."

"What could possibly give you that idea?"

Han pointed down at the muddy shore of the lake with his toe. "They wouldn't hang around after dark with these near."

Leia stifled a cry—what she had taken to be a mud puddle

was in fact a footprint nearly a meter long, something incredibly big, with five toes.

At the dinner table, Isolder sat with his mother and Luke, feeling glum, disappointed. His mother had arrived only this morning on *Star Home,* and in the course of a few hours she had achieved something that Isolder hadn't been able to do in a week: learn where Han had taken Leia. She had rightly reasoned that the various rewards for Solo—offered both by the New Republic, which wanted him alive, and by various warlords, who wanted him dead—made the offers far too tempting. Rather than settle for a part of the pot by releasing information, everyone with a clue as to Solo's whereabouts would hunt him down themselves. So her spies had concentrated on tracking outbound ships, following various disreputable pilots. Omogg had accidentally tipped her hand by purchasing a new heavy weapons system for her personal yacht—the kind of system someone would use only for a very dangerous mission.

Now, Isolder was waiting for his mother to revel in her victory, make some seemingly inconsequential but pointed remark designed to show the superiority of the female intellect over that of a male. The women of Hapes had an old saying: Never let a man become so deluded as to believe that he is the intellectual equal of a woman. It only leads him to evil.

And Ta'a Chume would never do anything that might lead her son to evil. Still, she remained remarkably cordial over dinner. She talked with Luke Skywalker, laughed disarmingly in all the right places. She kept her veil down, yet managed to be seductive. Isolder wondered if the Jedi would sleep with her. It was obvious that she wanted him, and like all the Mothers before her, she kept her age well. She was very beautiful.

But Skywalker seemed not to notice either her beauty or her veiled attempts at seduction. Instead, his pale blue eyes seemed to scrutinize the ship, as if he wished he could take a gander at its technical readouts. The first queen mother had begun constructing *Star Home* nearly four thousand years earlier, basing the floor plan for the ship on her castle estate. Plasteel interior walls were all covered with a facade of dark stone, and the minarets and crenellated towers were all capped with crystal domes. The castle on *Star Home* perched on a great hunk of wind-sculpted basalt that the ancients had hollowed out so that they could hide the dozens of giant engines and hundreds of weapons in its arsenal.

Though *Star Home* was no match for one of the new Imperial Star Destroyers, it was unique, more impressive in its way, and certainly more beautiful. It tended to awe foreigners, especially at times like this, when they were dining peacefully near some planet, and the brilliant light of dancing stars refracted in the ancient crystal domes.

"It must be fascinating to do your kind of work," Ta'a Chume said to Luke as they finished the last course. "I've always been very provincial, staying close to home, but you—traveling across the galaxy, searching for records of the Jedi."

"I really haven't been doing it long," Luke said, "just the past few months. I'm afraid I haven't found anything of value. I'm beginning to suspect that I never will."

"Oh, I'm sure there are records on dozens of worlds. Why, I remember when I was younger, my mother once granted refuge to some Jedi, a group of fifty or so. They hid out in the ancient ruins of one of our worlds for a year, running a small academy." Her voice became rough. "Then Lord Vader and his Dark Knights came to the Hapes cluster and hunted the Jedi down. After Vader killed the Jedi, he merely sealed them in the ruins at Reboam, I hear. Perhaps they kept some records of their doings, I don't know."

"Reboam?" Luke asked, suddenly intense. "Where is that?"

"It's a small world, harsh climate, relatively uninhabited—not unlike your own Tatooine."

Isolder could see a sudden, unreasoning hunger in Luke's eyes, as if he wanted to discuss this more. Ta'a Chume offered, "When this is all over and you've rescued Leia, come to Hapes. One of my counselors, who is getting quite old now, could show you the caves. You would be welcome to keep anything you find in them."

"Thank you, Ta'a Chume," Luke said, and he stood, obviously too excited to eat. "I think I'd better prepare to go now. But before I do, may I ask you one more small favor?"

Ta'a Chume nodded, inviting him to ask.

"May I see your face?"

"You flatter me," Ta'a Chume said, laughing lightly. Behind her golden veils, her beauty was hidden, and in all of Hapes no man would ever have been so bold as to ask. But this Luke was simply a barbarian who did not know he was asking for something that was forbidden. To Isolder's surprise, his mother pulled up her veil.

For one eternal moment, the Jedi gazed into her startlingly dark green eyes, the cascades of red hair, and held his breath. In all of Hapes, few women could vie with the Ta'a Chume for beauty. Isolder wondered if perhaps Skywalker had noticed his mother's discreet advances after all. Then Ta'a Chume dropped her veil.

Luke bowed low, and in that moment his face seemed to go hard, as if he had peered into Ta'a Chume and did not like what he'd seen. "Now I see why your people venerate you," he offered casually, and he left.

The hair prickled on the back of Isolder's neck, and he recognized that something important had just happened, something he had missed. When Isolder saw that Luke was well out of hearing range, he asked, "Why did you tell the Jedi that lie about an academy? Your mother hated the Jedi as much as the Emperor ever did, and she would have relished hunting them down."

"The Jedi's weapon is his mind," Ta'a Chume warned. "When a Jedi is distracted, when he loses his focus, he becomes vulnerable."

"So you plan to kill him?"

Ta'a Chume rested her folded hands on the table. "He represents the last of the Jedi. Listen to him talk of his precious records. We don't really want to see the Jedi rise from their graves, do we? The first band was troublesome enough. I won't have our descendants bowing to his, ruled by an oligarchy of spoon benders and readers of auras. I have nothing against the boy personally. But we must make certain that those of us who are best trained to rule, continue to rule." She shot Isolder a glare, as if daring him to challenge her reasoning.

Isolder nodded. "Thank you, Mother. I think I had best get ready for my journey." He rose from his chair, hugged his mother and kissed her through the veil.

He knew that he should have left *Star Home* immediately, headed for his own ship. Instead he hurried down to the guest docking bay, found Skywalker at his X-wing fighter, preparing to disembark. "Prince Isolder," Luke said. "I was just getting ready to leave, but I can't find my astromech droid. Have you seen it?"

"No," Isolder said, glancing about nervously. A technician came in from a side corridor with the droid.

"Your droid started throwing sparks," the technician said. "We found a shorting circuit to his motivator."

"Are you all right, Artoo?" Luke asked.

Artoo whistled the affirmative.

"Mr. Skywalker," Isolder said, "I . . . wanted to ask you something. Dathomir is what, sixty, seventy parsecs?"

"About sixty-four parsecs," Luke answered.

"The *Millennium Falcon* will have to travel a twisted course through hyperspace to make that kind of jump," Isolder said. "What kind of man is Solo? Will he take the most direct route?"

Computing a jump in hyperspace was a laborious task. The nav computers tended to take "safe" routes, routes where the black holes, asteroid belts, and star systems were well charted. But such routes were often long, tediously twisted. Still, a long route was far better than a short, dangerous trip through uncharted space. "If it were just him," Luke said, "yeah, Han might take a shorter route. But he wouldn't put Leia at risk, not knowingly, anyway."

Luke had an odd tone to his voice, as if he were not saying all that he knew. "Do you think Leia is in danger?" Isolder pressed.

"Yes," Luke said huskily.

"I heard of the Jedi Knights when I was a child," Isolder said. "I was told that you had magical powers. I have even heard that you can pilot starships through hyperspace without the aid of a nav computer, and that you can take the shortest routes. But I have never believed in magic."

"There's no magic to what I do," Luke said. "The only power that I have is what I draw from the life Force around us. Even in hyperspace I can feel the energy inherent in suns and worlds and moons."

"Do you *know* that Leia is in danger?" Isolder asked.

"Yes. I've felt a sense of urgency for her. That's why I came."

Isolder made up his mind. "I think you are a good man. Will you take me to Leia? Perhaps you could shave a few parsecs off our trip. We might even be able to reach Dathomir before Solo."

Luke studied the prince, said doubtfully, "I don't know. He's got a big head start."

"Still, if we could reach Han Solo first . . ."

"First?"

Isolder shrugged, gestured to the fleet of Star Destroyers and Battle Dragons just outside the energy field. "If my mother reaches Solo before we do, she will kill him."

"I suspect you're right, and she does not wish me well, either, though she seems friendly enough," Luke said, surprising Isolder. So the Jedi *had* sensed his mother's intent.

"Take care of yourself, Jedi, and meet me on my ship," Isolder whispered, knowing that in all probability his mother would hear of his betrayal of her within the hour.

"I'll be careful," Luke said, and he patted his R2 droid lovingly and stared at it, as if gazing through its metal exterior.

Chapter

11

Leia stormed up into the *Millennium Falcon*, threw her helmet to the floor so that it bounced and clattered into a corner. Han followed her up the ramp, around to the lounge where Chewbacca and Threepio were playing games on the holo board.

"Great, Solo, great!" Leia shouted. "What have you gotten us into? I'll tell you why Zsinj's men aren't searching for us: they figure we're all going to die, so why bother!"

"Look, it's not my fault!" Han shouted. "They're trespassing on my planet. They're all trespassing! And as soon as we get out of here, I'm going to figure some way to evict the whole bunch!"

Chewbacca growled questioningly.

Han said, "Aw, nothing much."

"Nothing much?" Leia shouted. "There are monsters outside. For all we know the planet could be crawling with them!"

"Monsters?" Threepio whined, rising from his seat, hands rattling. "Oh dear, you don't suppose they eat metal, do you?"

"I don't think so," Han said sarcastically. "Outside of space slugs, I've never heard of anything *that* big that eats metal."

Chewbacca growled, and Threepio asked, "How big are they?"

"Let me put it this way," Leia said, "we haven't seen them yet, but if the footprints are any indication, one of them could probably eat all three of us for breakfast and then use one of your legs to pick his teeth."

"Oh dear!" Threepio shouted.

"Aw, come on now," Han said, "don't frighten the droid. For all we know, these could be harmless herbivores!" Han tried to put an arm around Leia's shoulder to comfort her, but she pulled away, waved a finger in his face.

"I sure hope not," she said, "because if that track came from a herbivore, then you can bet there's something even bigger around here that eats it." She turned and looked away. "I don't know why I let you bring me here. How could I be so stupid? I should have made you turn yourself in. Warlords and monsters and who knows what else? I mean, what can you expect from a planet you won in a card game?"

"Look, Leia," Han said, touching her shoulder again, trying to get her to turn to him for comfort, "I'm doing the best I can!"

Leia spun and talked directly in his face. "No! I'm not going to let you sweet talk me. This isn't a game. This isn't a fun ride. Our lives are on the line. And right now, whether you love me and want me to marry you, or whether I love Isolder and want to marry him—none of that matters anymore. We've got to get out of here. Now!"

Han had seen Leia like this only very few times—always when her life was in danger. He had often thought that with his relaxed attitude, perhaps he enjoyed his life more than she enjoyed hers. But when he saw her fierceness rise to the surface, he realized that she loved life more passionately, more deeply than he could. Perhaps it was her Alderaanian heritage surfacing, her culture's legendary respect for any life, something Leia was forced to lay aside in her fight against the Empire. But always it surfaced, and Han kept finding that Leia was like that: she hid her feelings deeply, so deeply that Han suspected even she didn't know what she felt.

"All right," Han said. "I'll get you out of here. I promise.

Chewie, we're going to need some weapons. Let's get out the heavy artillery and the survival packs. We saw a city not more than a few days over the mountains, and where there is a city, there's got to be transportation. We'll just steal the fastest ship available and blast out of here."

Chewbacca whined his concern over leaving the *Falcon.*

"Yeah," Han answered. "Let's lock her up tight. Maybe someday we can make it back, salvage her." He swallowed hard, unable to speak anymore. Two or three seasons out here in the mountains, in the rain and snow, and the wiring would get so rusted and shot that the *Falcon* would be practically worthless. And chances were that the New Republic wouldn't win its way this deep into Zsinj's territory for another ten years.

Leia stared at him, unbelieving.

"You always said that the *Falcon* was my favorite toy," Han said. "Maybe it's time to give it up."

He went to the storage locker, pulled out an extra helmet, some snap-on camouflage battle fatigues to hide Threepio's golden exterior. He went to find Threepio and get him dressed, but the droid was already standing at the bottom of the gang-plank, his golden eyes shining as he gazed out into the forest in the dusk. Leia and Chewie were shutting down the *Falcon,* preparing her for storage.

"I've got something for you," Han said to Threepio. He pulled out the battle fatigues. "I hope they don't baffle your sensors or impede your mobility or anything."

"Clothes?" the droid asked. "I wouldn't know. I've never worn clothes before, sir."

"Well, there's a first time for everything," Han said, moving behind Threepio to snap the fatigues on. Somehow, it made him feel uncomfortable. In some homes, the wealthy had droids dress them, but Han had never heard of anyone dressing a droid.

"I think it would be best if you leave me here, sir," Threepio volunteered. "My metallic surface might act as a lure for predators."

"Oh, don't worry about that," Han said. "We have blasters. There's nothing out there that we can't take care of."

"I'm afraid I'm not designed to travel in this kind of terrain," Threepio argued. "It's too wet and rugged. In ten days, my joints will squeak like a roonat, if they aren't frozen altogether."

"I'll bring some oil."

"If Zsinj's men come looking for us," Threepio said, "they'll be able to home in on my circuitry. I'm not equipped with any kind of electronic countermeasures that would let me conceal my presence."

Han bit his lip. Threepio was right. His very presence could likely get them all killed, and there wasn't a thing they could do. "Look," Han said. "You and I have been together for a long time. I never turn my back on a friend."

"A friend, sir?" Threepio asked. Han considered. In all likelihood this trip would kill the droid, and though they'd never been friends, he didn't really hate Threepio *that* much. Out in the darkness, some animal gave a whooping call. It sounded peaceful, not at all threatening, yet for all he knew it could be the alien call of some giant predator saying, "I smell dinner."

"Now don't you worry about a thing," Han said as he finished dressing the droid. He placed the helmet on Threepio's head, and the droid turned to him, looking somehow forlorn in the bulky clothing. Han tried to think of some way to get Threepio to stop worrying. "You're a protocol droid, and if you really want to be helpful, you'll help me figure out how to get Leia to fall in love with me."

"Ah," Threepio said, obviously excited by the idea. "Don't concern yourself, sir, I'm sure I'll think of something."

"Good, good," Han said, and he walked up the gangplank just as Leia came out with a pack and rifle.

As he turned the corner, he could hear Threepio telling Leia, "My, have you noticed how dashing King Solo looks tonight? He's incredibly handsome, don't you think?"

"Oh, shut up," Leia snarled.

Han chuckled, got his pack, a heavy blaster rifle, an inflatable tent, infrared goggles, and a handful of grenades that he thought might be especially effective if he tossed them down a giant predator's throat. Then he walked outside, and they raised the gangplank, sealed the *Falcon*, and headed into the dark woods where moonlight silvered the white bark of trees.

Overhanging branches left the grass and underbrush high-
lighted in a patchwork where light furtively played tag with the
shadows.

The woods smelled clean, the way that they will in early
summer when the sap is still fresh, the leaves new, and summer
dryness puts a halt to the decay of leaf mold. And yet, despite
the calming familiarity of the woods, Han felt keenly aware that
he was on an alien world. Gravity here was too light, adding a
springiness to his step, a feeling of power, near invincibility.
Perhaps, he thought, the low gravity had led to the evolution of
larger creatures on the planet. On such worlds, the circulatory
systems of large animals did not become strained, bones did not
snap under their own weight. But Han could feel the alienness
in the trees—too tall and willowy thin, rising eighty meters
above, swaying in the warm night air.

They saw little in the way of animals. A few piglike rodents
in the underbrush scurried away when they got near—barreling
through the foliage so fast that Han joked that they must have
had hyperdrive units built into their posteriors.

They hiked for three hours, and at the top of a barren
mountain pass where rocks broke through a thin skin of grass,
they took a breather and looked out toward their destination,
the halo of a lighted city. Brown clouds had blown in, and blue-
purple lightning crackled and flashed in the distance. As the
thunder rolled over the shoulders of the mountains, it sounded
almost like the roar of ancient cannons.

"It looks like a thunderstorm heading our way," Leia said.
"We'd better hurry down off this ridge and put up a shelter."

Han studied the clouds for a moment, dark blue lightning
suddenly flicking like a strobe. "Not a thunderstorm, more like
a dust storm or a sandstorm maybe, blowing up out of the
desert." It seemed odd for the storm to be all concentrated in
one place, as if a giant tornado had blown in from the desert
and now was dropping its weight here at the feet of the mountains.

"Yeah, well, whatever it is, I don't want to get caught in it,"
Leia said, and they scurried down the ridge, scree sliding under
their feet.

Once under the canopy of trees again, Han somehow felt
more secure. They picked a campsite beside a fallen tree, among

myriad boulders washed smooth by a mountain stream. The size of the boulders—many of them taller than a man—gave mute testimony to the ferocity of the floods that must have washed through here during the rainy season. Camping there didn't seem wise with a storm on its way, but it was a calculated risk. The huge boulders all around gave Han a sense of security. A person could easily hide here in case of an attack.

They set their tents, ate a light meal from their packs and sterilized some water. "You and Chewie take the first watch," Han said, throwing Threepio a blaster rifle.

The droid fumbled with the weapon. "But sir, you know that my programming doesn't allow me to harm a living organism."

"If you see anything, just shoot at its feet and make a lot of noise," Han said, and he went to sleep. He planned to lie on his air mattress and think a while, but he was so tired that he just swirled away into blackness.

Only moments later, it seemed, he woke to the sound of blaster fire shattering rocks and Threepio shouting excitedly, "Yoohoo, General Solo, I need you! Waaake uhuuup! I need you!"

Han grabbed his blaster and jumped out of his tent just as Leia climbed out of her own. Something big and metal creaked. Not a dozen meters away stood an Imperial walker, a scouting vessel with a two-person crew. It perched on a rock like some long-legged, steel bird, twin blaster cannons aimed at Han and Leia. Han wondered dimly how in the world it could have sneaked up on the droid.

Within the carrier, shielded behind transparisteel, the pilot and his gunner watched, their faces dimly lit green by their control panels. The pilot raised a mike, shouted in a gravelly voice. "You two, drop your weapons and put your hands on your heads!"

Han swallowed hard, looked around. There was no sign of Chewbacca with his bowcaster. "Uh, is there some kind of problem here?" Han asked. "We were just out for a little fishing expedition. I do have a license."

The pilot and gunner looked at each other. That split second was enough. Han grabbed Leia's arm and jerked her away, jumped behind a boulder for cover, fired at the transparisteel window, hoping his blaster would pierce through and hit the pilot, or at the very least blind the gunner momentarily. The shot bounced off the window. His little hand blaster didn't have the kind of power he needed, and he realized he'd left his grenades in the tent. They crouched behind the boulder for cover.

"You two come on out of there, or we'll shoot your droid!" the pilot shouted.

"Run!" Threepio yelled. "Save yourselves!"

The gunner cut loose with a barrage of blaster fire that sent rock shards flying around Han. Ozone and dust filled the air. A fragment bounced off a boulder behind them, drove a splinter into Solo's hand. Leia leaped out the other side of the boulder, fired with her blaster rifle, jumped back for cover.

Solo searched frantically for some sign of Chewie, saw a shadow moving against the lower limbs of a silver tree, climbing stealthily. Chewie was there with his bowcaster. He crouched, fired a bolt that splattered against the Imperial walker's hull in a shower of green light. Metal screamed in protest.

The pilot tried to swivel his cockpit to look behind them. Leia jumped from her cover, fired three rapid shots into the vulnerable hydraulics assembly at the walker's lowest joint. Chunks of metal flew from the walker, and it twisted from its perch, flopped to its side. The giant metal legs kept kicking.

Han ran up to Threepio, took his heavy blaster and rushed to the windows. The walker's blaster cannons couldn't reach him. Han said, "Now, you two just crawl on out of there real slow. You aren't going anywhere in that thing, unless you're going to die."

The pilot frowned, raised his hands. The gunner popped the hatch above his head, and the two crawled out. Han muscled the two so that they stood side by side, stuck the barrel of his blaster up the pilot's nose.

"This is an interdicted planet!" the gunner shouted at them. "You'd better get off!"

"Interdicted?" Leia asked. "Why?"

"The natives don't take kindly to strangers," the pilot said. Leia and Han looked at each other, and the pilot said in wonder, "You mean you didn't know?"

"We'll take our chances," Han grumbled.

"These natives don't happen to have five toes and foot-prints a meter long, do they?" Leia asked.

The pilot's face took on a closed look. "Lady, those are just their pets."

From the overturned walker, a voice issued over the radio, "Strider seven, report your status. Verify, please: is this General *Han* Solo you've captured?"

Chewie came from behind the shadows of a boulder, shot his bowcaster into the Imperial walker's radio, then grabbed each prisoner by the head and banged their helmets together hard enough so that the crack echoed through the woods. He growled and looked up the hill, asking them to hurry.

Leia had already begun packing the tents.

Chapter

12

W hen Isolder's Battle Dragon, the *Song of War*, prepared to drop out of hyperspace, Isolder was full of hope. Luke had managed to pilot them to Dathomir in seven days, saving ten days from the shortest route that the Hapan astrogation computers could devise! In fact, Isolder realized that he might even beat Han Solo to Dathomir.

Yet when they dropped out of hyperspace, his heart left him. Ten kilometers of shipyard docks were being guarded by two Imperial Star Destroyers and a host of ships in dock.

Automatic alarms began ringing, and all across the Battle Dragon, crew members rushed to their posts.

Luke Skywalker stood at the bridge, gazing at the view-screen. He pointed up to a Frigate that had peeled away from the docking system and was plunging into Dathomir's atmosphere, flames shooting out of its sensor towers. "There—" Luke shouted, "Leia's in that burning ship!"

Isolder studied the monitor quickly. "She's on that?" Isolder said, astonished. *Even with all our rush,* he wondered, *have we arrived only just in time to watch her crash?*

"She's alive!" Luke said firmly. "And she's terrified but

hopeful. I can feel it. They're going to try to land! I've got to get down there." He rushed off, heading for his fighter. Already Isolder could see dozens of old Imperial TIE fighters launching from Zsinj's Star Destroyers, pinpricks of light flaring out from their engines.

"Launch all fighters!" Isolder ordered. "Knock out that Super Star Destroyer at the docks along with anything else you can get. I want this to be messy!" The *Song of War's* ion cannons opened fire as torpedoes screamed from their launch tubes. Though the Imperial Star Destroyers were three times the size and more heavily armed than a Hapan Battle Dragon, the Imperials had designed their ships using old-fashioned stationary gun emplacements. After a blaster cannon or ion cannon fired, it took several milliseconds for the cannon's giant capacitors to recharge. The net effect was that the gun was stuck idle 80 percent of the time.

Not so with the Hapan Battle Dragon. Because the Battle Dragons were designed as huge saucers and the gun emplacements rotated rapidly around the rim of the saucer, idle guns moved on to recharge while fresh guns swung into place.

Both Star Destroyers immediately retreated from the onslaught. Isolder glanced momentarily at Luke's back as the Jedi left the control deck. Though the Hapan Battle Dragon was a fearsome opponent, it would be no match for Star Destroyers once their fighters scrambled. The fighters would be able to penetrate the shielding and knock out the rotating gun emplacements after they idled. Isolder's own fighters could keep Zsinj's war birds at bay for a time, but the Hapans couldn't hold them off indefinitely.

"Captain Astarta," Isolder said, glancing at his bodyguard. "Take over the attack. I'm going down to the planet."

"My lord," Astarta objected, "my job is to protect you!"

"Then do your job well," Isolder said. "I need enough confusion to cover my escape. My mother's fleet won't be here for ten days. Warn them what to expect, and jump back into the fray with them. I'll be monitoring radio signals from the planet. If I can, I'll rendezvous with you at the first sign of your attack."

"And if you don't fly up within five minutes," Astarta choked, "then I'll kill every one of Zsinj's men in this solar system, and we'll scour this planet until we find you!"

Isolder grinned, touched her on the shoulder, then ran from the control room, down the corridors of the *Song of War*. So much of the ship's power was being diverted to guns that the corridor lighting had dimmed, and he made his way to the flight decks by marking the emergency light buoys. The decks were pretty much empty, the normal complement of fighters having scrambled.

Skywalker was already powering up an X-wing—not his own, Isolder noticed. A dozen launch techs were checking his guns, lowering his astrogation droid into its seat.

"Problems with your fighter?" Isolder shouted across the room.

Luke nodded. "Weapons didn't check out. Can I borrow one of yours?"

"No problem," Isolder said.

Isolder grabbed a flak jacket and helmet from their hangers and tied his own personal blaster on. The launch crew saw him and began readying his own fighter, *Storm*. A glowing feeling of pride stole over him when he glanced at his fighter. He'd designed and built it himself.

In one startling moment of clarity, Isolder realized that he was much like Solo, perhaps too much. Solo had his *Falcon*. Isolder had *Storm*. Both of them had worked as pirates, both loved the same strong woman. And all through the trip to Dathomir Isolder had asked himself why he was coming. His mother knew where Han had run to; the Hapan fleets could retrieve Leia. Isolder didn't *need* to risk his life in this senseless encounter.

But when Isolder considered it, he realized that part of him wanted to beat Solo senseless, yet he wanted something more. Solo had thrown down a challenge that Isolder could not refuse. There on the flight deck, Isolder suddenly realized: he'd come to *steal* Leia back from Han Solo, take her away at gunpoint if he had to.

Luke settled into his fighter, and Isolder shouted, "Skywalker, I'm coming with you. I'll be watching your tail!"

Luke turned to Isolder, did not take off his helmet as he gave a thumbs-up.

With a surge of adrenaline, Isolder ran across the flight deck, leaped into *Storm*'s cockpit and fired up the control panel.

Overhead, the flight techs battened down the transparisteel bubble as Isolder activated the turbogenerators and armed his missiles and blasters. The techs were taking extra time, rechecking his systems, and Isolder revved the generators as if he would take off, sent them scrambling for cover. Then he erupted into space.

He flipped his transponder settings to identify himself as a Hapan fighter, then screamed over the *Song of War*'s top saucer.

From space, he could more easily see how the battle was going: the Star Destroyers had backed off in unison and spread apart so that Astarta was forced to choose one of them as a primary target. Instead, she had taken the Battle Dragon over the docks at the shipyard and had begun pummeling the helpless Super Star Destroyer that waited for repairs, doing more damage to the costly machinery in one strafing run than she could ever have accomplished in a pitched battle.

Neither of the active destroyers was hurrying to stop her.

Two of the Victory-class destroyers at the docks must have been partly operational, for TIE fighters and old Z-95 Headhunters were scrambling from their decks. The skies were littered with swarming fighters, chunks of twisted shrapnel, and scattering debris from destroyed ships.

Isolder flipped a switch on his radio, let it search the Imperial frequencies until he could hear the chatter of the enemy fighters. Luke Skywalker was already circling out past the edge of the Hapan Dragon, and Isolder followed the Jedi out, closing on his tail.

"Red One to Red Two," Luke called over the radio. "There's a lot of debris falling from the shipyard." Just as he spoke, a kilometer-long section of scaffolding took a hit, went spinning down into the gravity well while other segments blew out of orbit. "I'm going to shut off my engines and follow some of it down in a minute. But before I do, I want to take out a couple of enemy fighters."

Isolder considered a moment. He and Luke couldn't land without being detected. He'd have to eject, then let his ship crash.

"I'm right with you, Red One," Isolder answered.

Luke accelerated to attack speed, spun out toward a phalanx of twenty incoming Headhunters that glowed red on the scopes like flaming gems. Isolder followed at his right wing, put double power to the front shields, listened to the Headhunters' chatter strategic codes over the Imperial bands. He hit his jammers, and the Headhunters went silent. He checked his head-up display, noticed something odd, called out, "Luke— your deflector shields aren't up!"

The Headhunters' jammers shot static at him, and Isolder shouted again, "Luke, your shields!"

Through the crackling static, Isolder heard Luke shout, "My shields *are* up!"

"No," Isolder shouted. "Your shields are not up!" but Luke threw a thumbs-up sign, trying to calm Isolder, and then the Zebra Headhunters were on them, blaster fire lighting up the skies. Isolder picked a target, fired simultaneously with ion guns and a homing missile, twisted his stick abruptly to the right. From the corner of his eye he watched Skywalker take a hit to the top-right wing, fall into a spin, simultaneously take a hit to the front sensor array. Skywalker's ship began tumbling through space, breaking apart, and the astrogation droid was hurled from the vehicle. The Headhunter in front of Isolder exploded, and four or five blaster shots hit Isolder's front deflectors. The shields collapsed. Isolder couldn't take another run.

Luke rattled around in his falling ship, thrown against the transparisteel like a doll. Isolder silently prayed, then aimed his life-sensors at the cockpit. Nothing. Skywalker was dead.

Isolder cursed, and knew that he could do nothing now but feign his own death. He ejected a thermal detonator out the back of his ship, counted to one. A brilliant explosion pierced the sky behind him, and he flipped off his transponder, powered down, and let the *Storm* drift and fall beside Luke's ship. The explosion should have fooled the enemy sensors, and with a pitched battle going on, Zsinj's men wouldn't have time to check the wreckage too closely.

Under Isolder's display console was a storage area. From it, he pulled a reflective blanket, unfolded it, and turned it so that it held his body heat in. Any sensors close enough to detect him would register that his body had cooled, show him as dead. For a moment, Isolder watched Skywalker's corpse tumbling in his ship, and little explosions seemed to go off in Isolder's brain. After all the help Luke had given, the Jedi was dead.

Isolder had warned Luke that his shields were down, and Luke hadn't believed him. Such things didn't result from technical glitches. The X-wing fighter had to have been sabotaged somehow. Isolder did not doubt that Ta'a Chume had murdered the young Jedi.

Isolder gritted his teeth, pulled the blanket over his head like a shroud, and waited to make planetfall.

Leia pushed through a tangle of creepers under the cover of darkness, looked up the slope to the top of the plateau. In the light of the double moons, she spotted several huge rectangular slabs of black stone. Somewhere in the midst of each rectangle, a hole had been carved in the shape of an eye, and within each eye socket, a huge round boulder served as the pupil to the eye. The rectangular slabs were jumbled, elevated at different levels, so that different eyes pointed half a dozen directions at once.

Leia halted, stared up there for a long moment, mystified. Up on the plateau in the brush beyond her line of sight, something roared, ran across the stone on slapping feet, leaped from the other side of the hill and landed in thick brush, then clambered off through the trees. Leia stopped, heart pounding.

"What was that?" Han asked, standing still to catch a breath. Chewie and Threepio had stopped just behind her.

"Something alive—about the size of the *Millennium Falcon*, I'd say." Leia sighed, grateful only that the thing had run off. "I'll bet it had five toes."

"At least it wasn't carrying a blaster." Han waved his blaster at the sculptures on top of the ridge. "What do you think this means—the eyes, pointing off in different directions?"

"I don't know," Leia said. She looked back downhill at Chewie and Threepio. "Any ideas?"

Chewie only whined, but Threepio looked around at the hills. "If I may say," Threepio answered, "I think it's a kind of symbolic writing used to instruct creatures of limited intelligence."

"What makes you say that?" Leia asked.

"My data files contain similar structures found on two other planets. You see, a lookout sits in a particular spot, watching in each direction indicated by an eye. In this instance, the eyes seem to point toward different valleys and mountain passes. Using this method, creatures with superior intelligence can use inferior beings as lookouts."

"Great," Han said, "so whatever just ran off, went to tell the boss that we're here."

"It would seem so, sir," Threepio said.

Han swallowed, looked back down the valley they had come from. The trees were extremely thick, and they had just hiked through a deep bed of plants with tall, thick stems and enormous round leaves. "Great. Well, I haven't heard any Imperial walkers since we went through that thick patch of jungle. I think that might have slowed them down."

"We've been running for hours," Leia said. "We've got to stop and rest, soon." She wiped the perspiration from her brow.

Chewie growled a question. "He wants to know why there aren't any speeders yet," Threepio translated.

Han nodded. "Yeah, I don't get it. If Zsinj wants us, he could send speeders through these woods pretty effectively. But so far they've just brought the walkers. That doesn't make much sense. Why just come at us with walkers?"

"Maybe Zsinj's men feel they need the armor," Leia said, "or the heavy guns."

"Or both," Han agreed. He pointed to the ridge top, the ancient stone statues of eyes that stared tiredly from the hill. "I want to go up there." He began scrambling up the steep hill, grasping roots and the trunks of small trees to pull himself along.

"Wait, Han!" Leia called, too late. Han was already a third of the way up. She ran up after him, fought her way through some heavy briars that would have sliced her hands to shreds if she had not noticed them in time.

When Leia reached the top of the moonlit ridge, Han stood on the lookout point. They were at the base of a mountain where three valleys met, and this small plateau was a single, smooth, windswept rock. A star carved into the stone marked the spot where a lookout would stand, and as Threepio had said, if Leia stood in that spot and looked out, the top of each eye marked a pass or a valley that needed to be watched. Very simple instructions—except that by triangulation Leia calculated that the lookout must have stood between twelve and fifteen meters tall. A hole gouged into the stone was filled with rainwater. Leia took a drink.

Han walked around the plateau, blaster drawn, gazing down the slopes with his infrared goggles. "Whatever was up here, it's gone. Still, in a place like this, there's not much to see. An army could walk through some of these forests and never be spotted."

"Maybe they're not so interested in watching all of the passes," Leia said. "Maybe this valley is strategically situated, and it's more important to be right here, to watch this spot, than it is to watch those ridges."

Distantly, over the mountains, borne on a slight breeze, came a roaring cry that shook Leia's bones.

"It's coming back," Han said with certainty. "I'd say it's two, maybe three kilometers away."

Leia ran off the small plateau, jumped downhill in a dozen strides. Chewie and Threepio were already backing down the hill. Han followed.

"Come on, come on, you guys!" Han said. "Let's have an organized retreat here."

"Fine," Threepio said, "you organize while I retreat." The droid took off down a valley through the brush as fast as his metal legs would move. Chewie shot one glance back at Han and Leia, then followed Threepio.

Han rushed past Leia, and she whispered at his back, "Some hero you are!" Han caught up with Chewie and Threepio and tried to get them to slow down, but both of them were running scared. Leia didn't want to be left behind, kept looking over her shoulder as they made their way down a hill, turned up a valley and began following a small creek through thick trees. At one point, Leia felt sure that she had heard a low grunt behind her, but the shadows under the trees were so deep that she could have imagined it.

How long is the night cycle here? she wondered, realizing that she knew nothing about the planet's rotation, its tilt, its seasons. It seemed that dawn couldn't be far off.

They were running uphill, toward two pillars of stone that

pointed upward like jagged canines. Chewbacca was in the lead but he stopped, wavered in his steps. They had been running in a group for the past few minutes, so scared that none dared to take a step without the other, and that proved their undoing.

Behind the stone pillars stood four Imperial walkers.

Floodlights blinded them, freezing them in their tracks. "Halt!" a voice shouted over a loudspeaker, accompanied by the boom of blaster cannons that exploded at Chewie's feet. "All of you, drop your weapons and place your hands on your heads."

Leia dropped her blaster rifle, almost relieved to see the Imperial walkers. Chewie and Han did the same. Better a prison camp than whatever lived out in those mountains.

Two of the walkers circled the pillars. Their searchlights played through the trees, then turned back to Leia and the others. "You, droid, pick up the weapons and carry them in your arms. Dump them over the side of the trail."

Threepio took the weapons from Han, Chewie, and Leia. "I'm terribly sorry about this," he apologized, piling the guns into his arms. He carried them to the side of the trail, tossed them into the brush.

Han's eyes smoldered as he glared at the walkers. All four walkers were two-person affairs, scouting models, the only size small enough to maneuver through this mountainous terrain.

"Turn around and head back the way you came," one pilot shouted over the loudspeaker. "Move nice and easy, and don't try anything! If any of you try to run, your comrades will be shot first."

"Where are you taking us?" Han demanded. "By what right? This is my planet: I have a deed!"

"You're in warlord Zsinj's territory now, General Solo," the pilot said over his mike. "And every planet in this sector belongs to Zsinj. If you want to protest this arrangement, I'm sure Zsinj would be happy to discuss it, at your execution."

"General Solo?" Han asked. "You think *I'm* General Solo? Look, if I were a New Republic general, what would I be doing here?"

"We'll be very happy to *pry* those answers out of you— along with your toenails—during your interrogation," the pilot said, "but for now, turn around and start marching!"

A cold chill went through Leia, and they began marching downhill through the woods, the tall trees with their silver bark graceful in the moonlight. The harsh glare of the bobbing headlights on the Imperial walkers made a surreal track. The skeletal rotting leaves at their feet seemed to dance and weave.

After a while, Leia realized that Zsinj's men weren't wholly preoccupied with their prisoners. While two of the walkers kept them covered, the other two played their searchlights on the path ahead and to the sides. From the lights of their control panels, Leia could make out the faces of the pilots and gunners, like the faces of frightened children, eyes darting back and forth, sweat dripping down their foreheads.

"These guys are more scared than I am," Han whispered in Leia's ear as they walked along.

"Maybe that's because they know something you don't," Leia shot back.

When they had been marching for two hours, Leia began to wonder in earnest when dawn would come. The night air felt cold on the back of her neck and her eyes felt gritty. The shadows of trees closed in about them like standing sentries.

Then the attack came: one second they were walking along, and the next she heard heavy footsteps rushing behind. The two walkers on the flanks got tackled from behind by creatures well over their seven-meter height. The middle walkers swiveled to fire their blaster cannons, and for a moment the gunfire flashed like lightning.

Leia spotted one of the huge beasts involved in the attack, its saberlike canines snapping the air.

Something enormous behind Leia smashed a walker using a huge club, grabbed the walker next to it and tossed all three tons of its armored hull toward a rock where it crashed in a heap of rent metal. A gunner kept firing into the air as a beast clubbed his walker, smashed it again and again—and in the gruesome blue actinic flashes, Leia saw the beast and her heart nearly stopped: it stood ten meters tall and wore a protective vest of woven ropes with bits of stormtrooper body armor tied on it. Yet in spite of its attire, there was no mistaking those oddly grotesque arms, the gaping curved fangs, the hunched stance of the warty beast with bony headplates. She had seen one before. It had been smaller than the ones here, perhaps only a juvenile, but it had seemed enormous at the time—in the prison beneath the palace of Jabba the Hutt. Rancors.

Han yelled, turned to run, and tripped. Chewbacca took off leaping through the woods, and one rancor chased him three steps and threw a weighted net. The net caught the Wookiee, knocked him to the ground. Chewbacca roared in pain and remained on the ground, holding his ribs.

Leia stood, heart drumming, frozen with fear. Yet the sight of the enormous beasts attacking in their wrath was not what frightened her.

In less than ten seconds, the blasters of the Imperial walkers were all silenced; the machines lay in smoldering ruins at their feet. Leia looked up at the three giant rancors, each more than ten meters in height. On the creatures' necks sat human riders.

One of the riders bent low, her dark hair shimmering in the light of the burning walkers. She wore a high-collared tunic of glittering red scales, and over it a supple robe made of leather or heavy material. On her head she wore a helm with fanlike wings, and each wing was decorated with ornaments that bobbled as she moved. She held a very ancient Force pike, its vibroblade rattling and in need of adjustment, the handle carved and decorated with white stones.

If the costume and mount were not impressive enough, the woman's very presence struck Leia like a blaster bolt to the ribs. The woman seemed to radiate power, as if her physical body were a mere shell, and beneath it hid a being of terrible light. Leia knew she was in the presence of someone strong in the Force. The woman swung her pike overhead, motioning for Leia and the others to stay, cried out in an alien tongue.

"Who are you?" Leia asked.

The woman bent low in the shadows and sang softly in her own language, then spoke cautiously, as if listening to her own voice, trying to catch the meaning.

"Is this how you form your words, offworlder?" Leia nodded, realized that the woman was somehow using the Force to communicate.

She spoke brief orders to the other two women. One of them scurried down from her rancor and began gathering weapons from the corpses of Zsinj's troops, while the other urged her rancor over to Chewie. The rancor unwrapped the injured Wookiee and carried him in one hand. Chewbacca cried out and tried to bite the rancor, but Han yelled, "It's okay, Chewie. They're friends, I hope."

The woman with the Force pike leaned over Leia, pointed at Han and Threepio. "Keep your slaves marching, offworlder. We will take you to the sisters for judgment."

Chapter

13

Isolder gritted his teeth, watched the desert swell toward him as *Storm* plunged toward the planet. There was nothing he could do to save his ship. Firing his engines would ensure that Zsinj's forces would detect him, so Isolder only hoped that he could eject at the last possible second, let his parachute open briefly and carry him down, hoping it would slow his fall enough so that he wouldn't break any bones.

Off in the distance, eighty kilometers to the west, a small city lit the darkness. Other than that, there were no bright spots in the desert, not even the headlights of a speeder to show a sign of habitation.

Isolder reached under the control panel to his fighter, pulled out a survival kit. Above him the parachute bolted onto Artoo's ejection seat opened, and the droid jerked upward. Luke's demolished X-wing tumbled through the atmosphere. Isolder cracked the transparisteel bubble of his fighter, let the wind catch it and fling it open. He unbuckled his safety harness, checked the small pack that held his parachute to make sure it was strapped tight, slapped his blaster, then leaped from the ship, soaring in freefall.

The wind whistled through the crenellations in his oxygen mask, and he watched as the ground rushed toward him. The ample light of two small moons let him see every rock, every wind-twisted tree, every gully and switchback. He waited until he could wait no more, flipped the release to ignite the explosive charges that would send up his parachute.

Nothing happened. He yanked the emergency cord, kept tumbling. He flailed his arms, shouting—and miraculously, some type of repulsorlift field hit him, slowed him so that he dropped as softly as a feather. For one wild moment he imagined that the flailing of his arms was somehow carrying him, and he dared not stop flapping till he hit the ground. The broken hull of the X-wing fighter dropped past him, several hundred meters off, crashed into the ground in a fireball.

When Isolder's feet hit rock, his knees shook so badly that he could hardly stand, and his heart raced. Isolder threw off his helmet, gasped the warm night air, looked around at the rocks and sparse trees of the desert.

Storm had also settled quietly to the ground, but nowhere could Isolder see a sign of the repulsorlift mechanism, no generators, no antigravity dishes aimed into the air. He looked all around, then saw something above: Luke Skywalker sitting with his legs crossed, eyes closed in concentration, and arms folded, floating to the ground. *Skywalker*, Isolder thought. *Perhaps that is how his ancestors got their name.*

When the Jedi had floated within inches of the rock, he opened his eyes and jumped, as if dropping from a ledge.

"How, how did you do that?" Isolder asked, the hair prickling on the back of his arms. Until that moment, Isolder had never felt like worshiping anyone or anything.

"I told you," Luke said, "the Force is my ally."

"But you were dead!" Isolder said. "I saw it on my scopes! You weren't breathing, and your skin was cold."

"A Jedi trance," Luke said. "The Jedi Masters all learn how to stop their hearts, drop their body temperature. I needed to fool Zsinj's soldiers."

Luke scanned the desert, as if getting his bearings, gazed up into the night. Isolder followed his line of sight. Far above he could make out the warships—pinprick flashes of blaster fire, tiny ships bursting into flames like distant stars gone nova.

"When I was a boy on Tatooine," Luke said, "I used to love to stay up at night with my binoculars and watch the big space freighters fly into port. The first time I ever watched a space battle was from my uncle Owen's moisture farm. At the time, I knew that men were struggling for their lives, but I didn't know it was Leia's ship or that I would become caught up in that struggle myself. But I remember the thrill it gave me, and how I yearned to be up there, in the battle."

Isolder looked up, felt that gnawing desire. Part of him wondered how Astarta and his troops were faring in the battle, and he wished that he could be up there in the fighter, protecting the ship. Overhead, the huge red saucer shape of the *Song of War* suddenly accelerated away, blurred into hyperdrive.

"You feel the pull, too, the bloodlust, the call of the hunt," Luke said, pulling off his flight suit. Beneath it, he was dressed in flowing robes the red color of desert sandstone. "That's the dark side of the Force whispering to you, calling you." Isolder stepped back, fearing that Skywalker had somehow learned to read his mind, but Luke continued, "Tell me, who do you hunt?"

"Han Solo," Isolder said angrily.

Luke nodded thoughtfully. "Are you sure?" Luke asked. "You have hunted other men before. I feel it. What was the man's name? What was his crime?"

Isolder didn't speak a moment, and Luke walked around him, watching Isolder carefully, looking through him.

"Harravan," Isolder said. "Captain Harravan."

"And what did he take from you?" Luke said.

"My brother. He killed my older brother." Isolder felt light-headed, dazed, to be so interviewed by a man he had thought dead only moments before.

"Yes, Harravan," Luke said. "You loved your brother very much. I can hear you, as children, trying to fall asleep in the same large room. Your brother sang to you at night, making you feel safe when you were frightened."

Isolder felt confused, and tears stung his eyes.

"So tell me," Luke said, "how your brother died."

"Shot," Isolder said. "Harravan shot him in the head with a blaster."

"I see," Luke said. "You must forgive him. Your anger burns in you, a black spot on your heart. You must forgive him and serve the light side of the Force."

"Harravan's dead," Isolder said. "Why should I bother to forgive him?"

"Because now it is happening again," Luke said. "Once again, someone has taken a person that you love away from you. Han, Harravan. Leia, your brother. Your rage, your hurt from one ill deed long past colors your feelings now. If you do not forgive them, the dark side of the Force will forever rule your destiny."

"What does it matter?" Isolder asked. "I'm not like you. I don't have any power. I will never learn how to float through the air or raise myself from the dead."

"You have power," Luke answered. "You must learn to serve the light within you, no matter how dim it may seem."

"I watched you on the ship," Isolder said, thinking back to Luke's behavior on their journey out. Luke had seemed inquisitive, but kept himself aloof. "You don't talk like this to everyone."

Luke gazed at him in the moonlight, and double shadows played over Luke's face. Isolder wondered if Luke was trying to convert him because Isolder was the Chume'da, the consort to the woman who would become queen. "I talk like this to you," Luke said, "because the Force has brought us together, because you are trying to serve the light side now. Why else would you risk your life, come here to Dathomir with me to save Leia? Vengeance? I think not."

"You are wrong about that, Jedi. I didn't come to save Leia, I came to steal her away from Han Solo."

Luke laughed softly, as if Isolder were some schoolboy who did not know himself. It was a peculiarly disconcerting sound. "Have it your way, then. But you will come with me, won't you, to rescue Leia?"

Isolder gestured to the desert, spreading his arms. "Where do we look? She could be anywhere—a thousand kilometers from here."

Luke nodded toward the mountains. "Over there, about a hundred and twenty kilometers." He smiled secretively. "I warn you, the trip will not be easy. Once you choose to walk in the light, your path will lead you places you do not want to go. Already the forces of darkness gather against us."

Isolder studied the Jedi, heart hammering. He wasn't used to thinking of the world in terms of forces of darkness, forces of light. He wasn't even sure he believed such forces existed. Yet here was a Jedi no older than himself who had floated from the sky like thistledown, who seemed to read his thoughts, and who professed to know Isolder better than he knew himself.

Luke looked off to the horizon. His droid was floating down on a parachute, a couple of kilometers off. "Are you coming?"

Isolder had acted almost without thought until now, but suddenly he felt frightened, more than he would have believed possible. His knees threatened to lock, and he found his face burning with shame. Something frightened him, and he knew what it was. Luke wasn't just asking Isolder to follow him to the mountains. Luke was asking him to follow his teachings, his example. And in the process, Luke promised that Isolder would inherit detractors, enemies, in the same way that all Jedi did. Isolder considered for only a moment. "Let me get some things out of my ship. I'll be right with you."

Rummaging through *Storm*, gathering a spare blaster, Isolder found that he became calmer. All of the Jedi's spooky talk really meant nothing, he realized. Perhaps there were no forces of darkness lurking out there. Following Luke around in the mountains really meant nothing. It didn't mean that Isolder himself would necessarily have to learn the ways of the Force. Luke could very well be deluded, a harmless crank. *But he floated from the sky.* "I'm ready," Isolder said.

During the first part of their journey, the country was incredibly rugged—gullies washed through ground split by crevices. The bones of huge herbivores littered the crevices, creatures with long hind legs, stubby tails, flat triangular heads and tiny front legs. The skeletons showed that the beasts had been large, perhaps four meters from nose to tail. Often the bones had dry, gray scales lying about them. Yet they found no living beasts. Instead, it seemed almost as if the creatures had died out in the recent past, within the last hundred years.

Little grew in this blasted desert. Short, twisted, leathery trees. Stubby patches of purple grass as pliant as hair.

Luke made light of the journey, sometimes jumping ten meters into a crevice where Isolder had to climb tediously down. Isolder soon found himself drenched with sweat, but the Jedi did not sweat much, did not pant, showed no sign of being remotely human. Instead, the Jedi's face was locked in concentration. It took the better part of the night to reach the droid, and Luke would not leave without it, showing uncommon devotion to the small lump of circuitry and gears.

So they made their way toward the mountains following a tedious route that the droid could navigate, until they reached a desert hardpan that ran over rolling hills.

There was no sign of water, and the sun began to rise over the desert, casting an ethereal blue glow. Luke said, "We'd better find some shelter for the day—back there." He pointed to one of the last cracks, went and pushed Artoo over, then jumped in.

Isolder followed them down into the crevice, rested on his haunches in the sandy soil and drank half of his water. Luke took a small sip, sat and closed his eyes.

"You had better get some sleep," Luke said. "It's going to be a long day, and a long walk tonight." With that, the Jedi seemed to fall asleep, breathing deep, evenly.

Isolder cast an angry glance at him. Isolder had been wakened in the early morning from his sleep cycle, and as far as he was concerned, it was only midday. He had always had difficulty changing his sleep schedule, so he sat with his arms folded, trying to feign sleep, or at least show some portion of control worthy of a Jedi's disciple.

Nearly half an hour later, just as the sun was breaking over the desert, Isolder heard the earthquake. It started as a distant rumble moving down from the mountains, growing louder and louder. The earth began to shake, and chunks of dirt broke from the sides of the crevice. The droid Artoo whistled and beeped in alarm, and Luke jumped to his feet.

"What is it, Artoo?" he asked, and Isolder shouted, "Earthquake!"

Luke listened to the sound a moment, shouted back. "No—not an earthquake—"

Suddenly a huge shadow flitted overhead, then another and another. Large reptiles with pale blue scales were leaping over the crevice. One tripped and nearly fell on top of them, used its tiny forelegs to pull itself upright and rush forward.

"Stampede!" Isolder shouted, throwing his arms over his head. Artoo whistled and wheeled in a circle, seeking shelter. Hundreds of reptiles leaped over the crevice.

The roaring quieted after several moments, and one huge reptile leaped into the ravine not a dozen feet from them, stood panting, loose folds of light blue flesh jiggling at its throat, as it studied them. The last of its fellows leaped away.

The beast had bloodred eyes and black teeth shaped like spades. The scales at the top of its head shone slightly iridescent, almost lavender. Its breath smelled musky, of rotting vegetation, and it stared down at them, curious.

"Don't worry, we won't harm you," Luke said, gazing at the creature steadily. It moved forward, put its nostrils to Luke's outstretched hand, and sniffed. "That's right, girl, we're your friends." Luke poured some water from his canteen into his hand, let the beast lap it up with its long, black tongue. The creature made belching noises, plaintive whining sounds.

"What are you doing?" Isolder said. "That thing is drinking all of our water."

"It's eighty kilometers through the desert to the mountains," Luke said, "a difficult journey even for a Jedi, and there is no water between here and there—only sand. But every evening, these creatures run to the hills to feed, and every morning, they run back here to hide from predators and the day's sun. That's why we saw so many skeletons here in the crevices, where their old ones have died. They call themselves the Blue Desert People. Tonight, they will carry us to the mountains. We won't need all this water."

"You mean they're intelligent?" Isolder asked doubtfully.

"Not much more so than most other animals," Luke said, gazing at Isolder, "but smart enough. They care for one another and have their own kind of wisdom."

"And you can talk to them?"

Luke nodded, stroked the reptile's nose. "The Force is within us all—you, me, her. It binds us together, and through it I can read her intent, make mine known."

Isolder watched them a moment, then sat down, troubled

for some reason that he could not express, could not quite grasp. He slept part of the day, ate from his pack, drank his water. All day long the beast slept beside them, laying its head out flat on the ground so that it could sniff Luke's feet.

That evening just before the sun began to set, the beast raised its head, made a honking noise. Several other beasts answered, came to its call.

"Time to go," Luke said. Isolder climbed up from the ravine while Luke closed his eyes, levitated Artoo up, then climbed up himself.

The Blue Desert People were everywhere, climbing out of their holes, snorting loudly and looking at the sunset. They seemed unwilling, or perhaps by some virtue of genetic memory were unable, to begin the journey until the sun had dropped below the mountains.

Under Luke's guidance, Isolder climbed on the back of a large male, set himself just beneath its arms. When the beast stood, it was a precarious position, but Luke carried Artoo up to the same spot on a larger male and seemed to balance fine.

As the bottom of the sun touched the top of the mountains, the Blue Desert People bellowed, lowered their heads, lifted their tails out straight behind them as a counterbalance, and raced across the sand on their powerful hind legs.

With the beast's head down, Isolder found that his position was quite stable, even comfortable, though Artoo whistled and groaned about it at first. The Blue Desert People thundered across eighty kilometers of pan and towering dunes, their red eyes seeming to glow a glittering black in the darkness, grunting and snorting. Isolder listened to them talk, realized that the grunting and snorting came from animals on the perimeters of the herd, and that they were issuing instructions. If reptiles snorted two or three times on one side of the herd, the herd would veer away. But if animals issued contented grunts, the herd would stay on course.

By early nightfall they reached a wide muddy river where tall grasses and reeds grew in the shallows. Birds with long necks and leather wings swooped low over the river in the moonlight, taking long drinks. Here the Blue Desert People stopped to water and feed among the rushes.

"This is where we get off," Luke said, and they dismounted. Luke patted the nose of each of their mounts, thanking them with soft words.

"Can't you make them carry us farther?" Isolder asked. "We've still got a long way to go."

Luke flashed an annoyed glance his way. "I do not *make* anyone do anything," Luke said. "I do not make Artoo follow me, just as I did not make you follow me. The Blue Desert People agreed to take us this far, and now that we have water, our own legs will suffice for the rest of the journey."

Isolder suddenly realized why he found Luke's behavior toward the Blue Desert People so discomforting: among the royal family on Hapes, they did not treat their servants so well. Women were accorded greater respect than men, industrialists more respect than farmers, royalty more respect than them all. But Luke treated his droid and these dumb animals as if they were Isolder's equals, or as if they were Luke's own brothers, and that . . . alarmed Isolder, to think that the Jedi saw him as no more important than a droid or a beast. And yet, Luke showed the Blue Desert People such tenderness that Isolder found himself feeling jealous of them.

"You shouldn't do this!" Isolder found himself saying. "The universe doesn't work this way!"

"What do you mean?" Luke asked.

"You—you're treating those beasts as *equals*. You show my mother, the Ta'a Chume of the Hapan empire, the same degree of cordiality as you give a droid!"

"This droid, these beasts," Luke said, "all have a similar measure of Force within them. If I serve the Force, how can I not respect them, just as I respect Ta'a Chume?"

Isolder shook his head. "Now I see why my mother wanted to kill you, Jedi. You have dangerous ideas."

"Perhaps they are dangerous to despots," Luke said, smiling. "Tell me, do *you* serve your mother and her empire above all else?"

"Of course," Isolder said.

"If you served her, you would not be here," Luke countered. "You would have been content to marry some local despot and sire your heirs. Instead, your heart is divided. You tell yourself that you have come to rescue Leia, but I believe you have really come to Dathomir to learn the ways of the Force."

A thrill coursed through Isolder as he realized that it might be true, and yet, the very idea sounded absurd. Luke was saying that Isolder's every small impulse, each mad decision, could be taken as evidence that Isolder was his disciple, a servant to some higher power that Isolder was not even convinced existed.

True, Luke had floated through the air, carried Isolder's ship to safety, but couldn't that power have issued from Luke's own twisted mind, rather than from some mystical Force? On Thrakia was a race of insects with genetically transmitted memories who worshiped their own power to speak. Apparently the insects all remembered that in the recent past they had communicated only through scent, and then one day they discovered that they had the ability to communicate by clicking their mandibles. After three hundred years they were all still overawed by the fact that they could communicate this way, and all of them took it as a sign that they had been gifted from some higher being. But it was just their stupid mandibles clacking!

As they walked off through the low hills, following the course of the river, Isolder watched the Jedi and wondered. Was Luke truly led by some mystical Force? Or did he simply follow his own conscience, fooled into believing that his strange powers and crazed notions came from some outside influence?

With each step they took toward the mountains, Isolder had to wonder: are my footsteps guided by the light side of the Force? And if so, where will this Force lead me?

Whatever answer Isolder found to that question, he knew it would change every future moment of his life.

Chapter

14

At dawn the morning fog blowing off the muddy river obscured Luke's vision so that he could not see more than a few meters ahead. The ground along the riverbank had turned swampy, hindering Artoo's progress. The trees along the river had all burned and rotted, so that limbs pointed up out of the fog like crooked fingers, in shades of ebony and ice. Large speckled lizards clung to the trees, sometimes as many as a dozen to a branch, watching the fog-shrouded reeds for prey or predators.

Behind Luke, Isolder did not speak. Several times Luke turned to see him, deep in thought, brow furrowed. Luke knew only too well what the young man must be thinking. Only a few years ago, Luke had followed Obi-Wan Kenobi off on a similar mad quest to take stolen blueprints to Alderaan.

For these past months, Luke considered, *I've wanted so badly to find the records of the ancient Jedi, to find some talented students and teach them of the Force.* Yet Luke realized the truth: Isolder had sought *him* out, even though the prince showed little talent.

This was Luke's chance to practice, to teach someone to follow the light side of the Force, without the pressure of having to worry about whether the student would become another Vader.

He picked his way through the mud, watching for quicksand, wondered if that is how it had happened with Obi-Wan Kenobi. Luke had always imagined that the old man had been waiting for Luke to mature, like a farmer watching over his field of grain. But now he wondered if Luke's sudden intrusion into Obi-Wan's affairs hadn't been as much of a surprise to Obi-Wan as Isolder's intrusion now seemed to Luke.

Isolder was obviously moved by the Force. That much Luke could discern, but he could feel no power in the prince. Perhaps the power was so new, so small, that Isolder could not feel it himself.

Luke reached a fork in the trail. One way was high and safe-looking, but the muddy path seemed to draw him. He followed his instinct down the muddy path.

Perhaps there had never been a Jedi academy, he thought. Certainly, Ta'a Chume had lied to him about an academy on one of her worlds. He sensed that.

Perhaps the Force directed acolytes to their Masters when they were needed. Perhaps the only true training of any worth that a Jedi could receive came only as he or she battled against darkness.

If this were true, certainly Dathomir would be the perfect academy. Luke could feel tremendous disturbances in the Force —yawning pits of darkness. He'd never run across anything remotely like it. Yoda's cave had held such a darkness, but here —he felt it all around him.

Ahead of them, reptilian avians croaked and flapped into the sky on leather wings. Luke stopped, realized that he had just come to the end of a peninsula that jutted into the river. He could go no farther, and the brackish water here bubbled. A tar pit. He cast his eyes about for a place to step.

Isolder said, "What's that?"

Luke looked up. Jutting above the fog in the river sat a huge metal platform, leaning at an odd angle. The flocks of avians flew around the platform nervously. The rising sun cast golden rays on the rusted metal, turning it bronze, and beyond the platform was an enormous exhaust nacelle, rotted through so that Luke could see parts of the heavy turbo generators still intact.

"It looks like an old spaceship crashed here," Luke said, realizing after he did so that the wreck was far larger than even one of the old Victory-class destroyers. Yet it must have lain here for hundreds of years.

A small wind blew over the river, stirring the fog, and Luke glimpsed a dome out beyond the exhaust nacelle, the transparisteel still intact.

He started to turn to leave when the name on the rusted exhaust nacelle caught his eye: *Chu'unthor.*

His mind did a little flip. It was not a race of people that Yoda had tried to free from the planet hundreds of years ago, but the spaceship. And in all that time, no one had ever gotten it off the planet.

"We've got to get out there," Luke said, his voice husky with excitement.

"What for?" Isolder asked. "It's just an old wreck."

Luke cast about through the fog, looking for a way to the ship. They walked back up the peninsula, circled through the mire for nearly a kilometer until they found two ancient wooden rafts made of logs tied together with rotting hide. They looked like something children played with. There were fresh marks on the bank where the rafts had been tied up.

"Someone was here recently," Isolder pointed out.

"Yeah," Luke said, "well, who could pass up the chance to look at a really neat wreck?"

"I could," Isolder said. "We don't really need to go out there, do we? I mean, we came here to rescue Leia."

Artoo whistled his agreement, issuing a bunch of clicks and beeps to remind Luke that every time the droid gets near water, there's a monster in it.

Isolder looked off toward the mountains, and Luke could see that the prince really didn't want to delay his trip. Yet the promptings of the Force had led Luke to the place, just as he allowed it to lead him in battle. He knew only too well that he must trust his feelings. Now his feelings told him to get out to that wreck. "It will only take a few minutes," Luke said, hopping onto one of the rafts. "Who's coming with me?"

"I'll wait here," Isolder said, and Artoo's eye swiveled around to look at the prince. The droid was shaking scared, but made a grinding noise at Isolder and rolled onto the raft.

Luke poled the raft out to the wreck. Huge brown fish lazily sunned themselves in the still water. The morning sun had begun burning the fog away, and as he got closer, Luke could see most of the ship—colonies of living domes, the engineering section. The hull around the hyperdrive engines had rusted through. The ship looked to be two kilometers long, a kilometer wide, and eight levels high. The space between the windows to the living quarters showed that the *Chu'unthor* had been heavily inhabited, almost a floating city, perhaps some sort of pleasure craft. It was definitely made to house people. By the tilt of the ship, most of it seemed to be well sunk under the tar pits, with only the upper decks showing, and they were pretty badly rusted.

Yet this was no ordinary wreck—there were no blast marks to show signs of battle, no gaping holes to show an explosion, no crumpled structure to indicate a violent landing. Rather, it seemed that the ship must have developed a technical problem, floated down peacefully, then tried to land in the tar pits.

As he got closer, Luke saw that the ship had been sealed tight. Entryways weren't just closed—they had been welded shut, and many of the transparisteel bubbles on the domes bore heavy scuff marks, as if something had tried to batter its way through the transparent material.

The ship was tilted at an angle, so Luke poled the raft around to the front, which had sunk deepest into the mire, then climbed up onto the wreck. Someone had indeed tried to break into the ship. Luke found many more scuff marks on the domes, bent pieces of crude iron that someone had used to try to pry open the welded doors, along with shattered pieces of giant clubs and broken boulders. Writing had been painted here or there in some strange tongue, and arrows pointed to the weaker welds. Someone had worked for years at breaking into the ship, had made it a great study, but their tools were ineffective.

Kids, Luke thought, but no child could have wielded those giant clubs.

Some of the domes had access sockets that Artoo could

have plugged into and opened, but the sockets were far too rusted. Anyway, the whole ship looked as if it had rotted inside too. The transparisteel was pitted by blowing sand, almost fogged. Many of the domes seemed to contain training rooms for gymnastics of some kind—huge balls littered the floors, as if someone had been playing a game when the *Chu'unthor* fell. Another dome had been a restaurant or night club. Beverage glasses and uneaten meals sat on rusted tables, covered with dust. Artoo wheeled along behind, working hard to negotiate the angle, whistling softly and studying all the damage.

"It looks like whoever was on this ship got out fast once they landed, and they never came back," Luke told Artoo.

The droid issued some beeps and clicks, reminding Luke of Yoda's message: "Repulsed by the witches." Luke could feel the disturbances in the Force here, like dark cyclones sucking in all light.

"Yeah," Luke said. "Whatever Yoda encountered on this planet, it's still here."

Artoo groaned.

Luke stopped, looked in at one bubble. Workbenches stood at the center, and several benches held rusted mechanical parts—corroded power cells, focusing crystals, handles for lightsabers—tools to make weapons that only a Jedi could use.

Luke's heart pounded. *A Jedi academy,* he realized, and everything suddenly made sense. *I searched forty planets and never found a sign of an academy, because the Jedi academy was in the stars.* Of course they needed a spaceborne academy. With so few people strong enough to master the Force, the ancient Jedi would have needed to scour the galaxy hunting for recruits. In each star cluster they might have found only one or two cadets worthy to join.

He pulled out his lightsaber, flipped it on, and began cutting through the transparisteel, feeling desperate. This old wreck, as rusted as it was, couldn't possibly hold anything of worth. But he had to look. Blue gouts of molten transparisteel bounced off the deck of the *Chu'unthor,* and Artoo wheeled back a pace.

Luke was so involved in trying to break into the spaceship, that he almost did not feel her presence, but suddenly there was a power behind him, rushing toward him. He turned just in time to see a woman—long reddish brown hair flashing, tawny hides from some alien creature, strong bare legs. She spun and kicked at him with a leather boot, and Luke felt the force of her intent, ducked, swung with his lightsaber.

He felt a ripple in the Force signifying an attack, but before he could respond the girl swung a club, smashing his artificial hand hard enough so that circuits shorted and the lightsaber spun away. She kicked at his belly and Luke dropped and rolled, used the Force to call his lightsaber back to his left hand.

The girl stopped, and her mouth dropped in astonishment as she saw what he had done. Luke could feel her Force—powerful, wild, like that of no other woman he had ever met. Her brown eyes were flecked with orange, and she crouched on the hull of the *Chu'unthor*, panting, considering. She could not have been more than eighteen years old, perhaps twenty.

"I won't hurt you," Luke said.

The girl half-closed her eyes, whispered some words, and Luke felt a touch, a probing finger of Force that rippled through him. "How can you work the magic, being only a man?" the girl said.

"The Force is in us all," Luke said, "but only those who are trained can become its Masters."

The girl studied him skeptically. "You claim to master the magic?"

"Yes," Luke said.

"Then you are a male witch, a Jai, from beyond the stars?" Luke nodded.

"I have heard of the Jai," the girl said. "Grandmother Rell says that they are unbeatable warriors, for they battle death. And since they battle for life, nature cherishes them, and they cannot die. Are you an unbeatable warrior?" The Force of the girl rippled, almost as if she would attack, but Luke felt a difference—the rippling was almost like a blanket, smothering him, binding him, and as Luke tried to imagine what it foreboded, an image came to mind.

He saw the girl hunting in the desert, searching desperately for something that others guarded, protected. He saw a hut made of twigs beneath the shelter of a red rock ledge, an evening campfire twisting in the wind, half-naked children playing beside the fire. And the girl was searching, creeping toward the hut, hungering for something within.

The girl smiled at him and began chanting, and the look in her eyes shocked him. He had never seen such fierce lust. *"Waytha ara quetha way. Waytha ara quetha way . . ."*

"Wait a minute!" Luke said. "You can't be thinking—" Broken bits of stones and clubs began rolling over the surface of the *Chu'unthor*, rumbling like an approaching storm. Behind the girl, the fog over the river swirled violently. *We were repulsed by the witches.*

"Waytha ara quetha way. Waytha ara quetha way!" Lightning crackled overhead and a dozen small boulders blasted toward Luke, hurtling through the air. Vader had tried similar tricks, but Luke reflected woefully that Vader hadn't been nearly as good at it. He swung wildly with his lightsaber, bursting several pieces of rock, but one caught him in the chest, throwing him backward a pace. *Repulsed by the witches.*

"Wait!" Luke shouted. "You can't just take men as slaves and mate with them any time you please!" Boulders thundered across the hull of the ship, hundreds of them, lunging toward Luke like a herd of living animals, and he realized that *this* woman could do just about anything she wanted. He raised an arm desperately, trying to turn the rocks aside with the Force, but his mind was a roiling sea and he could not gain his focus. *Repulsed by the witches.*

A log whirled toward him, spinning, and he ducked, stones leaped at him in such numbers he could hardly see them whiz past, and suddenly *she* was before him, whirling and swinging a club. He hadn't even felt her move toward him, yet her club smacked his skull, lights flashed in his head, and he reeled to the ground.

Groggily, he heard the girl yelling at him, realized that she straddled his chest, locking his arms with her strong legs, but Luke was too weak to fight her off. She held his jaw and shouted triumphantly, "I am Teneniel Djo, a daughter of Allya, and you are my slave!"

. . .

In the early morning Han struggled up the treacherous flight of steps carved into the sheer mountain cliff. As on most low-gravity planets, the volcanic mountains rose tall and sheer, and they were walking along a cliff face two hundred meters above solid black rock. The stone steps were wide enough even for a rancor, and thousands of feet had worn them smooth. During the night, cold water dripping from the mountaintop had deposited a thin crust of ice over the steps, making them treacherous.

Behind Han, the rancors snarled and paced slowly, grabbing at the bare rock cliffs for support, terrified of falling but driven mercilessly by their riders. Chewbacca didn't look good. He held his ribs and moaned softly as the rancor carried him along.

In the clear morning light, Han could see the three women clearly now. Under their robes, they wore tunics made from colorful reptile skins. Each hide tunic flashed in colors of green or smoke blue or yellow ocher. Over these, they wore thick robes woven of fiber, intricately trimmed with yellow plant fibers or large dark beads made from seedpods. Yet their most ornate decorations were the helms. What he had first thought were antlers in the darkness, he saw now were merely headdresses of blackened metal, curving up like some odd insect wing. Drilled into the helms were holes. A child's playground of ornaments dangled in each hole, swaying with each step the rancors took. For ornaments he saw what looked like pieces of agate and polished blue azurite, the painted skulls of small carnivorous reptiles, a small petrified fist from some creature, bits of colored fabric, glass beads, a piece of beaten silver, a bluish-white orb that might have been a dried eye. None of the women wore the same style of helm, and Han knew enough about various cultures to be wary. In any given society, the most powerful members tended to dress the most elaborately.

Han kept hold of Leia and Threepio, concerned that if one of them fell, they might all tumble from the cliff. His breath came ragged, steam puffing from his mouth. They turned one last treacherous corner and looked down into an oval-shaped valley hidden in the folds of mountain cliffs. Stick shacks with thatch roofs dotted the valley, and checkerboard squares of green and tan showed growing crops. Men, women, and children worked the fields, fed huge four-legged reptiles in their pens. A large stream ran through the fields to a small lake, then tumbled over a cliff into the wilds below.

They descended the stairs, passing a phalanx of ten women, all mounted on rancors. The women were all dressed in similar styles—in rough lizard leather with robes suitable for the cold mountains, helms with antlers. Most of the women had blaster rifles, though others were armed only with spears or throwing axes tucked into their belts. None of them seemed to be younger than twenty-five, and somehow the dirty faces of the women chilled Han more than the mountain air. They did not smile, did not show grief or worry. Instead, they were cold, brutally impassive, like the faces of shell-shocked warriors.

Above the narrow valley, carved into the basalt, were fortifications—turrets and parapets and windows. The women had placed slabs of plasteel from the hulls of broken spaceships over the rock like a mosaic. A couple of odd blaster cannons pointed out from the mountain stronghold. Black scorch marks and pits in the rock showed that these women were indeed at war. But with whom?

The group reached a landing of stone, and on orders from one of the women, one rancor gingerly carried Chewbacca, leading Leia up toward the fortress, while other rancors marched Han and Threepio down into the valley on a muddy trail, past pens filled with herds of giant dirty reptiles that sat quietly munching fodder, sullenly staring at Han.

They came to a circle of huts made of twigs and mud, and at the opening of each hut was a tall stone urn that Han guessed held water. Through open doors he could see colorful red blankets hanging on the walls, baskets of nuts on small wood tables, various wood hay hooks.

His guard led him to the back of the huts, where he found dozens of men and young women and children. In a sandy lot filled with weeds the villagers had dug holes and filled them with water from buckets, making small puddles. Each adult sat gazing intently into the puddle while children stood quietly outside the circle, watching.

The rancor stopped, and the warrior astride it reached

down and tapped Han on the shoulder with her spear, pointed at the puddles. *"Whuffa,"* she said. *"Whuffa!"* indicating that he should go look into a puddle.

"Do you have any idea what they want?" Han asked Threepio.

"I'm afraid not," Threepio said. "Their language is not in my catalog. Some terms of their dialogue may be ancient Paecian, but I've never heard the term *whuffa.*"

Paecian? Han wondered. The Paecian empire had foundered three thousand years back. Han went to one old graybeard, looked at his mud puddle. The puddle was small, perhaps half a meter around and only a finger deep.

The man sneered up at Han, growled, *"Whuffa!"* He handed Han a copper blade, indicating that Han should use it to dig, and gave Han a bucket of water, pointed toward a free space in the field.

"Whuffa, right. I've got it," Han said, and he took the items to the clear spot, away from the others, and scraped out a small hole, poured in the water. It smelled terrible, and Han suddenly realized it wasn't water at all, but some form of crude fermented beverage. *Great,* he thought. *I've been captured by weirdos who want me to stare into a puddle until I have a vision.*

He looked at his reflection in the puddle a moment, realized his hair was mussed up, and used his fingers to comb it. The warriors did not seem to know what to do with Threepio; they left him on the sidelines with the children, who gawked at the droid curiously, but not worshipfully. Up at the fortress, Leia had already gone into the shadows of an open doorway. Distantly, Han heard a TIE fighter screaming through the atmosphere, and the women on rancors searched the sky nervously, hands shadowing their eyes.

It seemed a good sign. If these women were having trouble with Zsinj, then at least Han was in the right camp. But considering the haphazard nature of the fortifications, maybe not. In any case, he didn't like the sound of being "judged." If these women were xenophobes, they might kill or enslave offworlders out of fear. If they thought Han and Leia were spies, they could be in even bigger trouble. Then there was the fact that the women had automatically assumed that Han was Leia's slave. He glanced at the warriors on their rancors. The women watched him coldly. He decided to pretend to be hard at work.

For an hour he sat gazing into his puddle of fermented goo, the sun shining on his back, until he realized he was getting mighty thirsty and wondered if it was permitted for him to drink some of the liquor himself. *Better not,* he decided. *It might not be allowed of slaves.*

Leia hadn't come down from the fortress yet. Han watched a woman come out to a parapet a hundred meters above the valley floor. She was an old woman, wearing a leather hide for a cape, carrying a bucket. She stood gazing down a moment, then waved her hands in the air and spoke, but her words did not carry. After a moment, a crystal ball rose from the valley floor to meet her. She leaned out over the parapet, held the bucket under the ball, and the ball dropped, splashing liquid over the rim of the bucket. The old woman carried the bucket back into the fortress, and Han sat astonished. It had not been a crystal ball floating in the air at all—but water. Yet it had not been a natural phenomenon. The ball of water had risen slowly.

Han heard a loud sucking sound, looked down at his puddle of liquor. Some form of large worm had risen to the hole and was drinking. Nearby, an old man whispered, *"Whuffa!"* and Han looked at the toothless geezer. He made grasping and pulling motions with his hands, telling Han to catch the thing.

Han looked at the worm. All he could see at the moment was a leathery, dark brown skin and a hole that it drank through. After a moment it oozed up a little, showed a head about the thickness of a child's arm. All around the crowd, everyone was watching him—children, adults, warriors on their rancors. All of them remaining absolutely silent, holding their breaths. Whatever a whuffa was, these people wanted one pretty badly. There might even be a reward in it.

After a moment, the worm eeled up a bit more, began rolling in the mud, sniffing for more liquor. Still, it looked pretty big, and there wasn't much to grab on to. Han waited for three minutes, till the worm got up enough courage to ooze farther out of its hole, heading for the bucket of liquor. Han figured it couldn't hurt to let the thing get a little drunk, so he let the worm stick its orifice in, begin draining the bucket accompanied by slurping sounds. The worm had long segments to its skin, no eyes. Han reached down and grabbed it with both hands, afraid he might break it.

The worm jerked back so hard and so quickly it pulled Han to the ground, but he didn't let go. "You're mine!" Han shouted, and suddenly everyone rushed around him, waiting to help, children leaping in delight and crying, "Whuffa! Whuffa!"

The worm twisted in Han's grip, turned its orifice toward him and spat a pitcher of liquor into Han's face, then began wheezing and hissing.

Han held on tight. He could feel the worm tensing, using the friction of the ground to pull itself back, but after a couple of minutes the worm exhausted itself, and Han pulled it forward a meter. Still, there was more in the ground, so he grabbed another handful and pulled. Sweat was running down his face, down his hands, making his grip precarious, but after another three minutes he got another meter of the whuffa up. Behind him, other men had grabbed the thrashing head of the thing and held it.

Han worked for half an hour before he realized that this was going to be a long job—he had twenty meters of whuffa out of the ground, and the thing hadn't begun to taper down or anything. Yet now he was developing a system. When the whuffa fatigued, he pulled out as much as he could as fast as he could, tugging up two or three meters at a time before the whuffa could reestablish its grip.

An hour later, Han was reeling from fatigue when he yanked on some whuffa and found that, miraculously, it seemed, he had reached the end. The force of his tug knocked Han down. Every kid and man in the village had a hold on the whuffa, which had now gone quite limp down near its head. Han estimated that it must be two hundred and fifty meters long. With great fanfare, the villagers paraded the whuffa down to an orchard. Old men clapped Han on the back and whispered their thanks, and Han followed them.

The villagers began draping the whuffa in a bare tree, and Han saw other whuffas there, drying in the sunlight. He went over and touched one. It felt dead, almost rubbery, but the supple leather of its skin felt good in his hand, strong, even elegant. The chocolate color was nice, too. On a whim, he tried to see if he could tear it—but the stuff wouldn't snap, wouldn't even stretch. He looked over at the women on their rancors, saw that saddles on the rancors' necks were tied in place with whuffa hide.

Great! Han realized. *So I caught a rope.* But the villagers here seemed to think it was a big deal. They were all ecstatic. Who knew what kind of reward they might give him? If they executed offworlders, maybe being Han Solo, the heroic Whuffa Grabber, had just saved his life. And even though it was just a rope, Han had to admit that it was a darned good rope. You could probably sell it offworld to fashion designers, and maybe there was more to it than just rope. What if it had medicinal properties? These people were at war. Maybe they applied whuffa hide to their wounds as an antibiotic, or boiled it to make antiaging drugs. Why, once Han thought about it, there was no telling what you could do with a whuffa!

"Han?" a woman called. He turned. A dark-haired woman sat astride the neck of a rancor at the edge of the orchard. "My name is Damaya. You will follow me." She tapped the rancor's nose with her heel, turned the beast.

Han's mouth felt dry. "Why? Where are we going?"

"Your friend Leia has been pleading your case to the Singing Mountain clan for the past two hours. She has won your freedom, but now your future must be decided."

"My future?"

"We of the Singing Mountain clan have chosen not to be your enemies, but that does not mean we will be your allies. We understand that you have a sky ship that may be repairable. If this is true, the Nightsisters and their Imperial slaves will want it. And, since you are a man of power in the outside world, they may want *you*. Our clan needs to know whether you want our protection, and if so, what you will pay for it."

Han followed Damaya, still panting, sweat dripping down his back. After nearly a day without sleep, his eyes itched and his sinuses burned as if he were allergic to something on the planet. The messenger led him up toward the fortress, and just before they reached the landing where the stone stairway diverged into three paths, a group of strangers came up from outside the valley—nine women, humanoid, with strangely blotched, purplish skin. They did not wear exotic helms like the warriors, but instead wore only dark, shaggy, hooded robes crudely woven from some plant fiber and covered with trail dust. He wondered nervously if these women had been called in to be his judges.

But Han watched the warriors guarding the trail and knew that the hooded women were enemies. The rancors growled and fidgeted, scraping the stone walkways with their huge palms. The warrior women held their blasters at the ready, unblinking, though the leader of the nine carried a broken spear, probably as a sign of truce.

Damaya got off her rancor and led Han up the steps toward the fortress.

The nine women hesitated at the landing to watch them pass, studying Han intensely. Their leader, an older woman with graying hair at her temples, had glittering green eyes, and the hollows of her cheeks were a sickly yellow hue. She smiled at Han, causing him to shiver.

"Tell me, offworlder, where your ship is," she said to his back.

Han's heart hammered, and he turned. "It's, uh, over—" he started to point, and the messenger Damaya spun violently on her rancor.

"Tell her nothing!" Damaya commanded, and her words were like a knife slicing through some invisible cord that held Han's throat. He realized suddenly that the old woman had used Luke's Jedi trick of commanding those with weak minds.

His face must have reddened, for Damaya said, "There is no need to be embarrassed. Baritha has a powerful gift for forcing minds."

The old woman, Baritha, laughed at him, and Han turned away, angry. She followed him two steps, then swung the haft of her spear up from behind, tapping his crotch experimentally.

Han spun, fists clenched, and the old woman whispered under her breath, chanting, and held her hand out in a clutching gesture. Han felt both of his fists caught in an invisible vise, and joints cracked under the pressure.

"Don't be so quick to anger, you morsel of a man," Baritha cackled. "Respect your betters, or next time, it will be an eye— or something equally as valuable to you—that I crush."

"Keep your filthy hands off me!" Han growled. Han's

guide, Damaya, casually pulled out her blaster, aimed it at the old woman's throat and said something in her own language.

The old woman released her grip on Han. "I was only admiring your prisoner. From behind he looks so . . . tasty. Who could resist?"

"We of the Singing Mountain clan suffer your presence here," Damaya said, "but our hospitality has limits."

"You of the Singing Mountain clan are weak-minded fools," the old woman croaked, sticking her head forward and raising her eyebrows so that her face unwrinkled somewhat. "You couldn't throw us out if you had to, and so you will suffer our presence, and submit to our demands. I despise your pretensions of civility! I spit on your hospitality!"

"I could shoot you in the throat," Damaya said longingly.

"Go ahead, Damaya," the old woman said, pulling open her robes, revealing a shriveled breast, "shoot your dear aunt! I don't love life anymore since you cast me out of your clan. Shoot me. You know how much you want it!"

"I won't let you goad me into it," Damaya said.

The old woman cackled, said in a pouting voice, "She won't let me goad her into it," and the robed sisters behind her laughed. Han found himself unreasonably angry, wishing that Damaya would raise the blaster and plug a few of them. Instead, she holstered the blaster, and tapped Han on the shoulder, urging him to walk ahead of her so that she placed herself between him and the nine hooded sisters.

The fortress turned out to be even more hammered than Han had seen from below. Everywhere around the patchwork of blast shielding the rock was cracked and pounded. Many of the cracks had been patched with some dark green, gummy substance so that the basalt took on a marbled appearance. Chunks of red sandstone lay scattered on the walkways outside, and Han wondered where the sandstone had come from— all the mountains nearby seemed to be volcanic in origin. Someone had to have carried the stones several kilometers.

Two guards at the door to the fortress peeled from their posts and led the way. Han glanced back: A dozen Singing Mountain warriors followed on foot, guarding the robed women. They entered the dark chambers of the fortress, which was honeycombed with halls and stairways. The walls were covered with thick tapestries and lit by sconces. They quickly turned to a room carved into the corner of the fortress so that windows opened on two sides.

The huge room was nearly triangular in shape, with six openings looking out to the prairie. Blaster rifles lay stacked near each window, flak jackets had been tossed in piles on the floor, and a solitary blaster cannon poked out toward the mountains to the east. A huge dent showed where something had smashed its housing, so that green liquid coolant lay puddled beside it on the floor. The cannon was useless. In the center of the room a cooking pit was filled with bright embers. A large animal roasted above the coals while two men basted it with a pungent sauce and turned the spit.

The room was filled with a dozen women in glittering robes of reptile hide, all in helms. Near the back of the crowd, dressed as one of the warriors, Han saw Leia.

One of the women stepped forward. "Welcome, Baritha," she said to the old crone, ignoring Han. "On behalf of my sisters, I, Mother Augwynne, welcome you to the Singing Mountain clan." The greeter stepped forward, and despite her kind words, her face was cold, somewhat guarded. Augwynne wore a tunic of glittering yellow scales, a hide robe with black lizard shapes sewn around its hem. Her headdress was made of smooth golden wood and decorated with cabochons of gleaming yellow tigereye.

"You needn't bother with formalities," Baritha said, and the old woman tossed her broken spear to the floor, the purple veins in her head throbbing. "The Nightsisters have come for General Solo and the other offworlders. We captured them first, and by all right they belong to us!"

"We found no Nightsisters with them," Augwynne answered, "only Imperial stormtroopers trespassing on our land. We killed them, and have offered their prey sanctuary among us as equals. I'm afraid we can't honor your claims to ownership."

"The stormtroopers were our slaves, working under our direction, as you well know," Baritha answered. "They were bringing the offworlders to prison for interrogation."

"If you only want to interrogate General Solo, then perhaps

I can help you. General Solo, why did you come to Dathomir?"
Augwynne's eyes flashed to the pouch at Han's belt, and he
took the cue.

"I own this planet and everything on it," Han said. "I came
to check out my real estate."

As one, the Nightsisters began hissing, shaking their heads,
and Baritha spat, "A *man* claims to own Dathomir?"

Han fumbled in his pouch for the deed, found the box and
pressed its switch. The holo of Dathomir appeared in the air
above his palm, his name clearly registered as owner.

"No!" Baritha shouted, waving her hand. The box flew
from Han's grip, tumbled to the floor.

"That's right," Han said, "I own this world, and I want you
and your Nightsisters off my planet!"

Baritha glared at him. "Gladly," she said. "Provide us a
ship, and we will leave."

He felt an odd tugging in his mind, fought the urge to
divulge the location of the *Falcon*.

"Enough of this," Augwynne said. "You have your answer,
Baritha. Tell Gethzerion that General Solo will remain with the
Singing Mountain clan, as a free man."

"You cannot free him," Baritha breathed threateningly.
"We of the Nightsisters claim him as our slave!"

Augwynne answered calmly, "He has won his freedom by
saving the life of a clan sister. You cannot claim him as a slave."

"You lie!" Baritha said. "Whose life has he saved?"

"He saved the life of clan sister Tandeer, and earned his
freedom."

"I have never heard of a clan sister by that name," Baritha
argued. "Let me see her!"

The women of the Singing Mountain clan parted, revealing
Leia in the shadows. She wore a tunic of shimmering red
scales, a helm of black iron decorated with small animal skulls.
Baritha studied her face doubtfully. "Have I seen this one before?"

"She is new to us, a spellcaster from the Northern Lakes
region, and an adopted clan sister. Speak the words to the spell
of discovery, and you will know that all I say is true."

Baritha glared at the women in the room. "I do not need

the spell of discovery to tell me what is true," she said. "You base your arguments for General Solo's ownership upon technicalities!"

"We base our arguments upon laws that you and your kind have never respected," Augwynne countered.

Baritha growled, "The Nightsisters dispute your right to these slaves. Release them to us, or we will be forced to take them!"

"Do you threaten bloodshed?" Augwynne asked, and suddenly the room filled with humming, dozens of women all around Han mumbling with half-closed eyes. The Nightsisters retreated into a circle, backs to each other, and held hands, chanting, eyes closed, heads half-concealed in the shadows of their robes.

Baritha shouted, "Gethzerion, we have found the offworlder. He has a starship, but the clan sisters will not give him to us!" Han could hear a humming in his ears, almost as if a fly buzzed within his skull. The hair raised on the back of his neck, and he knew for a certainty that no matter how far away this Gethzerion was, she had heard Baritha's call and was now giving the woman instructions.

Han started to back away from the Nightsisters, seeking shelter, but Baritha lunged from her circle and grabbed Han's arms, her purple-skinned fingers biting into his shoulder like claws. He twisted and tried to pull free. One of the warriors of the Singing Mountain clan raised a blaster and fired at Baritha's face, but Baritha merely released her grip, muttered a word, and used her hand to deflect the blaster bolt into the ceiling.

As one the Nightsisters turned and leaped through the open windows, their black robes flapping. Han's heart skipped a beat at the thought of those bodies smashing on the rocks two hundred meters below. But for a moment Baritha hovered in the air, twisted to sneer at them.

"We will have blood!" she roared and the sound of her threat filled the room so that the very stone trembled. Then she let herself fall.

Han ran to the window, looked out: The Nightsisters lightly dropped to the ground, scurried off like insects into the cover of the underbrush.

Several clan sisters reached for blasters, but Augwynne said softly, "Let them go."

She came up behind Han and touched his shoulder lightly, looking at the blood that ran from his wounded biceps. "Well, General Solo, you should consider yourself fortunate that Gethzerion wants you alive. Welcome to Dathomir."

Chapter

15

Teneniel Djo watched her offworld spellcaster struggle at his bonds. She'd placed his hands in a wood stock, then tied them with whuffa leather. The stupid offworlders—both men—struggled secretly when they thought she was not looking, and this pleased her. The handsome one, he was no more than a commoner, beautiful but unable to cast spells. But this male witch, he was a catch to prize.

She herded them through the foothills, unconcerned about whether her captives might try to escape. She had not bound their little *machine*, their droid. Oh yes, Teneniel knew what a droid was, though she had never seen one close. She feared its escape least of all. Like her other prisoners, it did not need a close guard.

Instead, she watched the brush on the hills to both sides, often stopping to turn her head as if listening for pursuit. Something bothered her, a tingling feeling at the back of her scalp, a coldness that clawed the pit of her stomach. She whispered the spell of discovery and felt the dark ones stirring all across the wilderness. For four years she had sojourned in this waste, knowing that she was too close to the Imperial prison, yet she had never felt so many of the Nightsisters stir at once. She concentrated only on the nearest. She would need all her energy to keep from getting caught.

She led her captives up to a thicket of short trees so that she could survey the trails ahead. She climbed out on a rock. The mountains here were nearly impassable, and Teneniel dared not take her captives on the rougher trails. The machine person would never be able to make it under any circumstances, and the men would need their hands free. Teneniel sang the discovery spell again. She could feel Nightsisters to three sides of them —one was two kilometers to the south, another three kilometers to the west, and one a kilometer straight ahead to the east. To the north, you could not climb the mountain unless you knew the spells for levitation, and Teneniel doubted she could persuade the others to let her levitate them. She whimpered softly.

"They're hunting us, aren't they?" the male witch whispered.

Teneniel nodded, studying the landscape. She wiped the perspiration from her forehead.

"Free me!" the male witch urged her. "Whatever is out there, I can help you." She glanced at him doubtfully. She had never met an offworlder she could trust. But if he did not even know what was hunting them, then maybe he did not know of the Nightsisters and their lackeys at the Imperial prison. Or maybe he was in league with the Nightsisters and only feigned ignorance.

"If I free your hands, do you promise not to run away?" Teneniel asked. Nearby, the handsome slave twisted his head around, listening to them.

"If I stay with you, what will you do with me?" the male witch asked.

"I will take you to my clan," Teneniel said honestly, "and all of my sisters will witness that I have caught you fairly. Once you are registered as my property, you will live in my hut and sire daughters on me. Do you agree to this?" She held her breath. She was offering him a good deal.

"I can't agree to that," the male witch said. "I hardly know you."

"What?" Teneniel asked. "Am I so ugly that you would rather be captured by the Nightsisters? Would you rather spawn with one of them and watch your daughters master their spells?"

"I . . . don't know what the Nightsisters are," the male witch said, yet his blue eyes opened wide with fear, and his voice was tight.

"You can feel them nearby, can't you?" Teneniel asked. "Isn't that enough? You will be a valuable breeder. Who has ever heard of a male spellcaster? Rather than let you—rather than let any of us—fall into their hands, I will kill us all." She pulled out one of their blasters.

The little mechanical person squealed and its metal housing rattled on its frame. Its single blue eye swiveled from Teneniel to the male witch.

"No!" the male witch said, nodding toward his friends. "It's not them that the Nightsisters want, is it? It's you and me. The Nightsisters are drawn to us. Let my friends go. The Nightsisters will not bother them. You and I can escape!"

"You will be my mate?" Teneniel asked hopefully. The male witch licked his lips, looked at her—not just at her face, but at her body, and Teneniel realized with a start that he thought she was attractive. Overhead a warm wind stirred the trees, and the leaves began to whisper.

"Perhaps," the male witch said. "But I won't make that choice unwillingly. I didn't come to this planet looking for a wife. I'm not your property, and I won't allow you to kill anyone here, including yourself."

The male witch's lightsaber flipped from her belt, activated itself and tumbled through the air, slicing his bonds and returning to his hand.

"I had to ask, at least," Teneniel said, glancing away. She had been wondering all day if it was possible to keep a male witch enslaved. The ease with which he'd just freed himself answered that question, and the fact that he could cast spells without voicing them or using gestures unnerved her. Some of the sisters could do that with simple spells, but this male witch did it with even complex spells. She didn't want him to see the fear in her face, or the hope. "Tell me, offworlder, do men on your planet have names?"

"I am Luke Skywalker, a Jedi Knight. These are my friends, Isolder and Artoo."

Teneniel laughed. "A Knight? You are not much of a warrior, Luke Skywalker." He used the lightsaber to cut the bonds of the handsome prisoner.

Teneniel told Isolder and Artoo, "Luke Skywalker and I will lead the Nightsisters away from here. As Luke Skywalker has said, they may not be interested in you. If you want shelter, then you must go to that mountain—the one that juts up like a wall." She pointed forty kilometers in the distance. "There you will find my clan sisters." She did not tell them that if they survived the journey, she would take them slave again. She was not interested in Isolder as a breeder, not with Luke Skywalker around, but she was sure she could sell him for a small fortune.

She tossed Isolder his blaster, hoping it would be enough to get him to the clan alive. He already had his pack with its food and tent.

"Come with me, Luke Skywalker," Teneniel said.

"Just call me Luke."

She nodded, took off through the woods at a run, heading east through a sunny glade where dewplates grew thick and green. Her discovery spell still worked; she could feel the Nightsister ahead, not half a kilometer off. Teneniel tried to form her plans, consider her battle spells, but somehow the effort of trying to run and think at the same time seemed too much. She felt confused, unsure even which direction she was running, and she wondered if she might not be under the influence of a spell herself—but the thought slipped away before she could grasp it. Teneniel's gift was casting the Force storm, and here in the trees such a storm should be able to hide them. She hoped to meet the Nightsister head-on, then slip past her in the storm. It seemed a daring plan to Teneniel, a brilliant plan, to rush toward the Nightsister. Once the plan was formed, Teneniel felt a great sense of ease, knowing she had made the right decision.

Luke ran effortlessly. At first she thought he must have great stamina, but after a few minutes she saw that he did not sweat like a normal person. Therefore, he must have cast a spell —some spell she'd never heard of, and Teneniel had the unnerving realization that he might be more powerful than she'd imagined. Truly, she had captured him easily, and he had trudged along through the day making a show of pulling at his bonds. But he could have freed himself at any time, and she could feel that he did not fear her. And he knew secret spells that none of the sisters had ever heard.

"Do you always use words when you cast spells?" Luke asked almost casually as he ran.

"Or gestures. Some learn to cast silently, as you do," Teneniel gasped, sucking for air. Luke gauged her as she struggled up the hill, sweating. Teneniel knew she did not look her best at the moment. When they got back to the clan, she could dress in clean clothes.

The Nightsister could not be far ahead, so as they ran for the top of a small wooded rise, Teneniel began chanting, eyes half-closed, preparing her spell. She stopped with Luke, and the wind above her trembled, feeling her power. She peeked over the hill into a small valley filled with young snowbark trees. Through the thick woods she saw the Nightsister dressed in purple robes, along with twenty of Zsinj's men dressed in the camouflaged armor of Imperial stormtroopers.

One trooper shouted, "Up there!" and raised a blaster rifle. Teneniel focused her spell. Immediately the magic wind rose— storming across the ground so hard that rotted leaves and twigs rose in a maelstrom, blinding her enemies. The trees swayed and cracked in the wind.

Luke would have stood watching, but Teneniel grabbed his hand and rushed through the storm, the wind following at their backs, unable to see more than an arm's length in front of them. The wind began to die a bit, and Teneniel worked harder, drawing energy from the land. The tempest grew black as Teneniel was compelled to blast topsoil from the ground, and all around them the maelstrom denuded the slender green leaves from the snowbarks.

The filthy wind blotted out the sun, and Teneniel dodged and wove through the trees, seeking a way past the Nightsister. Teneniel could still feel her, twenty meters to their right, and just when Teneniel was sure she was past, a bolt of blue lightning pierced through the haze, struck Teneniel in the breast, jarring her mind, lifting her in the air.

The Nightsister stood before them, flames flying from her fingertips, and Teneniel recognized the hag: Ocheron, a woman who had been powerful in her clan, a woman gifted at deception. Too late, Teneniel realized that Ocheron had caused them to run into her trap.

Ocheron laughed and the blue lightning arced from her fingertips, sucked Teneniel's breath away. She shrieked for help. The flames dug into her like fiery claws. The world reeled, and the blue lightning played over her. It touched a breast, and the breast went so cold it felt as if it had been severed. Tongues of lightning played up her left arm, and the arm seemed to die and wither instantly, like a cut ola vine. A bolt of lightning sizzled into her ear, and all sound left her, another arc touched her eye and half the world went black.

The lightning sucked the very life from each limb it touched—slicing parts of her away like a giant blade. She could not fight it, could not run away. She felt so helpless, she could not even scream as she collapsed.

Time seemed to slow as she fell. Ocheron cackled and the killing fire streamed from her fingers. Teneniel's spell faltered: the wind hushed. Soot and debris still filled the sky like a dark fog, but twigs began to rain down in the storm.

Then there was a flash of blue and the smell of ozone as Luke pulled his lightsaber, switched it on and lunged. Ocheron's eyes widened in surprise at his attack, and she tried to turn her attention to him—too late. The lightsaber struck off her head. Purple flames erupted from her neck like water thundering down a mountain stream, and Luke covered his face, trying to shield himself from the touch of the dark power he'd unleashed.

Four stormtroopers rushed through the dark fog, firing their blasters. Luke deflected bolts with his lightsaber and attacked, killing the men swiftly.

Teneniel found her voice, tried chanting again. Luke grabbed her arm and pulled her as the wind rose around them. She stumbled along blindly, mumbling her spell in desperation until they reached the top of another hill and stepped out of the swirling maelstrom.

Teneniel fell silent, and Luke half-carried her through some deep woods along a hillside. Teneniel remembered an old cave, pulled him to it, and they stumbled inside.

There Teneniel lay on the ground panting. Luke studied her wounds. The blue lightning had left deep burns. The wounds were searing hot, and Teneniel coughed. Blood flecked out of her mouth, coming up from a wound in her lungs, and she began to cry, knowing she was about to die.

Luke pulled at the charred leather of her tunic until it ripped, then traced his fingers over the wound on her breast. His hand was cool, soothing like a balm, and she faded into a deep, uneasy sleep.

In her dreams, Teneniel was a girl, and her mother had died. The sisters of the Singing Mountain clan had laid the corpse out on a stone table to dress it and paint her mother's face in flesh tones. But Teneniel knew she was dead, could not bear to watch the sisters try to create the illusion of life. She ran up a flight of gray steps, past a woven mat that bore the image of a clan sister in yellows and white, holding a war spear. Beyond it was the warriors' hall, a room where commoners— those without the spellcasting ability—or mere apprentices like Teneniel were never allowed entrance, no matter if their mother had been war leader, no matter what their level of talents.

Teneniel let the mat close behind her, and stopped, staring in horror at the sheer enormity of the room. The ceiling seemed to stretch up endlessly, and the far walls were lost in shadows. The war room had been excavated through much of the mountain, and even the echoes of Teneniel's rough breathing came soft and diffused, lost in the distance. In the wall to the left a lookout window had been carved. The window was large enough so that perhaps twenty women could stand at it abreast, and was shaped in an oval, like the opening of a huge mouth. A row of spears lay propped against the lower sill, reminding Teneniel of the ragged, uneven teeth of a rancor.

For a long moment, she felt the yawning emptiness of the room, felt the yawning emptiness inside her. *Swallowed, I've been swallowed.* Teneniel closed her eyes, tried to forget her mother's stiff and purpled body, the rigid fingers curled into claws. Yet the yawning horror could not be closed out. Somewhere, she could hear a little girl shrieking in terror. She ran, and everywhere Teneniel went, she pulled aside the hanging curtains to expose rooms. Witches fed in the rooms, reclining on soft leather cushions. Witches talked daintily, laughing and casting spells. And all the while, Teneniel could hear the young girl crying, but no one seemed to notice.

When Teneniel woke, hours had passed. It was night outside the cave, and Luke had placed a small mechanical light on a rock beside her. Teneniel's tunic was off, and the Jedi had covered her with a blanket from his pack. She felt no pain, only a deep sense of ease, unlike anything she had ever felt in her life.

Teneniel touched her breast, her face. The scars were hot to the touch, but she could see with her eye, hear with her ear. She looked around the cave. Its walls were crudely painted with stick images of women in various poses—some resting their hands on the heads of others, one woman hovering above a crowd, another walking through flames. The cave went back only twenty meters, and human bones littered the floor near the back. Atop the pile of human bones was another skeleton— larger, with horrific teeth and a humerus longer than a man. The skeleton of a rancor.

But the Jedi had gone, leaving his pack. Teneniel got up, drank some water from her gourd. Her feet were cold, so she packed some straw into her boots, then lay back to rest. She still felt weak. Her head spun from more than fatigue. The Jedi had healed her wounds, never chanting a spell. Among the sisters, none who had the healing gift could do such a thing. The healing spells were the most difficult to master, and they were sung in such a flamboyant manner that Teneniel often thought the sisters put on more of a display than they needed. Still, all agreed that the healing spells must be sung. If the Jedi had cast such spells without so much as a word, he must be truly powerful indeed.

Often, while camping under the stars, Teneniel had wondered what it was like on other worlds. She had heard from her sisters of the stormtroopers at the prison, so secure with their armor and their weapons. But these weak stormtroopers did not understand spellcasting, and they fawned over the recreant Nightsisters. Yet Teneniel had often dreamed that somewhere up there on another world were men like Luke.

Teneniel reached up under the blanket, touched her breast where the Jedi had rested his fingers. *Someday,* she thought, *someone will fill this emptiness inside me.*

Outside the cave, she heard a scuffling. Luke came in, followed by Isolder and Artoo. Luke sat at her side, stroked her cheek with his palm.

"Are you feeling better?" he asked. Teneniel grabbed his hand, nodded, unsure what to say. She looked into his pale eyes. She had lost him. He had saved her life, and now she could no longer claim ownership.

"The Nightsisters met where we did battle," Luke said, "but then turned back. I'm not sure if they are leaving for reinforcements, or what."

"They know there are two of us," Teneniel said, "and you killed Ocheron, one of their stronger warriors. They may be afraid that we can overpower them."

"What about the stormtroopers?" Isolder asked. "They must have had a hundred troops with them." Being only a human, he did not understand.

"They don't count," Teneniel said, and she wondered. Perhaps these offworlders did not understand the situation as well as she thought, so she explained, "Stormtroopers are easy to kill."

"I don't like this," Isolder said. "I don't like the idea of being backed into this cave."

"The Nightsisters will not fight us here," Teneniel said. "This place is sanctified by the blood of the old ones." She sat up, nodded toward the human skulls littering the floor beneath the skeleton of the rancor.

"You really think that they'll keep clear of this place?" Isolder asked.

"Even the dead have some power," Teneniel said, nodding toward the piles of skulls. "The Nightsisters would not court their wrath."

Luke nodded. At least the Jedi understood. He asked, "What were your ancestors doing here? How did they get here?"

Teneniel wrapped her arms around her legs, and stared into his eyes. "Long ago," she said, "the old ones came from the stars. They were warriors, masters of machines who built forbidden weapons—machine warriors that looked like men. And they sold them to others, cheap.

"Your people cast them out of the sky for their crimes, and sent them here. The warriors were given no weapons—no metal, no blasters. So they fell prey to rancors." Teneniel half-closed her eyes. She'd heard the story so many times that now she envisioned that distant past, saw the prisoners sent to Dathomir. They were violent people who had committed gross crimes against civilization and who, therefore, merited only a life outside civilization. Many of the prisoners considered themselves above the law and thought of their weapons only as toys. So the ancients had considered it just to strand them on a world without technology.

"For many generations they lived like beasts, and were nearly hunted to extinction, until the star people cast out Allya."

Luke had a faraway look in his eye, the way old Rell did when she saw visions. "This Allya was a rogue Jedi," Luke said with certainty, leaning forward. "The Old Republic did not want to execute her, so the Jedi exiled her, hoping that given time she would turn away from the dark side."

Teneniel said, "She used her spells to tame the wild rancors and hunt food. She taught her daughters all of her lore, and taught them to hunt for their mates, even as I hunted for you. While rancors dined on others, the daughters of Allya prospered from generation to generation, teaching their own daughters the spells. We divided into clans, and for a long time the clans vied for men in friendly competition, stealing mates. We governed ourselves, punished anyone caught using the night spells. In my grandmother's day, we pushed the wild rancors from these mountains. My grandmothers hunted the last of them. We hoped for peace at last.

"But in my mother's time, the outcast Nightsisters gathered together. At first, they were not many, but . . ."

"Some of you tried to fight them, using their own tactics," Luke offered. "And those who did became Nightsisters themselves."

Teneniel looked up at Luke. "So, does this thing happen on other worlds too? Some of the sisters say it is only a disease, an illness that we catch, which turns us into Nightsisters. Others say it comes from using the spells—but I do not know which spells they are talking about. Our spells have been tested over generations."

"It is none of your spells and all of your spells," Luke said. "Tell me, how old were Allya's daughters when she died?"

"The oldest was sixteen seasons," Teneniel said.

Luke shook his head. "A mere child—too young to learn the ways of the Force. Listen, Teneniel, it isn't the spells themselves that give you power—you are drawing on the Force, a power created by all living things around us. Because the daughters of Allya were strong in the Force, they mastered it somewhat. But it isn't the words you speak that give you power, nor is it any one spell that corrupts you: it is the intent with which you cast your spells, the nature of your desires. If your heart is corrupt, your works will be corrupt. If you listened to your heart, then you would know this." Teneniel fidgeted. "I think you *do* know this," Luke continued. "You could have killed that Nightsister and the stormtroopers a few hours ago. Instead you simply tried to cover your escape, sneak around them. Your . . . generosity surprised me."

"Of course. If I killed the Nightsisters, I would be as evil as they are," Teneniel said flippantly, trying to hide her fear that she might become one of them.

"You listened to the Force, let it guide you," Luke said. "But in other ways you are cruel. You tried to kidnap me and Isolder. Do you really think you could take a man slave, or pummel me with rocks, and still hope to retain your innocence?"

"I wasn't trying to kill you when I hit you," Teneniel said, "just catch you! I wouldn't even have hurt you badly!"

"Yet you know it is wrong to take another person captive?"

Teneniel glared at him, fidgeted. "I—hoped to love you. And if I did not love you, then I could have sold you to someone else who wanted you more. It's not as if I were going to make you do anything bad. The daughters of Allya have always hunted for mates this way."

Luke sighed, as if exasperated. "Do all of the daughters of Allya do this, or just some of them?"

"If a woman is rich enough," Teneniel answered, "she can buy a man she likes. I am not rich."

Isolder leaned forward. "These Nightsisters, what are they doing with the stormtroopers?"

"Eight seasons ago, a leader from the stars sent stormtroopers to build a new prison. An outcast from our clans, a Nightsister named Gethzerion, took employment from the stormtroopers, helping to catch runaway slaves. At first the Imperials liked her, promised to train her as a warrior and give her glory. But when they began to see her power, they feared her and decided to strand her on Dathomir. The Imperials blew up the ships at the prison, stranding their own soldiers in the process. It is rumored that Gethzerion killed the leaders at the prison, and the stormtroopers are so terrified of her that they obey her every whim. She has promised them freedom if they will help her escape to the stars, for now that she has seen how weak the Imperials are and how much they fear her, she believes that she will someday rule worlds without end. But for now Gethzerion contents herself by making war with the clans, killing some of our sisters, enslaving others. Many of the clan sisters have joined her."

"What does she do with the unfortunate captives there at her prison?" Luke asked.

"She keeps them as slaves, hoping someday to barter them," Teneniel said.

Luke half-closed his eyes. "Gethzerion knows what she is doing. She hopes to turn all of your sisters to the dark side. With an army of them at her back, she really could become a power in the galaxy." He looked at Teneniel. "How many Nightsisters are there?"

"No more than a hundred," Teneniel answered. For a few moments she dared hope that Luke knew how to get rid of them—but he paled at her answer.

"And how many spellcasters are in your clan?"

Teneniel seldom visited her clan, had not been home in three months. With so many of her sisters killed recently, and so many having been captured by Gethzerion, Teneniel was afraid to give an answer, yet perhaps the Jedi would think it was enough.

"Twenty-five or thirty."

Chapter

16

That evening, flames flickered in the cooking fire and juice sizzled and popped over the coals as men carved the beast and heaped it on earthenware platters with tubers, nuts, and uncooked shoots. Han sat on leather cushions on the floor with Chewbacca, Leia, and Threepio in the fortress of the Singing Mountain clan. Han found that his weariness, the coming dark, and a full stomach made it hard to keep his eyes open. Yet Chewie fed hungrily, bandages wrapped over his ribs. The Wookiee's marvelous regenerative powers let him heal more in a day than a human would in two weeks.

Outside, through the open portals, Han could see fierce storm clouds in the distance, flashing lightning. The stars here burned fiercely above the tree-covered mountains.

Around him, the witches laughed and taught their daughters spells in the shadows. The young girls wore shirts and pants of simple hides, not the elaborate costumes of the fully trained witches. Yet the witches seemed more casual, more cozy around their children. They removed their headdresses and let their hair down. Without their full attire, they weren't so intimidating, and reminded Han only of rugged peasants.

The witches' husbands worked silently, dressed in tunics of woven plant fibers, serving meals to the women so quietly that Han almost felt as if they must be communicating telepathically.

Augwynne sat nearby so that she could speak softly to Han and Leia. She noticed how Han frequently eyed the distant storm. "Do not worry yourself," she said. "That is only Gethzerion, thrashing in impotent fury. But she is too far away. There will be no Force storm tonight."

"Gethzerion is making that lightning?" Threepio asked, his eyes suddenly bright. "Why, I wonder how much power output she can produce."

Augwynne looked at the distant clouds, unconcerned, and a brilliant branch of orange lightning with many tongues arced up into the sky, as if expressly for her to see. "Oh, she's very powerful, and very angry. But for tonight, she will not come. She's gathering the sisters of her clan and won't move against us until they are all safely together.

"So," she said, as if to change the subject, "this deed to Dathomir that you own. Is it really worth anything?"

Leia said, "It will be when the New Republic wins back this sector."

"And how soon will that be?" Augwynne asked.

"That's hard to say," Han answered, nervously eyeing the sky. "It could be three months, it could be three decades. But it's a pretty sure thing. Zsinj is a great warrior, but he's not a good governor. The more we whittle away at his fleets, the faster his worlds will slip from his grasp. As soon as his commanders see him falter, they'll be at his throat."

Chewbacca roared a confident agreement.

"Chewie believes Zsinj will fall within a year," Threepio said. "But my programs indicate that at the current rate, he could hold on to his power for considerably longer than that. I estimate that he'll fall in fourteen point three years."

"I think Chewie's guess is closer," Han said. "But things could still be rough for a while after that."

"Tell me," Augwynne said, her voice edged with excitement. "How can I buy this planet from you? Do you value gold, gems? There are plenty of both here in the mountains." The room suddenly quieted around him, as witches nearby listened for Han's answer.

Leia shot Han a knowing glance, waiting for him to name a price. "Well," Han hesitated. "Since I own everything on this planet, those gold and gems are pretty much mine. The planet is valued at three billion credits. Of course that's just for the real estate. That doesn't include improvements—buildings, fixtures . . ."

Augwynne studied his face a moment, nodded, not realizing that he was joking. She looked at the faces of her sisters. "We of the Singing Mountain clan have no money," she said, "but we would offer you our service in payment. Tell me three things you desire, and we will grant your wishes, if it lies within our power."

"Well," Han said, looking at the expectant faces of the witches. He had not forgotten Damaya's words earlier. Though these witches were not his enemies, they had also not chosen to be his allies. That could come only with a price, and now they were naming the coin. He wasn't taking them too seriously. "The first thing I wish, is that I could get off of this planet." He looked up at the vaulted stone ceilings. "Then, I guess I'd like some of the gold and gems you were talking about—say as much as a grown rancor could carry. And last of all . . . if you can convince her, I want Leia's hand in marriage."

Augwynne looked at Han and Leia, nodded thoughtfully. "Leia told us you would ask for these three things," the old woman said. "The Singing Mountain clan will do all that it can to meet your purchase price, but Leia is not part of the bargain. We cannot force her into a marriage. We will have the gold and gems by dawn. At this very moment, three sisters have gone to retrieve your ship so that you and your hairy Wooka can fix it."

"Now wait a minute!" Han said, realizing he had spoken too soon, not realizing the witches were serious.

"You're too late!" Leia gloated. "You've just sold yourself a planet!"

Han began to object, and Chewie growled, but Augwynne raised a hand. "Do not regret your price, Han Solo. The sisters of the Singing Mountain clan will gladly pay it, though it cost many of us our lives. Gethzerion may fight us in hopes of capturing you and your ship. That is why the Force storm rages out over the desert. But we have already considered your terms, and we accept."

Already considered your terms, Han wondered. So that was why Leia had spent so much time with them earlier in the day while he had worked in the fields. The witches had been pumping her for information, scheming ways to get this planet from him, and they'd agreed to fight the Nightsisters in his behalf. They'd probably even timed it so that they brought Han and the Nightsisters upstairs together so that Han would see what the opposition was like. In other words, they had manipulated him from moment one. This Augwynne was pretty slick. Han asked, "What would you do even if you owned this planet?"

"We would sell land to settlers," Augwynne said, "and hire teachers to come to us from the stars. We would join the New Republic and learn your ways so that in time our children will no longer be outcasts, living in these rough hills."

She did have things planned. In fact, it sounded to Han as if Leia might have done some recruiting before Han was brought up from the fields. Threepio said, "Excuse me, but might I inquire as to how you are going to retrieve the ship?"

Augwynne said, "The sisters took three rancors. They will cut down some trees and make a skid, then pull the ship back here. We will cast a spell and lift it up into the mountain, where we can conceal it while you work on it. Would this be adequate?"

"I suppose," Han said, taken aback. He didn't like the idea of selling his planet, but now that he thought about it for a moment, considering the Nightsisters, he suspected this might be the best offer he could get. "If the rancors are as big as the ones I've seen, then, yeah, three or four could pull it. But I wouldn't want it banged up any more than it is."

Augwynne pursed her lips, studied him thoughtfully. "Our sisters should have it back here by dawn. I must warn you, you will be in great danger: Now that Gethzerion knows you have a starship, she will not relent in her pursuit of it. She will send the Nightsisters to capture it at the very least."

"If the Nightsisters plan to launch an attack," Leia asked, "how long will it take?"

"The Nightsisters are cautious," Augwynne said. "I think they will launch a full attack only if they believe that their forces can overwhelm us. We have cast spells to learn of their plans. Right now, some of the sisters are scattered and are in the process of returning to the city. Once they combine their numbers, I believe they will march as soon as possible. We have perhaps three days. You will need to repair your ship and leave before then."

"Or what?" Han asked.

"Or we might all die," Augwynne said seriously. "If the Nightsisters attack, I do not believe that our clan will be able to withstand them. There are a dozen other clans in the mountains, but even the nearest is a four-day march. I have sent runners to the sisters of the Frenzied River and the Red Hills clans, asking for aid, but it will come only after we retreat. You must leave before the Nightsisters can attack!"

Han looked at Chewie, Leia, and Threepio. He'd gotten them into a real jam this time. The best thing for the clan here would be if he simply blew up the ship so that Gethzerion would have no reason to hunt him down. But if he did that, they might never get off of this planet. Han could handle being marooned here, but what of Chewbacca? The Wookiee had a family, and though he would stay here if Han required it, Han couldn't demand that kind of sacrifice from him. Threepio? Without his oil baths and spare parts, he'd fail within a year. And of course there was Leia. He'd forced her here against her will and now felt obligated to take her back. Yet he knew she would not value her freedom above the lives of others.

Han sat cross-legged, rested his hands on his knees and rubbed his eyes. *I covered my trail pretty darned good,* Han thought. *But sooner or later, someone is going to track us down.* Omogg might figure out where he'd gone. The Drackmarian was smart. She might even sell such information to some bounty hunters. Han was sure the New Republic would put a price on his head. Sooner or later, someone would come looking. There might still be some hope for escape from this planet. "I don't really want Gethzerion trying to run off in my ship any more than you do," Han admitted. "But maybe we should just give it to her."

Chewie roared and Augwynne said, "We can't give Gethzerion a ship. She is too powerful. You can't give her access to the stars."

"Han," Leia said, "Augwynne has filled me in on a few things. I believe the Emperor himself was afraid of the Nightsisters. That's why he interdicted this planet. Years ago, he started a nice little penal colony here, not knowing about the Nightsisters. When he learned about them, he blew the planet's airfield from orbit and stranded hundreds of his own people here, along with the prisoners, rather than risk letting Gethzerion escape. That's how frightened he was of Gethzerion.

"Those warships up above us were put there to keep people on this rock as much as to keep them fenced out. And now that Zsinj is in charge of this sector, he's still afraid. The Imperials who got stranded at the prison might still be able to cobble some kind of a ship together, and Zsinj has to watch out for that."

Han sighed, "Maybe we should just blow the *Falcon*. Then Gethzerion wouldn't have any reason to come hunting for us."

"Never concede to evil," Augwynne said. "That is our oldest and most sacred law. When we concede to evil, even in a small way, we feed it, and it grows stronger. Gethzerion has grown powerful because we of the clans have not challenged her for far too long. We should have fought her years ago, when we saw what she was becoming, but we always hoped that we could turn her from her ways. If we need to fight her now, then we will do it, for it is the right thing for *us* to do. And you must fix your ship and leave. That is the right thing for *you* to do. I for one will do all in my power to protect you."

Han fumbled in his pocket, pulled out the deed for Dathomir, and extended it to Augwynne. "Here," he said, "you take this." In that moment, Han wondered how he could have ever been so deluded as to think that Leia would choose a husband based on the material goods he could offer.

"No," she objected, pushing his hand away. "We have not earned it yet."

"Take it for safekeeping then," Han said, "until you feel you've earned it."

Augwynne cradled the cube in her hand, lovingly. "Someday," she whispered.

Han sighed. He remembered the explosions as the orbiting warships pounded the wreck up by the lake, destroying any trace of it. Parts would be hard to come by. If he had all the parts—the wiring, coolant, and a nav computer—then he and Chewie could probably fix the *Falcon* in a few hours. But that was starting to look like a big *if*. He could strip wiring from anywhere—a couple of crushed Imperial walkers would do. He toyed with the idea of draining coolant from the walkers' hydraulics, but decided it wasn't worth the risk: the mixture might not meet the rigors of trying to cool a hyperdrive generator on a spacefaring ship. Still, if the prison had had even a modest shipyard, they ought to have a couple of barrels of coolant, maybe a spare astrogation brain or even a whole R2 unit. "In the morning, I'll check out my ship, figure out exactly how damaged it is. I know right now that it's going to need some parts. We'll need to leave for the prison tomorrow to scavenge. Augwynne, can you send someone to guide us?"

Augwynne studied him for a moment, dancing flames reflecting from her dark eyes and graying hair. "I think it is time for you to rest. You can look at your ship and make your plans in the morning."

Han yawned, stretched. Leia watched the ground by the fire. At first, Han thought she was thinking, but he realized after a moment that she was just exhausted, half-asleep, letting her mind drift. He got up, pulled off her helm, surprised to find that it was actually quite light in his hands. "Come on. Let's go to bed."

She looked up at him dully, a hint of anger or confusion in her eyes. "I'm not going to bed with you!"

"I just meant—I thought you'd like it if I fix a bed up for you."

Leia looked away angrily, and said, "Oh."

"You all look tired," Augwynne said. "I'll take you up to your room." She lit a candle in the fire and then led Han, Leia, Chewie, and Threepio away from the noisy diners, up the drafty stairs to a large sleeping chamber. An opening led from the room out to a stone parapet overlooking the valley. The room itself held dozens of straw beds spread out on the floor, covered with heavy blankets. Augwynne's male servant lit a fire in a small hearth, while Augwynne went out on the parapet for a moment and watched the distant lightning. She sang softly. When she returned, she muttered, "Gethzerion is restless, and she has posted Nightsisters quite close to the fortress. I'll increase the guards tonight. Sleep soundly."

"Thank you," Threepio said, patting her back as she left. "Well, she seems hospitable enough," he remarked after she'd gone. "I wonder what they have in the way of oil around here." The droid paced the room, studying his surroundings.

Leia took off her robe, pulled out her blaster and set it under her blanket, then lay down on a mat to sleep. Chewbacca went into a corner, put his back against a wall, then sat down with his bowcaster in hand, hung his head and closed his eyes. Han glanced around the room, took a mat by the window where the fresh mountain air blew in. His sinuses were definitely bothering him. *Great,* he thought, *I win a planet in a card game, and to top it all off, I'm allergic to it.* Outside, he could still hear the booming of thunder, the songs of the witches in their halls below, and water dripping on the parapet outside the window.

It was quiet, and Han could not quite get to sleep. Threepio walked around the room nervously and then said, "Princess Leia, would you like some relaxing music to help you sleep?"

The golden droid stood in the center of the stone room, eyes shining, head tilted to one side.

"Music?" Leia asked.

"Yes, I've written a song," Threepio said, "and I thought you might appreciate it if I sang it to you." His tone said that he'd be offended if she didn't listen.

Leia frowned, and Han rather pitied her. He'd never heard Threepio sing, but he couldn't imagine that it would be much good. "Sure," Leia said hesitantly, "but, maybe just the first verse."

"Oh, thank you!" Threepio said. "I've titled my song, 'The Virtues of *King* Han Solo'!"

A musical intro with horns and strings began playing, and Han found himself a bit surprised. He knew that Threepio could mimic other voices, and he'd heard the droid give some nice sound effects when telling stories to the Ewoks, but he'd never heard music coming from the droid. Threepio did a rather convincing impression of a full symphony orchestra.

Then he began swirling in dance, doing a soft-shoe that scraped and echoed over the stone floors, and the droid sang in a deep voice that sounded an awful lot like Jukas Alim, one of the galaxy's more popular singers:

> He's got his own planet,
> Although it's kind of wild.
> Wookiees love him.
> Women love him.
> He's got a winning smile!
> Though he may seem cool and cocky,
> He's more sensitive than he seems,

(*Chorus sung in accompaniment with three women who all sound like Leia*)

> Han Solo,
> What a man! Solo.
> He's every princess's dream!

Threepio ended with a flourish of horns and drums and a tap routine, then took a bow to Leia. Leia just stared at him with an expression somewhere between bewilderment and horror.

"Hey, that's pretty good," Han said. "How many more verses do you have?"

"Only fifteen so far," Threepio said, "but I'm sure I can come up with more."

"Don't you dare!" Leia said, and Chewie roared his agreement.

"Well!" Threepio huffed. He powered down for the night.

Han lay back and smiled to himself. The chorus "Han Solo, / What a man! Solo," kept ringing through his mind the way that stupid jingles will, and he took a strange sort of pleasure in knowing that Threepio had gone to so much trouble.

He listened to Chewbacca's deep breathing as the Wookiee fell asleep. Yet Han lay, restless.

"Han," Leia whispered.

"Yeah?"

"That was nice of you, offering her the planet."

"Oh," Han said, almost choking on the words, "it was nothing."

"You're a pretty nice guy sometimes," Leia said.

Han raised an eyebrow, looked across the room to where Leia rested on her mat, blankets pulled tight against her throat. "So, uh, does that mean you love me?"

"No," Leia said flippantly. "It just means that sometimes I think you're a pretty nice guy."

Han lay back, smiled, and breathed the sweet night air.

When Augwynne returned to her council chambers, the children and men were still there, but the sisters of her clan had formed a circle. "Well," she said to the sisters, made nervous by the presence of the men and children she had sworn to protect, "you have all seen what the offworlders offered. Now we must decide how best to meet their price."

Old Tannath said, "Moments ago you quoted the *Book of Law,* saying that we should not concede to evil. But when have we of the Singing Mountain clan ever stopped conceding to evil? Gethzerion is powerful because we of the clans have not challenged her for far too long. When she began following her dark ways, we could have put an end to her easily."

"Hush," Augwynne said. "That was long ago, the mistake cannot be unmade. We were right to hope that she would turn from her ways."

"She violated all of our laws," old Tannath said. "Those who commit evil are supposed to go into the wilderness alone to seek cleansing, but she sought to unite the forsaken ones and create the clan of Nightsisters. We could have killed them all when there were less than a dozen. And when she and her cohorts went to work for the Imperials, we could have warned the offworlders at the least. Yet even then we did not fight her. Admit it, Augwynne, you have loved Gethzerion too much, and we have feared her too much. We should have killed her years ago."

"Tannath, do not question past decisions here," Augwynne said, letting her tone of voice carry her anger, "in the presence of men and children. We would not want to upset them."

"Why not? Will my words upset them any more than

Gethzerion's attacks?'' Tannath asked. '' 'Never concede to evil.' I ask that the council obey its own law.''

"We have all agreed to this already, earlier this afternoon," Augwynne said. "We have all agreed to help Leia and the offworlders."

"You agreed to help them, but did you agree to pay the full price? Even if we can help them fix their ship and escape, do you think Gethzerion will just allow us that small victory? No, she will seek vengeance."

The room became silent as the witches held their breath, thinking. If a sister from another clan stole a male slave to take as a husband, it was considered unseemly for the man's owner to steal him back. You allowed the victory. But Augwynne could see that Tannath understood the Nightsisters too well. The Nightsisters would not allow the Singing Mountain clan even a small victory.

Sister Shen was nursing her baby, and she looked up, suddenly frightened. "We will have to prepare to escape," the young woman said. "We can evacuate the children and the old now, send them to the Frenzied River clan. We should prepare to retreat if we are attacked."

"And leave the ship in the hands of the Nightsisters?" Tannath asked.

"Yes," another answered. "If Gethzerion left the planet, we would be rid of her."

"For how long?" Sister Azbeth asked. "She dreams of power and glory. Yet she would know that we are her enemies. No, she will hunt us down. We would gain nothing, in the end. No, we must fight her."

"But if we ran—" one of the sisters said.

"Then the Nightsisters would only chase us, fight us in the open where we have no advantage," Tannath said. "No, we must prepare to make our stand here, at Singing Mountain, where our weapons and fortifications will be some help."

"Sisters, you are talking war," a witch said from the back of the crowd.

"And what choices do we have, really?" old Tannath asked.

"But I am afraid it is a war that we cannot win," Augwynne said.

"If we choose not to fight, then we will have only chosen to lose without fighting," the old one answered. "I for one will fight. Who is with me?"

The old witch looked around the room, and the clan was quiet, even the sound of breathing was stifled. Augwynne looked at the rigid expressions, the set eyes of the women, and could see that this decision was one they regretted having to make. It was a decision they had put off too long.

Sister Shen juggled her nursing child to the other breast, said, "I am with you," and at the back of the room two more answered, "I am with you," and their small voices fell like the first tumbling stones that signify an avalanche.

Hours later, Han woke to the sound of distant thunder in the moonlight, the smell of some sweet perfume. The fire had died in the hearth, and outside the window, out on the parapet, Leia stood facing him. Her long robe draped to the stone, and the scattered light of moonbeams made a halo of her hair.

"Han, come here," she said. Her voice rang in his ears, unnaturally loud in the still room, but not unpleasant.

He got up from the straw mattress, slowly. He cleared his throat, and said, "What's going on? What are you doing out there?"

She put a finger to her lips, glanced down the side of the cliff. "Come," she whispered.

Han hurried over, nervous. Leia seemed so—at ease, rested. Not her usual self. Han wondered if it was just the darkness widening her pupils that made her eyes seem so large, so liquid. Leia took his hand. Her small fingers were cold, more heavily calloused than he remembered. She walked out to the edge of the parapet. "Come with me," she said more loudly. "I won't let you fall." She began singing lightly, swaying in dance, and it felt as if a warm woolen blanket fell over his mind, making his thoughts muzzy. She took a step out and stood in mid-air, and Han thought he should be surprised, yet somehow it seemed natural for Leia to be standing in the air. He wanted to follow, but somehow his throat tightened, his face felt hot, and his knees wobbled.

"Don't be afraid," Leia whispered. "The drop is not so far as it seems. I won't let you get hurt."

Han's knees seemed to strengthen, and the warm burning in his cheeks and ears lessened. He took a careful step.

A blurring figure dressed all in hides leaped from the dark doorway behind them. The steel of a vibro-blade hummed in the air, slashed down through Leia's face. She shrieked and dropped, clinging to Han's wrist, pulling him over the edge.

Suddenly Han recognized his danger. He jerked away reflexively as Leia fell shrieking to the rocks two hundred meters below.

The figure in black pushed Han to the ground, pulled a blaster and began firing at the cliff face. There were women crawling up the rock wall, clinging impossibly like spiders. All of them looked like Leia. Han gasped, watched them scurry backward, then leap away and drop safely to the ground. Other guards rushed out to the parapets and began firing. Within seconds the Nightsisters disappeared.

The woman who had saved him pulled back her hood, stood panting in a cloud of pale blue smoke and ozone from the blaster. "I knew they'd come for you," Leia said, glancing sideways at Han, and only that dangerous fire in her eyes and the sure way she gripped the blaster let him know that it was the real princess. "They'll be back."

Chapter

17

The next morning as Isolder sat at the campfire cooking a clutch of lizard eggs, he looked up at the cave walls, at stick figure paintings of women that danced on the rough stone. The smoke above the fire gathered at the top of the cave, an ominous blue cloud. Outside the sun had just risen, and flecks of sunbeams beat through the wiry trees. A long green lizard on a nearby tree flapped its gills and made spitting noises.

At the back of the cave Teneniel stirred, propped herself on one elbow. "Thank you for staying with me," she said, blinking sleep from her eyes.

"It was nothing," Isolder said.

Teneniel argued softly, "You could have run away."

Isolder nodded, looked down at the fire to avoid seeing the gratitude in her eyes. Teneniel seemed thoughtful. In the corner, Artoo's lights suddenly flashed as he powered up for the day. The little droid looked around the cave, whistled and chimed.

After a moment, Teneniel said, "Your metal friend asked to know where Luke is."

A chill ran down Isolder's spine. Every time he turned

around, it seemed that Luke or Teneniel was doing one more superhuman thing. Teneniel had first come upon him by the river, danced around him, singing to him coyly, then held a rope out for him. He'd thought perhaps it was some odd custom, and as he reached to take it, the thing had leaped in the air and wrapped its coils around him so fast he'd thought it was a snake. Before he'd even thought to yell, Teneniel had stuck a gag in his mouth. Later in the afternoon he'd seen the devastated forest where she'd battled Zsinj's troops—trees stripped of leaves, denuded of bark; even the ground had been gouged. Now she was interpreting some cybernetic code for him. It gave him the chills to be in the presence of beings with such power.

"Luke just went to fill the canteens. He'll be back in a moment. How much farther till we reach your clan?" He turned the eggs, listened to them sizzle and pop.

Teneniel got up, wrapped her robe around her naked body, and walked over to the fire. Isolder thought she would sit to warm herself, but instead she leaned over and cupped his chin in her hands, then kissed his lips tenderly, experimentally. He was so surprised that he did not pull back. On all of Hapes, no woman had ever treated him that way: so casually forceful. Instead, the women around him had been respectful but distant. When she finished, she stepped back, licked her lips as if to taste him. "You are very handsome," she said. "I wish you were Luke, and not just some commoner."

Isolder had to think for a moment. He'd never been called a *commoner* before, being the prince of the hidden worlds, yet when he saw her power, he understood how she could think of him that way. "Luke's . . . a good man—a *great* man," Isolder agreed. "I can see why you would like him."

"All night long I dreamed about him," Teneniel said. "You could never take his place in my heart."

Isolder thought it such an odd thing to say that he suddenly realized that more was going on than he understood. Luke came in at that moment. "I've got the water bottles filled, and the trail ahead seems clear. Let's go."

Isolder scraped the rubbery eggs from the pan, gave several each to Luke and Teneniel. Teneniel wrinkled her nose in disgust, but Luke said, "They're pretty good. You ought to try them."

"I do not know what you eat on your worlds," Teneniel said, "but it is obvious that you do not know how to cook." She did not eat the eggs.

They broke camp and walked a kilometer through the forest, then came to a wide, lightly graveled trail leading north and south. Teneniel led them south on the trail for four kilometers, then took a better road east, following a river. By midmorning they came to a low valley where fog climbed up the stone mountainsides. Teneniel led them up a winding stone trail, still wet from the night's rain. She took Isolder's hand and held it the rest of the way, as if he were some schoolchild that might slip off the face of the cliff. When they reached the top, he thought they had come into a valley of oddly shaped stones, but as they walked through the fog he saw the witches, dark shapes in the white fog, straddling shadowy monsters.

Isolder stopped to stare at the women with their helms, their intricately embroidered cloaks and glittering tunics of scaled leather. Luke's R2 unit began to rattle in its housing and moan softly. Teneniel gripped Isolder's wrist tighter, pulled him urgently, and Luke followed.

As they passed between the monolithic mounts, the women stared down at Isolder and gave a loud ululating cry, smiling at Teneniel and laughing. He could not doubt the meaning of the hoots and chatter. These women cheered him as if he were a stripper.

Teneniel led them to a landing, then up a flight of stairs to a stone fortress marred from battle. Apparently their presence was causing some kind of stir, for a crowd followed behind.

There, at the doors of the fortress, an old woman came out, bearing a staff of golden wood with a great white gem near a knob at the top.

"Welcome, Teneniel, my daughter's daughter," the old woman said. "It has been months since you last visited us. Did you find what you seek?"

"Yes, Grandmother," Teneniel said, still holding Isolder's wrist. She dropped to one knee. "I hunted near the old wreck at the throat of the desert, guided by a vision, until I almost despaired. But I captured this man from the stars, and I claim him as my husband." She raised Isolder's wrist in the air. "His name is Isolder, from the planet Hapes!"

Isolder was stunned. He pulled his wrist down and backed up a step, but the women around him crowded close, cooing in admiration. "All of you sisters see this man," the old woman said. "Do any of you dispute Teneniel's ownership?"

A tenseness to Teneniel's stance told Isolder that this was a dangerous moment. The old woman searched the faces of the crowd, and Isolder looked at the warrior women. Many had dark looks on their faces, openly envious. Others smiled at him playfully, lustily.

"I do!" Isolder said, because no one else spoke up.

The old woman jerked back a step. "You claim that some other sister of the Singing Mountain clan is your owner?"

"He came with me peaceably!" Teneniel argued. "He could have run away, but he gave himself!" Her voice was filled with such pain, such betrayal, that Isolder did not know how to answer her.

"I—I only wanted to help you!" he said, looking to the old woman to referee. "She was injured. I only wanted to help care for her!"

From the recesses of the stone archway, Leia appeared in a gown of glittering red scales. "Isolder? Luke?" she called, and Isolder's heart swelled inside him.

He choked back a cry, and Leia rushed into his arms, hugged him. "Are you all right?" Isolder asked.

"Fine," Leia said. "I can't believe you came all this way. I can't believe you found me! Luke," she cried, and she hugged the Jedi. Isolder stared at them agape a moment. Somehow, he had never realized that they were so close.

The old woman said to Leia, "Do you know this man? Is he *your* slave?"

"No, Augwynne," Leia said, separating from Isolder and Luke a bit. "He's a friend. Where I come from, we don't have slaves."

Augwynne thought a moment. "So, Teneniel captured him fairly. This one belongs to her."

"Isolder once saved my—" Leia began to argue, then tensed as Augwynne gave her a hard look.

"What?" Augwynne asked. "You would plead for his freedom on the same ground that you did for Han Solo?"

"We were attacked," Leia said. "Isolder saved me."

Augwynne studied Leia's face and said skeptically, "You seem uncertain. Why? What is the whole truth?"

"It was a brief melee," Leia answered regretfully. "I'm not sure who our attackers were firing at—me or Isolder."

"Thank you for answering honestly," Augwynne said, patting Isolder's hand.

Augwynne glanced at Luke. "What of this one?" she asked Teneniel. "He's not bad looking. Will you also take him for a slave?"

As one, both Teneniel and Leia said, "He saved my life," and Teneniel added, "This one is a male spellcaster, a powerful Jedi. He slew Nightsister Ocheron."

At those words, many of the clan sisters hissed and stepped back, gauging Luke skeptically, and some of them began whispering to one another in their own language. From the cautious glances, the frowns, the whispered voices, Isolder guessed that more was going on here than he knew. It was almost as if they found Luke's presence to be . . . portentous.

Augwynne studied Luke carefully and then glanced at the other women. She shook her head and laughed, feigning dismay. "Bah! Three new men in the village, and only one of them eligible—and him just barely? It sounds to me as if every man up there in the stars must have saved Leia at least once. All of my life I've wanted to travel offplanet, but now—I wonder how I'd fare. Tell me, Sister Leia, are people always trying to kill you?"

Isolder could not miss the uncomfortable tone in her voice. She was nearly begging Leia to change the subject. "Well, the last few years have been pretty rough," Leia admitted.

"Perhaps some evening, you will have to sit by the fire and spin your tale," Augwynne said. "But for now, I must make a ruling. I give this man Isolder into custody of Teneniel Djo, to keep as her husband."

"What?" Leia asked so loudly that Isolder jumped.

Augwynne whispered into her ear insistently, as if to keep her quiet. "He belongs to Teneniel. She hunted for him, she caught him, and she is very lonely."

"But, you can't just take him as a slave!" Leia said.

Augwynne shrugged, waved at the women around her as if to give proof. "Of course we can. Every woman on the council owns at least one man."

"Don't fear," Teneniel said, trying to calm Leia, "I won't use him harshly."

"Luke," Leia urged. "You've got to stop them! You can't let them do this!"

Luke meditated a moment, shrugged. "You're the New Republic's emissary. You know galactic law better than I do. You handle it."

Leia stopped speaking a moment, looked at Luke and Isolder. Isolder thought about it quickly. Under New Republic law, the normal administration of affairs on any planet would be handled by the planetary governor, whoever that was, or by regional heads of office in case there was no planetary governor. In this case, Augwynne was a regional head of government, and all the New Republic could do was lodge a formal protest.

"I protest this," Leia said. "I protest this very strongly!"

"What does that mean?" Augwynne asked. "Do you wish to fight Teneniel Djo for right of ownership?"

Isolder shook his head no, and Leia held his eye a moment. "What kind of fight?" Leia asked. "Are we talking to the death, or what?"

"Perhaps," Augwynne said, shaking her head. "You might be wiser to offer to buy him . . ."

Luke shook his head at Leia and said, "Don't worry, Leia, it will be all right."

Leia waited for a long time, and said, "Teneniel Djo, I wish to buy this servant. What would you require for him?"

Teneniel glanced around the crowd, and Isolder suddenly realized that she might have more than one bidder.

"He is not for sale—yet," Teneniel said.

Leia looked at Isolder, and said, "I'm sorry."

Teneniel took Isolder's hand, looked up at him, and her eyes shone in a strange shade of copper that Isolder had never seen on Hapes. Isolder let her hold his hand, and he did not feel uncomfortable. That in itself seemed odd. Everything in him, all of his training, screamed that he should fight these barbaric customs, yet on some deep level he didn't fear Teneniel, and in fact trusted her implicitly.

Luke hugged Leia to comfort her, and Artoo came close enough so that she could pet his sensor window with her hand. Luke said, "So where are Han and Chewie? I thought they'd be with you."

"They should be down soon," Leia answered. "The sisters dragged the *Falcon* in early this morning. Han is checking the damage now. It got pretty well trashed during the ride down to Dathomir, but it looks like the only way off this rock. What about your ship?" Leia had an undertone of warning in her voice when she asked about the ship.

"We could probably sell whatever is left of it for scrap," Luke said, but Isolder noted that the Jedi did not mention that Isolder's fighter was still intact. Isolder took it as an unspoken warning. The fog was continuing to climb up the mountain even as they spoke, and now it hung over their heads by an arm span, like some celestial ceiling.

Isolder felt someone touch his buttocks, turned. The witches were pressing close, brushing against his back. He thought perhaps they were trying to get a better look at Leia, but suddenly realized that they weren't trying to get a view of Leia or Augwynne, they were trying to get a closer look at him. One young witch patted his hip and whispered lustily, "My name is Ooya. Let me show you where I sleep."

"I think we'd better go in to talk," Leia told Teneniel, grabbing the witch's arm with her left hand. Leia also grabbed Isolder's hand possessively, pulled him along. "Come on, let's go find Han," she said, glancing over her shoulder at the other women. Isolder thought it odd how much Leia's grip was like Teneniel's. She had not been on the planet two days, and already she was mimicking the witches' body language—the way they held their heads high, their peculiar strut. In another week he imagined that she would fit into their clan as if she'd been born to it. It was the type of subtle thing that only a diplomat with a great deal of training could manage.

They went into the fortress, and though many of the witches did not follow, some of the women began whooping and making lusty ululating cries. Isolder felt his face going red.

As they walked through the door of the fortress, Augwynne touched his arm momentarily, stopping both him and Luke. "Go visit your friends," she said to Luke, "but come see me immediately afterward. Your coming here is no accident."

Leia led them through a maze of stone passageways up six flights of stairs, then down a hallway to a huge cavelike room. The *Falcon* filled almost the whole space. Isolder could see no large opening, no way that they could have brought the ship in.

He studied the walls for a moment, saw that several huge stones had been cracked on the far side. Which meant that the witches had somehow broken a hole through the stone wall, hoisted the *Falcon* vertically over two hundred meters in the air, then resealed the wall once they had gotten the *Falcon* inside under the cover of fog. The witches had done a lot of work. Given the simple Iron Age technology of the place, all of these feats seemed impossible, and Isolder realized that somehow, in the back of his mind, he did not want to know how the women had accomplished so much.

The *Falcon* lit the room with one headlamp, and the ship's running lights were on. Han couldn't have powered up so many systems outside without worrying about detection from orbit, but Isolder realized that the thick rock would cover the electronic signature.

They went up the ramp into the *Falcon*, found Han and Chewbacca in the cockpit running diagnostics. A protocol droid was messing with fried wiring around the main generators.

"Han!" Luke said, as they entered the cockpit, but Han didn't return the enthusiastic greeting; instead, he turned back to his computer, and Isolder realized that Han felt guilty, couldn't face Luke at the moment.

"So, you found us, kid? Well, I figured it was only a matter of time. Things have gotten pretty sticky here. You didn't happen to bring any spare parts, did you?"

"What's going on, Han?" Luke asked. The Wookiee patted the Jedi on the shoulder, growled affectionately. "You don't just kidnap Leia, drag her halfway across the galaxy, and then say hi, as if nothing happened."

Han spun in his captain's chair, looked up, smiled a controlled smile, as if he would scream if he did not smile. "Well, see, it happened this way: I won a planet in a card game and really wanted to see it badly. Meanwhile, the woman I love was planning to run off with another man, so I convinced her to take a short trip with me. Only when we got here, I found the skies full of warships that shot me down—because no one bothered to warn me that the planet was interdicted—and after we crashed, a bunch of witches decided to start a war over who gets the wreckage of my ship. So I'll tell you, Luke, I've had a really bad week so far. Now, to top it all off, I suppose you're going to lecture me, or arrest me, or beat me up. So tell me, how is your week going?"

"About the same," Luke said. He held his tongue a moment, looked at the control panel. "What's wrong with your ship?"

"Well," Han said, "we blew our anticoncussion field generators, cracked the sensory array window, fried the brains out of my astrogation computer, and leaked about two thousand liters of coolant from the main reactor."

"I brought Artoo," Luke offered lamely. "He can navigate the ship." Luke looked back at Isolder, as if asking him to speak. Isolder could see that now was not the time for reprimands or fisticuffs. Right now, they needed to work together. But it was all he could do to keep from bashing Han Solo in the mouth.

"I've got my fighter here," Isolder said, and Teneniel took his hand. Isolder didn't want to speak about it too loudly, and he glanced behind him. None of the other witches had followed them into the ship.

"You've got a working ship on this planet?" Han asked. "How many people can it hold?"

Isolder considered his answer. If he told him two, would Han try to steal the ship and take Leia with him? "Two."

Luke looked at Isolder curiously, and Han drew a breath in relief. "I want you to get Leia and fly her out of here, right now!" Han said. "There's a bunch of people here who would kill for that fighter, and believe me, you don't want to meet them!"

"He's testing you," Luke casually said to Han. "His fighter holds only one, and we've already met the Nightsisters." Han's face got dark with anger, and his eyes looked hollow, haunted.

"You passed the test, General Solo," Isolder said.

"We're in serious trouble here," Han warned Isolder. "Don't play so rough with me."

Isolder didn't like Han's tone of voice. "You're lucky I don't play rougher," Isolder said. "I'd gladly beat your face in for what you've done here. You'll be lucky if I don't."

Luke watched Isolder calculatingly.

"Go ahead and try it," Han said, "if you think you can handle me."

Isolder glanced at Chewbacca. Wookiees specialized in their own form of hand-to-hand combat, and when a Wookiee disarmed an opponent, the opponent was literally *disarmed*. And if that didn't subdue you, the Wookiee would go ahead and rip off your legs, too. Isolder wanted to make sure the Wookiee didn't join in the fray. Chewbacca shrugged, whined something in his own language.

"Hold on, now," Leia said. "We've got enough problems here without fighting among ourselves. Isolder, I came here with Han willingly . . . sort of. He asked me to accompany him as a friend, and I agreed."

Isolder glanced at her, disbelieving, not sure what was going on. He'd seen the holo vid clips of the alleged abduction, but he couldn't call Leia a liar. "Uh," he said, embarrassed. "General Solo, I think I owe you an apology."

"Great," Han said. "So, let's get back to work. Why don't you start by coming up with a way to get us out of here?"

"I've got a fleet on its way," Isolder said. "They should be here in another seven or eight days."

Han asked, "When you say fleet, how big a fleet are you talking?"

"About eighty destroyers," Isolder said.

Han's jaw dropped, but Leia said, "Seven days isn't quick enough. If Augwynne is correct, the Nightsisters will attack in three."

Isolder put his arm around Leia. "My astrogation droid can pilot the ship for a jump. We could send Leia home."

"I don't think so," Leia said. "I'm not going without the rest of you. Han—if you had all of your spare parts, how soon could you get this ship fixed?"

Han calculated. Plugging the rupture to stop the coolant

leak would take only a few minutes. You might even be able to pour the coolant in while in flight. The R2 unit could patch in on a moment's notice to navigate. Installing new anticoncussion field generators might take two hours. The easiest thing would be to put on a new sensory array window. Two hours, if everyone helped and they hurried.

"Two hours," Han answered.

"I suggest we cannibalize Isolder's ship," Leia said, "fix the *Falcon*, and get out of here."

Isolder looked at the *Falcon* skeptically. It was a big ship compared with his fighter—four times the length. With all the extra shielding and cargo space, it had to be forty times the mass. "What kind of anticoncussion field generators are you using?" Isolder asked.

"I've got four banks of Nordoxicon thirty-eights. All of them are down. What are you running on?"

"Three Taibolt twelves."

Chewbacca roared something.

"Yeah, that's a bust," Han admitted. "What about your sensory array window?"

"Point six meters across," Isolder said.

"That's a little small for us," Han grimaced, "but if we had to, we could weld some plate over my current array, make the window narrower. It would cut our sensor capabilities a little."

"Yeah, that would work," Isolder agreed. "But where are we going to get a big enough field generator?"

"Could we fly without it, sir?" Threepio asked.

"Too dangerous," Han said. "We're not just worried about missile attacks, we've got to deflect micrometeorites. If one tore through the sensor array, it could take out a lot of sensitive instrumentation."

"Maybe there's some kind of field generators near the prison," Han said, throwing his hands up. "An armored gun emplacement, a wrecked ship, something. I'll just have to go there and see."

"If we can find some generators to steal, it will be a four-man job just to pull them, and we might need a sentry to watch for trouble," Isolder said. "Then there's the problem of transporting the stuff. We're talking nearly two metric tons of equipment here."

"We can worry about moving the stuff once we get it," Han said. "The prison's got to have some antigrav sleds at least."

"You can count me in," Luke said.

"I'm already in," Leia added.

Isolder considered a moment. They wouldn't be able to take the Wookiee into the city. Chances were that no one on this planet outside of the soldiers had ever seen one. The same was true of Threepio. That left them short-handed. He didn't like the idea of having Leia endanger herself, but they were running short of options. He looked back at Teneniel, pleading. The witch appeared to be frightened but determined.

"I'll guide you to the prison," Teneniel said. "But I've never been inside. I don't know what you are looking for, and I don't know where to find it."

"Have any of your clan sisters been inside the prison?" Leia asked.

Teneniel shrugged. "Augwynne would know such things better than I. I'll get her." Teneniel took off, returned a few minutes later with the older woman.

"None of our clan has been inside the prison," Augwynne said, "except those who have become Nightsisters." She was silent for a long moment.

"What of Sister Barukka?" Teneniel said hesitantly. "I heard that she has become forsaken."

Augwynne hesitated a long time, then looked up at Leia. "There is a woman of our clan who joined the Nightsisters, but has recently left them at great price. She now lives alone as one of the forsaken and has petitioned to rejoin our clan. Perhaps she could help guide you, tell you where to find what you seek."

"You seem reluctant to recommend her," Leia said. "Why?"

Augwynne answered, softly. "She is fighting to cleanse herself. She has committed unspeakable atrocities that have left a great mark upon her. She is forsaken. Such people are . . . untrustworthy, unstable."

"But she's been inside the prison?" Han asked.

"Yes," Augwynne said.

"Where is she now?"

"Barukka lives in a cavern called Rivers of Stone. I can send one of our warriors to guide you."

"I'll take them, Grandmother," Teneniel offered, placing a hand on Augwynne's shoulder. "Perhaps you could escort them to the war room and get some lunch. You could show them the map and plan our route. I'll have some children prepare mounts." She took Isolder's hand. "Come with me, please," she said. "I'd like to speak with you." She pulled him along as if she expected him to follow.

She took him down some stairs through a maze of corridors and stopped to pick up a pitcher of water, then led him into a small chamber that held a single mattress and a trunk. A large mirror made of silver sat on one wall, with a sink beneath it. "This used to be my room, when I lived here with the clan at Singing Mountain," Teneniel said. She opened the trunk, pulled out a soft tunic of red lizard hide, another of green. She held them up. "Which do you think Luke would like the best on me?"

Isolder didn't dare tell her that the whole idea of wearing lizard hides seemed rather barbaric. "The green goes better with your eyes."

She nodded, casually stripped off her torn and soiled tunic, pulled off her boots, and stood gazing in the mirror as she took a rag and gave herself a sponge bath. Isolder swallowed hard. He knew that on some planets, humans had different notions of modesty, and the businesslike way in which Teneniel bathed seemed to indicate that she really wasn't trying to entice him.

"You know, I don't understand your customs," Teneniel said. "Yesterday morning when I captured you, I thought you wanted me, and the idea flattered me. I gave you every opportunity to escape first, and you took the capture rope in your own hand. I knew that you had come seeking a woman. I could feel that about you." She frowned, glanced over her back at him. "But now I see that it is this Leia woman you want."

"Yes," Isolder said, looking at the sculpted muscles in her back. Teneniel was not a beautiful woman by Hapan standards —in fact, she was rather plain—but Isolder decided that she had some rather fascinating musculature. She was definitely athletic. He'd seen few women on Hapes with her kind of build

—not the compact, beefy muscles of a bodybuilder, nor quite the leanness of a runner or swimmer. Instead, she was something in between. He asked, "Do you like to climb a lot?"

Teneniel shot a smile over her back. "Yes," she said. "Do you?"

"I've never tried it."

Teneniel toweled off, slipped on her tunic, pulled her long hair back over the top of it and began combing the tight curls from her hair. "I like the feel of climbing rocks," Teneniel said, "getting all sweaty. When you get to the top of the mountain, if the weather is right, you can take off your clothes and bathe in the snow."

Although he really felt no attraction for the girl, he realized he would have to be pretty tired not to dream about her tonight. "I suppose you could."

When she finished combing her hair, she put on a headband of bright white cloth, turned to him and smiled. "Isolder, I would give you back your freedom outright, but if I did, the other clan sisters would only capture you. So until you leave, I think it best if I give you your freedom in all but name."

Isolder knew she was trying to be kind. "You're very generous."

She gave him a friendly kiss on the forehead, and took his hand again, led him down to the war room.

Leia and the others stood around a huge map on the floor, molded of clay and painted. A clan sister was plotting a route through the mountainous countryside, a route that would keep them away from established trails that Gethzerion's spies might be watching. The route would take them on a tortuous path over a hundred and forty kilometers of mountain and jungle, to the edge of the desert where the prison lay. Only the strongest rancors would be able to make such a journey in just three days.

Isolder looked at Leia, kept wondering about her, wondering if she were really all right, wondering if Han had really kidnapped her. She did not seem to be angry with Han or frightened of him. Yet Isolder could not imagine that she would simply run away with him on some wild fling. He swore in his heart that if she had chosen Han, he would win her back. He casually made his way to her side, held her hand. Leia smiled up at him, gazed at him fondly, and though they stood there for ten minutes while the witch marked their trail, Isolder studied only the curve of Leia's neck, the color of her eyes, the scent of her hair.

After they had eaten, Augwynne took Luke and Isolder to a side bedroom where a toothless crone with wisps of white hair sat wrapped in a blanket, snoring. Her seat was a stone box with a cushion atop it, and two elderly women attended.

"Mother Rell," Augwynne whispered to the crone, lightly shaking the woman's shoulder. "We have two visitors to meet you."

Rell caught her breath, opened her eyes and squinted at Luke. Her leathery skin was spotted purple with age, but her eyes gleamed like brown pools. She tenderly took Luke's hand. "Why, it's Luke Skywalker," the crone smiled in recognition, "who started the Jedi academy all those years ago." Luke flinched, for the crone had not been told his name. "How are your wife and children? Are they well?"

Luke stuttered, "We're all fine." The hair on the back of Isolder's neck stood on end. He had the odd feeling that he was looking into a brilliant light.

The crone smiled knowingly and nodded. "Good, good. If you have your health, you have much. Have you seen Master Yoda lately? How is that old flirt?"

"I haven't seen him lately," Luke answered, and Rell's grip went slack, her eyes dimmed. She seemed to forget that Luke was even standing there.

Augwynne directed her attention to Isolder. "Luke brought another friend to see you," Augwynne said, and she put the old woman's spidery fingers in Isolder's hand.

"Oh, it's Prince Isolder," the old woman said, leaning close to peer at him. "But, I thought Gethzerion killed you. If you're alive, then . . ." She studied him a moment, then her face went dark with realization and she looked up at Augwynne. "I've been dreaming again, haven't I? What century is it?"

"Yes, Mother, you've been dreaming again," Augwynne answered soothingly, patting the old woman's hand, but Rell would not loose her grip on Isolder's hand. Her eyes lost their focus.

"Mother Rell is nearly three hundred years old," Augwynne explained, "but her spirit is so strong that it will not let her body die. When I was a child, she used to tell me that someday a Jedi Master would come with his pupil, and that when he did, I should bring them straight to her. She said she had a message for you, but she is not lucid at the moment. I'm sorry."

Augwynne seemed tense, and she tried to pry the old woman's grasp free from Isolder's hand. Rell smiled at them all, her white head bobbing like a float on the water. "It's been pleasant visiting you," Rell told Isolder. "Please come see me again. You're such a nice young girl or boy or whatever you are. . . ."

Augwynne got the old woman to free Isolder's hand, and she took the men from the room, ushering them hurriedly.

"She sees the future, doesn't she?" Luke said.

Augwynne nodded mechanically, and Isolder became extremely uncomfortable, for if the old woman was right, Gethzerion would kill him within the next few days. "Sometimes she gets lost in it as easily as she becomes lost in the past," Augwynne explained.

"What else did she tell you about me?" Luke said.

"She said that after you came," Augwynne answered softly, "she would let herself die. And she said that your coming would signal the end of our world."

"What did she mean by that?" Luke asked, but Augwynne only shook her head and went to the hearth. Her manservant ladled some soup into her bowl. Luke must have seen the fear etched into Isolder's face, for he put his hand on Isolder's back.

"Don't worry," Luke said. "What Rell saw is only one possible future. Nothing is written. Nothing is written."

Chapter

18

After lunch, Teneniel led the group down to their mounts. Though the noon sun did not seem particularly warm, the rancors were already bathing in the ponds below the fortress, wading around on the bottom with only their nostrils showing.

Some of the boys from the village were shouting orders to the rancors, and soon four of them came up out of the water. The boys put breastplates on the rancors, hauling up the heavy mail made of pieces of bone and bits of armor all tied together with whuffa hide. Once they got the armor on the rancors, the boys climbed up on their bony headplates and tied on the saddles. The saddles were situated in a shallow depression just in front of the headplate, and were held in place by means of ropes tied to the beast's fangs, then strung back between its nostrils to the thorny bones at the top of its head plate. Two saddles were put on each mount.

Leia chose to ride an old sow, a herd leader named Tosh, who had pale green lichens and moss growing in her warty brown skin. Han gave her a boost up on the rancor so that she could climb up its knobby arms to the bony plates on its shoulders, then leap over to the saddle. Then Han helped Isolder and Luke lug the droids up onto one of the mounts and tie them in. Taking the droids was difficult, but they needed Artoo's sensors.

Once they finished, Teneniel climbed up on one of the mounts and Chewie on another. Han came to Leia's mount and started looking for a foothold to climb up, but Luke hurried over.

"Say, uh, Han," Luke said softly. "I was sort of hoping to ride with Leia. It's been a long time since I've seen her, and I sort of wanted to get caught up on a few things." Leia could feel an unusual tenseness in Luke.

"No way, buddy," Han said. "She's mine. Why don't you ride on that rancor over there?" He nodded toward Teneniel. "That Teneniel is definitely hot for you."

"Her?" Luke said. "I wouldn't know about that." Luke blushed, and Leia suddenly understood: Luke was feeling shy, and yet she could feel that he was pulled in two directions. He liked the girl but didn't want to get close.

"You can't tell me you haven't noticed her," Han said. "I mean, that woman is definitely put together just right."

"Yeah, I've noticed." Luke smiled weakly.

"So, what? You're telling me you don't want her?" Han asked in disbelief.

"We're just from such different worlds," Luke said.

"But you've got so much in common. You're both from strange little backwater planets. You both have odd powers. You're male and she's female. What more do you need? Believe me, buddy, if I were you, I'd go right up there and ask her if she wants to ride on my rancor."

"I don't know," Luke said. Above them, Leia could feel some of the tension ease out of him. Han had nearly talked Luke into it.

"Okay, if you don't want to ask her to ride with you, maybe I should ask her to ride with me," Han said, glancing up at Leia.

"Oh, you're so juvenile," Leia shot back, "trying to make me jealous. Well, it won't work."

"Hey," Han said, "*I'm* the jilted lover here. If you want to ride with His Highness Isolder, that's your prerogative." He waved toward Isolder, who was standing over by Teneniel's rancor. "But if I go looking for some lovely young lady to comfort me while I'm on the rebound, why should you care?"

"I don't care—much," Leia said. "It's not you I'm worried about. I just don't want you using another woman that way!"

"Me?" Han said, throwing his arms wide and shrugging in a gesture of disbelief. He turned to look at Teneniel, but Luke was already climbing the rancor to sit next to her. Isolder had sneaked back around Leia's mount, and he scurried up in that instant, leaped in the saddle beside Leia.

"Too bad, General Solo," Isolder said, patting Leia's knee. "It looks as if you will have to ride beside your hairy Wookiee friend. But I know that won't bother you, since you two are so close."

Han glared up at Isolder, and Leia definitely did not like the look in his eyes. The day didn't get much better from then on.

They started by taking a back trail over Singing Mountain so that the rancors had to climb down a hundred-meter cliff. They proved to be terrible mounts in many ways—when a rancor looked around, the creature's entire head plate shifted right and left or bobbed up and down, depending on its line of sight. If it walked upright, its awkward gait tended to be jarring enough so that an inattentive rider could easily get thrown, and when it dropped to all fours and loped through the thick brush, just staying mounted became an incredible feat. All in all, riding a rancor proved to be as physically demanding as any task Leia had ever undertaken. Yet by nightfall she was convinced that a person could never travel in these mountains without one.

Twice they came to great canyons a trained climber would be afraid to scale, yet the rancors dug their huge claws into ancient handholds and toeholds carved in the cliffs, and shinnied up and down the stone. During one such incident, Han's rancor knocked free a stone that barely missed crushing Isolder. The prince glared up at Han, and Han smiled down weakly. "Sorry."

"Perhaps not sorry enough! If you cannot steal her from me, do you think to murder me?" Isolder said, jaw clenched.

"Han wouldn't do that. It was only an accident," Leia assured Isolder, but the prince scowled up at Han nonetheless.

Isolder remained quiet for a long time, but when their rancor was marching well ahead of the others, he said, "I still don't understand why you came here with Han so abruptly." He did not say any more, did not pry, but his tone spoke of his frustration, demanded an answer, an answer that she did not want to give.

"Does it really seem so odd that I would run off with an old friend like Han?" Leia asked, hoping to change the subject.

"Yes," Isolder said rather vehemently.

"Why?" Leia asked.

"He's rather abrasive . . ." Isolder said, cautiously, as if thinking.

"And?"

"Oafish," Isolder concluded. "He's not good enough for you."

"I see," Leia said, trying not to let her rising anger show in her voice. "So, the prince of Hapes thinks that the king of Corellia is an abrasive oaf, and the king of Corellia thinks that the prince of Hapes is slime. I can see that you two won't be forming a mutual admiration society anytime soon."

"He called me 'slime'?" Isolder said, shock evident on his face.

A moment later, in heavy brush where a man would have spent hours cutting his way through even with a vibro-blade, the rancors simply crashed through the foliage. As Isolder's mount pushed through some trees, Isolder held a branch to keep it from scratching Leia, then let it swing back, whacking Han and Chewbacca. Han shouted, "Hey! Watch it!"

Isolder flashed a smile. "Perhaps, General Solo, you should watch out for yourself. This is a very dangerous planet you've led us to, filled with all manner of dangerous species of *slime*."

Han's face darkened. "I'm not worried!" he said. "I can take care of myself."

They rode on for most of the rest of the afternoon without incident, perhaps too weary to fight. Leia listened to Luke and Teneniel talking softly, Luke instructing her in the ways of the Force, the girl telling of hunting a horned beast she called a drebbin in these mountains. Apparently the creatures preyed on rancors, though Leia found that hard to imagine.

When the party came to a mountain river in the late evening where floodwaters roared, the rancors leaped in and swam with long strokes, only their nostrils showing above water, their tails floating behind them. Leia began mindlessly humming a tune, then realized she was humming, "Han Solo, / What a man! Solo," and she stopped, embarrassed.

Han brought his rancor up beside Leia and Isolder, smiled at Leia broadly. The rancors swam side by side for a moment, then the current pushed Han's rancor so that it nudged theirs. Isolder responded by turning his rancor into Han's so that for a moment the two rancors swam shoulder to shoulder jostling one another.

Leia glared at Han and Isolder and shouted, "Cut it out, both of you!"

"He started it!" Han yelled, and Isolder slapped his reins into the water, splashing Han.

Behind them, Teneniel began singing lightly and a water spout rose from the river, carrying twisted sheets of brown foam forty meters into the air. It whirled toward the group, then collapsed, drenching Han and Isolder. Luke and Chewbacca broke out laughing, and Leia smiled back at the witch.

"Thank you," she said. "Maybe someday you can teach me that spell."

Leia felt a sudden sense of bliss and desire, realized she had touched Luke's emotions. He'd seldom felt that way about a woman before, she was sure. Leia winked at him.

"We can camp soon," Teneniel said when the rancors climbed out of the stream. Artoo had his antennae dish extended. "The caves are nearby."

"Artoo isn't picking up any Imperial signals," Threepio said, his golden eyes shining unnaturally bright against the dark foliage of the forest. "Though he is getting a great deal of radio traffic above us."

"What's going on?" Luke asked, and Artoo began twittering and beeping.

"Apparently, sir," Threepio informed them, "several Imperial Star Destroyers just jumped out of hyperspace above us. Artoo is trying to get a count of the ships now. So far, he's detected signals from fourteen ships."

Leia glanced up nervously at the sky even though it was still far too light to make out a spaceship, and Isolder said, "I shouldn't have brought in a Hapes Battle Dragon. After our little attack, they've got only two choices—reinforce or bug out. It looks as if they plan to reinforce."

Leia almost asked, "What are the chances that Zsinj's men will figure out that we're down here?" but decided she'd better not say it. She didn't want to cause the group any concern, just in case no one else had thought of it. But she looked at Han, knew by the frown lines what he was thinking. The guards from prison had already broadcast his name over the air. It was a good bet that Zsinj's men knew Han was alive down here. And like all good New Republic officers, Han carried a price on his head. The only question was, did Zsinj want him badly enough to break his own interdiction order and send a ship down?

Leia looked back at Isolder. "I think you're right. I don't like the idea of having all those destroyers above us." The chances that the ships' sensors could detect the droids' electronics was remote, but still there was a chance, so she added, "Let's get to those caves and hide for a while."

In less than ten minutes, Teneniel led them up a hill through the thick trees, till they came to a yawning hole in the ground half-concealed by twisted red vines with pungent white flowers. Teneniel got down from her rancor, went to the cave mouth and shouted, "Barukka? Barukka?" But no one answered. She stood for a moment, nervous, then closed her eyes and began to sing softly. When she opened her eyes, she said, "I can't feel her anywhere near."

"If we don't find her," Threepio said, "how will we get any information about the prison? Artoo, scan the area for human life forms!" Artoo whistled and began aiming his antenna dish along the horizon.

Teneniel peeked inside the cave, walked in. A moment later, she came back out. "There are some clothes there, some pots. It looks as if she may have left several days ago."

"Great," Han said. "Where would she go?"

"Hunting for food?" Teneniel guessed. "Or maybe she has rejoined the Nightsisters. This is a dangerous time for Barukka. As one who is forsaken, she is supposed to remain here in the wilderness, remain alone and consider her past, her future. But often the loneliness becomes too much."

The sky was beginning to darken as the sun set. "Let's camp here," Luke said. "We can wait for her."

He urged his rancor into the dark, and Teneniel began setting stones in a semicircle around the cave's mouth, apparently to signify that it was occupied. Somehow, the whole idea of going inside bothered Leia. She felt as if she were violating Barukka's privacy.

Isolder urged his rancor forward into the shadows. Once inside, the caves proved to be a glimmering wonderland of stalactites and stalagmites encrusted with garnet in hues of pale citrine streaked with metallic green and ivory. It looked like seawater splashing all around, and Leia understood why the witches had named it Rivers of Stone. The roof of the cave reached high enough so that the rancors could have stood on one another's shoulders. Water flowed through the caves in a shallow stream.

Teneniel dragged some logs in from a cache by the door, and Han started them afire with his blaster. During the day, the group had remained quietly alert while riding, keeping a lookout for scouting parties from the Nightsisters. Now that they could talk, Leia found she was too tired.

The rancors, however, seemed not to be tired. They hunched around the fire in their gruesome breastplates of bone and stormtrooper uniforms, and warmed their knuckles near the fire, growling softly. Tosh spoke to the younger ones, gesticulating with her claws, the firelight playing over her teeth and the warty bone plates on her shoulders.

Chewbacca curled up on a mat and slept; the droids went to the mouth of the cave so that Artoo could monitor the countryside with his sensors. Han took off exploring the back of the cave with a torch. Luke and Teneniel talked softly as she put some large green nuts in the coals of the fire to roast in their shells. Isolder lay against a garnet-encrusted pillar, eyes half-closed, playing with his blaster.

The rancors made a moaning sigh, and Teneniel nodded up toward Tosh. "She's telling her children how her ancestors first met the witches," Teneniel said. "She says that a sickly female met a witch that healed her, and the witch rode on the rancor's back, learned to speak its tongue. By riding the rancor's back, the witch was able to spot food better with her sharp eyes that

see well even in the daylight, and the rancor thrived and became huge. In time, she became a herd mother, and her herds
prospered while others died out. Back then, the rancors did not
know how to make fine weapons like spears or nets. They did
not know how to protect themselves with armor. Because the
witches have taught them such great things, she says, the rancors must always love the witches and serve them, even when
we make unreasonable demands to give us rides through the
wilderness or ask them to fight the Nightsisters."

Leia studied Teneniel thoughtfully, realized the girl must
have felt her curiosity about the rancors. "I think Tosh loves
your people," Leia said.

Teneniel nodded, reached up to scratch the rancor's hind
leg. "Yes, she's very grateful that her herd is strong, but none of
the rancors are happy about the Nightsisters."

"You told me earlier that the rancors will not serve the
Nightsisters," Luke said. "Why is that?"

"The Nightsisters treat them badly, as if they were mere
slaves. So the rancors always run away."

"I find it interesting," Isolder said, "that you treat your
rancors as friends but treat men as slaves. You have an interesting power structure with men at the bottom, but I find it all
rather barbaric."

"It's often easier to see the barbarism in alien cultures than
it is to see it in your own," Luke said. "The witches have built a
hierarchy based on power, as do most cultures."

Isolder nodded.

"For example," Leia said, "I find the whole concept of rule
by birthright to be rather barbaric. Don't you, Isolder?"

"That's an odd statement, coming from you, Princess,"
Isolder said. "You come from a family that has been bred and
trained to lead for generations. It is only right that you should
lead, and all of your people know it. Even when your title and
throne have become little more than a token honor, your people
still clamor for you to serve as the ambassador for Alderaan."

"So you claim that we are leaders not by birthright, but
because we inherited those skills?" Leia asked in dismay. "I
think that's pretty farfetched."

"No, it isn't," Isolder affirmed. "We breed animals for intelligence, for beauty, for speed. Among social carnivores, the

herd leaders often select the strongest and smartest mates. As a result, their offspring usually 'inherit' a dominant position in their pack, if you will."

"Even if I gave you that point," Leia said, "it really doesn't have any bearing on human behavior. Humans aren't social carnivores."

Isolder glanced into the shadows. "If you knew my mother better, you would not argue *that* particular point." Leia wondered at those words.

"Certainly many groups of humans see themselves to be social carnivores," Luke said. "Look at any speeder pack, and you can't help but see something of that attitude. Then of course there are the warlords."

"And the Nightsisters," Teneniel said.

"Luke, I can't believe you're arguing against me on this!" Leia said. "You're the gentlest person I know."

"All I'm saying," Luke said softly, "is that as distasteful as it may sound to you and me, Isolder might have a point. Intelligence, charisma, decisiveness—all of these traits are likely to have genetic components. And so long as these traits breed true, then perpetuating a guild of leaders might not be a bad idea."

"I think it's a terrible idea," Leia said. "You've seen it, Isolder. You've seen businesspeople on your planets who could lead as well as you."

Isolder hesitated. "I suspect they might serve well as leaders—they are certainly leaders in commerce—but I'm not certain they should be allowed to lead governments."

"How could you not be certain?" Leia asked.

"Our business leaders tend to measure everything in terms of growth, profits, output. I have seen worlds operated by businesspeople, and they take little thought for those people who are seen as a drain on their economy—the artists, the priests, the infirm. I would prefer to let such leaders run their businesses."

"You complain about a mercenary attitude among businesspeople, yet only a moment ago you called your mother a predator?" Luke said. "What is the difference between her and someone in business?"

"My mother was a good leader for her time," Isolder said.

"Your Old Republic was falling apart. We needed someone bru-
tal to fend off the Empire, and when we could not fend them off
any longer, we needed someone strong enough to hold our
worlds together under the pressure of Imperial rule. My mother
met those needs. But her day is past. Now we need a queen
mother strong enough to fight off my aunts, yet gentle enough
to lead through kindness."

Teneniel was still rubbing the rancor down, and the huge
beast leaned into her, seeking her ministrations. "I don't profess
to understand all of your argument," Teneniel said, "yet you
call us barbarians because women rule this world and you men
have no power. But if you are led by a queen mother, then how
can you be any less barbaric than us? Men hold no power on
either of our worlds, so what is the difference?"

"In a sense, I hold ultimate power," Isolder said. "For although I am only a man, I will choose the next queen mother."

Leia gritted her teeth. It was the same stupid argument that
repressed people came up with in every society. One way or
another, they satisfied themselves that they held some control
even though they relinquished it to others. You often couldn't
argue with people who were so thoroughly grounded in their
own culture.

But Leia realized that something else made her angry: The
fact that she happened to fit all of Isolder's specifications for a
perfect queen mother. He claimed to love her, and he was one
of the most attractive men she'd ever seen. But maybe he was
one of those people who only let themselves fall in love when
they met someone who had the right qualifications. If this were
the case, Leia didn't know how she felt about that.

Perhaps Teneniel had the right answer. She just looked at
Isolder and laughed. " 'I will choose the next queen mother,' "
she mocked, feigning his accent surprisingly well. " 'I have all
the power!' " She shot a wicked smile over her shoulder as she
rubbed down the rancor, and she laughed, "You're so dumb!"

In the back of the cavern, Han suddenly began shouting
and firing his blaster. Luke leaped to his feet, pulled his lightsaber. "There's a monster back there in the pond!" Han yelled
as he rushed up to the fire, blaster still smoldering. "It's big and
green and it's got tentacles! It tried to eat me."

"Oh, yes," Teneniel said, "I forgot about her."

"You mean you *knew* there was a monster there," Han shouted, "and you didn't tell me about it?"

"The clan sisters put her in the lake several years ago," Teneniel said. "We thought when she grew large enough, she would make a good meal for the rancors."

Teneniel patted Tosh's flank, whispered into her ear. The rancor regarded her calmly a moment, a feral light gleaming in her eyes, then she roared and the small herd took off at a run, heading for the lake. The humans moved in close to the fire and began eating roasted nuts.

The fire was cozy, warm, and they talked softly among themselves for a few minutes as the last of the sunlight faded and the cave seemed to darken and close in around them. For a while, Leia felt comfortable, but suddenly her heart began to pound, and she felt stifled, suffocating. She stood up, looked behind her. A woman in black stood at the mouth of the cave, holding a great staff.

"What are you doing here?" Barukka demanded, walking toward the light. When Leia had first spotted her, the staff had made the woman appear old and infirm, but as she got close, Leia saw that Barukka was a young woman, perhaps no more than thirty. Still, Leia could feel an aura of dark power around her, something that made her feel worn, ageless. Barukka's piercing blue eyes were very intent, and she watched them all warily from beneath a hood. "I must warn you that I am forsaken, and that this is my house you have entered. I cannot welcome you or offer you shelter."

"Then perhaps we can welcome *you*, and offer you shelter and some dinner," Luke said, rising from his seat.

"Please," Teneniel said, "we've come for your help!"

Barukka stayed outside the light of the fire, watching them like some wild animal. Her face was badly bruised. "You are in danger," Barukka said at last. "Gethzerion has been summoning the Nightsisters for a war. I can *feel* her summons, pulling at me. You are her enemies." Barukka's voice was strangely contemplative, as if she were studying her own feelings.

"But we are not *your* enemies," Luke said.

"Mother Augwynne told me that you petitioned to join the Singing Mountain clan," Teneniel said. "We would like to welcome you back fully as a sister some day."

"Yes," Barukka said distantly. "She has chosen to leave the Nightsister clan." She said it as if she were speaking of someone else, someone who was not in the cave, and Leia knew that this woman was not sane.

"*You* chose to leave the Nightsisters," Teneniel said.

"Yes," Barukka whispered, as if remembering.

"Will you help us?" Teneniel asked. "We need to go to the prison, to find some parts for a ship. Can you tell us where to look?"

Barukka stood unmoving for a long moment, frowning in concentration. She began to tremble, and whispered, "No, I can't."

"Why can't you?" Luke said. "Gethzerion has no power over you."

"She does!" Barukka said. "Can't you hear her calling me? She hunts me! Even now, she is stalking me!"

"Does she call to you?" Luke asked. "Do you hear her voice in your head?"

"Yes," Barukka said.

"What does she say?"

"She rails against me, curses me," Barukka answered. "Sometimes I hear her at night, as if she is standing by my bed."

"You two must have been close," Luke said.

Teneniel said, "Gethzerion is her sister."

"Barukka," Luke said softly. "She *was* your sister, but the part of her that you loved is either gone or has been hidden very deeply."

Barukka looked down at the floor, as if gazing into the depths of the earth, then looked up at Luke. "Who are you? You are more than you seem. I *feel* your presence."

"He is a Jedi Knight from the stars—" Teneniel said.

"—Come to put an end to our world!" Barukka hissed, suddenly fierce. "Yes! Yes! The prison! I have been there!" She spun into motion, began to make hissing and spitting noises. She pointed her staff at the cave floor and swirled it. Leia's heart pounded in fear, and she suddenly realized that the spitting sounds were words, an incantation. The ground at Barukka's feet buckled and rose to form a miniature chain of mountains as high as her knees, stretching from one side of the cave to the other. Suddenly the dust swirled darkly and buildings arose at Barukka's feet: nestled in the mountains was a long building with six sides, with a great courtyard in the center. Cell blocks ran around the inside of each wall, tiny windows and doors showing in minute detail. Small round guard towers rose at each corner of the prison, and perfectly sculpted guard droids swiveled in chairs, keeping watch with their miniature blasters. Small Imperial walkers stood guard at one end, figures made of dust that walked impossibly along the grounds. Outbuildings rose near them, and at last a single large tower formed from the ground near the prison, with a walkway of dirt leading through the air from the upper levels of the prison to the top of the tower. On the far side of the prison, the dust roiled in waves, as if a small lake had formed.

Chewbacca roared in fear and pointed: tiny humanoid figures of dust walked around the perimeters of the prison, some dressed as stormtroopers, others dressed in the robes of witches. Barukka stood over her creation, sweat running down her face, panting. Her eyes were glazed, and the firelight flickered in them. Leia could tell that only a great act of concentration let the woman manipulate the dirt this way. It was a talent beyond anything that Leia had ever seen in Luke, and it frightened her. If Barukka could do this, what kind of power did some of the other Nightsisters have?

"These are the entrances to the prison," Barukka said, stabbing toward doors on the east and west of the prison. "And here are its guardians." She stabbed the tower guards with her staff, smashed the Imperial walkers, squashed an outpost on the western edge of the desert.

"Gethzerion has long sought to assemble a complete ship so that she can escape," Barukka said, "and she keeps the components here, in the basement beneath her tower." She jabbed her staff into the base of the tower.

Han and Luke went to the living map, studied it thoughtfully. "That tower is too heavily guarded for us to come at it in the open," Han said. "In fact, the whole eastern valley here is just too exposed."

They looked at the lake to the west of the hills. "I'd say our best bet is to hike through the hills here on the north or south," Luke agreed, "then sneak to the prison from the back side. Once we're in, it's an easy walk through the prison blocks, over the walkway and into the tower."

"Yeah," Han said. "And they've got a hover craft and a couple of speeder bikes parked out front. Once we get our parts, we should be able to just load them up and leave."

On top of the tower, a tiny figure of a Nightsister walked through a door, stood looking up at the sky for a moment, as if staring directly into Barukka's face. Barukka suddenly shrieked, "Gethzerion!" and spun, smashing the figure with her staff.

The perfect living replica of the prison crumbled into sand, and Barukka fell to her knees, sobbing. Luke reached over to her, gingerly touched her back, and held her.

"It's all right," Luke said. "She won't hurt you anymore. She won't hurt you anymore."

Barukka looked up at him, and her face was a mass of purpled bruises. "But what of me?" she cried. "When will my scars heal?"

Luke touched her face. "Those who use the dark side of the Force to harm others often do harm to themselves," he said softly. He ran his fingers over the bruises, and immediately the puffiness diminished. "Sit with me tonight," Luke said, "and together we can begin your healing."

For a long time that night, Leia stretched out on a blanket. The chorus "Han Solo, / What a man! Solo," played over and over in her mind until she had a fierce desire to take a hammer to Threepio. Had he known it would affect her this way? Had he known it would get caught in her mind and play over and over again until she thought she'd scream?

To calm herself, she lay awake and listened to Luke as he taught Teneniel, Barukka, and Isolder. "The Jedi uses the Force only for knowledge and defense, never to injure or gain power."

"But with the spells of our clans," Teneniel countered, "the words of the spells are the same whether we cast them for darkness or light. How will we know whether we are using them rightly?"

"It's not the words that give you power, it is your intent," Luke said. "When you remain calm, when you feel at peace, when you show mercy and justice to those who make themselves your enemies, then you will know that you are using the Force correctly. But if you surrender to hate, or despair, or greed, then you give in to the dark side and it will dominate your destiny, take control of you."

"I have . . . friends among the Nightsisters," Teneniel said. "As a child I played with Grania and Varr, and I considered them dear friends. Even Gethzerion gave gifts to me during Winterfest. We cast her out of our clan only seven years ago. I cannot think of them as all lost."

"Some of them you may win back from the dark side," Luke said. "If you feel good in them still, then you must awaken them to that if you can. But don't be fooled. The dark side can be compelling, and some turn completely from the light, become agents of evil. Remember the good that was once in them if you can, love them for it, but don't let them sway you. The agents of evil seldom reveal themselves willingly."

"You said that those who follow the dark side can be won back. But what if you yourself become tainted?" Barukka asked quietly. "How can you free yourself?"

"Then you must turn away from the dark side with your whole heart. Give up your anger, give up your greed, give up your despair."

Leia looked over at Barukka, saw that the woman's brow was furrowed and a tear glimmered in her eye. Though Leia could not imagine what was going through the woman's mind, she somehow felt grateful not to have Barukka's problems.

Luke reached out and touched Barukka's chin, raised her face and said softly, "And in time, you must give up your guilt."

Chapter

19

G ethzerion isn't with them," Teneniel said with certainty
the following evening as they looked from the hills
toward the prison. She nodded toward a long line of
marching stormtroopers and Imperial walkers that picked their
way across the brown flatlands like a flock of ungainly metallic
birds. Secretly, she'd wished that Gethzerion were with the
small army. Teneniel did not like the idea of going into the
prison complex knowing that she might meet Gethzerion
around any corner. The flatlands around the complex appeared
dry. What was a lake in winter became a plain in summer.
Patches of cane grew tall around frequent mud holes where
burra fish had dug down into the lake bed, hoarding water as
long as possible.

"I count about eighty Imperial walkers and maybe six hundred stormtroopers," Isolder said. "Too bad we don't have a
way to send a message back to the clan sisters."

I can send a message," Teneniel said. She closed her eyes
and half-whispered, half-sang the spell for talking at great dis-
tances. "Augwynne," she said. "Hear my words, see with my
eyes. These are the forces that the Nightsisters send against

you." Teneniel felt the easy sense of contact with Augwynne, let the woman see the marching Imperials from her own eyes.

"How long do you think it will be before they reach Singing Mountain?" Isolder asked. Teneniel broke contact.

"Two days," Teneniel said. "We should get back before they do." They stood on a hill, hidden by the green fanning leaves from tall waxbrush. Eight kilometers off, the lights of the prison gleamed like stars on the horizon. A tall guntower that seemed made of glass thrust up from the earth like a thorn. The black steel walls of the prison squatted on the green hills. Teneniel whispered a slight spell to sharpen her vision, looked off toward the prison. She could see several witches in their black robes outside the fortress. On towers over the prison walls and at the top of the gleaming city, guardian droids swiveled constantly, covering the prison compound with their guns. A large craft floated in the air in front of the compounds. It looked just as Sister Barukka had showed them.

Luke took his macrobinoculars from his utility belt. "They've only got one speeder out there, and the hover car is gone. I see some sensor arrays up on the towers, nothing fancy. Still, Artoo and Threepio will need to stay here. We can't risk having them get a whiff of our electronics. This being a prison, we've got to figure that they'll have a full array of biosensors. If we're going to make it in unannounced, we'll need to stay out of their range as long as possible, circle south to the hills. Once we make it there, the rock will screen us out."

Artoo began whistling and rocking in his housing. "Sir," Threepio translated, "Artoo is picking up communications between Zsinj's starships and the prison."

"Well, what do they say?" Han asked.

"I'm afraid the transmissions are coded," Threepio answered. "However, the code does appear to be based on one that the Rebel Alliance broke several years ago. If you give me a few hours, I may be able to translate it for you."

"Sorry, Threepio," Luke said, "I'd like to know what they're saying, but we can't wait that long. Why don't you work on it while we're gone?"

"Very well, sir," Threepio said. "I'll devote my full resources to the task."

"Good," Luke said. "Chewie, you take care of the droids for us. We'll see you soon."

Chewbacca growled and patted Han on the back as they said their good-byes. Teneniel unharnessed her rancors, told them to go into the forest to hunt. As always here on Dathomir, the sun fell away suddenly, and in the purple twilight Han, Leia, Luke, Isolder, and Teneniel headed across the plain, keeping the cane patches between them and the towers of the city. Teneniel whispered spells to sharpen her hearing and her sight, but for the first few minutes, the only sound was the occasional croak of a lizard or the splashing of burra fish in their mud holes, until in the distance, she heard Tosh roar, a lonely wailing call bidding them farewell.

They headed for the barren hills to the south, reached them in two hours just as the first of Dathomir's small moons rose, and then raced northward through the washes and gullies. The rocks and soil reflected the dull silver light of the moon and still radiated dry heat from the day, but a cool wind from the mountains whispered through the dead grasses. In one wash, they met a pair of horned creatures digging their way out of the sand, and Luke stopped. The husky saurians thrashed their tail spikes in surprise, but did not seem frightened enough to fight. Instead they retracted their heads beneath their armored shells, shook the last of the dirt from their backs, then ambled over a hill, heading toward the cane fields for dinner and a drink.

Soon after that, the company turned a corner in a wash and found the guard post—a white, covered tower perhaps fifteen meters high. The tower had two chairs on a platform, and a mount for a blaster cannon. But the cannon had been taken off its mount, and no one was stationed at the guard post.

"What do you think is going on?" Leia said. "Where are the guards?"

"We saw quite a few stormtroopers marching off," Han said. "Maybe the prison is only running a skeleton crew, so some of the guards got pulled."

"No," Luke said. "Look at the sensor array up on that tower. The dish is rusted over." He suddenly realized that none of the others could have spotted that kind of detail in the dark. Luke was straining his Jedi senses to their fullest. "I don't think they're using this post at all anymore and haven't put a guard out here in years. Think about it: since the Emperor interdicted this planet, everyone here is a prisoner. Even if someone runs away, they can't really go anywhere."

"Still," Leia said, "they wouldn't want murderers and thugs running loose." There was a wrongness to her thought, and Luke considered, trying to decide what it might be, but needed to focus his attention elsewhere at the moment.

Luke sighed. "Well, this is it. Let's go see what we can find," and he headed up the draw, past the guardhouse. A moment later they came out of the draw and found a wide brown river. He'd expected a lake. During their trip through the winding gullies, they'd actually crossed the small chain of hills.

Up to the north a kilometer, a dozen giant droids bristling with arrays of shovels and clippers and multiple hands worked at moving irrigation pipes over several well-manicured fields. Barukka's map had not shown the droids. So there were subtle differences. Beyond that, he could see only the east wall to the prison, a lofty black wall that even a rancor couldn't climb. On each of two towers, vaguely humanoid droid gunners handled the blaster cannons. Both droids faced inward, guns trained on the courtyards.

"I don't see much out there," Luke said, surveying the ground with his macrobinoculars. "There's some harvester droids and a pumping station. I see the sally port at the back of the prison, but it's hard to tell how well guarded it might be."

Luke began to put his macrobinoculars away, but Teneniel snatched them, held them up and smiled to see that the amethyst light showed the world better than even her spells could.

"Let's go in that door," Isolder said.

"We can't just walk up to it," Han objected.

"We can hijack one of the harvester droids," Isolder said. "They're pretty basic droids. If you jump into their hoppers, they'll think that they've harvested a crop and take you right into the food-processing plant."

"Are you sure it will work?" Han asked. "What if the guards at the sally port check the hopper? What if those droids on the wall see us and take a shot? What if the harvest droids have built-in shredders to mulch the crop? I can think of a million things that could go wrong!"

"Do you have a better idea?" Isolder countered. "First of all, guards work at trying to keep people from getting *out* of prison. They don't worry about people trying to break in. Second, we don't have to worry about the guards on the walls seeing us, because we're going to crawl in low, under the crop cover. And third, I know those harvest droids don't have internal shredders because those are Hapan model HD two thirty-four C's!"

Han glared at Isolder, and Luke glanced at Leia to see her reaction. Obviously the two men were trying to impress her, and Isolder had just scored the first point—if his plan worked.

"Fine," Han said. "I'll lead." He unholstered his blaster and followed a ridge downhill, keeping a spur of land between them and the guard droids on the wall. When they crept to the edge of the muddy fields, he ran low between rows of tall vines, thick with berries. Several times he snatched large berries and popped them in his mouth.

They quickly reached a harvester droid. It had dozens of small claws, and it used them to feed berries into a mouthlike hopper. It stood only three meters tall and walked on stubby legs. Han looked up at it dumbly while Isolder climbed a little access ladder on the droid's side, lowered himself experimentally partway into the droid. The droid seemed unaware of him and kept feeding berries into the hole, so that Isolder had to push them back out. "Come on in," Isolder said. "This one is nearly empty."

Han, Leia, and Luke quickly followed. Teneniel hesitated, and Luke could sense her fear. She didn't like the idea of going into that mouth, dropping into a dark room.

The droid turned and began walking toward the prison, apparently satisfied that its hopper was full. Luke stuck his head out the hopper and whispered, "Teneniel, hurry!"

She raced up the ladder and leaped in.

The hopper was pretty cramped with five people in it, and Luke found himself standing in berries up to his knees, wedged tightly between Teneniel and Isolder. Luke sensed Teneniel's desperation, held her hand and whispered, "It's all right. You'll be all right."

Han lifted himself up, looked out the droid's "mouth" as it marched them toward the prison walls. "Looks like two guards at the sally port," Han whispered, then dropped back.

Teneniel's heart was beating wildly, and she tried hard to still her breathing, feel calm, feel the Force as Luke had told her. Luke studied her effort. At long last, she breathed easier, and Luke whispered, "Good," and squeezed her hand.

A light shone overhead through the mouth as they reached the sally port, and the droid stopped. Its metallic voice grated, "I have a load of hwotha berries for delivery to the processors."

"So soon?" one of the guards queried. "Those vines must be snapping under the weight. Go on ahead."

The droid marched into the prison, and dimly Luke could hear the guards talking. "With that many berries, do you think we'll get some?"

"Nah," the other said. "The brass will eat them all."

The droid trudged through brilliantly lit halls, past machines that hissed and spat steam, then stopped momentarily. The floor dropped out beneath them, and Luke found himself sliding through the dark down a smooth metal tube. Teneniel made a noise, frightened, and Luke grabbed her hand, whispered, "It's all right."

Conveyer wheels pushed them along in a tangle as nozzles built into the roof squirted them with water. They passed through the washers and suddenly jets of freezing air squirted over them.

And then there was light from an opening in the tubing just ahead. Luke rolled off the processor and pulled Teneniel with him, and they all lay amid a heap of machinery that clanked and droned. Metal legs held the food processors up at waist level. The air was moist and warm, but Luke could not see much. He listened intently. He could hear voices off to his right, echoing down a narrow hallway.

"Where are we?" Teneniel asked.

"We're under the kitchens, in the service tunnel for the food processors," Han answered. "Now all we have to do is find a way out of here."

"This way," Luke whispered, listening to the sound of voices. He led them crawling through a forest of metal legs and machinery, under a ceiling of pipes, over a carpet of dust balls.

After six minutes they reached an opening—a heavy grate bolted to the floor. Through it he could see hundreds of people milling about in a large dining room, all of them wearing orange jumpsuits. Many of them were humans, but several were hairless reptiles with enormous eyes mounted on a face that curved out like a ladle. "Ithorians," Han grunted.

"What are Ithorians doing in a prison?" Leia said, and she stopped and gazed out. A green woman walked by. Up on a catwalk overlooking the kitchens, armored Imperial stormtroopers strolled with blaster rifles in hand, watching the prisoners.

Luke looked down through the forest of machinery, saw another light. "This way," he said, moving on. Several minutes later they came to the second grate. Beyond that they could see a lighted room that smelled hot and wet. An elderly man supervised several droids that were hanging uniforms on racks. Behind Luke, the others scrunched up, looking out at the exit.

"What now?" Han asked. The old launderer ordered the droids to wheel the clothes out an exit, and the droids soon left.

Luke said loudly and calmly to the lone occupant of the room, "You, come and open this grate!"

"Oh, please, Luke," Leia whispered urgently, "don't try that trick. It never works for you!"

The man walked over to the grate, looked in. "What are you doing down there?"

"You must open this grate!" Luke said, letting his Force flow into the old man.

"I don't know the access code," the old man whispered conspiratorially, "or I'd be glad to help you. What are you doing in there? Did you get lost or something?"

Luke suddenly realized that his Jedi tricks would not work on this old man, yet the prisoner would be happy to help them.

"Wait a minute, Luke," Han said. "I see the access plate right up here. Maybe I can hotwire it!"

"Don't bother!" Leia said. "You'll probably just set off an alarm!" Han whipped out his blaster, demolished the plate. A few blue sparks bit into Luke's face. Everyone held their breaths, listening.

"See," Han assured them. "No alarm."

"You got lucky," Leia whispered. "Now you'll want to fiddle with the wiring for an hour, and then you'll set off an alarm!"

Han reached up with one hand, said "Ow!" as he touched the hot metal. Immediately the grate slid up. "See," he whispered. "Easy."

"Braggart," Leia hissed as she crawled into the laundry room.

"You only say that because you find it so hard to express your true admiration," Han said.

"Good job," Luke said as he crawled through the hatch. The laundryman helped him up, gawking.

"What are you doing?" the old man asked.

"We're breaking in," Han said.

By the time Teneniel got out, the old prisoner stood looking at them. "Hmmm . . ." he said, studying Isolder. "You folks can't go running around in here dressed like that. What will you wear?"

"What have you got?" Han asked.

"Just about everything comes through here," the old man said. "Uniforms for prisoners, guards—even that local junk the witches wear. So where you folks from?"

"All over," Han said suspiciously. "Why all the questions?"

"Lighten up," Luke answered. "He's harmless."

"How can you be so sure?" Han said. "He's a criminal, after all."

"Wait a minute, Han," Leia said. "I feel it, too. What are you in here for?"

"I objected to the Empire," the old laundryman said. "I ran an aerospace engineering firm on Coruscant. When they tried to steal some of our designs, we burned our buildings to the ground. I'm afraid that if you're looking for dangerous felons, you've come to the wrong facility."

"Political prisoners?" Han asked.

"And conscientious objectors," Leia said. "Potentially too valuable to the Empire to lose and too dangerous to let remain free and join the rebellion."

"That's why the Empire imprisoned them here," Luke said, "on a virtually uncharted planet. If they were dangerous felons, they'd be sent to a maximum security facility where the Empire could boast that they'd never escape. But these are people that the Empire wanted simply to disappear."

Leia studied the face of the old man, a kindly face. "How many like you are here?"

"Three thousand," the laundryman said. "But please, we can talk while you dress. Quickly! What are you doing here? Where will you need to go? Are you trying to take prisoners out?"

"We'll need free access to the compound for right now," Han said.

The laundryman sorted through stacks of clothing, pulled out two black robes for the women, guard uniforms for the men. But he stopped short when he heard someone approaching through the corridor. Two burly stormtroopers passed the open door, and everyone in the group stood still, tried to appear casual. The stormtroopers stopped, backed up and looked in the laundry room, fingering their rifles.

"Hey, you two!" Han shouted. "Get in here! On the double!"

"Are you talking to us?" one of the stormtroopers said, pointing to himself with his thumb.

"Yes, I am, soldier," Han said. "Now get in here!"

The stormtroopers glanced at each other, cautiously stepped into the room.

"I'm Sergeant Gruun," Han said, stepping forward, "external security! My people just infiltrated your prison here, right under your noses! In all my years in security, I've never seen such sloppy work. Tell me, who is your commanding officer?"

The stormtroopers looked at each other, pulled their blasters instantaneously. Han grabbed both blasters by the barrels, twisting them so that the shots fired into the ceiling. Isolder and Luke jumped the guards, bowling them over. Han threw the blasters to the floor, whimpering, "Oh, oh, hot!"

In close quarters, the stormtroopers' body armor hindered their movement, and in a few seconds Luke and Isolder pried their helmets off. A couple of well-placed blows quieted the guards. Leia gagged and tied them while Han and Isolder stripped off their armor, then dumped the bodies into a laundry bag. The old worker pushed them into a back room.

Luke, Han, and Isolder donned stormtrooper outfits. As

they dressed, the laundryman watched them but did not question them at all. Sometimes, Luke knew, it was better not to know the answers. If he were tortured later, the laundryman would not be able to reveal any vital information.

"Thanks," Han said, patting the laundryman on the shoulder when they finished. "We won't forget this. If we make it off this rock, we'll come back for you."

Luke watched the old prisoner, knew that he'd suffer for his part in this unless the guards were neutralized. "Wait!" Luke said, and he went to the sleeping guards, placed a hand on each of their heads, let the Force wash through them, submerging their memories of the brief struggle. When he finished, he was breathing heavily. "Dump the men in the tunnel under the grate. When they waken, they won't remember you being here. At least they won't remember for a few years."

The old man nodded solemnly, gazed at Luke. "I know what you are. I've seen men like you before. I remember the Jedi," he said, and he clasped Luke's shoulder. "Thank you."

"Thank you," Luke said, standing up. He swayed a little with fatigue under the weight of all his armor. Altering another's memory was a difficult task, and Luke worried that he might have overextended his powers for the day. It would have been easier to just kill the guards, but he could not allow that. He hoped he would not regret his decision as they made their way into the prison compound.

Chapter

20

O h dear," Threepio said point four seconds after he broke the Imperial code. He had hoped to engage Chewbacca in an extended conversation, describe exactly how he had reasoned out the more subtle nuances of the code, but realized that all of this would have to wait. "Zsinj has learned from monitoring radio broadcasts that General Solo is here on-planet," Threepio hastened to explain, "and Gethzerion has negotiated to sell Han to Zsinj's men. She says she found the skid marks showing where the sisters of the Singing Mountain clan towed the *Millennium Falcon,* so she anticipates that Han will come to the city looking for spare parts. She has set a trap for General Solo!"

Chewbacca growled, shaking his bowcaster in the air.

"We must warn them!" Threepio shouted, and Artoo emitted a burst of static, squealing his agreement.

A whistle blew over the prison's intercom, and in the plasteel corridors a jet black droid wheeled along, shining its artificial eyes to the right and left. It had a small hand blaster of the kind that could injure but not kill built into its helmet, and as it wheeled down the hallway, it shouted, "Count! Count! Count!" The inmates scattered, trying to stay out of the blaster's path, but the droid nailed two men who weren't fast enough to make it to their cells, and the hapless prisoners screamed in pain.

Han and Isolder followed it down the corridor, dressed in their stormtrooper attire. Leia and Teneniel followed close behind, disguised as witches. Luke followed last, slow with fatigue. Teneniel took his hand, urged him to walk close behind. Still, Luke stretched his senses to the maximum. They were getting closer to the witches' tower. He could feel them there, ahead. The prison corridors seemed strangely quiet, lacking guards. The prisoners had been locked in their cells for the night.

The guard droid let them pass without comment, and they walked through the empty halls, footsteps ringing against the plasteel. As they passed a side hallway that led between tiers of cells, Leia paused.

"Wait a minute . . ." she whispered, peering into the first cell. "I know that woman! She's from Alderaan! She served as senior weapons technologies adviser to my father."

"Keep moving," Luke said softly. "We can do nothing for her at the moment."

"But she's supposed to be dead!" Leia said. "Her ship was found crashed."

"Move along," Luke said softly.

They came to a sealed door with an electronic lock beside it. Through a window in the door they could see a second door. Han looked at the number pad for the electronic lock, pushed in a four-digit sequence at random. A red light flashed above the pad, indicating that he'd hit the wrong combination.

"Don't!" Luke said. "Let me see if I can get it." He walked to the pad, put his hand on it, closed his eyes in concentration. Dozens of guards used the pad daily. He could sense which four keys they pressed, but did not know the precise order. Hesitantly, he pressed the four numbers in the order he hoped would be correct. A green light flashed at the top of the pad, then the door swung open.

Luke pressed a button to open the next door. It led to a tiny elevator. When the others stepped into the tiny room, Teneniel stood staring at them a moment, frowning.

"Come on," Luke said. "It's an elevator. It will take us up to the walkway that leads to the tower." Teneniel blushed and hurried in.

When the elevator reached the top, the door opened into a glass causeway that spanned over the dark prison walls. The glass was so clear, so perfect, that Luke could see stars above him. Down outside the towers was a work yard, a few metal shacks, some Nightsisters walking under brilliant electric lights.

And a smothering sensation hit Luke. He could feel Night-sisters near, just ahead in the towers. Isolder and Han took the lead, headed over the causeway, but Teneniel stood rooted in terror.

"It's all right," Luke whispered. "Let the inner calm come to you. Draw your strength from the Force, let it wrap around you like a cloak. We have to get past them, if we're going to get to their shipyard. The Force can hide you from her."

At the far side of the causeway, a door opened. Four Night-sisters in black robes, their cowls down low, walked toward them. The one in the lead walked with stiff legs, slowly, hands clasped over her belly. Luke breathed deeply, slowly, and let the Force flow through him.

The others walked ahead, and Teneniel heaved her legs forward, woodenly. The Nightsisters passed in the narrow corridor, and one woman's black skirts slapped against Teneniel's. And then they were past.

The Nightsisters stopped, and Luke could feel Teneniel's fear, could feel how she wanted to run.

"Halt! You there!" a Nightsister shouted at their backs, her voice dry and crackling like rotted leather. As one the group stopped. The Nightsister demanded, "What were you doing so late at the prison?"

Han turned, answered through his helmet microphone. "Trouble in cell block C."

The Nightsister nodded her head thoughtfully, began to turn away, but looked back at them. "What trouble? Why wasn't I notified?"

"A minor scuffle between inmates," Han said. "We did not wish to disturb you."

The Nightsister pulled her hood back, and in the brilliant lights, Luke was struck with horror. Her white hair was unkempt and matted. Her bloodshot eyes were a vivid crimson. But most horrible was her face—a purplish monstrosity from ruptured blood vessels, gray and dead in the cheekbones.

"I feel your fear," the Nightsister said. "What would a Nightsister have to fear here—in our domain?"

"With so many guards gone, there are rumors of an impending riot," Han said, stepping forward, inserting himself between Teneniel and the Nightsisters. "I'm afraid there may be some truth to those rumors."

The Nightsister nodded thoughtfully. Luke could feel her trying to probe them, and he almost pulled his blaster. Instead, he channeled the Force, let it flow into the witch, quiet her suspicions. "I will pay a visit to block C. My presence should cow the rabble," she said. "Thank you for alerting me."

Han nodded, and the Nightsister turned, pulled up her hood and proceeded to the elevator.

Han led the way into the glass tower. He opened a door and marched them through some kind of common room.

A dozen Nightsisters dressed in black robes lounged on plush couches in a circle, engrossed in the spectacle of watching ghostly floating images of beautiful men and women. The Nightsisters sat snacking on exotic foods, and did not even seem to notice them pass.

Han led them to an elevator, and as the door closed, Teneniel nearly collapsed. "The Nightsister we passed," she said. "That was Gethzerion. I was sure she'd recognize me." She swallowed a deep breath.

Luke stood looking at the elevator door, and suddenly he felt as if he were very high in the air, looking down at Dathomir below, and all of it was black. All of it was frozen. Every bit of it. Everyone, everything was dead. He closed his eyes, tried to rest for a moment, thinking that perhaps his fatigue was affecting his vision, but the blackness remained, and a tremendous sense of despair and urgency filled him. He stared into the blackness, knowing it for what it was: A vision of the future.

"What?" Leia said, turning to Luke. "What is it?"

"We can't leave here," Luke said, the words feeling dry in his mouth. "We can't leave this world yet—not this way."

"What do you mean?" Isolder asked, and Han said, "Yeah, what do you mean? We've *got* to leave!"

"No," Luke said, staring away. He pulled off his helmet, gasped for breath. "No, we can't. Everything here is so wrong. There's so much darkness." He could *feel* the darkness coming, the cold, seeping into every fiber of his muscles.

"Look," Han said. "We're going to get some spare parts for the *Falcon*, then the whole bunch of us are going to fly our tails back to safety. As soon as we get back to Coruscant, we can send a fleet in, you can command a million troops—whatever it takes!"

"No," Luke said with certainty. "We can't go." He was frightened. But he had no plans. He couldn't go back up to the Nightsisters and attack them. They couldn't afford a confrontation now.

"Listen to Han," Isolder said. "These people have been trapped here for years! They don't need us to martyr ourselves for them tonight. They'll last until we can get back to rescue them."

A pale light of certainty seemed to flash through Luke, and the Jedi turned to Isolder, glanced quickly at all of them. "No, they can't. Watch, and you'll see. Believe me, the powers of darkness are gathering rapidly. Isolder, you said your fleet will be arriving in six days. But if we don't stop it before then, this planet will be destroyed!"

Han shook his head doubtfully. "Listen, kid," he said. "Don't go getting all crazy on me. I know you're under a lot of pressure. You've got a few problems now—and I really do sympathize—but if you keep talking like that and scaring these folks, I'm going to have to bust you in the chops."

Luke could feel Han's nervousness. He didn't want Luke upsetting the others. Perhaps rightfully so. The elevator jarred as it hit bottom, and Luke hit a keyplate. The doors hissed open, but Luke still had his back to the door. "Go ahead, Han," Luke said, gesturing at the immense storage chamber behind him without bothering to turn around. "Here is what you want."

Luke turned to see three dozen damaged ships—three nearly demolished Imperial lift-wing carriers, a dozen TIE fighters melted halfway down to slag, parts of broken hover cars. Han surveyed the damaged vehicles, and gasped. In the center of the junkyard, with footlights shining under them, sat a nearly completed TIE fighter and a stock light freighter that looked almost exactly like the *Millennium Falcon*. Most of the forward sensor forks were painted rust-orange, while the hull was a faded olive and the rear drives were an old space-pirate blue. Weld marks showed where parts of three ships had been cobbled together.

"They've almost got themselves a ship!" Han said, pulling off his helmet to get a better look. "It looks like all they need is a few more cells for the sublight drives."

"We couldn't be that lucky," Leia said.

"Hey, these old Corellian stock light freighters were some of the most popular in the galaxy in their day," Han said. "And you still can't find a ship that's more durable."

Isolder pulled off his helmet, took a deep breath of the fresh air. "More overweight and clunky, you mean."

"Same thing," Han said.

Han headed down a shallow ramp toward the ship, and Leia said, "Wait!"

Han stopped, and Leia studied the shipyard suspiciously. "These are pretty valuable pieces of equipment," she said. "They're here underground, lighted. Don't you think it's odd that they aren't guarded?"

"Who needs guards?" Han asked. "These ships won't fly. Besides, you saw the stormtroopers marching off. The place is a little understaffed tonight."

"What about alarms?" Luke asked. He picked up his macrobinoculars, scanned the room, adjusted the dials. "I don't see any laser alarms, but this place could be rigged with any-thing—motion detectors, magnetic field imagers—and in this junk pile, we wouldn't even know where to begin looking."

"So what do you want us to do," Han asked, "just stand here? We've got to check this ship out."

"Come on," Leia said, touching Luke's shoulder. "He's right."

Han and the group crept forward, scanning the ground, the surrounding junk piles. The Corellian freighter's hatch doors were closed, and Han stopped a moment, studying the access keypad. "If I were going to guard this ship, the place where I'd put the alarm is right here," Han said. "If someone punches in the wrong sequence, *bzzzt*. The alarm goes off."

"What's the right sequence?" Teneniel asked. Luke placed his hand over the keypad, but no one had touched it in a long time. He couldn't feel the sequence.

"I don't know," Han said, studying the characters. "Every captain has his or her own code. But of course the port authorities have overrides, depending on what systems you're registered in. Here are the licenses." He pointed out a column of characters. Some of the alien scripts were tiny, delicately curved. Others were in pictographs, while still others were blockish and bold with crude knife shapes, as if they'd been designed by some warrior race. "Whoever ran this ship did a lot of traveling in the Chokan, Viridia, and Zi'Dek systems. I used to know some of those port access codes back in the days of the Old Republic, but this character was running for the Imperials. They changed all of the codes. Damn, I wish I'd done more pirating."

Isolder stepped up to the ship, punched in the code fifteen-zero-three-eleven. The hatch swung down. "Chokan Imperial port authority code," Isolder said, smiling.

Han looked at him, astonished. "You worked the Chokan system? Even with that nasty plague?"

Isolder shrugged. "I knew a girl there."

"Must have been *some* girl," Leia said.

Han hurried up into the ship. "I'll go run diagnostics and make sure these parts are worth stealing. Isolder, you and Leia find some wrenches and get the sensor array window off, then go down in the hold and start pulling the AC generators off their mounts. Luke, run get a couple of barrels so we can drain the coolant."

As the others went inside, Luke stood with Teneniel a second, patted her on the shoulder, his face tense. "This is going to take some time," Luke said. "Keep your eyes open."

Leia and Isolder got some tools out of the ship, and pulled off the sensory array window. Luke went to a far wall where huge metal containers were stored, rolled a barrel across the room. Teneniel whispered some spells to sharpen her senses, but found that it did no good. Somehow, subconsciously, she had already tapped into the Force. With her heightened senses, she could hear every thudding movement and clank of tool, Han's excited delight from the cockpit as he whispered, "Jackpot!" the echoing *pings* as Luke rolled the barrel over the floor, crunching bits of sand and dirt. Luke went inside the freighter, grunting as he worked a hand pump to transfer the coolant to the barrel. Leia and Isolder carried their window inside and fired up some torches to cut through frozen bolts. The flames hissed and squealed as they cut through the metal.

Teneniel walked away from the ship so that she could hear better, wished she had a blaster rifle if only to make her feel more comfortable, better armed. There were so many scrapped spaceships in the room that she felt as if she were in a rocky cave. She really couldn't see much from the floor.

She decided to climb up the side of a transport that was more molten slag than it was ship. She went to it, looked for a handhold. The tang of oxidizing metal bit into her nostrils. She found a knobby lump, grabbed it and began pulling herself up, but could have sworn she heard the swishing of skirts, a mumbled word.

She glanced around the room, lit only by the footlights at the base of the two partly repaired ships. There were a lot of deep shadows. The high ceilings mildly echoed the thumps of Han and the others as they worked. Teneniel quickly and quietly hurried to the top of the ship, sat looking over the junkyard. From here she could see everything—the storage area, the elevators, a door that opened to a stairway on the south wall. At the far north end of the room a rectangular opening led outside. The opening was silvered by moonlight. The darkness, the creepy feel of the place, the muted echoes, the mouth leading outside. All of it came crushing in on Teneniel. It was so much like the warriors' hall she'd entered as a child when her mother died.

She felt that same suffocation here, the same yawning emptiness. She looked off into the shadows at a far corner of the room—thought she glimpsed movement, dark shapes running in the shadows. She stared at the place but could see nothing.

She began chanting softly, a spell of detection, and a bolt of cold fear pierced her. She could *feel* them there—in the darkness, closing in with deadly intent.

Teneniel scanned the room, searching vainly. Something was wrong with her sight. She could feel a cool pressure over her eyes, a stuffiness in her ears, and she tried wiping it away with her hands.

Suddenly her vision cleared. Baritha stood at the foot of her pile of rubble, with three other Nightsisters at her side. One of the women chanted softly, and she held her thumb and forefinger out, pinching them together.

Invisible fingers seized Teneniel's throat, choking her.

"Welcome, Sister Teneniel," Baritha said. "So, we set a trap, and look who has fallen into it! What happened, did you finally tire of hiding in the mountains?"

Teneniel gasped for breath, found herself struggling. Her ears thudded and rang; her lungs burned. She tried to sing a counterspell, but could get no air.

"Too bad I cannot let you live another moment," Baritha said. "I'm sure that Gethzerion would have enjoyed tormenting you!"

She gave a hand signal, and the Nightsister at her side sang louder. She balled her purpled hand into a fist. Teneniel felt her windpipe wrench terribly, and Luke's words rang through her ears. "Let the Force flow through you."

There were no spells she could sing, no chants, not even a funeral dirge. The Nightsisters thought her powerless. Teneniel tried to calm herself, let the Force flow through her, open her throat. The pile of slag on which she stood seemed to twist and buck beneath her like a frightened rancor, and Teneniel dropped to her hands and knees. The Force was not there, nowhere to be found. Her heart pounded wildly with terror, and with all her will she tried to shriek for help before she died.

The world twisted, and she dropped into the dark void, swallowed by blackness like her mother before her.

Luke heard Teneniel's scream in his mind, shouted for Han, and ran down the gangplank.

He saw the Nightsisters huddled in their robes a hundred meters from the ship, Teneniel lying in a heap on the carrier above them. "Stop!" Luke shouted. "Let her go!"

He let the Force surge through him, opened Teneniel's trachea. The girl gasped for breath.

"What?" Baritha asked. "A puny little *man* seeks to command us?" The witches turned toward him.

"Leave this place!" Luke said. "I warn you: Tell Gethzerion to take the Nightsisters away and set your slaves free!"

"Or what, offworlder?" Baritha said. "Or you'll bleed all over us when we pop your head open? Has your stay on our world been so short that you don't know what we are?"

"I know what you are," Luke said. "I've battled your kind on other worlds."

One of the Nightsisters grabbed Baritha's arm, a warning gesture. Behind Baritha, two of the Nightsisters began to sing softly in harmony, and their images faded. Luke let the Force flow through him, realized they were trying to alter his perceptions.

"You cannot hide yourselves from me," Luke said. "No matter where you run, I would hunt you down. Your only chance to live is to leave now, peaceably."

"You lie!" Baritha shouted, throwing back her hood. At the top of her voice she began yelling her spell, *"Artha, artha!"*

Luke pulled his blaster and fired. Baritha cut short her spell. She reached out with a gesture and slapped the blaster bolt away.

"You are no spellcaster!" Baritha shouted, and one of the Nightsisters rushed toward him. Luke pulled out his lightsaber, flipped it on and threw it, so that it tumbled end over end. The Nightsister grabbed for the handle, and Luke used the Force to twist the lightsaber in mid-air, killing the hag. He called the lightsaber back to his hand.

Baritha and the Nightsisters drew back a pace. One of the women shouted, "Gethzerion, sisters—come to us!" And Luke knew that she was summoning reinforcements.

Teneniel lurched from the top of the wreck, took a flying leap toward Luke.

"No!" Baritha shouted, and she began chanting her spell

again. A solar panel broke free from a TIE fighter, went spinning toward Teneniel, caught her in the back and knocked her to her belly. She slid next to Luke's feet, but rose to her knees. Baritha chanted her spell and another solar panel flew across the room.

Teneniel ducked beneath it and glared at the old woman. "You really don't want to try this with *me!*" Teneniel warned viciously. Behind them, the engines to the freighter roared to life, and Luke had to question the sanity of trying to fly the thing with over half its sublight drive cells missing while overhead the Star Destroyers were poised to blow any outgoing craft from the sky. But at the moment, he really didn't feel like arguing.

A sensor array broke free from the TIE fighter, went swirling toward Teneniel. Luke shouted, "Come on!"

But the girl stood her ground, began singing a counterattack. The computer array twisted in the air, hurtled toward the Nightsisters. Baritha jumped aside to dodge hardware, but one Nightsister got hit and went flying to the ground.

"Damn you, Gethzerion!" Teneniel shouted to the air. "I'm sick of the way you hunt us. I'm sick of trying to stay out of your path! I'm sick of the way you hurt and kill. I'm sick—" Luke looked at Teneniel's face, realized that she was enraged, mad beyond reason. He could feel the force of her wrath. Her face was red and tears streamed from her eyes. Teneniel began muttering her song, and a hurricane blew through the room. A TIE fighter flipped over under the force of the onslaught, tumbled toward the Nightsisters. The witches ducked and raised their hands, gesturing a warding spell.

"No! Don't give in to anger!" Luke shouted, grabbing Teneniel's shoulder. "That's not Gethzerion! That's not her!"

Teneniel turned, looked in his face, gasping for breath, and suddenly seemed to realize where she was. Han fired the freighter's forward blasters into a heap of slag, throwing shrapnel and creating a cloud of smoke and ionized gases that blew toward the Nightsisters like a storm.

Luke grabbed Teneniel's hand, pulled her up the gangplank and hit the close switch, rushed to the cockpit. Han was there alone. Luke could not hear the witches singing any longer, but through the viewscreen he saw them, fists outstretched in a gripping gesture. Han slowly pulled the thruster stick, trying to raise the ship.

"Man, these drives are in worse shape than I thought," he said doubtfully. "I don't think this bucket can even lift off."

At the far side of the room, figures in black robes flowed from a doorway. Luke said, "Get us out of here—now!"

Han struggled to lift the stick. "This throttle is stuck!" he shouted, grasping it with both hands. Luke looked at the witches with their gripping gesture, channeled the Force through him, then reached down and pulled the throttle up easily. The ship rattled and rose, and Luke spun it around, threw the sublights on full power as they surged toward the portal on the far side of the building.

The witches behind were caught in the flash of tailfire as the thrusters ignited. The ship burst out of the building, and the freighter shuddered and rolled to the sound of blaster fire.

"Don't worry," Han said. "It's just the sentries on the prison towers. The shields can hold them." Han took the throttle, and they rumbled over the plains. The freighter was sluggish, definitely sluggish.

Han shouted over the intercom. "Hey, Your Highnesses, have you about got those generators loose?"

"Negative," Isolder said over the intercom. "Give us a few more minutes."

"Might I remind you that this is an interdicted planet?" Han said. "And we have a sky full of Imperial destroyers above us who are no doubt arming missiles at this very moment in hopes of blasting us to pieces."

"Affirmative," Isolder said. "We're working on it!"

"I don't want you to work on it," Han said. "I want you to get those generators out of there—now!"

"I'll go help," Luke said, and he hurried down the corridor. Teneniel was still standing by the hatch, looking at the door. Her face was pale. She glanced away guiltily.

"I'm sorry," she told Luke. "I won't let it happen again."

Luke nodded, crawled down into the hold, up into a snug corner of the right sensor array fork. Isolder had already unbolted two generators from the mounts, and he had a huge wrench and tried vainly to loosen another bolt. Leia was pulling on the generators, trying to squeeze them past Isolder's body.

"Pull those generators out of the way if you can," Luke urged Isolder, firing up his lightsaber. "Leia, get up there and cap the coolant." Luke slashed the heads off the remaining six bolts, then gave the last two generators a good kick. Both of them tumbled off the mounts. He and Isolder dragged the generators up to the main deck. They worked desperately to wrestle them onto the hatch gate, and just as they got the last one up, Leia finished capping the barrels of coolant. They dragged all the coolant to the hatch at once.

"Evacuate ship!" Han called over the intercom.

He had hardly said the words when he ran out from the cockpit. "We'll be flying over a lake in about thirty seconds. I saw it on my screens!"

Han hit the open latch on the hatch, and as the entry ramp dropped away, the coolant and generators went spilling out. Luke was surprised to see that they were only traveling five meters above ground at perhaps sixty kilometers per hour.

A blast rocked the ship, and Han looked up. "Those Star Destroyers know we're here. Let's hope the shields can hold for thirty seconds."

A sudden barrage sent the ship bouncing, and Isolder grabbed the sensory array window and slipped down the ramp. He caught himself halfway, dropped the window, tried crawling back. A second barrage rocked the ship, sent him sliding farther.

Leia screamed, grabbed his hand. Moon-silvered water flashed beneath them, and Luke grabbed Teneniel's hand and pulled her from the ship. All five of them dropped together.

Luke plunged into the water, and his feet hit mud. He bobbed back up to the surface, looked around desperately for the others. Teneniel came up beside him, Han and Leia twenty yards away. Beyond them, Isolder floated up on his back.

Leia swam for Isolder. Luke looked out at the ship, flying over the lake. After several more missile hits, the shields died, and the ship exploded in a green fireball that mushroomed up into the night.

Luke swam to Leia and Isolder, found Isolder's face

muddy. He'd hit the shallows and was coughing dirty water. "He's lucky he didn't snap his neck," Leia said.

Luke touched him, felt life still strong in him. "He'll be all right."

They walked a hundred yards through the shallows, lay down on the beach. Luke could feel a tremor in the Force, like a thin probing finger of thought, Gethzerion stretching out with her mind, trying to find them. They were less than ten kilometers from the city, in fairly clear view, and the Nightsisters had surely seen the ship blow up, but Gethzerion was using the Force to search for survivors. Luke cleared his mind, let Gethzerion's touch wander past him. He looked at Teneniel, saw her struggling for control. She suddenly relaxed, and Luke felt that the danger was over, at least temporarily. The probing touch moved out farther over the lake.

"Well," Leia panted. "That wasn't so hard!"

"Yeah," Isolder agreed, still coughing. "Maybe we should go back, try it again."

"We need to hurry and get out of here," Luke said. "Gethzerion will be sending stormtroopers to look for survivors and see if she can salvage the wreck. I don't want them to find anything but our tracks."

Luke's words seemed to sober the entire group. Luke tried to catch his breath.

"Luke, let me see your macrobinoculars," Han said. Luke reached down to his waterproof pouch, pulled out the macrobinoculars. Han lay panting, looking up into the sky.

"What? What's up there?" Isolder asked.

"I don't know," Han said. "I saw it as we flew out. Something funny on the sensors."

"What?" Leia asked.

"Satellites," Han said, "Zsinj's men have released thousands of satellites overhead."

"Like what?" Isolder asked. "Orbital mines?"

"Maybe," Han said. "Probably. Whatever they are, there's a lot of them."

Leia looked up at the sky, searching among the stars. "I don't know," she said. "I've got a bad feeling about this." Luke followed her gaze. He could see the satellites, thousands of dim stars, as if the number of stars in the sky had doubled within the past few hours. He thought back, realized that the satellites must have been released near the same time he had his vision in the elevator. He closed his eyes, saw the vision again—eternal night.

Chapter

21

A pale pink sun was just rising under clear skies and Luke was struggling to patch a breached container of coolant when the rancors came loping across the flats. The group had been working for less than fifteen minutes, and Luke sensed that they needed to leave soon. Gethzerion's stormtroopers would be here in another half hour.

Chewbacca bellowed in greeting, and Threepio shouted, "Oh, thank goodness we found you!" He turned to Chewie and Artoo. "See, I told you they would be all right. His Highness King Solo would never allow himself to get blown up!" His head swiveled back around. "So, what are you doing out here?"

"We had to bail out of the ship before it got shot down," Luke said. "But we broke open a canister of coolant. I put some steel tape on it, but I'm waiting for the adhesive to dry. We're glad you showed up."

"I'm the one who found you," Threepio bragged. "Thanks to my superior AA-one Verbobrain, I was able to crack that Imperial code!" Artoo squealed derisively, and Threepio added, "With Artoo's help, of course. We were just on the way to the city to warn you!"

Han grunted, sat down on the barrel. "Warn us of what, Mr. Verbobrain?"

"Gethzerion!" Threepio said. "She planned to set some kind of trap for you!"

"Yeah, we sort of figured that out on our own," Han said, "when she sprung it."

"But there's more," Threepio said. "Show them the latest message, Artoo."

Artoo squealed, leaned forward on the rancor and focused his holo cams. Two images appeared on the mud flats standing side by side: Gethzerion and a young officer wearing the slate gray uniform that identified him as one of Zsinj's generals.

Gethzerion said, "General Melvar, you may inform Zsinj that we have captured General Han Solo, and we of the sister-hood await the shuttle he promised in trade." The old witch stood silently, hands folded over her stomach. General Melvar calmly regarded her with a thrill-killer's glimmering eyes, scratched his jaw with a platinum fingernail shaped like a claw. Such cuticle implants were costly and painful, and those who wore them often cut themselves accidentally. General Melvar had the thin white facial scars to prove it.

"Warlord Zsinj has reconsidered his offer," Melvar smiled coldly. "He wishes to express his sorrow at having had to bomb the ship that left your compound, but now that Solo's *Millennium Falcon* has been destroyed, matters have changed. It was Solo's ship that we destroyed?"

Gethzerion nodded. Her eyes were half-closed, secretive.

"Who was on it?" Melvar asked, his voice threatening.

"Stormtroopers," Gethzerion lied. "They saw that we were repairing the ship and tried to fly it before the repairs were completed. If you had not killed them, I would have."

"I suspected as much," Melvar smiled triumphantly. "Although I must admit that I had rather hoped *you* were aboard." He took a deep breath. "So, you have General Solo, and you wish for a shuttle."

Gethzerion nodded stiffly, her dark hood hiding her eyes.

"You realize that now that Solo's ship has been annihilated," Melvar said, "your bargaining position has weakened. Therefore, Warlord Zsinj wishes to make a counterproposal to your ratty band."

"As I fully expected," Gethzerion answered. At this, the general averted his eyes, tried to hide his annoyance at being anticipated. She continued, "After all, it is well known even on our remote world that Warlord Zsinj never keeps his word when doing so might inconvenience him. I rather expected that he might scoff at releasing the Nightsisters from Dathomir. So tell me, what lesser bauble does he offer?"

"Warlord Zsinj offers to retrieve General Solo from your sisterhood in thirty-six hours. He will be coming personally to collect the general. In return he will refrain from destroying your planet."

"So, he offers us nothing?" Gethzerion asked.

"He offers you your lives," Melvar grinned. "You should be grateful to receive even that."

"You do not understand the Nightsisters," Gethzerion scoffed. "We don't value our own lives. So you see, he offers us nothing of value."

"Nevertheless," Melvar said, "we demand that you release Han Solo to us at once. Extinction is such a permanent condition. Take a few moments to decide."

"And you may tell Zsinj that we of the Nightsisters have an offer of our own: tell Zsinj that in return for our release from this world, our sisterhood will serve him."

Melvar's eyes brightened with interest. "How can he be sure of your devotion?"

"We will bring him our daughters and our granddaughters —all our females under the age of ten. He may keep them where he will, as his hostages. If we displease him, he may kill our children."

"Only a moment ago you admitted that life held no value for you," Melvar argued. "If this is true, then wouldn't it be reasonable to assume that you would sacrifice your own children to gain your freedom?"

Gethzerion's voice grew rough with emotion. She said softly, "No mother could be so evil. Tell Zsinj to consider our offer, as we must consider his."

The holograms flickered off, and Han stood up, looked around. "So," Han said, "what do you think Zsinj has planned? Aerial bombardments, what?"

Leia refrained from answering. "He said he'd destroy the

planet—not just the Nightsisters or their city." She breathed deeply. "Could he be working on something big?"

"Like another Death Star?" Luke asked. "I don't think so."

"I don't know about this," Han said. "Gethzerion's playing Zsinj for a sucker—telling him that she's taken me hostage, destroyed my ship. Obviously, she'll do just about anything to get off this rock."

"And Zsinj sounds like he's willing to do just about anything to get you," Leia said.

"Yeah," Han agreed. "The really scary thing is, that if we could just introduce Gethzerion and Zsinj, they have so many personality traits in common that I think they'd really hit it off."

Leia looked at Han, frowning in concentration. "I don't get it. Zsinj sure seems to want you bad, Han. Coming here personally? He's going to an awful lot of trouble to extort the Nightsisters. What has he got against you?"

Han scratched his jaw uncomfortably. From atop the rancor, Chewbacca roared, encouraging Han to continue. Somehow Luke knew it would be bad.

"Well, you know after I destroyed his Super Star Destroyer, I sort of—well, called him personally on holo vid, and, uh, gloated."

"*Gloated?*" Leia asked. "What do you mean, gloated?"

"I, uh, don't remember the exact words, but I personally took credit for blowing up his ship and said something like, 'Kiss my Wookiee!' "

Chewbacca broke into deep laughter and nodded vigorously.

"Let me get this straight," Isolder asked. "You said 'Kiss my Wookiee!' to the most powerful warlord in the galaxy?"

"All right! All right!" Han said, sitting down on the generator. "I'm sorry! You don't have to rub it in. I admit that I screwed up! I, I just did it in the heat of the moment."

Isolder slapped Han's back. "Ah, my friend, you're even dumber than I thought—heck, maybe you're dumber than anybody thought—but I wish I'd been there!" Luke felt rather surprised at the way Isolder had called Han his "friend."

"Yeah," Leia said. "Me, too. You could have sold tickets to that."

Han looked up into Isolder's eyes. "Really? Oh, you should

have seen the look on Zsinj's face—you know, he's got little fat red cheeks, and the spittle was dripping out of his mouth, nose hairs twitching! It was great! Do you know he really is a genius? He can curse fluently in nearly sixty languages. Now I have heard some obscenities in my time, but this man has a special talent."

"Oh yeah," Isolder smiled. "You know he's going to put your head on a platter, don't you? And considering Zsinj's reputation, he might even eat it."

"Yeah, well," Han said, "it keeps life interesting."

"We can worry about Zsinj later," Luke said. "Right now, we had better get these parts back to the *Falcon*. Let's not get caught out here in the open. When Gethzerion finds out that we made it off the ship alive, she'll be right on our tails." Luke looked at the barrel of coolant, feeling uncomfortable. Even with the patch, they'd lost half the barrel, and he knew that they needed every drop to make a safe jump.

Leia patted Luke's back reassuringly. "We'll have to make do."

He nodded, agreeing only because that was all he could do. They had the rancors quickly load the generators and barrels of coolant into sacks woven from whuffa hide, and then the rancors slung them on their backs. The monsters didn't even seem to notice the load, and in ten minutes they made it off the mud flats and into the shelter of the foothills.

After a day and a night without sleep, the whole party was exhausted, but the rancors were rested, so they rode until near sunset, then made camp. Yet Luke could not rest. He walked off into the forest and paced. It was early evening. He stood on a hill looking out over the plains, and when he blinked his eyes the plains seemed dark, frozen, void of life. *Eternal night*, a voice whispered in him. *Eternal night is coming.* He wondered if the visions were symbolic, a representation of his own impending death.

He stretched out his senses, felt the stirrings in the Force. Already, the army of Nightsisters was over halfway to the clan at Singing Mountain. Gethzerion had her landspeeder, and a trip that took three days for her army would take her only an hour. She and the rest of her clan could spend those three days laying strategy.

Often, Luke had found that in the past he could imagine a battle as it might go, rehearse it in his mind. When he did so, the Force would guide him, give him insights he might not otherwise have had. But this time it was different. His skirmish beneath the towers had taught him little about the Nightsisters' capabilities. He wished that Yoda or Ben would appear to counsel him, yet the only image that came to his mind was Yoda on the holo tape, *Repulsed by the witches.*

Yoda had been a greater Jedi Master than Luke ever hoped to be, yet the witches had withstood him and others like him. Luke felt unsure of his power. The Force. Where did it really come from? Yoda had said that life created it, that it was energy. But could Luke use it in good conscience? If he was drawing energy from other living things, sucking them as if he were some leech bleeding them dry, how could he really justify what he did?

And there was a further matter. In his battles with Darth Vader and the Emperor, Luke felt he had never truly tested his powers to the limits. Vader had sought only to turn him, had kept Luke alive. Yet Luke had no illusions that Gethzerion would be so lenient.

"What's going on here, Ben?" Luke whispered, staring back into the deep green jungle. The dying sunlight flashed on the leaves. "Is this some kind of test, or what? Are you trying to find out if I'm ready to stand alone? Do you think I don't need your help? What's going on here?"

Yet Ben did not answer. An evening breeze rustled through the tops of the trees so that leaf shadows danced over the ground. Luke looked up at the setting sun, found himself surprised. The forest carried the scent of leaf mold and some type of fruit in the upper branches of the trees. The evening was warm and perfect, the sun shining on him. Overhead, oblivious to the Nightsisters or Zsinj, lizards jumped among the upper foliage of the forest. In spite of everything, Luke realized, Dathomir really was a beautiful world. If the map in Augwynne's war room was correct, humans seemed to have explored perhaps only one-hundredth of the livable surface of the planet. And for most of the creatures here, and on millions of planets elsewhere in the galaxy, Gethzerion's schemes mattered less than the scattering of a handful of sand in the desert.

.   .   .

As Luke wandered into the forest, Isolder sat and listened to Han talking to his droid. Leia soon fell asleep, but Isolder woke a bit later, noticed Teneniel sitting by the fire, outside the circle of light, watching the stars. He went and sat by her.

"Sometimes at night when I'm out in the desert," Teneniel said softly, "and there are no clouds, no trees to obstruct my view, I lie awake at night and look at the stars, wondering who lives there, what the people are like."

Isolder studied the points of light above them. In his pirating days he had worked this part of the galaxy, and he had a gift for astrogation. By noting a couple of major stars, he was able to picture where he was in space. "I've often done the same," he said. "Except that between my history books and lessons in diplomacy and a little travel, I've learned a great deal. Pick a star," he waved at the stars. "I'll tell you about it."

"That one," Teneniel said, pointing at the brightest one on the horizon.

"That's not a star," Isolder said. "That's just a planet."

"I know," Teneniel smiled at him, "but I had to test you. All right, there are six stars up there right next to each other that form a circle," she said, pointing directly above them. "The brightest one is blue. Tell me about it."

Isolder studied the star a moment. "That's the Cedre system, and it's only about three light-years from here. There is no life around that star, for it's too young, too hot. Pick another star—a yellow one, or an orange."

"What about the dim star to its left? That one?"

Isolder considered. "That one is really two stars, a double system called Fere, or Feree, and it's pretty far away. Two hundred years ago, the people there had a very great culture, and they built some of the better starships in the galaxy—small luxury cruisers. I have an uncle who collects antique starships, and he has a restored Fere."

"Don't they build ships anymore?"

"No, during some wars a lot of people were moving around, checking out new worlds to hide on. Someone accidentally carried a plague to Fere and wiped out the planet. Still, if you had a powerful enough telescope, you could view the people there as they once were. The Fere were very tall, with soft skin a rich ivory, and six delicate fingers on each hand."

"How could I see them, if they are all dead?" Teneniel asked, disbelieving.

"Because with a telescope, you would be seeing light that reflected off their world hundreds of years ago. Since the light is just reaching us, you would be looking into their past."

"Oh," Teneniel said. "Do you have such a telescope?"

"No," Isolder laughed. "We don't make them that well."

"What about the dim star beneath it?" Teneniel asked.

"That's Orelon, and I know that star very well," Isolder said. "It's big, and it's bright, and from here it is the only visible star from my home cluster, Hapes. There are really sixty-three stars very close to each other in that cluster, and my mother rules over them."

Teneniel remained quiet for a long time, thoughtful. "Your mother rules sixty-three stars?" she asked, her voice shaking.

"Yes," Isolder said.

"Does she have soldiers? Warriors and starships?"

"Billions of warriors, thousands of starships," Isolder said. She drew a deep breath, and Isolder realized that his answer must have frightened her.

"Why did you never tell me this?" she asked. "I did not know I had captured the son of such a powerful woman."

"I told you that my mother was a queen, and you knew that when I chose a wife, she would be queen."

"But—I thought she was the queen of a clan village," Teneniel gasped. She lay back on the grass and held her hands up to her head for a moment, as if dizzy. Isolder decided to give her time, let her become accustomed to life on his grand terms. "So," Teneniel said thoughtfully, "when you leave Dathomir, if I look up at that star, I will know where you are?"

"Yes," Isolder said.

"And when you are on your home world, will you ever look up in the sky at night and see my sun, and think about me?" Her voice was choked, desolate.

"From Hapes, we cannot see your sun. It's too dim. Hapes has seven moons, and they drown out the light from stars this dim," Isolder said, wondering at her tone of voice.

He turned to the side, studied Teneniel's face in the starlight. As with most Hapans, his night vision was poor; the light of seven moons and a brilliant sun made night vision unnecessary, so over the millennia his people had gradually lost the ability to see well in the dark. Still, he could make out her silhouette, the tight lines of her face, the curve of her breast. "I don't understand you," Isolder said. "What do you think I am to you? You say that I am your slave. You say that your people kidnap men to be husbands, and the fact that you own me gives you some kind of status in your clan, if I understand correctly."

"I would never force you to do anything against your will," Teneniel said. "I . . . I couldn't. As I have said, if some other woman captured you, perhaps you would not be so lucky." Isolder recalled Teneniel's enigmatic smile as she had first approached him, shyly walking around him, singing softly, yet watching him intently, copper eyes never flicking away. He had smiled in return, thinking only to be cordial, and then as he reached out to take the cord she offered, it had entangled him. Now he understood. She had given him every opportunity to escape, and he had let her catch him.

As far as mating rituals went, this one was not particularly complex, but the players on both sides had to understand the rules.

"I see," Isolder sighed. "What if you and I did not like each other? What if the marriage didn't work? Then what would you do?"

"Then I could sell you. If you preferred another woman, then an honorable master would try to sell you to her, setting whatever price seemed reasonable given the purchaser's wealth and circumstances. Or, if there was no one you liked in our clan, you could arrange to be captured by someone outside the clan—or you could run away up into the mountains, to let me know you were not satisfied, and if I thought it could still work out, I would hunt you down again. There are many things you could do."

Isolder considered. Though it sounded barbaric on the surface, the witches' way of mating sounded no less onerous than most other systems. As on his own world, the women dominated, but the men here had recourse. He tried to imagine this world as it had been for thousands of years—small human bands battling the rancors without weapons. Given such an alternative, marrying a witch, gaining her protection even if only to become a slave, would have been a great boon.

And now Teneniel was giving him his freedom. She would let him run away, try to make it off this planet, and she wanted only one thing in return: to be remembered, to be thought of fondly.

Given the grasping nature of his aunts, the avarice of his mother, he wondered how many women on his own world would have been so generous, so understanding. She had a beauty to her that he had seldom seen matched.

Isolder got up on his elbows, crouched over Teneniel, and kissed her softly on the cheek, knowing that he was kissing her good-bye. He found that her face was wet. She'd been crying. "If I ever make it back to Hapes," he said, "I'll remember you. I know where you are, and sometimes I will look toward Dathomir, and I'll wonder if you are looking across the heavens at me."

An hour later, Luke woke the others, and they mounted the rancors and rode hard, driving the rancors mercilessly through the forests, over mountains and through deep canyons. Late in the night, they halted again deep in the woods just fourteen kilometers from Singing Mountain. The rancors were too exhausted to move any farther. Luke could feel a sense of urgency, wanted to hurry, but the rancors were too tired and the whole camp was exhausted.

"We'll rest here for a bit," Luke said, and as one the group sloughed off their mounts, and lay on the ground with blankets. Both of the droids had already powered down for the night.

Luke ate some meager rations in near silence without a fire, and the rancors stood heaving from exhaustion in the shadows, sleepy-eyed. They weren't recovering well from their exertions, so Teneniel filled a water skin, and as the others in the party slept, the monsters bowed down to her and let her sponge their faces with a wet rag. Luke wondered at their behavior, then realized that since the rancors had no sweat glands, the rigors of the trip left them suffering from the heat. He went to Teneniel.

"Here," he said. "Use the Force to help them. It can cool their bodies." He touched the first rancor, let the Force wash over the creature. It sighed contentedly, touched him with a great muddy claw, as if to pet him.

Teneniel shook her head in frustration. "I still don't see how you do it," she said. "It seems to me that it would be so much easier with a spell."

"If saying some words helps you concentrate," Luke said, "then I don't see that it would do any harm. But the Force cannot be bound by words, encapsulated in words."

"I'm sorry—for what I did back at the prison," Teneniel said. "I almost killed them. I . . . suddenly, when I was angry, it seemed that nothing you had said made sense. I only wanted to kill them, put an end to their evil, yet your *rules* prevented me."

"They wanted you to try to kill them. They wanted you to give in to hate."

"I know," Teneniel said, "but in that moment, I couldn't see how the light side of the Force was stronger than the dark."

"I've never said it was stronger," Luke answered. "If it is power that you want, it may be that both sides serve equally well. But look at the Nightsisters—look at what the dark side offers: fear instead of love, aggression instead of peace, dominion in place of service, and instead of contentment, consuming appetite.

"If you crave easy power, then the dark side of the Force offers what you desire—at the expense of all else that you value."

Luke touched each of the rancors in turn, cooling them. Teneniel put her arms around Luke's chest, hugged him from behind, her cheek nuzzling his shoulder.

"And what if I crave love more than anything else?" Teneniel asked. "Will the light side of the Force lead me to it?"

It was hard not to understand her question, but Luke was tempted to feign confusion. Luke found her attractive, but to profess love . . . would be misleading. "I don't know," Luke said honestly. "I believe it could."

"Before you came," Teneniel said, "I saw you and Isolder in a vision. I'd been lonely for so long, living in the wilderness, and I only wanted to find a husband, rejoin my clan. For many days I worked at casting the seer's spells, and then I saw you in my dreams. I think perhaps you are my destiny."

Luke took her clasped hands in his, held them. "I don't believe in destiny. I think we forge our own path in life through the choices we make. Look, I have something I have to say, but I haven't said it because I don't want to hurt you: I feel like we hardly know each other. I think, that we need to just calm down."

"You mean *I* need to calm down," Teneniel whispered. "Among my people we choose our husbands quickly, often in the flashing of an eye. When I saw you, I knew in a moment that I wanted you. I haven't changed my mind. But you act as if love must come tentatively."

"I'm not sure it comes tentatively," Luke said. "It's just that sometimes it grows, but usually it dies a quick death."

"So?" Teneniel said. "If our love dies a quick death, what have we lost?"

"I can't do that," Luke answered. "Love is more than a mere curiosity or a momentary excitement. I don't think that two people can know it's real until they've spent time together, until they have a history together. But I have a duty to fulfill. I'm going to finish my Jedi training, and after I leave this planet, the truth is that I'll probably never see you again. You and I won't ever have much of a history."

Luke wanted to say more, wanted to tell her that someday he hoped to meet a girl like her, but over in the deeper shadows under the trees, Han stirred in his sleep, raised a hand in the air, and said loudly, "No! No!" Then he pulled a hide to cover his head and rolled over.

Luke thought it strange. He'd never seen Han talk in his sleep before. Then Luke felt it, a disturbance in the Force, as if something invisible had moved under the canopy of the trees with them. He could feel it floating nearby, and wondered if some kind of animal lurked in the shadows. He turned to look up, and a pressure encircled his head, as if a dark helmet had been placed upon it. A chill ran down his spine, and he fought to remain calm, invisible. He recognized that it was some sort of probe.

"What's going on? What is it?" Teneniel asked, and Luke

waved his hand, gestured for her to remain silent. He held still for several minutes, fighting for control, drawing upon the Force. Then the feeling faded.

Teneniel gasped, as if she'd suddenly been struck by cold water. She tried to cover her head with her hands, then looked up at the night sky and laughed. "Gethzerion, you'll never learn anything of value from me!"

Gethzerion's brittle voice rang through Luke's ears, filling the woods, coming from everywhere and nowhere. "But I already have," Gethzerion said. "I've learned that Han Solo is alive, and that he dreams with hope of repairing his ship. I must confess, I am glad he was able to salvage his precious generators. Believe me, I want as much as you do for him to get that ship running smoothly."

Luke reached out with the Force, tried to touch Gethzerion's mind. He saw a brief image of Imperial walkers marching in the darkness, and then Gethzerion recoiled, hiding herself.

"Get the saddles back on the rancors," Luke said, feeling grateful that he had been able to heal the beasts of their discomfort, even if only for a few moments. "We've got to leave now. Gethzerion has been marching her troops through the night so that she can attack your clan at dawn."

Chapter

22

The group hurried to mount their rancors for one last ride. Something subtle had changed during the night. Teneniel and Isolder rode together, as did Han and Leia. Luke rode with Artoo, and realized that his talk with Teneniel had sobered the woman somewhat. She'd given up on him, and in a sense, he felt relieved.

As the rancors raced toward the clan stronghold at Singing Mountain, plunging through the jungle at breakneck speed, their macabre chain mail rattled and clacked, making the only sound to disturb the night. No reptiles leaped through the branches or croaked in dismay at the sound of their approach. No birds flapped from their limbs. Instead, it seemed almost as if the animals of the jungle had died, dropping silently from the vines, they were so quiet.

They ran the rancors for another hour, climbed over a chain of hills, and stopped, gasping, to look into the bowl-shaped valley where Singing Mountain lay five kilometers off. Overhead the sky was a dull red, firelight reflecting from smoke-filled skies. The Nightsisters had set fire to the jungle on the surrounding hills, so that the mountain looked as if it sat in a tureen of smoldering embers. Very clearly, Luke heard Augwynne's voice call in his mind, "Luke, Teneniel, come quickly!"

And Luke shouted in return, "We're on our way!" He urged the rancors to run faster so that dirt flew up behind as their claws ripped the forest floor.

Luke could feel the darkness hurtling toward them. In the pit of his stomach, he could feel the wrongness, like a sickness. The air carried the scent of flames and soot. Ash and smoke drifted in the copper-colored sky. Luke regretted that he had to lead the group in a huge semicircle, come at the mountain from its northern rim. A terrible sense of urgency drove him, but he could not take them to the more assailable south side of the mountain where the Nightsisters would be gathering for their attack.

The rancors circled to the cliffs at the north slope of the mountain, and Luke could feel the presence of Nightsisters nearby. He raised his hand, silently ordered the rancors to halt, and looked up the sheer face of the rock cliffs, wreathed in smoke. Firelight reflected on the rock, lighting all but the deepest crevices.

Luke gazed steadfastly at the cliff. They couldn't go up there without exposing themselves to attack.

The brown smoke hung ominously above like a pall to cover the world, yet it was utterly motionless. Somehow, the Nightsisters were manipulating the smoke, using the Force to wield it like a hammer. The air felt charged with static electricity.

Luke said, "Artoo, do a sensor scan, tell me if you pick up any electronics." Artoo raised his antenna dish, let it rotate.

"Master Luke," Threepio commented, "the air is very highly charged, and the ionization is wreaking havoc with my circuitry. I doubt that Artoo will be able to pick up much. This is no weather for a droid."

"This is no weather for anyone," Luke said, sniffing the air. The clouds were not the gray of storm clouds filled with heavy rain or the white of billowing clouds that promise summer sprinkles. These were dense clouds of dirt and soot rather than of water. He looked up, and suddenly the clouds above the valley swirled, as if a hand had waved above a cooking fire.

Gethzerion's face filled the sky, a face made of reddened smoke that frowned down upon them, eyes twitching. Then the face dissolved, but Luke was left with the uncanny feeling that Gethzerion was still up there, hidden behind the clouds, watching them. The rancors snarled and backed away from the cliff.

"Don't worry," Teneniel soothed the group. "Gethzerion is only trying to frighten you."

"Yeah," Han said, "well, it's working."

Artoo rotated his antenna uncertainly, finally began shaking, pointing southeast. He squealed and gave an electronic blip.

"Artoo can read several Imperial walkers in that direction," Threepio said.

Luke glanced southeast, then looked back up at the mountain. The shadows in some of those crevices above them were dark enough that human eyes might not be able to see the rancors if they crept up through the deeper cracks. But Luke knew that the life-sensors on an Imperial walker would spot them in a second. He would need to take out those walkers so the others could climb the cliff, and he didn't have much time.

Luke reached down, patted his rancor. The beast was overheating again. He could feel its fatigue, its dizziness. He let the Force flow through him, cooled the rancors and took away their thirst, then spoke to them. "Tosh, have your best climbers get my friends up to the clan stronghold. I will stay down here with two of you to fight, and I will join the others as soon as I can."

Tosh began grumbling orders to her children, and the two smaller males took the generators from her pack. Tosh and her daughter unstrapped their pikes and nets from their backs as they prepared for battle.

"Han," Luke said, glancing over at Han and Leia on their rancor. "Get Leia and the droids up into the *Falcon* and start working on the ship." To emphasize his words, Luke raised his hand, and Artoo floated from Tosh's back over to sit between Han and Leia. "There's nothing you can do down here. Teneniel, they might need your help."

"What do you mean?" Han said. "I'm staying with you. I've still got my wits and my blaster."

"And they won't do you any good," Luke said.

Han looked a bit dismayed, "Yeah, but—" Thunder rumbled over the clouds, echoed from the mountain wall. Purple lightning spat at the cliff face above, exploding like a blaster bolt, sending splinters of magma flaming down in an arc.

"You don't get it, do you?" Leia said. "The Nightsisters are coming for the *Falcon* because they know it's a sure ticket off of this planet. The best thing we can do for these people is to get that ship fixed as fast as possible and fly it out of here so that there's nothing left to squabble over!"

"I know that," Han said in a hurt tone. "I can see that! I'm right with you!" But Luke knew that in his heart, Han couldn't stand the thought of deserting a friend who was in need.

Chewbacca and Threepio climbed off the larger female and sat uncomfortably behind Isolder and Teneniel. On the huge rancors, even four riders could fit easily on the bony headplates above the eyes. Luke did not worry so much about overburdening the rancors with riders as he worried about the heavy packs with the generators and coolant. The rancors would have to climb the mountain with those packs.

"Will you be okay?" he asked the rancors, and the two small males grunted reassuringly.

He looked up, saw Leia's face lit in a sudden splash of lightning. He could feel her concern.

"Don't worry," Luke said. "I'll take out those Imperial walkers for you."

"That's not what I'm worried about," Leia answered. "Just take care of yourself. No heroics. There are some bad people out here. Even *I* can feel it." The silence stretched out between them, and Luke didn't quite know what to answer. If ever there was a day when they'd need heroics, this was it.

"I'll try to be careful," Luke said.

Luke nudged Tosh back, left the others behind in the forest as they remounted. Tosh ran for a hundred meters up a gently sloping hill, then stopped, stood tall and sniffed the air. The thick brush ahead was a solid black mass. Tosh grumbled softly, and Luke felt her sense of urgency. She wanted him to get off so she could move quickly in a fight. She crouched low, and Luke leaped to the ground.

He probed the darkness ahead. He could see nothing, smell nothing—even when probing with the Force, he felt nothing. Yet the rancors quietly crept to their left, circling the brush.

Luke followed noiselessly, using the Force to guide his footsteps.

They came to a trail that led into the deeper brush, and the ground was lit with reflected firelight. Luke could see scuff marks. Only the clawed metal toes of Imperial walkers left the ground so gouged and trampled. He peered toward the brush again. It was lighter here, the foliage above somewhat bare, and Luke realized he was on a little promontory, and no brush could be that thick.

A stormtrooper ahead shouted over his helmet mike, "Look! Up on the cliff!" Luke glanced over his shoulder. The two male rancors were scurrying up the nearly vertical rock, grasping ancient handholds with their huge claws. Luke could barely see the shapes that were Han, Leia, and the others.

Almost immediately, blaster cannons opened ahead of him, and in the blinding flash of the guns, Luke saw that what he'd thought was brush was really an Imperial camouflage net, hiding a gun emplacement. A dozen stormtroopers, four Imperial walkers, and a single Nightsister hunkered there. Luke knew that there must be dozens of outposts like this, hoped that taking out this one would afford Leia and the others enough of a chance to make it up the mountain.

Tosh and her daughter gripped their halberds and ran forward, using the sound of cannonfire to cover their assault. Luke nervously watched Leia, saw both rancors on the cliff swing magically away from the attack, placing a rock outcrop between them and the gunfire. It took Luke a moment to see that they had swung away by grasping ropes of whuffa hide that hung like creepers.

Luke charged in behind Tosh and her daughter. Tosh met the Imperials first, smashing into two Imperial walkers at once, knocking them into the gun emplacement. Frightened stormtroopers fired into her with blaster rifles, and Tosh roared in pain as the shots bounced off her thick hide. Luke pulled off three rapid shots, putting the Imperials down. Tosh's daughter swung her great halberd, cleaving a third walker in half.

The fourth Imperial walker spun malevolently and fired its twin blaster cannons into the young rancor. Ichor spattered across the installation, and the rancor's right arm fell away at the shoulder, splinters of yellow bone protruding through the dark tangle of meat. The rancor stared at her wounds in shock, grabbed her net with her good hand and hurled it at the last Imperial walker, then collapsed and died. The weight of its throwing stones bowled the walker over, and Tosh jumped up, slapped a retreating stormtrooper into oblivion with one paw, then rushed to the Imperial walker and slammed a fist into its cannons.

Flames and blue sparks erupted from the crumpled walker as its power plant melted down, yet Tosh smashed her fist into it again and again, crumpling the hull. No one could be alive in there, yet Tosh screamed and pried at the metal, seeking to rip out the gunner's corpse.

Luke fired into two more stormtroopers, and heard the Nightsister singing. She was huddled near the ground, frightened, retreating from Tosh and the carnage. Luke drew his lightsaber.

"You!" he shouted, and the Nightsister turned to him, her hood falling back. She was young, nothing more than a child really, perhaps sixteen. Luke could not imagine her being truly evil. He could feel her terror.

She began singing, and Luke raised his free hand with a gesture, used the Force to close her windpipe. The singing stopped, and she stood frozen, horror etched on her face.

"Don't make me kill you!" Luke said. "Promise me you'll leave Gethzerion and her clan forever!"

The girl stared at him, lit by the fires of burning Imperial walkers, eyes wild with terror, strangling. She nodded dumbly, and Luke could taste her animal fear. He let her go.

She dropped to the ground, looked up at him with rage. Luke could feel her surprise at her own impotence. With a single swatting gesture she cast a spell, knocking the lightsaber from Luke's hand.

Luke pulled out his blaster, fired. The girl screamed a curse, tried to ward the bolt away with her palm, but she was young and too weak. The blaster bolt tore into her flesh, leaving the hand blackened and burned. The girl looked at her own hand in horror, shouted.

The lightsaber leaped from the ground, swung at Luke's head. Luke channeled the Force, turned it off just before the blade arced into his face, then grabbed his weapon in midair.

"Please!" Luke shouted, but the girl began singing another spell. Suddenly Tosh reared up behind her, smashed the Nightsister with one great blow that thundered into the ground with the wet smack of pulping flesh and the crackling of bones.

Luke stood in shock, unable to comprehend his foe's own self-destructive behavior, unwilling to believe that one so young could have turned so completely to the dark side.

Tosh grabbed Luke in one claw, swung him up on her back, and raced through the jungle.

Luke could see black scorch marks in her flesh along the bony ridge behind her head. Some of them were deeply pitted, bleeding. Tosh was roaring in pain, not the pain of battle, but the pain of having watched her own daughter die. The rancor dodged through the trees, took him to the cliff and began climbing up in the darkness toward the clouds of fire-lit smoke.

Fires ringed the mountain, and thunder pealed around him. When Tosh reached the clifftop, Leia and the others were off in the distance, rancors standing hip-deep in a cane field. Leia was watching to make sure he got up all right, then she took the reins to her rancor, ordered it forward. The rancors raced, running through grain fields on their knuckles across the bowl-shaped valley toward the south rim and the fortress carved of stone. Old Tosh roared a battle challenge, and the rancors ahead joined her cry. Han and Isolder took up the cry for the human hosts.

As Luke reached the south side of the valley, he saw fifty rancors standing like shadowed monoliths along the sides of the cliff, wielding great poles and maces. A small army of men and juveniles dressed in their simple leather aprons slaved to carry huge throwing stones to the lip of the bluff, setting them beside the rancors.

When Leia reached the cliff, she urged her rancors upstairs to the great fortress. The rancors could not make it through the doorways, so Han, Leia, Isolder, the droids, and Teneniel stopped, began lugging the generators up the stairs. Yet Luke could still feel the urgency behind Augwynne's call of nearly an hour ago, and he left the others, rushed upstairs three steps at a time, passing room after room where huddled children and the village's invalids squatted in fear, until he reached the warriors' hall.

The clan sisters waited inside, dressed in their robes and headgear, standing above the sculpted maps of the terrain, intoning the words, *"Ah re, ah re, ah suun corre. Ah re, ah re, ah suun corre."*

Augwynne greeted Luke soberly, her face a carefully controlled mask, "Welcome, Luke Skywalker," she said as the others continued chanting. "I'd hoped you would hurry. We are doing a reading, trying to learn the locations of the Nightsisters so that we can discover their strategy." She used the end of her carved wood staff to nudge a scale model of Gethzerion's hover car closer to the fortress. If Augwynne were right, Gethzerion was only two kilometers from the mountain, moving between two groups of warriors. Luke guessed that Gethzerion must be using the hover car to take orders to each group personally. "Was your trip successful?"

"As well as can be expected," Luke said.

"Good," Augwynne breathed. "How long will it take for Han to repair his ship?"

"Two hours," Luke answered. "He's up there now, trying to mount the generators. Gethzerion knows he has a repairable ship."

"She was bound to figure that out," Augwynne said. "We'll try to fend off the Nightsisters until Han finishes."

One clan sister bent down, placed seventeen black stones at the western foot of the mountain. Luke studied the map. The Nightsisters' strategy seemed so odd as to be freakish. They had placed guard posts consisting of one sister each at twelve points of the compass. Since Luke had recently taken out such a post, he knew exactly what each installation contained. But in addition, Gethzerion had placed three assault squads evenly around the mountain. One was directly in front of the main stairs—the only easily accessible entrance—and two more teams were at 120-degree angles. Gethzerion's assault plans apparently did not take into account such mundane notions as terrain, fortifications, defensibility of the clan's positions. She seemed instead to expect her troops to swarm over any barrier. But Luke knew the power of the Force, and knew that her plans could work.

"Many of the Nightsisters are unaccounted for," Augwynne commented, looking at the map. "We shall have to beware." She moved the figure representing Gethzerion's hover

car nearer the southern base of the mountain, then went out to
wait on the balcony.

Luke ambled up beside her, and the other witches filed
behind. It was almost sunrise, and the clouds above had begun
to lighten. Still, there was so much smoke above them that Luke
was not sure if a real sunrise would dawn this morning. They
had traveled so much in the last night, with only two brief
stops, that Luke felt he hadn't slept in days. Down in the forest,
he could see Imperial walkers deploying in the woods, stormtroopers like white rats scurrying about for cover. Augwynne
said, "Do you have any words of wisdom for us, Jedi? Any
advice?"

"Use your powers only in the service of life," Luke said,
"to protect yourself or those around you."

"Do you mean to say that we should not kill the Nightsisters?" one of the women asked.

Luke looked down at the forces massing at their feet. "If
you can avoid it, yes. In this case though, I have already warned
Gethzerion and her band."

"As have we," Augwynne said. "Those who fight against
us this day will die with their blood on their own hands. I for
one will show no mercy."

They waited, and Teneniel came to Luke and held his hand.
"They're working up there on the ship as fast as they can. I felt
as if I were in their way. I thought I might be more help down
here."

Luke looked at her, and the firelight brought out the color
of her copper eyes, reflected red highlights in her hair.

Teneniel swallowed hard, and a breeze gusted. Luke had
thought that perhaps Gethzerion would come forward, make
some sort of speech to announce her presence, but the only
announcement came from Augwynne: "Here they come!"

The clan sisters around Luke began chanting, and far below, down in the shadows of the wood, the Nightsisters sang
loudly. The air swirled around the balcony, and Luke felt dust
sifting in his hair, suddenly realized that something was dropping on him from above. He looked up, and the clouds of soot
were raining down around him. He reached into his utility belt,
grabbed some goggles, and then felt a tremor rip through the
Force.

The winds surged, and Luke found himself in a maelstrom of blowing soot and gravel. He put on his goggles, and the clan sisters hid their eyes as they backed away from the balcony toward the shelter of their stronghold.

Teneniel Djo began singing, *"Waytha ara quetha way. Waytha ara quetha way . . ."* Blaster fire ripped into the parapet beneath Luke, and a lone Imperial walker rose into view, blasters blazing. The Nightsisters were using the Force to levitate it.

Teneniel threw her hand out, fingers splayed, focusing her spell. The dust around them swirled off like water in a drain. Grit and pebbles surged against the Imperial walker, and the static charge that they built caused a bolt of lightning to erupt from the mountain, reaching out like a finger to touch the walker. It exploded into flames and the Nightsisters let it fall so that it suddenly screamed out of sight, crashed in a blinding flash that showed Imperial walkers and stormtroopers rushing up the path to the fortress.

Luke leaned out for a better view, and through the swirling smoke glimpsed rancors at the top of the stairs, rolling boulders down the path like marbles. He watched the first boulder smash into an Imperial walker, sending it sprawling backward so that the walkers and soldiers behind it were swept over the cliff.

He marveled at the brazenness of Gethzerion's assault. It was a phenomenal waste of lives and equipment. Two clan sisters gazed down at the wreckage, muttering spells. Behind him, Augwynne shouted orders, "Ferra, Kirana Ti, go to the front doors. The Nightsisters are upon us!"

Luke looked about, saw no sign of Nightsisters, but used the Force, felt a tremor from above. He glanced up, saw three Nightsisters clinging to the rocks three meters overhead as if they were spiders. As one they dropped to the balcony.

Luke shouted a warning, whipped out his lightsaber and danced back a step. One witch beside him did not have time to react; a Nightsister landed beside her, shot the girl in the face with a blaster, then flipped a somersault as she leaped off the balcony.

Luke dodged a similar shot, sliced a Nightsister in half as she touched down beside him. On the far side of the balcony, Augwynne struggled with a Nightsister and Luke drew his own blaster. Augwynne pushed the woman over the balcony, and Luke jumped after the Nightsisters in hot pursuit.

The air was a gritty maelstrom, and as he fell past the stairs he saw Imperial stormtroopers spread out on a death road like pieces of white confetti. Blaster fire ripped past him as Imperial walkers shot at the stone-hurling rancors above.

He saw the ground coming up fast, two black-robed Nightsisters standing on the rocks. Luke dropped beside one of them. He shouted in warning. A Nightsister turned, readying a spell. Luke fired. She stood as if angered, flames smoldering from her cloak, and he realized that the Force must be strong in this one. The other ran off into the haze.

The lone witch glared at Luke. Gethzerion pulled back her hood to show the purpled veins in her face. Her red-glowing eyes were wide with surprise. "So," she said loudly to be heard over the sounds of battle, "we meet. I have been aware of the stirrings of your Force. I have always wanted to meet a Jedi, yet here I passed one in the halls of my own prison and never recognized him." She studied Luke momentarily, as if waiting to confirm that he was a Jedi.

"I've met your kind before," Luke said. "Listen to me, Gethzerion: turn away from the dark side before it is too late!"

Gethzerion nodded thoughtfully. "Pardon me if I say that I don't find you to be very impressive, young Jedi. It's a shame that you must die before you have a chance to witness how I make your friends writhe."

She pointed a finger at Luke, and before Luke even recognized her evil intent, a ripple of Force slammed into him. White lights exploded behind his eyes, and the right side of his face felt as if it had been smashed by a hammer. His left arm and right leg crumpled under their unbearable weight, and he dropped to the ground on one knee, stunned. All the noise and blaster fire and screams of pain died away, became a distant roaring. Gethzerion pointed at him again, twitched her finger, and his eyes lost focus. He felt the hammer blow to his left temple, dropped to his side and rolled over to his back, gasping. Luke stared up at the sky, watching streams of rocks hurtling above him—some propelled by the Force, others hurled by rancors.

Time seemed to slow. His head throbbed, pounding to the

same rhythm as the beating of his heart. His face had gone cold, numb, and Luke realized distantly that Gethzerion's spell had ripped open blood vessels in his brain, and he was about to die, one among hundreds of fatalities on this battlefield.

So this is how it would have been, if Vader had tried to kill me. Who had Luke been kidding? Teneniel had been right, Luke was no warrior. *Ben,* Luke thought. *I failed you. I've failed you all.* And suddenly there was a wave of pain, and Luke tried to remember who he'd just been talking to, tried to think of a name, someone he could call for help, but his mind was numb, empty, like the vast deserts of Tatooine lying naked beneath setting suns.

Chapter

23

Isolder hurried to grab the new sensor array window. Chewbacca was already using the power wrench to pull off the old window, while Leia and Han labored in the cramped space of the *Falcon*'s hold to get the anticoncussion field generators in place. The droids were inside the *Falcon*, dumping coolant for the hyperdrive. Outside the fortress, a war was in full swing. The stone floors rumbled and shook under the assault of blaster fire and hurtling rocks, while a wind sang through the honeycombed corridors.

It felt to Isolder as if the whole mountain would shake down to dust at any moment. He almost wished that the room had a window, a parapet like so many of the other rooms here in the fortress, so that he could see what was happening outside. But at the same time he felt safer secluded here in this sealed room, with only one door to guard.

Isolder carried the window to Chewbacca, held it up for a moment as the Wookiee searched with his hairy paws to grab a bolt so that he could fasten the new window to the *Falcon*. The Wookiee's hands were shaking in fear.

Behind them, Isolder heard a voice that sounded almost

distant, even though the woman shouted, "Gethzerion, I've found them!"

Isolder spun, dropped the window. A Nightsister stood in the doorway, panting. Isolder pulled his blaster, fired, and the Nightsister waved her hand, knocked the blaster bolt away.

"Well," she said. "You're a pretty one. I think I'll keep you."

Chewbacca roared and leaped at the Nightsister, and she backed up a step. Chewie dodged aside as if to pass her while retreating from the room, and the Nightsister lurched back. The Wookiee had snatched off the Nightsister's arm so fast that Isolder had never even seen it.

She gazed at the bloody stump of her shoulder, and Isolder fired again. The Nightsister went down.

Chewbacca howled, began looking frantically on the floor. Even though Isolder didn't understand Wookiee, he realized that Chewie had dropped the bolts. "Go inside and get some more!" Isolder shouted. "Hurry!"

Chewbacca scrambled to the *Falcon*. Isolder followed him up to the gangplank, nervously fingering his blaster.

He heard a hammering sound above his head. The stone walls burst open as if a giant fist had slammed against them. Isolder put his hands over his head to shield himself from falling rock, and a swirling hurricane of choking dirt and smoke whipped through the room.

Through the scream of the wind, he heard women's voices singing all around. He squinted his eyes and hit the close button on the *Falcon*'s hatch, shouting, "Go! Save yourselves!"

And in that moment, he knew that Rell's prophecy would come to pass. If he stayed here a moment longer, he would die. In the red glowing skies outside, he saw shadow shapes of women crawling along the rock, dropping through the rent in the torn wall.

Isolder ducked under the *Falcon*, rolled away, and made a run for the door, hoping to reach safety. A Nightsister came through the door to meet him.

She held up her hand, and an invisible force hammered into him.

·   ·   ·

Teneniel had watched Luke leap over the edge of the balcony, following the Nightsisters into the swirling mists, but she dared not follow. She heard screaming within the fortress, children shrieking in terror, and she rushed down a flight of stairs, leaving six of her sisters to fight on the balcony.

There had been three guards at the doors, and Teneniel followed hard on the heels of Ferra and Kirana Ti down the winding stairway. Ferra rushed around a corner and shouted in horror as her head suddenly, and without apparent cause, twisted around sharply, snapping her neck.

Kirana Ti stopped, pointed a blaster, waiting for someone to come up the stairwell, but a madness took Teneniel. Without voicing her spell, Teneniel sent a wind screaming through the stairwell powerful enough so that Ferra's corpse tumbled away. Below her, the Nightsisters shouted in dismay and Teneniel rushed down around the corner, saw two Nightsisters clinging to the handrails in order to avoid being swept downstairs.

A black rage filled her mind, and Teneniel pounded the hags with the Force wind, ripped the handrail from the stone walls so that the Nightsisters went shrieking into oblivion, bouncing down the winding stairway.

She let the wind fade, and Kirana Ti sat hunched on the floor, looking up at Teneniel's face in fear, weeping. Teneniel wondered why the stupid girl didn't get up, go out and fight.

"What are you looking at?" Teneniel shouted. "You miserable weakling!" Upstairs, one of their clan sisters shrieked, her voice cut short. "Get out of here. Go on and fight! Your sisters are dying!"

"Your face," Kirana Ti whimpered. "You've burst a vessel!"

Teneniel stopped, touched her cheek, felt the tender bruise beneath her eye. The mark of a Nightsister. Her mind reeled at the thought, and she realized that she'd murdered those Nightsisters in rage. She turned and ran blindly up the flight of stairs, past the warriors' chambers, and her footsteps rang on the stone.

She turned a corner at the top of the stairs, heard Nightsisters above her singing their spells. She looked around, surprised to find them so high in the fortress. There were no more open rooms this high—nothing but a few sealed sleeping and storage chambers. If the Nightsisters had not come up the stairs, they could have entered only by using the Force to break through the stone walls. And the only thing of value up this high was the *Millennium Falcon.*

Teneniel raced upstairs, running silently in the guttering torchlight past the faded tapestries of clan sisters long dead, rounded the corner to the upper chamber where the *Falcon* was stored.

The Nightsisters huddled there—twelve hooded figures muttering their spells, hands outstretched. They had torn the north wall asunder, and the cracked stone opened into the maelstrom.

Into the storm the Nightsisters sent the *Falcon,* floating on a field of Force. It was halfway through the crack in the wall, drifting out through space. The hatch door was closed. On the far side of the room, a lone Nightsister crouched over the still form of Isolder, binding his wrists, unable to resist the impulse to steal such a handsome slave.

Teneniel halted, backed against the wall, thinking. She could not fight so many, and if she tried to stop them from stealing the *Falcon* now, breaking their concentration on the spell, the ship would simply tumble out the rent in the wall, fall over the cliffs. Even with her powerful gift, her ability to move objects, she could not manage to save such a heavy ship and still fight the Nightsisters.

Her only hope was that Leia and Han were all right, hidden inside the ship. She reached out with her mind, calling for Leia. "Please," she whispered. "Fire your engines."

She inhaled a deep breath, turned and ran through the room, and channeled the Force to Isolder, using it to levitate his unconscious body. She bowled his captor aside, grabbed him and leaped against the stone wall, shielding Isolder with her body.

The *Falcon's* engines flamed, filling the room with white fire. The Nightsisters shrieked in the inferno, but Teneniel channeled the Force, let the flames flow around her. The *Falcon* shot off through clouds of brown smoke.

Teneniel slumped to the floor. The flames had burned her, singed her clothing. She did not feel damaged so much as just in pain.

The flames had blasted the rooms. A shelf of parchments

burned in one corner. Tapestries of ancient clan sisters smoldered. Among the Nightsisters, only one woman had been strong enough to survive the fire. She crawled, stunned, on her hands and knees, hair singed, face reddened as with a sunburn.

Leia piloted the *Falcon* through the dust and swirling debris of the Force storm. They had been working desperately to get the anticoncussion field generators on line, and had not even managed to get the first generator mounted. The gravel crashing into the *Falcon*'s sensor array forks was taking its toll, yet Leia didn't dare try to rise above the storm. The flashing lightning from the static electricity, the soot and accumulated garbage in the sky, was all she had to protect them from being detected by Zsinj's warships above the atmosphere.

She circled the fortress once, twice. From this altitude, she could see the sun rising through the storm, so she headed back over the valley beneath the fortress, flying low. Han rushed up from the hold and shouted, "What are you doing to my ship? You can't stay in this storm!"

He took the copilot's seat, and they headed low over the valley. Artoo was whistling and beeping in the back, and Threepio came out. "King Solo, Your Highness, good news! I've emptied all the coolant into the hyperdrive generators!"

"Great, Threepio," Han muttered. "Can you think of a way to stop this storm?"

"I'll have to work on that," Threepio said.

Leia looked down at the ground, at the tilled fields of the Singing Mountain clan. Just ahead, at the limit of vision, a dozen Imperial walkers and perhaps two dozen Nightsisters marched down a wooded road. Han spotted them.

"Boy, I hate messing up a good road," Han said as he launched his proton torpedoes. Leia only hoped the energy shielding would hold through the blast.

The proton torpedoes blossomed into a field of white, and Leia looked away. An incredible sonic boom shook the ship, echoed between the hills over and over. When the light faded enough so that she could see, gravel and soot began raining from the sky, long trails of debris that glittered in the morning sun like golden waterfalls.

Han whooped and laughed, ran his fingers through his mussed hair. For one eternal moment, Leia realized that they had struck a major blow. The Force storm was over. Han's torpedoes had taken out some of the Nightsisters' major talent.

In the fortress, Teneniel sat up, and the whole mountain suddenly shook with a huge explosion. Down below her in the valley outside, a cheer of victory arose. As quickly as the Force storm had erupted, it stopped. Soot and debris rained from the sky in dirty streams. Yet out above the residue of clouds, Teneniel watched the sunrise, a golden seam where land met sky.

Teneniel crawled to the wounded Nightsister on the floor where the *Falcon* had been repaired, and the hag looked up, tried feebly to whisper a spell, but collapsed. Teneniel flipped the woman onto her back, looked into her eyes. The Nightsister flinched, frightened. Her breath rasped through burned lungs, weakening. She had been standing in the wrong place, right behind the *Falcon*'s exhaust ports as it blasted off.

"Don't worry," Teneniel said, stroking the creature's soot-stained face. "I won't hurt you. I've killed too many of your kind already today. No matter what you do to me afterward, I want you to have this." Teneniel looked at the horrible woman, a victim of her own evil, and Teneniel channeled the last of her strength, granting her enough life force that given time and care, the Nightsister might live.

Han gazed at the streaming sunlight, and his heart leaped within him. For one moment, he thought he'd won.

Then, the darkness blossomed. On the far horizon, a circular black spot appeared, and then another beside it, and another, as if the sky had been lit with ten thousand glowglobes and someone suddenly was switching them off.

Within thirty seconds, the *Millennium Falcon* hovered beneath a sky void of light. Only flames from burning fields and crops illuminated the ground below. Chewbacca roared and shook his head in frustration, eyes wild.

"King Solo, help!" Threepio shouted urgently. "My photoreceptors are registering a most startling phenomenon: Dathomir's sun appears to be going dead!"

"No kidding," Han said.

"Hey," Leia said, her voice betraying her nervousness. "What is this?"

"Something far beyond the power even of the Nightsisters," Han answered with certainty, looking up at a ceiling of perfect night.

Chapter

24

Han set the *Falcon* down, shut off the engines. The night was absolutely black, and he looked up at the sky, wondering if perhaps something was wrong with the viewscreen. He thought about pounding it, just to see what would happen.

He glanced at sensor panels. "Oh man," he said. "That little ride of yours through the storm cost us dearly. The sensors are gummed up bad. I can hardly get any readings at all."

"Would you rather be dead?" Leia asked.

"No," Han conceded. "Where's Isolder?"

"I don't know," Leia answered. "He went out to put up the sensor window. I think the Nightsisters got him."

"Got him? What do you mean, got him? Killed him?"

"I, I don't know. He was lying on the floor when we blasted off. Teneniel was with him. She told me to get out of there."

Han looked at her; the ship's lights revealed the lines of dread etched in her face. What she'd done was tantamount to human sacrifice, and she knew it. He said, "We'd better get the medkit and go back. Make sure he's okay. How far do you figure we are from the fortress?"

"I did a lot of circling," Leia answered. "It couldn't be more than half a kilometer."

Han turned to Chewie. "Leia and I are going back to the fortress. You and Threepio see if you can get those generators mounted. Artoo, see if you can get some sensor readings, tell us what's going on. If you learn anything, I want to hear about it immediately."

Chewie roared an affirmative, and Han went back for the medkit, grabbed a heavy blaster and a helmet. He gave Leia a flashlight, and together they hurried down the gangplank, through the valley.

Dust and soot still filtered down on them, and here and there across the valley they could see fires burning. On the far side of the valley, green running lights showed four Imperial walkers scurrying off in retreat, ghoulish little figures running beside them.

Leia didn't turn on the flashlight. Instead, they ran along the road guided only by the feeble light from fires. What had seemed a long, bumpy ride in the *Falcon* turned out to be only a short run back to the fortress. When they reached it, the battle was over.

Grim-faced men milled about the fortress, torches in hand, staring at the total darkness with trepidation. Rancors roared in agony on the stairs, and Leia flashed her light over them. A dozen of them lay in a bloody heap like small hills at the top of the stairs, and Tosh struggled to drag the corpse of her son away, roaring her anguish.

Han and Leia hurried upstairs in the fortress, running past the dead. In the upper chamber, they found Teneniel sprawled over the body of a Nightsister. Leia flipped Teneniel on her back, and the girl breathed deeply. Han examined her. Outside of burn marks on her robe, he could find no injuries.

"Where's Isolder?" Leia asked, but Teneniel didn't move. Leia played her light across the room. A splash of white revealed Isolder in a corner. Leia rushed to him.

Han brought the medkit, but when he got near, he found Isolder snoring. Leia shook him awake, and Isolder snapped to sudden awareness.

"Where am I?" he asked. "What's going on?" Then he scanned the room, noticed the bodies of the Nightsisters, seemed to recall. He gazed into Leia's eyes. "Wow! What a beautiful face to wake up to." Isolder put his arm around Leia, kissed her quickly.

"All right," Han said. "No mushy stuff. We've got work to do." Han glanced up through the breach in the stone wall, saw the fires out in the surrounding valley. It was like gazing out of some primitive observatory.

Augwynne said, "There you are!" Han turned. The clan leader held a torch, and several children stood at her elbow. She moved feebly, as if weary. Leia helped Isolder up, and Augwynne stopped to inspect Teneniel in the darkness, said to one of the children, "Go, run get the healer."

"What's going on?" Han asked.

Augwynne looked out at the night, nodded. "I was hoping you could tell me," she said. "Gethzerion has retreated to the city. I saw the headlights of her hover car speeding through the forest. Over a dozen of our clan sisters lie dead, and several others are missing, as is Luke Skywalker."

Leia started, gave an involuntary whimper, looked around the room as if Luke might suddenly appear.

"Do you have any idea where Luke is?" Han asked Augwynne.

"We saw him chase after some Nightsisters when the attack first started," Augwynne said. "He leaped down over the cliffs."

"Luke can take care of himself," Han said, trying to sound confident for Leia's sake. "Let's give him a few more minutes. I'm sure he'll make it back." But Leia was frowning, staring out over the valley into the blackness.

Augwynne limped over to the crack in the stone wall, searched the sky fearfully. "Few of our common folk were hurt, and for that we can be grateful. I fear that this darkness is all that saved us. It turned back the Nightsisters' attack.

"I'll be down in the war room," Augwynne said. "I'll wait for my sisters to regroup." She walked wearily downstairs.

Han and Leia waited for the healer. An old woman came, passed her hands over Teneniel's body three times and sang softly, then sat holding Teneniel's hand. Teneniel's eyes fluttered open, and the woman said, "Rest, now. You gave some of your life to save another. Who was it?"

"A Nightsister," Teneniel said weakly, looked over to the shadows behind her. "There."

The healer went to the Nightsister, felt at her neck for a pulse, then considered for a long time. At last, she got up, walked downstairs without ministering to the woman.

Leia said loudly to her back, "You plan to just leave her? You'll let her die?"

The witch stopped, her back stiffening. She spoke without turning. "I have little enough talent, and others of my clan need my service. If Gethzerion desires to revive the creature, she may send another healer. But I would not place much hope in it."

Leia's eyes flashed with outrage, and Han placed a hand on her shoulder to comfort her. Leia said, "I'm going to speak to Augwynne about this."

Isolder gathered Teneniel in his arms, and Leia nodded at Han. "Take her down, too." Han lifted the Nightsister and carried her downstairs to the warriors' hall, following Isolder. The Nightsister's robes smelled dirty, rank, as if from soured fat. Han placed her on cushions near the fire while Leia quarreled loudly with Augwynne. The remaining witches had gathered around the fire, and all of them were dazed, listless. The men brought the dead to the hall, and began washing and dressing the bodies, preparing them for the funeral pyre.

At last Augwynne consented to heal the Nightsister, and placed her palm over the Nightsister's leathery face, then sang long and softly until the Nightsister's eyes opened. The creature lay on her cushions, looking up at them from green eyes cracked to mere slits. Han could not tell if she were sick or merely feigning illness. She looked as trustworthy as a viper. He suddenly realized that he would have preferred her dead.

"Han," Leia said uncomfortably, looking at the Nightsister, "I'm really worried about Luke. He should be back by now."

"Yeah," Han said. "I'm worried, too."

"I, I can't *feel* him. I can't feel his presence anywhere," she choked. "I *have* to go look for him."

"You can't," Isolder cut in. "It's too dangerous out there right now. Just because Gethzerion has left, it doesn't mean that the others have gone. The Nightsisters can't be far away."

Augwynne studied Leia with eyes dulled from fatigue. "Isolder is correct. You can't go out. The Jedi left over the cliff, and I doubt that he could have survived. Even if he is only hurt, he is still beyond your grasp."

Artoo appeared in the doorway, swiveled his eye around and whistled.

"Artoo," Han asked, "what's up? Did you get any readings on what's causing the darkness?" He listened carefully to bleeps and whistles, unable to decode the droid's answer, but Artoo raised up on his wheel pads, leaned forward and showed a split-image holo.

Gethzerion stood under a light, chest heaving from exertion, gazing up at her holo camera. "Zsinj, what is the meaning of this?" She waved her hands, indicating the sky.

Warlord Zsinj, a pudgy human, reclined in a large captain's chair, while colored monitor lights flashed behind him. The warlord, a balding man with a large gray moustache and penetrating eyes, smiled. "Greetings, Gethzerion. It's so good to see you again after so many years. This . . . darkness . . . is my gift to you: It is called an orbital nightcloak, and I thought a nightcloak sounded like an appropriate gift for the Nightsisters. It's really quite fun. The cloak consists of thousands of satellites chained in a network—each designed to distort light, bending it in toward the satellite. It's quite a marvelous toy."

Gethzerion glared at him, and Zsinj continued. "You told my men over two days ago that you had Han Solo. You will release him to me today. If you do not, the nightcloak will remain in place, and Dathomir will begin to cool. By this time tomorrow, you will have snow in your valleys. Within three days, all plant life will wither. In two weeks' time the temperature will drop to a hundred degrees below zero. You and everything on your world will die."

Gethzerion bowed her head in token of acknowledgment so that her hood concealed her face. "And if we release Han Solo to you, will you remove the nightcloak?"

"On my word as a soldier," Zsinj said.

"Your reputation is widely—regarded," Gethzerion said. "Have you considered our offer to you? Our offer of service?"

"Indeed," Zsinj said, leaning forward in his chair with interest. "I have considered where I might place you in my organization, and I regret that I can't seem to find a suitable position."

"Then perhaps you will consider offering us a position outside your organization," Gethzerion said.

"I don't understand."

"You are at war with the galactic New Republic. It is a foe so widespread that you cannot defeat it. I have foreseen it. Therefore, perhaps you would consider giving us access to travel to the New Republic worlds. You could name the star cluster. There the Nightsisters would carve out a niche for themselves, carving into the heart of your enemies, never to bother you again."

Zsinj folded his hands in his lap, sat thinking again. He studied Gethzerion's face for a long moment. "It is an intriguing offer. How many of your sisters would need transport?"

"Sixty-four," Gethzerion answered.

"How soon would you be ready to leave?"

"In four hours."

"We will work the exchange this way," Zsinj said. "I will drop two transports on your grounds in four hours. One ship will be unarmed, the other will be armed to the teeth.

"You will bring Han Solo to the armed transport, alone. The transport will depart with General Solo, and you will then be free to board the remaining ship, and leave for a destination that I will choose. Agreed?"

After a moment of reflection, Gethzerion nodded, "Yes, yes. That would be quite adequate. Thank you, Lord Zsinj."

Both holographs faded, and Han looked around the room at the faces of the witches. "Bah!" one old woman growled. "Both of them are liars. Gethzerion does not have Han or anything else to offer Zsinj, and Zsinj has no intention of releasing this planet or of letting Gethzerion leave."

"Did you *read* him," Augwynne asked, "or is this a guess?"

"No, of course I couldn't read him," the old woman said, "but Zsinj lies so poorly, one does not have to."

"He's no diplomat, that's for sure," Leia said.

Augwynne shot her a curious glance. "What do you mean by that?"

"Simply that Zsinj is rumored to be a pathological liar, yet even with all his practice, he sure seems transparent."

"Yes," Augwynne said. "I agree. Plots within plots. Perhaps this Zsinj is more devious than you imagine."

"Maybe Zsinj is bluffing," Isolder said. "He's built his orbital nightcloak, but those satellites up there would be pretty easy to knock down."

"You're right—" Leia agreed. "What did Zsinj say? He called it a chain of satellites."

"Meaning it can be broken," Han said. "Like a string of lights in sequence. You shoot down one or two satellites, and the system could collapse."

"I could go up and knock out some satellites with my fighter," Isolder said. He was volunteering for tough duty, Han knew. Zsinj had well over a dozen destroyers up there to protect his nightcloak. A lone fighter didn't stand much of a chance, unless it could knock out some satellites and then run for hyperspace.

"It doesn't sound like much of a weapon," Leia said, considering. "Any planet with spaceflight capabilities, or even a radio to call for help—"

"Would be able to fight against them," Augwynne said. "And so the weapon is good only for subjugating planets like Dathomir, primitive worlds without technology. Here, it is adequate."

"Three days," Isolder grunted, staring into the fire.

"What's in three days?" Augwynne asked.

"We only need to make it through three more days," Isolder said, "and my fleet will arrive. If we can take control of this planet, even for a single day, we could evacuate."

"We don't have that long," Han argued. "In three days, if that orbital nightcloak stays up, this planet will pretty much be a chunk of ice. And don't forget, this is still my planet. I'm not going to let that happen!"

"Yeah," Isolder admitted, "I'm sure you'll think of something. But even if you don't, at least we could get the people off."

Augwynne said hopefully, "Do you think so? Our people are very scattered."

"And when temperatures start hitting a hundred below," Leia said, "they're going to hole up in caves, burrowing as deep as they can get."

Han considered. There was no way they could wait for three days. Someone needed to get up there soon and take out some of those satellites, bring down the nightcloak long enough to stall Zsinj. *With a great deal of luck,* Han thought, *I might even be able to fly Leia out of here.* He imagined flying through the satellite net, blowing away a few satellites, then trying to blast free of the planet. But the fact was, once he began firing on those satellites, he'd have to vector off to follow their orbital path, and he'd have to maintain a slow attack speed to hit those satellites.

Considering the firepower up there, whoever tried to take out those satellites would be committing suicide.

He looked at Isolder, and the prince stared at him, and Han knew they were waiting for one another to volunteer. "Should we draw straws?" Han asked.

"Sounds fair enough," Isolder admitted, biting his lower lip.

"Wait a minute," Leia said. "There's got to be another answer! Isolder, what about your fleet? You left the same time that they did. Is there any possibility that they could get here sooner?"

Isolder shook his head. "If they stay to the prescribed route, no. Those ships are worth trillions. You don't fly that kind of equipment through hazardous routes."

Isolder was right, of course. More than one general in history had sent fleets through proscribed routes, hoping to shave a few parsecs off their trip so that they could win some advantage through surprise, only to find that their entire fleets got wiped out by flying through an asteroid belt.

Han glanced toward the stone door, realized he was waiting for Luke, and he shook his head. It wasn't like a Jedi to leave them all hanging, and Han felt more than a little worried. He fought the impulse to run down the mountain, shouting Luke's name. Leia folded her arms across her stomach, almost in a fetal gesture.

Han felt pulled in several directions at once—he wanted to find Luke, even if only to find him dead. He wanted to fly out of here and blow some satellites out of the sky. But what he did was go to Leia, wrap his arms around her shoulders.

She began to sob, her chest heaving. "He's not here," she said. "I can't feel him. He's not here anymore."

"Hey," Han said, wanting to offer some words of comfort, knowing that he could say nothing. Leia's ability to sense Luke's presence, to touch his feelings and know his thoughts, was too strong to doubt. Leia began shaking, and Han kissed her forehead. "It will be all right," Han said. "I'll . . . I'll—" He could see no way out, nothing left that he could do.

Suddenly, something shoved its way into his consciousness, as if an invisible hand had pushed through his skull. It was an odd sensation that left him feeling violated, dizzy. Very clearly, an image formed in Han's mind, a vision of dozens of men and women in orange coveralls, standing in a well-lighted room. They were looking up curiously, gazing around at walkways above them. On the walkways stood stormtroopers with blaster rifles. Han recognized the prison.

General Solo, Gethzerion's voice crawled through his mind. *I hope you will find this amusing. As you see, I am here at the prison with dozens of your kind below me. I trust that you are a compassionate man, a caring man. I suspect you are.*

As you know, I have struggled through various means to cause you to come to me. Perhaps this will convince you.

A hand waved in front of his face, a hand partly concealed by a black robe, and Han perceived that he was viewing the scene through Gethzerion's eyes. The stormtroopers looked at her waving hand, began firing into the crowd. Men and women screamed and scattered, trying to run from the blaster fire, but the gates back to the cell blocks had closed, and they could not escape.

Han threw his arm in front of his eyes, tried to blind himself to the atrocities, but the vision persisted. He could not close his eyes against it, for the vision remained even when his eyes shut. Nor could he turn away, for the images followed him: a woman ran shrieking below the parapet, and Han saw Gethzerion's hand go up, blaster aimed as if he were staring through the laser sights, and she snapped a shot into the woman's back. Gethzerion's victim spun with the impact of the blast, then collapsed, stunned, as Gethzerion pulled off another shot. A man beside the dying woman raised his clasped hands, pleading for Gethzerion to spare them. The witch fired high into his right leg and the prisoner was thrown to the floor to die slowly as he bled to death.

These fifty people are already dead, Gethzerion said, forcing Han to continue viewing the murders. *They die because of your stubbornness. When my stormtroopers finish with them, I will round up five hundred more just like them, bring them to this room to die.*

But you can save them, General Solo. I will send a Nightsister to pick you up at the foot of the fortress in my personal hover car. If you are not there to meet her in one hour, then those five hundred people will die, and you will get the privilege of watching. If you do not surrender after that, you will watch the deaths of another five hundred, and another. As I said, I trust that you are a compassionate man.

At first Leia thought Han was crying when he backed away, covering his eyes with his arm, but then he gasped for breath and his muscles went rigid. He gazed around the room, unseeing, and she'd never witnessed such a look of utter desolation in his eyes.

She took his hand and said, "Han! Han! What's happening?" but he did not respond.

"It is a sending," Augwynne said. "Gethzerion is speaking to him."

Leia looked at the old witch. Augwynne had removed her headdress and now sat on a stool by the fire, looking like nothing more than a dowdy old woman.

Han gasped and pulled his hands from his eyes, stood looking around the room. "I've got to go," he said. "I've got to get out of here."

He turned and ran, leaping blindly down the stairs. "Han, wait!" Leia called.

She chased after, followed the echoing retreat of his footsteps down the corridors. Artoo whistled for them to wait, but Leia ignored the droid. Han ran outside, pushed his way through the crowd of commoners that huddled by the doors, and took off at a full run.

Leia stood on the stone landing and watched him disappear, swallowed by the shadows. Isolder came out with the flashlight, pointed its powerful beam at Han's back.

"Where is he going?" Isolder asked.

"To the *Falcon*," Leia said, and she followed him.

They did not reach him until they got to the *Falcon*. By then he was already down under the right front sensor fork, working with Chewie on mounting the last generator. When he saw Leia and Isolder, he glanced up for a moment.

"Isolder, I need your help. We've got to get this ship flying and get out of here. Go back to the fortress and get that sensor array window." Isolder stood a moment, as if to wait for further instructions, and Han shouted, "*Now*, damn you!"

Isolder took his light, ran off through the darkness.

"What are you doing?" Leia asked. "What's going on?"

"Gethzerion just upped the ante on me," Han said. "She's killing innocent prisoners." He finished bolting the last generator down, threw the wrench on the ground. "I'm sorry I ever brought you here! You were right. If I hadn't come here, Zsinj wouldn't have his orbital nightcloak up, Gethzerion wouldn't be killing her prisoners! Zsinj, Gethzerion—these people don't even know me. They're fighting against Han Solo the New Republic general, against what the New Republic stands for!"

"So what are you doing?" Leia asked as he rushed inside the *Falcon*. "Running away? Is that your answer? Augwynne's people are desperate. You're supposed to be some kind of military genius—stay here and fight back. They need you and your blaster." She followed him up the gangplank, and Han remained silent, but instead of heading for the tool compartments as she expected, he ran down to the command console, set the ship's radio to standard Imperial frequency.

"Gethzerion?" he said quickly, and an unfamiliar voice answered.

"This is Prison Control. Do you have a message to relay to Gethzerion?"

"Yeah," Han said. Sweat dotted his face. "This is General Han Solo, and I have an urgent message. Tell her I'm coming in. I surrender. Do you copy? Tell her not to kill another prisoner. I'll meet her at the foot of the stairs to the fortress, just as she asked."

"This is Control One, we copy you, General Solo. What of your companions? Zsinj has been asking about any traveling companions you may have brought with you."

"They're dead," Han said. "They all died in the battle, not more than an hour ago."

Han threw the mike down, pushed his way past Leia, hurried down the access tube. Leia stood, watching his back for a moment, too surprised and confused to speak.

"Wait a minute," she said. "You can't do this! You can't just walk in there! Zsinj doesn't want you alive. He wants you dead."

Han shook his head. "Believe me," Han said, "I'm not happy about it either, but it was bound to happen sometime." He turned the corner, went to his bunk and angrily pulled up a mattress, exposing a hidden weapons locker that Leia had never seen. It held a nasty assortment of laser rifles, blasters, old-fashioned slug throwers—even a portable laser cannon. All the weapons were highly illegal, especially in the New Republic. Han reached under one of the rifles, pushed a button, and the bottom of the compartment rose, revealing a second hidden compartment filled with an odd assortment of grenades in various styles. Han grabbed a very small, but very deadly brand: a Talesian thermal detonator powerful enough to destroy a large building. It fit nicely in his palm.

"This ought to do it," Han said, tucking the detonator down under his belt. Detonators like this were used only by terrorists, those who no longer valued their own lives as much as they valued the destruction of their enemies. Han couldn't touch the thing off without killing himself. He pulled out his shirt so that it hung loosely over the detonator, concealing it.

"There, how does that look?" he asked calmly.

Leia couldn't see a sign of the detonator, would never have known he carried it if she hadn't watched him tuck it into his belt. Yet she couldn't answer him. Her heart raced, and she couldn't find her voice. She watched him through tears.

"Hey," Han said, "don't take it too hard. You're the one who said I had to grow up, take responsibility for who I am. *General* Han Solo, hero of the Rebel Alliance. I figure if I play it smart, I can take out Gethzerion and all her damned cronies with her. I'll have to leave it up to Isolder to do something about Zsinj. He's a good man. You made a good choice. Really."

Leia heard the words distantly, realized with a shock how strange they sounded. She hadn't thought about her involvement with Isolder for three days, hadn't really believed she had ever made a *choice*. Because she hadn't made a choice. Deep in her heart, she'd still been waiting to see if she loved Han.

Yet, she knew that that wasn't true. She had chosen Isolder, out of necessity. Her people had needed her to wed the Hapan worlds, and she'd responded to those needs. As long as the Empire remained a threat, she hadn't been able to see any other path she could take.

She glanced down at Han's belt line, tried to sound calm, controlled. "Yeah," she said. "That ought to do it. I've got to say, you really look good with a bomb strapped to you."

Han bent down and kissed her fiercely, passionately, and the blood thundered in her ears. Leia suddenly realized how much she had missed this, missed feeling such raw, elemental fervor for a man. She looked over his shoulder. Chewbacca was putting tools away. The Wookiee looked at her mournfully, and Leia closed her eyes, leaned into Han and kissed him harder.

He broke away, minutes later, gasping. "Han—" Leia began to say, but Han raised a finger.

"Don't say anything," he told her. "Don't make me regret this more than I already do." Han went to Chewbacca, talked softly to the Wookiee for a moment and gave him a hug. Leia sat down on the holo board and began to sob, trying to get her emotions under control. She could hear Threepio's voice, too loud and distraught, trying to talk Han out of it. Then Han returned to the lounge, squeezed her hand good-bye.

"I've got to go now," he said. He walked outside.

Leia tried to stay a moment, but she followed him down the gangplank, stood in the light thrown from the ship. Most of the little fires around the valley had burned down to nothing, and the skies were perfectly black, darker than any night she had ever imagined. A cold wind whipped through the mountains, and she hugged herself, realized she could see her breath in the chill air.

She watched Han's back as he walked away, disappearing into the darkness. "Han!" she called.

Han turned, looked at her. She could barely see his face at this distance, dark and insubstantial, almost an apparition. "I like some things about you," Leia said. "I like the way your pants fit."

Han smiled. "I know." He turned and began walking again.

"Han!" Leia called again, and she wanted to say, "I love you," but she did not want to hurt him, did not want to say it now, and yet could not bear the thought of leaving it unsaid.

Han turned to her, flashed a weak smile. "I know," he called softly. "You love me. I've always known." He waved good-bye, and jogged off into the deeper shadows.

She heard his running footsteps for several moments after. Leia sat on the grass in the light from the doorway and wept. Chewbacca and Threepio came out; Chewie put a hairy paw on her shoulder. Leia waited for Threepio to say something. He always told comforting lies in desperate situations. But the droid remained silent.

Oh Luke, Leia thought. *Luke, I need you.*

Chapter

25

As Luke's life drained away, a soft buzzing filled his ears. His muscles relaxed like never before. Overhead, rancors still tossed stones. He saw a blinding flash as one boulder hit an Imperial walker, and the machine split, giving off a fierce actinic glare as it burst.

Overhead, part of the mountain exploded outward, tearing away. Luke could see Nightsisters there, climbing the steep cliffs, halfway suspended by use of the Force, like great black arachnids dangling from their webs.

A sharp ache throbbed through his temples, and Luke turned to his side. A boulder dropped beside his arm, shattered, and distantly he could still hear screams and, mingled with them, Teneniel's voice.

"The Jai never die," she said. "Nature cherishes them. Nature."

A body fell beside him with a thud—the corpse of a clan sister, her metal helmet askew, the tiny gems and skulls bobbling. The sun was getting brighter, he noticed as he watched the dark red blood draining from her mouth.

Luke did not feel like he was dying so much as expanding.

He could hear noises all around, minute digging sounds of some salamander scratching beneath the rocks, worms burrowing beneath his head, a bush scratching a rock as it tussled with the wind. Everywhere was life, everywhere he could feel it, see the light of the Force glowing around him, in the trees, in the rocks, in the warriors above him on the mountainside.

The salamander raised its head above the soil, and it glowed with luminous Force. *Hello, my little friend*, Luke thought. The salamander had green skin and fierce little black eyes. It opened its mouth, and a white mist came out, stroked Luke as if it were a finger, and Luke understood that he was *seeing* Force, not just feeling it. *A gift*, the lizard whispered. *This is a gift for you*, and the gentle light stole over him, reinforced Luke's waning Force. Above him, the bush that scratched the rocks seemed to twist, and twigs of light bent down to cradle his head. *Here, here it is*, the bush whispered. *Life.* A nearby rock glowed white, and on the distant plains, one of the Blue Desert People raised its head as it fed in the rushes by the river, and its red eye stared across the leagues. *Friend*, it said, offering support.

Luke seemed to hear Teneniel's words, "Nature cherishes them," and he did not know if he was subconsciously controlling the Force, or if the life around him actually sought to heal him, but he saw the Force all around him, and he grasped those threads more easily than he'd ever done before.

To control the Force, to use the Force, was not such a violent thing as he had imagined. It was everywhere, more abundant than rain or air, offering itself. He had hoped someday to become a Jedi Master, yet now realized that there were levels of control he had never envisioned, far beyond anything he had dreamed.

The sweet power stole through him, and he did not know if he commanded it, or it commanded him. He knew only that he felt something heal in his head as ruptured veins closed, and then the vision ended.

He lay for a long time with his eyes closed, unable to do more than breathe, and wait for the Force to strengthen him.

Leia called his name, and Luke's eyes snapped open. The sky was so magnificently black that it seemed a perfect night had fallen. There were no more chaotic sounds of battle. On the mountains, he could see lights, torchlights in the hands of villagers, and one person walking down the treacherous mountain path, torch in hand. He thought Leia must be up there. "Leia," he called. "Leia?"

On the mountainside, the torchbearer held the torch aloft, looked down over the cliff. "Luke?" Han called. "Luke, is that you?"

"Han," Luke called weakly. He lay back in the blackness, felt at his side for his lightsaber, mustered energy to thumb the switch, hoping Han would see its light.

Distant voices came to him indistinctly. Someone grabbed him, shook him. A bright light shone in his eyes, and Han said, "Luke! Luke! You're alive! Hang on. Hang in there."

Han sat for a moment, holding Luke's hand, and Luke could feel Han's terror. "Listen, buddy," Han said. "I've got to go. Leia is waiting for you up top. Take care of her for me. Please, take care of her."

Han tried to pull away, and Luke could sense the terror and desperation that raged in him. "Han?" Luke said, grasping his wrist.

"I'm sorry, friend," Han said. "You're not in any shape to help me, this time." Han pulled away, and Luke felt as if he were swirling in darkness.

After what seemed an eternity, someone grabbed him, lifted him up. Luke managed to open his eyes, but could keep them open for only a moment. He was in the hands of peasants, a dozen rough peasants in simple leather tunics, torches held high. Han told them with deep concern, "Get him out of here! Carry him back up to the *Millennium Falcon!*"

The voices buzzed in his head, questioning. "Yeah, yeah, the *Falcon*, my spaceship," Han said. "Take him there. I've got to go!"

Then the hands lifted Luke, and the peasants carried him, and Luke let himself rest.

Chapter

26

In the uppermost chamber of the fortress, Isolder found the sensor array window just where he had set it. The corpses of the Nightsisters lay scattered on the floor, and either that or the total darkness set his nerves jangling.

He reached to pick up the window, heard a rustling in the corner, played his light in that direction and pulled his blaster in one fluid move. It was Teneniel Djo, sitting in the darkness. She glanced at him, then turned away. Her cheeks were wet from crying.

"Are you all right?" Isolder asked. "I mean, do you still feel weak? Is there anything I can do? Anything you need?"

"I'm fine," Teneniel said, voice rough. "Fine, I guess. So, you are about ready to leave?"

"Yes." Isolder directed the light away so that it would not shine in her eyes. He wasn't sure yet of Han's plans, but at this point about the only thing that made sense was for them all to bug out, get off this rock. Teneniel had taken off her helm and exotic robes, wore only boots and a simple summer tunic of orange hide, similar to the one she'd worn when they first met. She looked out into the starless sky. The fires below had died down, but the villagers' flickering torchlights still cast a soft yellow-orange glow.

"I'm leaving, too," she said.

"Oh," Isolder asked, "where are you going?"

"Back to the desert," Teneniel said, "to meditate."

"I thought you wanted to stay here with your clan. I thought you were lonely."

Teneniel turned, and even in the faint light he could see the bruise on her cheek. "The clan sisters all agree," she said. "I've killed in anger, violated my oaths. So now I must cleanse myself, or risk becoming a Nightsister. I'll be banished. At the end of three years, if I still desire to come back, then they will accept me." She wrapped her arms around her knees.

Teneniel's hair was brushed out straight down her back, cascading in tiny waves. Isolder stood for a moment, not knowing if he should say good-bye, or offer her a word of comfort, or if he should just pick up the window and hurry back to the ship.

He sat beside her, patted her back. "Look," he said. "You are a very tough woman. You'll be all right." Yet his words felt hollow. What did she have to look forward to? In three days, the Hapan fleet would come here, blow Zsinj's forces all to hell. But by then this world would pretty well be ice. At the very least, the summer crops would be ruined. But Isolder expected that beyond that, ecosystems would collapse, whole species of plants and animals would die off. Even if the orbital nightcloak were knocked out in three days, this planet might never completely recover.

And, of course, there were the Nightsisters. Few of the Singing Mountain clan survived, and they would be no match against the Nightsisters.

Perhaps these thoughts were making their way through Teneniel's mind, too, for she breathed raggedly. Her lower lip trembled and she tried to hold back a sniffle.

"Look," Isolder said. "A Corellian stock light freighter like Han's can carry up to six passengers. That means there's an empty bunk, if you want it."

"But where would I go?" Teneniel said.

"To all those stars out there," Isolder said. "Just pick one out of the sky and go there, if you want."

"I don't know what's out there," Teneniel said. "I wouldn't know where to go."

"You could come to Hapes, with me," Isolder said, and he knew even as he said it that he wanted nothing else. He gazed at her long hair, at her bare legs. At this moment, even with all the craziness and death on this world, nothing else that happened on this planet was more important than her pain. At this moment, even though he was nearly engaged to Leia, he craved nothing more or less than to put his arms around Teneniel.

Teneniel looked at him angrily, and her eyes flashed. "And if I came with you to Hapes, what would I come as? An oddity? The strange woman from backward Dathomir?"

"You could come as a bodyguard," Isolder said. "With the Force as your ally, you could . . ." Teneniel frowned at the thought. "Or you could come as an adviser, a trusted counselor," Isolder said, thinking frantically. "With your powers, you would be my greatest asset. With the Force, you could penetrate the subtleties of my aunts' plots, frustrate their plans . . ." Isolder had not considered it before, but as he thought, he saw that indeed she would be a great asset to his people. He *needed* her.

"And what else would I be?" Teneniel asked. "Your friend? Your lover?"

Isolder swallowed, knew what she wanted. On Hapes she would be considered a commoner, without a title or inheritance. If he married her, there would be public humiliation, embarrassment. He would have to relinquish his title, let one of his murderous cousins take the throne. The welfare of the Hapan worlds hung on his decision.

He put his hand on her back, hugged her good-bye. "You've been a good friend," he said, then he remembered that by her law, he was still her slave, "and a good master. I wish you nothing but happiness."

He got up, retrieved the sensory array window, looked back. Teneniel sat watching him, and Isolder had the creepy sensation that she was looking through him, reading his thoughts.

"How can I be happy if you leave me?" Teneniel asked.

Isolder did not answer. He turned his back, began to walk away, and she said, "You've always been such a brave man.

What will you think of yourself now, if you turn your back on the woman you love?"

He halted, wondering if she had read his mind or if she was just reading his emotions. *Can you hear me?* he asked silently, but she did not answer.

He thought of her long, naked legs; of the earthy smell of the hides she wore; of her copper eyes in a color unlike anything he'd seen among Hapan women; and of those full lips that he wanted to kiss so badly.

"Why don't you do it?" Teneniel asked.

"I can't," Isolder said, refusing to turn and look at her. "I don't know what you're trying to do to me. Get out of my mind!"

"I've done nothing," Teneniel said, her voice frank, innocent. "You're the one who has done it. You and I are connected. I should have realized that in the desert when I first saw you: I knew immediately that you had come to that spot looking for someone to love, just as I had. And I've felt the connection growing stronger for days. You can't fall in love with a witch of Dathomir without her knowing of it—not if she loves you in return."

"You don't understand," Isolder said. "If I tried to marry you, there would be public disapproval, repercussions. My cousins—" Isolder's blaster crunched in its holster and sparks flew from it. He looked down, saw it crushed into a ball, then looked up and saw the anger in Teneniel's eyes. A wind whipped through the room, tearing tapestries from the wall, lifting stones in a cyclone. The wind carried the stones and tapestries through the breach in the wall, sent them flying down over the cliffs.

"I'm not afraid of your cousins or public disapproval," Teneniel said. "And I don't want your planets. Pick a neutral world for us if you like." She got up, sauntered over to him, and stood before him, looking up into his eyes. Her breath whispered against his neck, and she leaned close to him. The very touch of her felt electric.

Isolder's heart pounded. "Damn you!" he whispered fiercely. "You're making a mess out of my life!"

Teneniel nodded. She put her arms around his neck and

kissed him, and in that endless moment, he remembered being with his father at age nine, playing in a virgin ocean on Dreena, an uninhabited world in the Hapes cluster. And Teneniel's kiss seemed as clean as those pure waters, washing away his doubts and uncertainties.

He kissed her fiercely, backed away. "Let's go. We're in a hurry!"

Teneniel grabbed his right hand, as if to help hold the flashlight, and they ran together down the fortress stairs.

When the villagers brought Luke to Leia, she was sure he was dead. He had a mass of bruises beneath the eyes, a slash on his face where blood had dried. The peasants set him on the grass, beneath the *Falcon*'s running lights, and Leia held his face in her hands.

He opened his eyes, smiled weakly. "Leia?" he coughed. "I heard you . . . call me?"

"I—" She didn't want to worry him, wanted only to let him rest. "I'm all right."

"No," Luke said, "you're not. Where did Han go?"

"He turned himself in to Gethzerion," Leia said. "She was taking hostages, killing prisoners. He had to go. Zsinj will be picking him up in three hours."

"No!" Luke said, fighting to sit up. "I must stop her! That's why I came here!"

"You can't!" Leia pushed him back down as easily as if she were knocking over a child. "You're hurt. Rest now, rest! Live to fight another day."

"Let me rest, for three hours," Luke said, closing his eyes, breathing deeply. "Wake me in three hours."

"Just sleep," Leia said. "I'll wake you."

Luke's eyes snapped open, and he studied her face angrily. "Don't lie to me! You have no intention of waking me!"

Isolder came up from the front of the craft where he and Teneniel had been hurriedly trying to clean the dirt and gravel out of the sensor array. Isolder crouched down, with Teneniel at his back. "Hey, friend," Isolder said. "Leia's right. Take it easy. You're too weak to do much for us now."

Luke laid his head back, shut his eyes as if he could no longer stay awake, but his voice suddenly became strong and commanding. "Give me time. You don't know the power of the Force."

Isolder put a hand on Luke's shoulder. "I've seen it," he said. "I know."

"No! No, you don't," Luke said desperately, rising up with unexpected strength. "None of us do!" Luke sat up for a moment, fell back. "Promise," he gasped. "Promise to wake me!"

Leia felt something, something in his words more than mere conviction—she felt something powerful in Luke, just under the surface, as if he were a raging fire. A new hope burned in her. "I'll wake you," Leia promised, and she stepped back, looked at Luke's battered form lying on the stretcher. She realized that she couldn't delude herself. Perhaps in a few days, a week, he really might be ready to battle Gethzerion.

Isolder put a blanket over Luke. "Teneniel and I can get him to a bunk."

Leia nodded. "Is the sensor array window back on?"

"Yes," Isolder said, "but I'm still having trouble with the long-range scanners."

Leia thought desperately. Everything in her cried out that she should go to rescue Han, but they didn't have enough time. If she used rancors, it would be a two-day trip. If they tried to fly the *Falcon*, even at top speed, they'd have a tough time making it more than halfway before the destroyers above homed in on their electronics and torpedoed the *Falcon* out of the sky. A thought struck her.

"Artoo, Threepio, come out here," Leia called into the ship.

Threepio hurried out. "Yes, Princess—how may I be of service?" Artoo rolled out, watching the edges of the gangplank with his electronic eye.

"Artoo," Leia asked, "can you get a count of the Star Destroyers up there for me?"

Artoo hesitated a moment, then a hatch flipped open and the droid extended his sensor dish. Artoo played the dish across the skies, then began emitting a series of electronic clicks and bleeps.

"Artoo reports that he cannot get a fix on any extraorbital

objects through any of his sensors other than radio waves. Apparently, the orbital nightcloak is blocking light at most wavelengths even through the ultraviolet and infrared ranges. However, he can verify twenty-six sources of radio emissions, and he suspects from previous counts that forty Star Destroyers are in orbit."

Isolder looked at Leia thoughtfully. "No wonder I can't fix the long-range scanners. There's nothing wrong with them."

"Right," Leia said.

"So as long as we fly under the orbital nightcloak and maintain radio silence, we're effectively a cloaked ship."

"Right!" Leia said.

Isolder nodded, glanced up at the *Falcon*'s array of conventional and proton torpedoes. "Let's go blast the hell out of those witches and see if we can rescue Han."

"No!" Leia said, glancing down at Luke, lying unconscious on his pallet. "Luke wants us to wait for him."

Han stood silently among the Nightsisters as the hover car dodged between the boles of giant trees lit only by its headlights. A full twenty Nightsisters were packed in the hover car, a solid, stinking mass in their dark robes.

They had tied his hands in front of him with a rope of whuffa hide, not even bothering to search him, they were so confident that he could not harm them.

The hover car shot over a hill, dropped with a stomach-wrenching thud and suddenly they were out of forest, racing over the clear desert toward the city lights.

Han closed his eyes, contemplated what he must do. He had to wait. He could blow the detonator at any time—but he wanted to get Gethzerion, had to get Gethzerion.

They drove into the city, and the Nightsisters jumped from the hover car, hurried toward their towers. Two stayed with Han, walked him to the abandoned airfield, took him into an old spaceport hangar whose roof had been blown away so that the dome walls rose around him like an impossible fence. "Wait by the back wall," one of the women said, dismissing him. The two stood by the door, talking quietly.

Han found his heart hammering, and he sat in the shadows on a hunk of rubble, waiting for Gethzerion to appear. He rested his thumbs in his belt buckle, palmed the thermal detonator.

She never came. Over the next several hours, the temperature dropped continually, until a light frost clung to the ground. Han kept checking his watch. Zsinj's four-hour appointment came and went. The shuttles never arrived, and Han began to wonder if Gethzerion was playing some kind of game with the warlord, perhaps trying to barter for a better deal.

As if to prove his worries true, Gethzerion's hover car made two more trips afield, each taking nearly two hours—just enough time to gather personnel from Singing Mountain.

After the third trip, a pair of stars appeared in the black sky, swept down toward the prison. The carriers extended their wings, then sledded in smoothly on antigrav, halted outside the tower. Han could see the ships' big stabilizer fins over the broken wall.

One Nightsister hissed, "Come on, General Solo. It's time."

Han swallowed, got to his feet, and walked to the exit. Lights from the carriers played over him, blinding him. Han walked slowly toward the lights, flanked by the two Nightsisters. He could not see the towers well. The ground was covered with Zsinj's stormtroopers, dressed in old Imperial armor. Han squinted, trying to see beyond them into the shadows on the other side of the carriers. If he detonated the bomb now, he would certainly take out the stormtroopers, and would probably damage one of the carriers—but he couldn't see for sure if the witches were there, unprotected.

"That's far enough!" a stormtrooper shouted, and the witches held Han's arm, halted.

An officer descended from the ship—a tall general with glittering platinum fingernails. General Melvar. He came within arm's reach, studied Han's face momentarily. He placed one platinum fingernail under Han's eye, as if to pluck it out, then raked a gash down Han's cheek.

He spoke into a microphone at his shoulder. "I've made visual identification. Han Solo is here."

Melvar listened momentarily, and only then did Han notice the microphone jacks behind his ears.

"Yes, sir," Melvar said. "I'll bring him aboard immediately."

The general grabbed Han roughly, digging his platinum nails into Han's biceps. "Hey, pal," Han said. "Don't be so hard on the merchandise. You might regret it."

"Oh, I don't think I'll regret it," Melvar said. "You see, causing others pain is, well, more than just a pastime for me. In my work for Zsinj it has become a cherished responsibility." He dug the claw of his pinky into a nerve center on Han's shoulder, then twisted. Fire blossomed all along Han's arm from the wrist up to the center of his back, and he gasped in pain.

"Hey, uh, that's some talent you've developed," Han admitted.

"Well," Melvar smiled, "I'm sure that I can convince Warlord Zsinj to let me demonstrate my talents more fully and at greater leisure. But come, we mustn't keep Zsinj waiting." He hurried Han toward the gangplank for the carrier, between a crowd of stormtroopers, and for one moment Han wondered if he would ever see Gethzerion.

He was halfway up the gangplank when the witch shouted, "Wait!"

General Melvar halted, glanced over his back. Gethzerion stood in the shadows at the base of her tower, a hundred meters off, flanked by a dozen Nightsisters. The old witch drew her robes up tight, stalked up to the carrier. Han surveyed the field. He'd surely take out the armed carrier with his detonator, along with General Melvar and Gethzerion, and at least the few Nightsisters outside the building. He'd hoped for better, but knew this was about all he'd get.

It felt odd, knowing that he was about to die. He'd expected to feel butterflies in his stomach, a tightness in his throat. But nothing came. He felt only numb, disheartened, regretful. After the life he'd lived, it seemed anticlimactic.

Gethzerion stopped at the foot of the gangplank, only an arm's length away. She looked up at Han, her leathery face still concealed by her hood. Han could smell heavy spices on her breath, and the scent of vinegary wine.

"So, General Solo," she said. "You led me a merry chase. I hope you enjoyed your stay."

Han looked at the old woman, said smugly, "I knew you

wouldn't be able to resist coming to gloat." He hooked his thumbs under his belt. "Why don't you gloat about this!"

He whipped out the thermal detonator and pushed the button. General Melvar lurched away, as did his guards. Melvar tripped over a stormtrooper behind him and both men went down in a tangle.

The detonator didn't go off. Han looked at it. The firing pin was broken.

"Having trouble with your explosive device?" Gethzerion opened her eyes wide and smiled. "Sister Shabell detected it before you ever boarded the hover craft, and she dismantled it with a word. You self-congratulating, strutting oaf! You never posed a threat to me or my Nightsisters! How dare you!" She reached out and made a grasping gesture, and the detonator flew from Han's fingers, landed in her palm. She offered it to Melvar. "I'll let you dispose of this, General. It still presents some danger. I thought it best to retrieve it before you depart."

Melvar got up, tried to recover his dignity, and took the detonator. "Thank you," he grunted.

"Ah, and allow me to do you one more favor!" Gethzerion whispered, stepping forward. "By giving you this—" Her eyes opened wide, blazing, and she made a raking motion with her index finger. Beside Han the general gasped, reached up to hold his temple, then staggered forward a pace. "A simple death!" Gethzerion cackled.

All around Han, a hundred stormtroopers crumpled simultaneously, some of them staggering a step or two, some firing blaster rifles in the air so that Han instinctively ducked. Within three seconds the stormtroopers lay on the ground like drugged birds, unmoving. Han looked up at the carrier, waiting for the gunners in the ship to open fire.

Nothing happened. The ship remained deathly still.

Several Nightsisters rushed from their tower, pushed past Han, made their way up to the carrier bringing dozens of Imperial prisoners with them to fly the ships. One Nightsister shoved Han aside, knocking him off the ramp. Han heard screams inside the ship, so that even though the gunner had never fired, he could tell that the crew was waging some kind of battle. Han figured the gunner must have died with the other stormtroopers. He found that he wasn't really surprised that the witches would attack this ship. Gethzerion wouldn't have been so stupid as to try to fly off this planet in a ship that had no armaments, no shielding—not with Zsinj's Star Destroyers in range.

Han waited beside the ramp, watching as Gethzerion approached. She pointed a finger at him and smiled. He glanced at a blaster lying near his hand, knowing that even if he managed to grab it, he would still die.

"Now, General Solo, what shall I do with you?" Gethzerion asked.

"Hey," Han said, raising his hands. "I have no quarrel with you. In fact, if you'll remember, I spent most of the last several days trying to avoid you. Why don't you and I shake hands and just go our separate ways?"

Gethzerion stopped at the foot of the ramp, looked in his eyes and laughed. "What? Don't you think it only fair now that I treat you as badly as you would have treated me?"

"Well, I—"

Gethzerion twitched her finger, and Han jerked upright, found himself with his feet dangling in the air, held by an invisible cord around his throat. Gethzerion watched him intently, began to sing, swaying from side to side. He felt the noose around his neck tightening.

Han choked, kicked, fought to break free.

"I wonder what your thermal detonator would have done to me," Gethzerion reflected, still swaying. "I suspect it would have blasted my flesh into scraps, and broken my bones, and fried me all at once. So I think I shall do all of these things to you—but not so hastily. Not all at once. I think we shall work from the inside out. First I'll snap your bones, one by one. Do you know how many bones there are in the human body, General Solo? If you do, just triple the number, and you'll know how many bones you'll have when I finish with you.

"We'll begin with your leg," Gethzerion said. "Listen carefully!" She twitched her finger, and the tibia in his right leg made crackling sounds. A painful spasm made its way up to his hip.

"Aaaghh," he cried—and saw something over the desert.

There about two kilometers off he saw the running lights of the *Millennium Falcon* speeding toward them, only meters above ground.

Gethzerion smiled in satisfaction. "There now, you have three bones where you had but one."

Han tried to stall her, tried to think of anything that would slow her for a moment. "Listen," he strained to speak. "You aren't going to do this to, to, to my *teeth*, are you?" he said, unable to think of anything else. "I mean, uh, anything but the teeth!" He glanced around the compound. Several Nightsisters were coming out the bottom of the towers.

"Oh, yes, the teeth," Gethzerion said, and she twitched her forefinger.

Han's right upper rear molar exploded with a popping sound, and the stabbing pain shot through his ear and upper face, until it felt as if Gethzerion had grabbed his eye at the socket and were intent on pulling it through the roof of his mouth. Han silently cursed himself for giving her nifty ideas. The *Falcon* wasn't getting here fast enough, and Han shook his head.

"Wait!" he cried. "Let's talk about this!" and Gethzerion wiggled her forefinger again. The upper left rear molar snapped, and suddenly there was a whooshing sound as the *Falcon* fired its missiles. The bottom of the tower exploded, tossing black-robed witches into the air. The tower began to lean as it collapsed.

Gethzerion turned, and Han dropped to the ground, released. Pain tore through his broken leg. A volley of blaster fire shot from the dorsal turrets with pinpoint accuracy. Gethzerion crouched as the bolt ripped through the air where her head had been. She leaped away from the ship, jumped and twisted just as another volley tore beneath her.

Han got a spooky feeling about this. Nobody could fire a ship's blasters with such accuracy. He rolled under the gangplank to take cover from flying debris. The heavily armored guard droids on all six prison towers spun on their turrets and opened fire on the *Falcon*, blasting with their cannons.

The *Falcon* rocketed over the prison, flipping in a complex quadruple spin that somehow managed to avoid all the incoming fire. Han had never seen anyone fly like that—not Chewie, not himself. Whoever was at the controls was an ace fighter pilot the likes of no one he'd ever seen, and he guessed it must be Isolder. The *Falcon* made a nearly impossibly tight roll a kilometer out, and shot back over the prison, upside down, all guns blazing.

Guard droids flared into mushroom clouds at the touch of the blaster canons. The unarmed carrier took a hit and crumpled, began to burn. The *Falcon* whizzed overhead, banked for another pass.

Gethzerion must have recognized that staying on the ground to fight was futile, for she leaped up the gangplank of the Imperial ship faster than Han would have believed possible. The carrier's turbines whirred to life before the gangplank even raised, and the air around the ship took on a blue sheen as shields activated. This was an Imperial personnel carrier—fully armed and shielded, nothing for the *Falcon* to toy with.

If Han remained under the carrier as it took off, he would get fried. Yet even if his leg weren't broken, by running he would have risked the *Falcon*'s blaster fire. He crawled for it, moving across the yard as fast as he could with a broken leg, then fell more than jumped over a bit of rubble from the tower, hoping the Nightsisters wouldn't shoot at him in their haste to leave.

The *Falcon* fired with its ion cannons, and blue lightning flickered around the carrier's hull, but the shields held. The carrier thundered into the air, white flames screaming from its exhaust nacelles.

The *Falcon* twisted around a hill, blasted a hole in the prison walls and skidded to a halt six yards from Han. The bottom hatch flew open, and Leia shouted, "Come on! Come on!"

Augwynne rushed down the hatch with two of her clan sisters, all three dressed in full helms and robes, and from the looks in their eyes, Han pitied the prison guards.

He crawled for the *Falcon,* and Isolder ran out, grabbed his shoulder and half-carried Han into the ship. Han looked at Isolder, confused. "Who, who's flying?"

"Luke," Leia said.

"Luke?" Han asked. "Luke's not that good!"

"Nobody's this good," Isolder said, slapping Han on the

back. "I've got to see this!" He ran back down the access tube to the control room.

Leia stared hard into Han's eyes, grabbed his face and kissed him. Pain flared from the broken molars and Han nearly screamed, but instead held Leia and closed his eyes, just enjoying it.

The ship jostled and swerved as Luke pulled maneuvers that even the accelerator compensators couldn't neutralize, and Chewbacca gave a terrified roar from the cockpit. Han limped in, holding onto Leia for support. He strapped himself into a seat, reached up and grabbed the emergency medkit from the compartment above his head, and slapped a painkiller patch on his arm. The dorsal quadruple blaster cannons fired, and Han looked around. Chewbacca, Isolder, Teneniel, and the droids were all in the cockpit, watching Luke.

"Who's up there firing the blaster cannons?" Han asked.

"Luke," Leia said, and Han looked down the hallway, confused. You could fire the blasters from the cockpit, but only with greatly reduced accuracy. Yet Luke had nearly taken Gethzerion's head off, with Han less than a meter away, while piloting this hunk of junk at full attack speed. The whole thing was too darned spooky.

Luke sweated from the effort of flying the *Falcon*. Levers and buttons on Chewie's control panel seemed to take on a life of their own as Luke manipulated them with the Force. The Jedi was doing the work of three—pilot, copilot, gunner. Luke fired a missile barrage without lowering the particle shields, and Chewie roared in terror and threw his hands in front of his face.

But as the missiles hit the fifty-meter mark, Luke dropped the shields and restarted them, so that they flickered for less than the blink of an eye. Han had never seen anyone with reflexes so sharply honed.

The carrier's rear shields erupted in a dazzling display of lights, and the witches finally managed to fire a barrage of blaster cannons on their own. Luke hit the thrusters and the *Falcon* leaped up, dodging. He fired his proton torpedoes, and the torpedoes accelerated toward the carrier in a white blur.

The Nightsisters shot their blasters at the missiles, and the torpedoes erupted in a sulfurous cloud. Han stared in disbelief at what the witches had done. No gunner was *that* good.

"Leia, Isolder," Luke shouted, "get on those quad cannons and open fire. Give them everything you've got."

"Give it up," Han said. "They're too heavily shielded! You're just going to get my ship all busted."

"And let these Nightsisters free on the galaxy? No way! I'm not giving up," Luke shouted. "Go on, Leia, get up there!"

Luke reached out, flipped on the radio jammers, sending out a storm of broadcast information. Han raised an eyebrow, wondering what Luke was up to. The witches certainly weren't going to try to call anyone, so the jammers served little function other than to warn everyone in the star system that a ship was there.

Leia ran down to the ventral cannon, began firing. Luke downed all shields and fired the ion cannons, risking that the carrier wouldn't lower its shields to return fire. Isolder began firing from the dorsal cannon, and the carrier accelerated, moving out of their range.

"They're getting ready to jump to lightspeed!" Han shouted, and he looked at the viewscreen. Space was a flat black curtain and the carrier accelerated into it.

"Not this close to the gravity well, they aren't!" Luke argued, and he accelerated behind.

Then Han understood. Luke knew his blasters and missiles couldn't bring down the carrier's shields. He'd turned on the radio jammers because he was calling for Zsinj. He wanted the Star Destroyers to know that the witches were hightailing it away, hoping to get enough altitude to make their jump into hyperspace.

They accelerated into the blackness of the nightcloak, Han holding his breath. The viewscreen went black; an onyx fog. Luke flipped off the jammers, and the *Falcon* roared into the sunlight, the carrier still ahead, and ten thousand stars glittered like jewels. So much light.

Han felt as if he'd just gotten a breath of fresh air.

Proximity indicators screamed in warning, and Han looked up, saw the slate gray V's of twin Star Destroyers converging ahead of them. Luke swerved to starboard, and a barrage of missiles ripped from the destroyers, punctured the carrier's weakened shields.

Han watched the missiles puncture the hull of the witches'

carrier. A plume of white-hot metal fragments burst from its right exhaust nacelle. For two full seconds, the carrier's running lights dimmed and the engines flared more brightly. Then it sputtered in midair and erupted into a ball of flame.

Han whooped in celebration as Luke accelerated wildly back toward Dathomir, into the protective covering of the orbital nightcloak, and once again the darkness swallowed them.

Leia was screaming for joy down in her turret, and Luke shouted, "Leia, Isolder, stay put. We're not done yet."

Luke flipped a switch, and the cockpit flooded with radio chatter. The screens picked up the sources, plotted them in tri-D on the head-up holo display. Han stared at the mess above them in dismay. The sky was full of ships. No matter which way they vectored, it would be a tight squeeze, trying to make it out of the gravity well. Apparently the nightcloak was fouling the scanners somewhat. Although the scanners showed the ships, they weren't picking up the transponder signals, and Han couldn't tell what kinds of ships were out there.

Han swallowed. "What are you thinking, kid, what are you going to do?"

Luke sighed, looked at the assembly of destroyers above them. "We've got to bring down this nightcloak," Luke said. "It's not just people down there—it's, it's trees and grass and lizards and worms! Life! A whole living world!"

"What?" Han said. "You want to get your head blown off for a bunch of lizards and worms? Don't flip on me now, kid! Find a hole in their net, and let's blast out of here."

"No," Luke said, breathing heavily. Chewbacca roared at Luke, yet Luke didn't respond. Instead the Jedi remained in the pilot's seat as if frozen, staring ahead in the smothering darkness as he flew.

Good, good, Han thought. *At least he's putting some distance between us and those other fighters.* Wherever they came out, Zsinj's men would not likely be ready for them. Luke closed his eyes, accelerated, as if in a trance, and smiled serenely. Han looked at his face, and though he was desperately afraid that Luke would get them all killed, right at this moment it didn't seem to matter. *Go ahead and get us killed,* Han thought. *We owe you our lives anyway.*

"Thanks," Luke said, as if Han had spoken the words.

Luke fired the quad blasters, and Han did not see their light trail. The darkness was so complete, that even that little bit of light seemed denied them. Luke waited a moment, and Han watched the targeting sights playing over the head-up holo display. Luke locked onto something, fired. Han couldn't see a target, nothing on the scopes, and he wondered if Luke really was hitting anything.

Again and again over the next twenty minutes Luke repeated the tactic, with no visible results. Threepio stood behind Han and whispered, "Pardon me, Your Highness, but do you think we're accomplishing anything? Perhaps you should take the fire controls?"

"Nah, let Luke do it," Han said, and he glanced back at the holo display. The radio signatures were rapidly increasing in number, and Han realized that Zsinj must have scrambled several hundred fighters. Apparently Luke's efforts had begun to worry the warlord.

And suddenly Luke fired a salvo and they came out of the blackness again, flying through the stars. It took a moment for Han to recognize that the orbital nightcloak had shorted out, and Dathomir once again turned below them, a shining world of turquoise oceans and dark brown continents.

Chewie roared, and Luke accelerated away from the planet.

Han gasped as the holo display began reading the transponder signals, showing the ships above them. There were hundreds of ships in the air—Imperial Star Destroyers and the rust-colored disks of Hapan Battle Dragons. TIE fighters and X-wings gyrated overhead in a deadly dance. Zsinj hadn't just scrambled fighters—the whole Hapan fleet had jumped out of hyperspace.

Huge silver orbs shot out in all directions from one Hapan Battle Dragon, and Han swallowed hard. The Hapans were mining hyperspace with pulsemass generators. It was a risky maneuver, because it stranded both the attacker and the victim in normal space for ten or fifteen minutes. It was a tactic that the Rebels had never used. One way or another, no one would be leaving this planet soon. The Hapans planned to either win or die.

Luke accelerated to attack speed, glanced up at the viewscreen and locked his sights on an enemy Star Destroyer that was besieged on either side by Hapan Battle Dragons. The sky around the Imperial destroyer was alive with TIE fighters— more than any one destroyer could carry, and the hair rose on Han's head as he realized that it must have drawn off support from other destroyers. Han checked the holo display. Two other Imperial destroyers were vectoring in, coming to the ship's rescue.

"Who is on that Star Destroyer?" Han asked, gazing at the highly protected ship.

"Zsinj," Luke answered softly. "That's the *Iron Fist*."

"Give me the helm, kid," Han said, mouth dry. "I want him."

Luke looked over his shoulder, and for the first time Han noticed that the Jedi's face was a bruised mess, but his eyes were clear. "Are you sure you can handle it?" Luke said. "That *is* a Star Destroyer up there."

Han nodded soberly. "Yeah, and that's my planet he's trespassing on! I want him—but don't be afraid to help me out, if I need it."

"Whatever you say, Your Majesty," Luke said, and the way he said it, it didn't sound like a joke. Luke got up from the pilot's seat.

Han sat down, pain spasming through his leg, leaned his head back against the headrest, and breathed deeply. For the first time in months, he felt at home. "Look, kid," Han said, flicking the stick so that he veered away from the *Iron Fist*, headed on a collision course with a TIE interceptor. "I don't know any of your Jedi tricks, but the best way to get close to a Star Destroyer is to sort of mosey on in, and try to act like you would rather be *anyplace* but where you are."

Han glanced down at his weapons display. He still had four Arakyd concussion missiles in his launch tubes, but his proton torpedoes were dry. He armed the concussion missiles, took remote control of the dorsal quad blaster cannons, and fired a couple of salvos ahead of the TIE interceptor, giving just enough lead. The little gray ship hit the blasts and flared into oblivion, and Han vectored toward another fighter that was hightailing it toward Zsinj's *Iron Fist*.

Han accelerated as if to attack, but hung back a good kilometer until he felt the *Falcon* shimmy. Tractor beams.

Chewbacca growled.

"I know," Han said. "Transfer power from the rear deflector shields. We won't let them hold us long."

Calmly, he accelerated toward the *Iron Fist* at full sublight-speed, jiggling the stick so that even though the tractor beams were pulling them in, the *Falcon* presented a moving target. He dove through a bevy of TIE fighters, and behind him he heard Luke gasp. They were coming up on that Star Destroyer mighty fast.

Han looked to see which port the tractor beam was pulling him toward. In half a second he spotted it, waited until he figured he'd passed through the ship's particle shields, then fired two of his concussion missiles.

The tractor beams pulled the missiles home. When they hit, an explosion blossomed on the *Iron Fist,* and Han hit the decelerators and tried to hang onto the stick as he turned.

He held his breath, tried not to let the others see him sweat as he skimmed over a turret that couldn't spin fast enough to fire on him.

"You're under their shields!" Isolder shouted over the intercom. "You can fire anytime!"

"Yeah," Han said. "I know!" A blaster cannon turret swung at them, and Han spun the ship, dodged the fire. He armed his last two Arakyds, then flipped his radio switch to standard Imperial frequency.

"Emergency message for Warlord Zsinj of the *Iron Fist*! Priority Red. Respond immediately! Do you copy! Priority Red. I have an emergency message for Warlord Zsinj!"

He waited for an eternity, weaving low through a maze of blaster turrets. At last Zsinj responded, and his face came up on the holo display.

"This is Zsinj!" he shouted, and the warlord's face was red, eyes frenzied from the battle.

"This is General Han Solo." Han nudged the stick, and the *Falcon* rose toward the forward command module of the *Iron Fist*. "Look up at your viewscreen, you vermin. Kiss my Wookiee!"

He waited half a second as Zsinj looked out his viewscreen to see the *Falcon* hurtling toward him. Realization dawned on Zsinj's face. Han fired his last two concussion missiles.

The top half of the *Iron Fist*'s forward command module disintegrated in a cascade of splintered metal. With its shields down, the destroyer became a sitting duck. A shot from a Hapan ion cannon bathed the *Iron Fist* in blue lightning, and with its complex circuitry down, immediately it fell victim to a hail of proton torpedoes.

Han accelerated away from the dying ship, out of orbit for a moment, content to leave any other dogfights to the Hapans. With Zsinj gone, he figured it would only be a few moments before the Imperial fleet surrendered.

There were no wild shouts of celebration behind him, no glee. Instead, only a profound silence.

He found that his hands were shaking, and his vision blurred. "Chewie, take the controls for a minute," Han said. And Han folded his arms over his chest. Months of frustration, months of doubts and worries and fears. That's what Zsinj had cost him.

Han felt Leia's thin hands on his shoulders, massaging them. His breath was coming ragged, and he leaned back in the captain's seat, let her knead some of the tension away. It was as if for the past five months, his muscles had been cramping tighter and tighter into little knots, warping him, and suddenly those knots began to unravel, work themselves out. *What a cramped little man I've been*, Han realized, wondering how he had not seen it, not noticed it himself, and promising himself that he would never let it happen again.

"Feel better?" Leia asked.

Han considered. Killing Zsinj was not something he could feel good about. Killing him was such a small, petty thing. Yet, he felt such a profound sense of relief. "Yeah," Han said. "I haven't felt this good since . . . I don't know when."

"The monster has one less head," Leia said.

"Yeah," Han said, "now that the papa shark is dead, all the little baby sharks will have to start gobbling each other."

"And pretty soon, there will be a lot fewer sharks," Leia said.

Han added, "And in the meantime, the New Republic can rush into Zsinj's old territory and take a few hundred star systems out of their hands."

Leia swiveled his seat around, and Han could see Isolder,

Teneniel, Luke, and the droids in the corridor. It was funny how most people wanted a crowd around celebrating a victory. Han always wanted to relish it alone.

"You won," Leia said, and her eyes were bright, full of tears.

"The war?" Han asked, wondering if she were just trying to make him feel good. "No. Not hardly."

"Not that—" Leia said, "our bet. Seven days on Dathomir? You said that if I fell in love with you all over again, I had to marry you. The seven days isn't over yet. You won."

"Oh, that," Han said. "Look—that was a stupid bet. I would never force you to do something like that. I release you from it."

"Oh yeah?" Leia said. "*Well, I don't release you!*" She took his chin in her hands and kissed him, a long slow kiss that seemed to penetrate every aching fiber of his being, making him whole.

Isolder watched them kiss. This whole episode would be a colossal embarrassment on Hapes. It wouldn't play well at all. And yet . . . he felt happy for them.

His comlink buzzed a secure channel that could only be accessed by Hapan security. He pulled it from his belt, flipped it open, saw the image of Astarta on the comlink's tiny screen. His bodyguard smiled in greeting.

"It's good to see you," Isolder said. "Yet I hadn't expected the fleet for three more days—which means that someone ordered them to fly through a proscribed route."

"Once I fled Dathomir," Astarta said, "I fed the Jedi's route to our fleet's astrogators via the holo vid. The fleet was able to shave a few parsecs off their trip."

"Hmmm," Isolder said. "An interesting gamble, but still it was dangerous."

"We did it on your mother's order," Astarta explained. "She's coming in with the Olanji fleet tomorrow. We've begun receiving surrenders from some of Zsinj's vessels. Since you are temporarily in command of the fleet, what are your wishes?"

Isolder's mind did a little flip, stunned that his mother would take such a risk on his behalf. "Accept only unconditional surrenders," he said, "and prepare to take any spaceworthy Star Destroyers back to Hapes. As for the Imperial shipyard—destroy it!"

"Yes, sir," Astarta said. "How soon should we be ready to pull out?"

Isolder thought for a moment. Zsinj may have sent for reinforcements. They'd have to get away from Dathomir as soon as possible. "Two days."

"Two days?" Astarta asked, the surprise in her voice showing that she thought it an extraordinarily slow retreat. "We will have to verify that with your mother."

"There are political prisoners on the planet, along with several thousand locals that may wish to be evacuated," Isolder said firmly. "We will need to contact them, give them the opportunity to leave."

Chapter

27

Han gathered sisters from all nine of Dathomir's clans for a feast the following evening, in the hall of warriors at Singing Mountain. The witches wore their finest helms and robes, but all of their finery seemed drab compared with that of the queen mother, who wore lavender silks and decorated her hair with rainbow gems from Gallinore. Ta'a Chume seemed mildly annoyed by the proceedings and rested uneasily on the crude leather cushions, as if the witches' finery were beneath her. She kept swatting at stinging insects, glancing toward the door distractedly, eager to get back to Hapes and her own business.

Han watched her through the evening, bemused by the beautiful face hidden behind the lavender veil, appalled at her bad manners.

At the height of the feast, Han presented Augwynne with the deed to Dathomir, and the old woman wept in gratitude, then had servants bring up the gold and gems she had collected, and the servants dumped the baskets onto the floor at Han's feet.

Han stood amazed for a moment, and said, "I, uh, forgot

about that. Look, I don't really want all of this." He looked into Leia's eyes. "I've already got everything I want."

"A bargain is a bargain, General Solo," Augwynne said. "Besides, we owe you more than we can repay. Not only have you freed us from Zsinj, but you helped destroy the Nightsisters. We will forever be in your debt."

"Yeah but—" Han started to object, but Leia nudged his ribs. "Keep it," she whispered. "We can use it to pay for the wedding."

Han looked at the gems at his feet, and wondered just how big a wedding Leia had planned.

"I have an announcement that also will affect your people," Prince Isolder said from a cushion beside his mother, and he rose to his feet, reached out his hand across the room. "Teneniel Djo, the granddaughter of Augwynne Djo, has consented to be my wife."

"No!" Ta'a Chume shouted, and she stood, glared at her son. "You can't marry a woman from this uncivilized little mud hole. I forbid it! She can't be the queen mother of Hapes."

"She's a princess, with her own world to inherit," Isolder said. "I think that is qualification enough. You've plenty of years left to sit on the throne, and in that time you can train her."

"Even if she *is* a princess—" the queen mother said, "something that I doubt you could successfully argue—her family has held deed to this world for less than five minutes! She has no royal blood in her, no lineage."

"But I love her," Isolder said, "and with or without your permission, I will marry her."

"You fool," Ta'a Chume hissed. "Do you think I would allow that?"

"No," Luke said, from the back of the room, "just as *I'm* sure that you never intended for him to marry Leia. Why don't you remove your veil and tell him who sent the assassins to dispose of her?" Luke's voice had that confident, commanding tone it took on when he used the Force. Ta'a Chume cringed as if she'd been touched with an electric prod, and she backed away. "Go ahead," Luke said, "remove your veil and tell him."

Ta'a Chume's hands shook as she pulled the veil back. She fought Luke's command. "I sent the assassins."

Isolder's eyes widened, and grief washed through him. "Why?" he asked. "You gave your permission. You sent your gifts and your entourage. I did nothing in secret."

"You asked for an alliance I could not approve of," Ta'a Chume said. "You chose a dowryless pacifist from a democracy. Listen to her talk of her vaunted New Republic! For four thousand years our family has ruled the Hapan cluster, but you would turn Hapes over to her, and in a generation her children would surrender control of the government, give it over to the rabble!

"Still, I did not want to deny you outright. I did not want to . . . compromise . . . your sense of loyalty to me."

"You would rather murder someone than risk losing my allegiance?" Isolder found his nostrils flaring. "Did you also hope that by doing this you could further distance me from my aunts?"

The queen mother's eyes narrowed. "Oh, your aunts have committed their shares of murders. They're every bit as dangerous as you believe. But Leia is a pacifist. I couldn't let you marry a pacifist. She would be too weak to rule. Don't you see? If Hapes had had a stronger military presence before the rise of the Empire—as I always advocated—we never would have fallen to the Empire. Mealymouthed pacifists and diplomats nearly ruined our realm."

"And the Lady Elliar," Isolder said with wonder in his voice, "she was a pacifist. Did you kill her, too?"

Ta'a Chume pulled the veil back over her face, turned away. "I will not be interrogated in this fashion. I'm leaving."

A note of wonder and horror came to Isolder's voice. "And my brother—was he too weak to rule? Is that it? Have you never intended to let anyone but *you* choose your successor?"

Ta'a Chume spun around. "Keep your assumptions to yourself!" she said vehemently. "Don't ponder things that you can't possibly understand. You are, after all, only a male."

"I understand murder!" Isolder shouted, nostrils flaring. "I understand infanticide!" But Ta'a Chume began picking her way through the crowd, heading for the door.

Teneniel took his elbow and said softly, "Let me reason with her. Ta'a Chume," she said softly, and Ta'a Chume stopped as if Teneniel had yanked her with an invisible cord.

"I'm going to marry your son, and someday I'll rule your worlds in your place." Ta'a Chume turned, and her eyes seemed to be burning lights as she glared through her lavender veil.

Teneniel continued. "Let me assure you that I am not a pacifist. In the past two days alone, I have killed several people, and if you ever try to harm me or mine, I will force you to confess publicly all of your crimes, and then I will execute you. I assure you, I find you to be that contemptible!"

Ta'a Chume's four bodyguards had been standing against the wall. Teneniel could not know it, but threatening the queen mother was grounds for immediate execution. The queen's guards went for their blasters, and Teneniel waved her hand. The blasters crumpled and clattered to the floor. One guard rushed forward, and Teneniel waved her hand and struck her from a distance with an invisible fist. The guard's jaw cracked with a sickening thud, and she fell backward, stunned.

Ta'a Chume watched the brief battle from the corner of her eye.

"Reconsider, Mother," Isolder said. "You once told me that you didn't want to risk the chance that our ancestors would be ruled by an oligarchy of spoon benders and readers of auras. But if I take Teneniel as my wife, there is a good chance that your grandchildren will *be* those spoon benders."

Ta'a Chume hesitated. Looked at Teneniel for a long moment. "Perhaps," Ta'a Chume said with conviction, "I was hasty in my judgment. I suspect that Teneniel Djo, princess of Dathomir, will make an adequate queen mother. Make sure you dress her in something appropriate before you bring her home."

She turned to leave, and Isolder said to her back, "One more thing, Mother. We are going to join the New Republic. *Now!*"

Ta'a Chume hesitated, nodded her head in consent, and stormed from the room.

The next morning, Luke stood on the parapet of the war room in the early sun, watching the shuttles rise in the distance, carrying the last of the refugees from the prison.

Augwynne came and stood behind him, watching the tiny ships leave. "Are you sure you won't go with them?" Luke said. "This will still be a dangerous sector."

"No," Augwynne answered. "Dathomir is our home. And we have nothing here that anyone would want—except you. We have something *you* want. I can feel that about you. What do you desire?"

"A wreck, out in the desert," Luke answered. "Once it was a spaceship, called the *Chu'unthor,* and the Jedi trained there. I'd like to come back someday and salvage it, see if any of its records are intact."

"Ah, yes. Our ancestors once fought a great battle there with the Jai."

"And you won," Luke said.

"No," Augwynne said, leaning her back against the stone wall of the fortress and folding her arms. "We didn't. In the end, both sides sat down and talked, negotiated a settlement."

Luke laughed. "So you got the ship, but it sat in the desert for three hundred years and rotted? What did you gain?"

"I don't know," Augwynne said. "Only Mother Rell was there, and her mind is nearly gone."

"Mother Rell?" Luke asked, and an odd sense of peace stole through him. Augwynne looked at him questioningly, and Luke hurried through the hall, down to Rell's room. The old crone sat on her cushion on the stone box as before, wisps of silver hair shining in the candle lights. She looked up at him vacantly.

"Mother Rell, it's me, Luke Skywalker," Luke said, and the old crone peered at him through rheumy eyes.

"What?" she asked. "Are the Nightsisters all dead? You killed them?"

"Yes," Luke answered.

"Then our world is ended, and a new one begun, as Yoda foretold." Luke found he was shaking with excitement. "I suppose you have come for the records?"

"Yes," Luke answered.

"We wanted them, you know," Rell said. "But the Jai would not give us the technology to read them. They said that the teachings were too powerful, and as long as there were Nightsisters on our world, we could not have them. Yoda prom-

ised that someday you would share them with our children."
She feebly got up from her seat, turned to the stone box and
pulled off the cushion, tried to open it.

"Help me, here," she said, and Luke heaved the box open.
Inside was a metal locker, corroded, with an ancient access control panel on it. The green run light on the box still shone. Luke
studied the box, punched in the two glyphs that spelled Yoda's
name. A hissing noise erupted from the locker as the lid popped
and air seeped in. Luke opened it.

The box was filled with reader disks—hundreds of them,
containing more volumes of information than any one person
could hope to study in a lifetime.

At noon that day, a Hapan shuttle came to pick up Teneniel
and Isolder. Luke, Han, Chewie, Leia, and the droids went to
see them off. Isolder found that he was hesitant to leave this
planet. Leia hugged them both and wished them happiness,
weeping openly until Teneniel reminded her that their paths
would cross from time to time, now that Hapes had joined the
New Republic.

Han shook Teneniel's hand, punched Isolder on the arm in
a friendly sort of way, and said, "See you around, Slime. Watch
out for pirates."

Isolder smiled back, held Han's eye. The witches and Luke
had done their best to heal Han's broken leg and teeth, though
he still wore a brace on his leg. Han looked like a pirate. He still
had that cocky air, the swagger to his walk. Even with a brace,
Han could swagger. "See you around, Oaf," Isolder said, but he
couldn't leave it at that. "So where do you two think you'll take
your honeymoon?"

Han shrugged. "I had hoped to take it here on Dathomir,
but things have quieted down so much in the past two days,
I'm afraid it would get boring."

"Perhaps you would like to tour the Hapan worlds,"
Isolder suggested. "I'm sure you would find this visit more
hospitable than your last."

"That's an easy promise to keep," Han agreed, "as long as
they don't shoot me on sight."

"We won't do that," Isolder promised, "though I might

have my people check your bags for stolen goods before you leave."

Han laughed, clapped him on the back. Chewbacca and Threepio said their good-byes, and then it was Luke's turn. The Jedi had hung back from the rest, watching them intently. He did not give them a tearful farewell. Instead, he took Teneniel's hand, held it for a moment and looked into her eyes—no, looked beyond her eyes. "You will give birth to a daughter first," Luke said, "and she will be strong and virtuous, like you. When you feel the time is right, perhaps you will send her to me for training."

Teneniel smiled, hugged him. Luke took Isolder's hand, held it. "Remember to serve the light side of the Force," Luke said. "Though you will never wield a lightsaber or heal the sick, you have some light within you. Be true to that light."

"I will," Isolder promised, and he wondered at how much his life had changed in the past few days. In a fraction of a second he had decided to follow Luke to this planet, and now he knew that he would be following Luke's path for the rest of his life. "I will," he said again, and he hugged the Jedi.

For a moment, they all stood staring at one another, and then Isolder looked around the valley once again, to the huts in the fields, the dark fortress above them, the rancors splashing in the pond, the bright sun shining over the southern valleys, the mountains and the deserts beyond. Isolder inhaled the sweet, clean air, tasting the rich scent of Dathomir for one last time, and he felt his sinuses burn just a little. He realized that he must have been allergic to something on this planet.

He took Teneniel's hand, and headed aboard the shuttle with his betrothed, taking her to other worlds, other stars.

Six weeks later, under the blue skies of Coruscant, Luke had just finished bathing and had dressed in a fine gray robe. As best man at Leia's wedding, he'd planned to arrive early, but then the shuttle driver dropped him at the Aldereenian consulate by accident, a building occupied by some insect race Luke had never heard of and which happened to be nearly two hundred kilometers from the Alderaanian consulate.

So he found himself arriving at the consulate an hour later

than he planned, and when he managed to get in the door, he raced down a long corridor paneled with great slabs of lustrous ancient uwa wood, toward the White Room. He turned a corner, and found See-Threepio running frantically just ahead.

Luke caught up with the droid and said, "Hey, Threepio, what's wrong?"

"Oh, Master Luke," Threepio said. "I'm so relieved to see you. I'm afraid I've gotten us all into a terrible mess! It's all my fault! We must stop the wedding immediately!"

"What's wrong?" Luke asked. "What are you talking about?"

"I just learned horrible news from the city computer. It was cross-verifying some files, and found that Han isn't royalty after all!"

"He's not?" Luke said.

"No! His great-grandfather, Korol Solo, was only a pretender to the throne—and got hanged for his crimes! We must warn everyone!"

"So that's why he got so embarrassed and walked out on the Alderaanian Council when you announced his lineage," Luke said. "He knew that his great-grandfather was a pretender all along!"

"Indeed!" Threepio agreed. "Stop the wedding!"

"All right! All right!" Luke said, placing his hand on Threepio's shoulder. "Don't worry about it. I'll take care of everything."

"Oh, that's so good of you, Master Lu—" Luke flipped the droid off, dragged him into an empty office, locked the door, then made his way to the White Room, opened one of its many doors.

The room had an enormous vaulted ceiling, ornately carved from one monolithic stone, and brilliant lights reflected from the dome, bathing everything in a soft, celestial glow. A thousand guests from a variety of planets sat to witness, and some of them turned to look at Luke. In the front row, Teneniel Djo and Prince Isolder sat together next to Artoo and Chewbacca, who was immaculately shampooed and brushed. The prince held a plant on his lap, a purple, trumpet-shaped arallute flower.

Luke stood at the back, staring up at the marble altar where

Han and Leia knelt across from one another, holding hands across the altar. The officiator stood in his emerald robes of office, leading Leia in her vows.

She turned and glanced at Luke, the diadems in her veil flashing in the light, and Luke could feel that she was not angry at him for having arrived late, only grateful that he had made it. And at that moment Leia was more serene, more content, than she had ever been in her life. And perhaps she was as filled with joy as anyone could be.